CURSED CHARM

ARCANE WITCHES BOOK 1

JALI HENRY

DIVERSE WORLDS PUBLICATIONS

Copyright © 2021 by Jali Henry

All rights reserved.

No part of this book may be reproduced in any form or by any electronic or mechanical means, including information storage and retrieval systems, without written permission from the author, except for the use of brief quotations in a book review.

❦ Created with Vellum

1

"Bree, our coffees si vous plait"

I rolled my eyes, and gritted my teeth, as my boss, Xavier, called up from the lower level of the factory. It wasn't actually a factory, that's just what they called it. An apt description, for a dank basement office, with no windows and a mould problem. They thought it sounded edgy and cool, when in fact, it just made it seem even more like a sweat shop.

I sighed and looked up at the industrial piping, adorning the ceiling. The espresso machine filter pipe had come loose for the third time today, spraying dirty water all over my best, white top. I got to work refitting the pipe and crossed my fingers, as I placed a cup beneath the spout. A chugging, slurping sound emanated from the machine and I held my breath. At this point, one of two things normally happened. Either I was lucky and coffee dripped down into the cup. Or, I was unlucky and the waste filter pipe came loose, with a loud pop, spraying dark, brown, gritty water all over me. Exhaling, I relaxed my shoulders, as dark liquid swirled into the cup. After making three more coffees, the only remaining hurdle was descending the stairs and placing them in front of each director.

Balancing the cups on the black, plastic tray, I walked carefully past the ping pong table. I'd been caught out before, by errant balls underfoot. I smiled smugly to myself.

Not today, ping pong balls. Not today.

Carefully stepping over each one, I reached the iron stairs and clomped down, my footsteps echoing off the cement walls. I'd made it to the final step, when, all at once, there was a yapping noise, as a white ball of fluff darted between my ankles.

Whoa!

I felt myself sway to the left. I rebalanced myself by bending forward, to the right. But the ball of fluff decided that was a good time to jump up against the backs of my calves. *Game over.*

Losing the fight against gravity, I toppled over, the entire tray crashing to the floor alongside me. The sound of clapping and whoops, from the odious Rafferty and his giggling sidekick, Ben, rang out around me, as I wallowed in my own humiliation, for a few moments. Lying face down on the cold, dusty, floorboards, I lifted my head and parted my curtain of pink hair. The fluff ball started licking coffee off my face and I winced and coughed, pushing it away. The scent of dog breath invaded my nostrils.

"Gigi! Are you okay my little squidgems?" Xavier's girlfriend, Galina, tottered over, on 6-inch heels, to pick up her pomeranian. "Oh look at you, you're all dirty. Did the naughty lady spill coffee over you, did she?" Galina nuzzled her nose into the dog's face as she puckered her pink, glossy lips and flicked her coiffed, blonde hair.

I picked myself up, off the floor, trying my best to paste a smile of serene politeness, on my face. It probably looked more like a grimace. And the dead-eyed smile Galina gave me in return, as she stroked Gigi, with one french-manicured hand, told me the feeling was mutual. Xavier wandered over, still talking on his phone, and gave Galina three air kisses before he clicked his fingers at me and pointed at the cleaning cupboard. I knew what that meant.

I trudged over to the cleaning cupboard to get the mop, desperately hoping no mice would jump out at me, this time. Then I walked to the bathroom, where I filled up the bucket with hot water. Slopping water over the floor as I lugged the heavy bucket back, I got to work, mopping up the spilt coffee. As I worked, I reflected on the drudgery of my life. If someone had told me that the price of entry, to a life in London, would be spending my days making endless cups of coffee, I might not have left Ireland. I had had such high hopes for my new life in the capital. Growing up in the two-horse town of Dunmoney, London had seemed like a magical place. I envisioned a melting pot of cultures, where nobody would look at me like I was weirdo. It was supposed to be my big chance, to make it as a social media marketing executive. Don't get me wrong, I was a social media marketing executive. But you'd never tell.

When I'd taken this job, I'd been really excited. Sure, the pay was shit, but at least I'd get experience and be able to get a better paying job after this. But what I hadn't expected, was to get here, and be treated as a glorified maid. When I'd tried to express these concerns to Xavier, he'd laughed them off. I recalled his exact words,

What's your problem? You get as much free coffee and beer after work as you like. And the offices are super cool, non?

The problem with Xavier was that his charisma and French accent kind of made everything seem like it was better than it was. That was most likely how he'd bamboozled the investors into pouring money into a startup, selling CBD-infused smoothies. Surely the market for that was already flooded? But he'd managed to convince some rich guys, somewhere, that this was a good idea. What really rubbed me up the wrong way, was that here I was, working for pittance, while every other day, Galina came in and took Xavier's company card, to go and buy more designer decor, to jazz up the office, in an attempt to make it look habitable. Xavier and Galina were clearly not familiar with the phrase, *you can't polish a turd*. But I was rapidly losing my patience with being treated like the office dogsbody. I wanted a career in social media marketing but did I really want it this badly?

Bringing my thoughts back to the task at hand, I stood up and wiped my forehead, as I inspected the floor. It was good enough. I picked up the bucket of dirty water and walked towards the iron-framed back door. Putting the bucket down, I rammed my body, sideways, into the door. With my diminutive frame, I needed to do it several times before it opened, bruising my shoulder in the process. The sound of rusty iron, scraping against stone always set my nerves on edge and I shivered, more from that than from the first chill of winter that permeated the late October air. I picked up the bucket and carried it to a waste water drain, in the dark alley, at the back of the office. Bending over, I tipped the water down the drain, scowling at the injustice of my life. Last time I'd poured it down the toilets. The water had overflowed and I'd spent the next half hour on my knees, trying to unblock it.

It was as I straightened up that I had one of my 'episodes'. Glittering, shapes of orange light moved through the air, in front of my eyes. I reached out to touch them and felt warmth and a tingling sensation pulse through my skin, whenever they made contact. The intricate shapes seemed drawn to me. They wound their fiery tendrils around my face, almost as if they had agency and intelligence. I allowed myself a few moments of joy, playing with the shapes, feeling their silky heat caress my face. All my cares seemed to melt away when I was with them. In their presence, I sensed infinite possibilities, although I couldn't understand why. I knew that what I saw and felt wasn't normal. If I told anyone else, they would say I needed to be admitted to a psychiatric ward. But I couldn't help how good I felt, when the lights were near me. It was my little secret, something I kept so close to my heart, even my own brother didn't know. Closing my eyes, I breathed in deeply. I could almost hear the lights, trying to communicate with me.

"Bree, what are you doing? It's bloody freezing out here and you're letting all the cold air in."

My eyes snapped open and I whirled around. With a sinking heart, I saw Rafferty standing at the doorway, smirking at me.

"You're such a space cadet." He turned his head back in the direction of the office. "Oi, Ben. Bree's having one of her flashbacks again." He walked over to me and tapped the top of my head. "That famed 'Irish crazy' is strong in you, isn't it."

I narrowed my eyes at him and clenched my jaw. "Say that again and it'll be the last thing you say today."

"Oooh! You're feisty this afternoon. What's wrong? Did you forget to take your happy pills?"

From inside, I could hear Ben's laughter getting louder as he walked out to join his crony. Rafferty was the most obnoxious member of the team. He didn't have to work, his Daddy was one of the investors. This was just a game to him and he never missed an opportunity to lord it over everyone. He only came into the office to play ping pong, mess around with Ben and drink the fridge dry every night. I wouldn't have cared so much, if he hadn't been such a monumental dick. It was hard enough working here, without having to put up with that bellend and his moronic buddy every second of every day.

"I'm warning you Rafferty, I'm not in the mood."

His piggy eyes swivelled slightly. "What you gonna do? Call your big brother to come and sort us out?"

I huffed and took a step closer to him, squaring up to his lumpen manboobs. I was inches away from him. His breath smelt like stale coffee, liquorice vape and garlic. My eyes bored into his. "I don't need Frank to take you out."

Ben started laughing and I cut him a murderous glare. His laughter abruptly stopped and he did the kind of burping hiccup that told me they'd started hitting the lager early today.

Rafferty cocked his head to the side as he sneered. "Yeah, right, princess."

It was as if someone flipped a switch inside me. I was fed up of being treated like shit. Fed up of the constant menial tasks, which were way outside of my job description. Fed up of being the butt of jokes. But most of all, I was fed up of staying silent. I decided right then and there that I was going to stand up for myself.

"Take it back, Rafferty."

He looked at me as if I'd gone mad.

"Take it back now and apologise or you'll be sorry."

He sucked his teeth and flipped his hand at me as his eyes narrowed with sarcasm. "Whatever."

That was as much of an invitation as I needed. Balling my hand into a fist, I casually stepped my right foot backwards, then powered my fist into his nose, with full force.

Rafferty's head snapped back then forwards as his eyes opened wide. His hands flew up to his nose, which gushed crimson blood. His face had gone bright red, and he was shaking. I looked at Ben. His chin gaped open in disbelief.

"You... you... BITCH!" Rafferty screamed, clutching his nose as blood streamed down his forearms. "You broke my nose."

Other members of the team rushed out, to see what the commotion was about. I knew that what I'd done was reckless. But I'd reached the point where I no longer cared. As I stood watching Rafferty, groan and shudder, I felt ten feet tall. Whatever was about to happen, it was worth it, for that one moment of victory. That delicious feeling I'd got, by wiping that shit-eating grin off his face. My exultation was short-lived, however. Xavier rushed outside. He took one look at Rafferty and one look at me. His expression turned thunderous and he said simply.

"You're fired."

Scowling, I got my bag, coat and helmet and walked out of the office, without a backward glance. I'd hated it here. The way the smell of mould clung to my clothes, permeating my bedroom long after a day of work. The endless lack of daylight which had totally messed up my sleep patterns. The thick cloak of anxiety that hung over every team member, making us all work later and later, just to keep our jobs. The fake camaraderie that forced us to pretend to enjoy drinks together every Friday night. I was thoroughly sick of it all, and had been for so very long. As I walked out of that office, I felt like I'd been carrying a heavy backpack for months, and had finally put it down. I felt lighter and clearer and I knew, deep down, that I hadn't made a mistake.

That job had been eating me up from the inside out and now I was finally free.

There was just one problem: my bank balance didn't agree with me. A chilly wind whistled through the cobbled street and I gathered my coat closer around my body, as I flicked my hair out of my face. My finances were on a knife edge. I'd been supplementing my meagre income by working nights as an EatsApp takeaway delivery driver. Sure, I could take on extra work through the app but it wouldn't be enough to cover my rent. I had to find another job, and soon.

Rounding the corner, I reached my scooter and gathered my hair, away from my face to put my helmet on. The moped had been a twenty-first birthday gift from Uncle Paddy and Aunt Siobhan. It was the best present anyone had ever given me and I thanked my lucky stars, every day, that I didn't have to spend some of my wages on public transport. The scooter also meant I could earn extra money delivering takeaways, on the side. Hoisting my fake-leather-clad leg over the bike, I started the ignition and took off through the streets of London. Traffic wasn't a problem for me on the scooter and within minutes I'd reached Tower Bridge. It was already getting dark and the sandstone bridge was lit up, casting golden lights over the Thames. I smiled as I took in the expansive view of the city. The beauty of London, at night, always captivated me. Skyscrapers competed with historic buildings and up ahead, the Tower of London came into view.

As I rode, I reviewed my options. It was highly likely that I wouldn't be paid for this month and rent was due in two weeks. If I couldn't pay, my flatmates would have no choice but to offer my place to someone else. I could sleep on Frank's sofa for a few nights but his flatmates wouldn't tolerate any longer than that. I refused to go back to Ireland. I'd sacrificed too much to get here. All those months spent saving up money from my part-time waitressing job, while at college. Worse than that would be having to show my face back home and admit that I hadn't made it here. I wouldn't be able to hide what had happened - I wasn't the only one from Dunmoney who'd come to

London. Frank wouldn't say anything but Conor would. Conor was a good friend but our relationship had always been weirdly competitive in a way that I didn't fully understand. There was no way he'd keep quiet about my reasons for returning home.

Turning right up Whitechapel High Street, I passed a group of middle-aged women, expensively dressed, laughing as they entered a posh restaurant. My stomach grumbled as the smell of steak wafted through the opening doors. I'd never been to a restaurant like that and I wondered if I ever would. Later, I would scoff a hastily microwaved jacket potato and baked beans, for my dinner, before starting my delivery shift.

Cutting through the back streets, around Dalston, I reached the two-bedroom flat which I shared with Agota and Tallulah. I hadn't known them before joining the flat share but Agota, in particular, had become a good friend and I got on pretty well with Tallulah too. After parking my bike, I let myself in and climbed the stairs to the second floor. The flat was tiny but at least it was in a newly-built apartment block, which meant there were rarely any problems with it. Opening the front door, I called out. "Hello. Anyone home?"

"Hey." Agota's voice called out from our bedroom. I walked through to see her lying on her single bed, flipping through her phone. "You're back early"

"Yeah, I got fired."

She sat up. "You what?"

Taking off my coat, I walked over and slung it on my bed. Then I bent down and put my bag and helmet on the floor, next to it. "I got fired."

Agota's eyes filled with sympathy. "Shit! That's terrible! How did it happen?"

"Rafferty." This needed very little explanation. I'd spent months moaning about Rafferty and by now, Agota was well-versed on exactly what a prize twat he was. I ran my fingers over my face. "I dunno, I just flipped. I couldn't take it anymore."

Agota's eyes opened wider. "What did you do?"

"I punched him in the nose."

Her hands flew to her mouth as a look of childish glee lit up her face. "You didn't!"

"I so did. I think I broke his nose - or he said I did. Right before Xavier came out and fired me."

"Bree, that is absolutely mental. Erm, I mean..." she started to backtrack. She knew how paranoid I was about being called insane. I had a deep-seated fear that I'd one day be committed, like my mother had been.

I smiled. "No, that's okay. You're right. It was a crazy thing to do. Crazy and stupid."

Agota cocked her head to the side, her hazel eyes suffused with compassion. "Come on, let's get a cup of tea. And I also have chocolate biscuits." She jumped off the bed and walked through to the kitchenette. The tiny flat was really intended for two people to live in. But who could afford that in Hackney? Sometimes, when I watched American TV shows, I heard them talking about their 'roommates' and I chuckled inwardly. They didn't mean actual roommates, but we did. There was me and Agota in one room, and Tallulah, in the other. Tallulah's room was scarcely bigger than a closet. Agota worked nights as a shelf-stacker so it wasn't as bad as it sounded.

I followed Agota through to the open-plan lounge and kitchenette. The best feature of the flat was the balcony which overlooked the street. It was only a couple of metres wide but in the summer, it was just big enough to have a barbecue out there. I spent many nights standing on that balcony, watching the world go by. Tonight I needed time to think more than ever. As the sound of the kettle spluttered and whistled, I wandered over and opened the balcony door to step outside.

Staring at the lights of the city, which cast an orange glow into the darkening sky, I mentally reviewed what had happened at work. Why couldn't I have controlled myself? Rafferty had been bullying me for months and I'd taken it. And he wasn't the first. Kids at school had always got a kick out of picking on me, especially after Mam had been admitted. I'd always had a problem with anger. Regular people would pass me on the street and I'd go into fight-or-flight mode and get these inexplicable feelings of rage - like I actually wanted to kill them. I'd never told anyone and had spent my life carefully controlling these urges. Nevertheless, some of the people I'd grown up with had somehow cottoned on that my brain worked differently to everyone else's. Names like 'Blowup Bree' and 'Bree the Bruiser' had latched onto me and stuck throughout high school. It was one of the reasons I'd started mixed martial arts training - not just to protect myself but also as a healthy outlet to channel my rage.

I thought I'd got better, since moving to London. I thought I could make a fresh start and leave the hurtful nicknames in my past. But today.... I'd just snapped. I sighed and shook my head. This was the real me. I'd spent months and months wearing a mask of placidity, taking Rafferty's bullshit when inside I was a seething ball of anger. The pressure cooker had finally exploded. It was my own fault. I'd skipped a few of my morning fight training sessions so that I could work late. That had been a mistake. I needed those sessions. They also offered me a regular chance to see my brother, Frank. His successful personal training business meant that I rarely saw him. Now, as I thought of Frank, I realised how much I missed him. He wouldn't offer me any comfort beyond the familiarity of home and family. But that was enough for me. I couldn't see him right now, he'd be at the gym, training clients. But I'd definitely go to MMA training tomorrow morning. I needed the release of thrashing out my feelings on my sparring partner.

My thoughts were disturbed by the sound of Agota's slippers, as she padded towards me, across the parquet floor. As I turned in her direction, my eyes caught a glimpse of the dancing lights again.

No. Leave me alone.

It was those bastard lights that had got me into this mess in the first place. But the lights weren't listening. They danced around my head, making intricate patterns and shapes that looked like a forgotten script. Their movements were seductive and as much as I resisted, I was quickly drawn in by their charms. I felt myself slip into a trance. As I stood, my head cleared of thoughts, reality drowned out by the entrancement of the lights.

"Bree." Agota touched my shoulder lightly and I gasped slightly and tensed up.

"Sorry, I didn't mean to startle you. Here's your tea."

"Thanks." I took it from her and smiled. Agota was my best friend in London and even she didn't know me properly. I'd never told her about the lights. I'd never told anyone. They were part of the many secrets that I kept locked inside of me. Secrets which included the horrors of my past. The only person that maybe knew, although we never spoke of it, was my brother. As I sipped my tea and followed Agota back inside, one fear pulled at my thoughts, tightening my belly. And I suspected it was this fear that had made me lose it when Rafferty had taunted me about being crazy. That tiny voice inside me that said.

Maybe he's right.

2

*W*ham! My head hit the floor, with a thud, as my sparring partner, Janice, pushed me to the mat. She jumped on top of me, her legs spread-eagle around my waist, grunting with effort. Anticipating what was coming next, I immediately brought my elbows up, to protect my face. Janice began raining punches onto my elbows, her breath hot on my face. I twisted my body from side to side, avoiding each punch, as I planned my next move.

The Brazilian Jiu Jitsu sweep

Quick as a flash, I reached up and clasped both of my hands around her torso, pulling her down, to bring her face closer to mine. The weight of her body was pressed against me and I knew that, as the heavier fighter, she had an advantage over me. But I could still get out. I kicked my right leg up to wrap around her left foot, then did the same with my left leg. Releasing my right hand, I hooked it over her left shoulder. Then I thrust my hips up in an explosive movement, while chopping up and across with my left arm. I simultaneously pulled her left shoulder down. The move swivelled her underneath me, before she even had time to realise what was happening. Now on top, and trapping her left arm, I pummelled her face with punches. She reacted by swiftly raising her right elbow to block me.

The bell sounded, signalling the end of the round and we got up and shook hands.

Janice grabbed her towel and undid her face guard to wipe her dripping forehead. "Nice work Bree - you almost got the better of me at the end there."

"Don't you mean I *did* get the better of you." I undid my face guard, picking up my water bottle to take a swig.

"Naargh, I'd have got out of that hold if the bell hadn't rung."

"Yeah, right."

Janice laughed as she raised her eyebrows and nodded. "Fighting talk. Okay, we'll see how you do in the rematch tomorrow. You're coming tomorrow, right?"

I twinkled my eyes at her. "Absolutely."

"Alright, see you then. I'm off to get ready for work" She walked off in the direction of the showers.

My heart sank a little bit and I felt my brow crease, as she mentioned her work. But I wouldn't want to do what Janice did. She was a hedge fund manager in the City. As far as I understood, it was well paid but very stressful and not fun at all. Plus she'd taken decades to reach her position. At forty two, Janice was twenty years older than me but she had the body and stamina of someone much younger. Like me, she'd been MMA training for years.

Frank walked over, readjusting his long blonde hair into a man bun. "Not bad at all, Sis. I think you could use a little more glute training though. It'll give you more power in the hip thrusts. Some sprints or barbell squats in your next weights session. We could meet up and train together if you like?"

I scrunched my face up. "I don't think so. The last time I did weights with you, I couldn't walk for three days. If I'd dropped a fifty pound note, I would've left it on the floor. *That* was how much agony I was in."

Frank chuckled then shrugged. "Only proves my point that you're skipping too many leg days."

Pouting, I rolled my eyes at him. But I knew he was right. My slight frame already gave me a disadvantage over almost every other fighter. If I didn't build more explosive power, I'd always be weak. Frank was only trying to help me. He had this never ending desire to protect me. I understood the place where this came from. It was an obsession that we both shared: the drive to never again be vulnerable. To never again be in a place where we couldn't physically defend ourselves. The familiar flutter of pain clutched at my stomach, in the way it always did when my thoughts nudged at the trauma of my past. I forced myself back into the room. Now wasn't the time for a trip down memory lane. I had immediate problems to deal with in the here and now.

Frank studied me. "Aren't you rushing off to get ready for work?"

"Yeah, about that…" I sighed. "I got fired yesterday."

"Fired? Why?"

"The short version is I punched Rafferty in the nose."

Frank's blue eyes widened as a broad grin spread across his blonde-bearded face. Then he burst out laughing as he held up his hand. "High five."

I slapped his hand and joined in his laughter.

He shook his head in respect. "That fucker has had it coming to him for so long. Honestly, if you hadn't done it, I was ready to storm in there and do it myself. Consequences be damned."

"Well, that's what I thought - in the heat of the moment. But the problem is, now how will I pay my rent?"

Frank batted his hand, as if swatting a fly. "You'll find something else. This is London. I mean, shit, you can stack shelves, like Agota does, if the worst comes to the worst. You still do the Eatsapp deliveries, right?"

"Yeah but that was to supplement my full-time income. You know that gig pays peanuts. Even if I work it all day, it'll never cover my rent."

Conor, walked over, swigging from a metal water bottle. "Did I overhear you saying you got fired, Bree?"

I nodded and smiled sadly at him.

His eyes swept up and down my body. "That's too bad. Why don't I take you out for lunch today, to commiserate?"

I raised my eyebrows. "I thought you were broke?"

He chuckled and ran his fingers through his dark hair. "I *was* broke, before I pulled off my first sale yesterday. Booyah!" He did a quick jab and cross, then gave a playful grin.

I frowned. "Don't you have to wait until the end of the month for the commission though?"

He shrugged. "Yeah but I can use my credit card. I know the money's coming. Anyway, stop thinking of reasons why not to come. I'm offering you both free lunch and the pleasure of my dazzling company."

"Well, if you put it like that, how can I refuse?"

"Good. Meet me outside Canary Wharf station at twelve thirty, okay?"

I nodded.

He looked at Frank and some of the other guys and raised his hand. "Guys, I'll see you tomorrow."

Frank's eyes narrowed as he watched Conor wander off, towards the showers.

I met my brother's gaze. "What? Say it, I know you want to."

He shrugged. "No, I'm done talking about it. You know I don't like him, I never have. What more is there to say."

"He's just a friend, Frank. A childhood friend, from our home town. I don't have many friends here."

Frank shook his head. "Yeah, see, that's just it. Don't you think it's a little convenient that a couple of weeks after moving to London, Conor just shows up in your life?"

I folded my arms. "Not really. Lots of people leave Ireland and come to London."

"He followed you here."

I threw my arms down in exasperation. "He did not. He always wanted to come to London after finishing college - same as me."

Frank wasn't giving up. "But he chose to come and train at the same gym as you. He follows you everywhere. He could've made his own life here."

"Well, maybe he wanted to be close to a friend. I don't see what's wrong with that."

"What's wrong is that I wish he would just state his intentions." Frank's voice was getting louder.

I burst out laughing. "*State his intentions?* You sound like an over-protective father. And keep your voice down. He'll hear you."

His chest moved up and down as he took a few calming breaths. When he looked at me again his face was etched with sorrow. "Maybe I am over-protective but you and I both know why. I'm not going to let anyone hurt you ever…"

I interrupted. To stop him from straying too close to the unmentionable subject. "I can look after myself, Frank. Don't you know that this is why I come here? Why I wake up at six most mornings and work my body hard, training to become as close as I can to being invincible?" I reached out and touched his tattooed shoulder lightly. The movement seemed to break his brooding and he flinched. Looking into his eyes, I softened my voice. "I'm not the little girl I was back then." I bit my lip. Now *I'd* strayed into the unmentionable subject.

My brother and I stood, facing each other, bound as much by blood as by the pain of our past. We were close in physical distance, yet with an invisible chasm of things, left unsaid, separating us.

He nodded slowly. "You're right. I'm going to back off and let you get on with your life. But if Conor, or any other man, hurts you - in anyway, I'm a phone call away. Got it?"

I half smiled. "I'm starting to see why Agota calls you the cave man."

His eyes flickered. "Really? She said that? What else did she say about me?"

My mouth dropped open as I felt my eyes widen. "You like her, don't you?!"

Frank shrugged as his face flushed. "No… not like that, I was just wondering."

"Just wondering... how she'd look naked?"

He playfully slapped me on the shoulder. "Oh stop it. You're killing me."

"That's my job. I'm your little sister."

We walked off together in the direction of the showers, with me ribbing him the entire way.

SITTING in a booth at Crouch's Steakhouse, I dipped the last piece of medium rare steak into the peppercorn sauce. As I put it into my mouth, I savoured the rich meaty flavour and slouched back into the banquette. A contented feeling of warmth and satisfaction spread through me.

Conor, sat opposite, smiling at me. "Full?"

I nodded. "I couldn't eat another bite."

"Really?" He cocked his head and raised one eyebrow, picking up the dessert menu. "So you have no interest in looking at this, then. I'll just put it over he..."

I grabbed the menu out of his hand. "I think we can just hang onto that for a little bit longer."

Conor chuckled. "You never change. Where do you put it all, that's what I want to know?"

I patted my stomach. "I'm a hard working girl. I trained like a maniac this morning."

"So did I, but I couldn't eat the size of steak you just did."

"There is nothing wrong with having a healthy appetite." I fluttered my eyelashes, playfully.

"Healthy? Yes. Obscene? No."

I reached forward and whacked him in the chest. "Shut up."

"Aargh! Waiter, please, she's attacking me." He looked around at the waiters, most of whom ignored us. One of the female waiters gave Conor a flirtatious look. I often saw women looking at him like that, especially here in London. He wasn't actually good looking, at least I'd never thought so. To me, he looked like every other, dark-haired, pale-faced boy I'd grown up with. It was the Irish charm. London women couldn't get enough of it. And if there was one thing I could agree that Conor had buckets of - it was charm. That was why he was good at sales. He had the gift of the gab. He could talk a bunch of teetotaling monks into buying a barrel of beer, if he wanted to. This was also what made him so much fun. Whenever we went on a night out, he'd persuade me to stay for 'just one more drink' and make it seem like the best idea in the world. And it would be - at the time. Then the next morning I'd be cursing him. Until our next night out came around and he was getting me drunk all over again.

I looked at him and corrected my expression. I wanted him to know how much I appreciated this lunch. This place was not at all cheap, and as much as he talked big, I knew he was still on the up, in London - the same as me. "Thank you, Conor."

He waved his hand and looked away. "Ah, don't mention it."

"No really. You didn't have to take me for lunch here. We could've gone to a 'greasy spoon' cafe."

Conor chuckled. "Yeah, but I know you've always wanted to come to one of these fancy restaurants. And you looked like you needed cheering up so..."

I made my face as serious as possible. "Well, I appreciate it." He smiled at me and I smiled back, before looking down at the dessert menu.

"Now, let's have a look at this, shall we?"

As I surveyed the list of desserts, I felt the air shift. It was often a precursor to one of my rage episodes and I braced myself. The familiar feeling washed over me. It was as if I could taste something different in the air. A faint smell and metallic taste, similar to rust. I'd smelt that before, at the onset of every rage episode, going back as far as I could remember. Often, the visual hallucinations accompanied it. I didn't lift my head, knowing that if the lights were there, I'd find them impossible to resist. Conor didn't know about my visions. When this happened, in his presence, I often claimed I was feeling unwell and rushed off. Over the years, this had made him think I was vulnerable and sickly. I guess I was kind of sickly but it wasn't a physical sickness. And I refused to acknowledge the other alternative.

As I sat, pretending to read the dessert menu, the metallic taste grew stronger. I clenched the menu, my knuckles turning white with the effort of controlling myself. This was the most powerful episode I'd ever had. Adrenaline surged through my body and I breathed deeply as a visceral ferocity caused my muscles to spasm. I wanted to lash out so badly. My mouth filled with blood as I bit my tongue, hoping that the pain would distract me. A gust of cold air interrupted my thoughts. I shivered and looked up to see a man enter the restaurant. Just as I'd suspected, intricate patterns of light swirled around my vision but this time I wasn't transfixed by them. My thoughts were pulled in another direction. I couldn't take my eyes off the man who'd just entered. All of my murderous intentions concentrated themselves, in his direction. A vision of myself, leaping over the banquettes, grabbing a knife as I went and stabbing it deep into his chest, flicked through my mind. I shook my head and blinked the urge away. The man smiled and shook the hand of the maitre d. He handed over his woollen, winter coat and adjusted his collar. His movements oozed confidence in a way that turned my stomach. I was both attracted yet repelled. He looked little different than any of the other rich, middle-aged guys, all around us. He was moderately handsome, in an obvious, slimy kind of way - with grey hair, a tanned complexion, average height and a slight paunch. But there was something different about this guy. Something that was beyond description yet unquestionably horrifying. I felt, in every fibre of my being, like I was staring at a monster.

As soon as this thought entered my head, his eyes locked onto mine. It was as if my hostile thoughts were a beacon, which had drawn him in - alerting him to my presence. My desire to inflict physical harm upon him intensified and I felt blood rush to my face. I ground my teeth with the effort of staying in my seat but I couldn't stop myself from narrowing my eyes at him. He must think I was a lunatic - I didn't care. In fact, I wanted him to hate me. If he attacked me first, I'd be justified in tearing out his throat. My gut told me that we were on opposite sides but in what war?

His smile dropped and his brow furrowed. I tilted my head and frowned in confusion. I didn't understand what was going on. But it seemed that he did. An expression of terror crept onto his face. His left eye twitched and his lip curled into a slight snarl. In that moment, I was certain that he hated me too. But why? I'd never seen him before in my life. Yet, the powerful feeling of hatred, which surged through me, was the greatest I'd ever experienced. My reaction to him was animalistic - almost instinctive. I finally managed to tear my eyes away and back down to the menu but I still couldn't take in a single word.

Now I really am losing my mind.

"Are you okay? You've gone red." Conor jolted me from my thoughts.

I looked back up, my eyes flicking briefly towards the man. He clenched his jaw, then swept back out of the restaurant, without his coat. My entire body deflated and it felt like I could breathe again as all my rage instantly dissolved. I looked at Conor and smiled. "I'm fine. I just felt a gust of cold air, that's all."

Conor continued to study me and I smiled at him politely. From the corner of my eye, I saw the maitre d come back with the man's coat ticket, only to find him gone. He exchanged words and gestures of confusion with the rest of the waiting staff. Conor's eyes were still on me so I forced my attention back to him and plastered a smile on my face. "How about some tiramisu?"

He smiled at me. "Sure, good idea. I'll have the brownie."

As he gestured towards the waiter to come and take our order, my thoughts returned to the strange experience I had just had. Who was that man? And why had my reaction to him been so all-consuming? What was different about him that had caused me to have such an intense episode? Was it time to finally confess, to my doctor, that I needed psychiatric help? Icy cold fingers of fear clutched at my belly. I would rather die than go into a mental institution. But if my episodes kept growing stronger, I may soon have no choice.

3

"Keep the change." The man winked at me, suggestively, as he put the twenty pound note into my hand. The takeaway cost nineteen pounds fifty but to see the self-satisfied expression on his face, you'd think he'd given me a tenner tip.

I smiled weakly back at him. "Thanks"

He grabbed the takeaway bag from my hands and shut the door in my face. I turned around and descended the stairs of the large, terraced house. I'd parked my bike on the street, directly outside. Looking at my phone, I reminded myself where my next delivery was. I had to be quick. My bike could fit two deliveries inside the seat. I'd delivered one but if I didn't make it there before the other one cooled down, my pay would be docked. The next stop was in Angel, quite a distance from where I was now. Quickening my pace, I jumped onto the bike and put my helmet back on.

Speeding off along the wide street, I passed a group of teenagers, dressed in Halloween costumes. I half-smiled. I'd been so absorbed by my problems, I'd forgotten that it was Halloween on Monday. Any other year, I probably would've been going out to a Halloween party myself tonight. But this year I couldn't afford it. Friday nights were the busiest for takeaways and I had to accept as much Eatsapp work as I could, until I found another day job. After lunch with Conor, I'd spent the rest of the afternoon applying for jobs online. I wasn't fussy. Whatever brought in money and wasn't sordid, or illegal, I'd do it. Hell, I'd even applied for garbage collection jobs. It was only a small step up from the work I'd been doing for Xavier's, cruddy, CBD start up anyway.

Stopping at some traffic lights, I pulled my collar up closer around my neck. The air was particularly biting tonight. Perhaps it was time to start wearing my winter thermals. Gripping the handles of my scooter, I revved the engine as the traffic lights changed. It started to rain and I cursed, opening my visor, before it started fogging up. Riding through rain, at night, presented a serious challenge and the last thing I needed was to end up having an accident.

Zooming up City Road, I looked at the street signs. The address was near here. Perhaps I should stop on the main road. Theft of scooters was common in London and parking on a quiet side street would be an open invitation. As I was considering it, a dark shape, in an alleyway, down one of the side streets, caught my attention.

What is that?

The delivery address was close enough that I could walk the rest of the way. So I switched off my engine and parked on the main road. My eyes were still on the dark shape. It was person-shaped and moving. I took off my helmet as I walked a little closer. Something about this made the hairs on the back of my neck stand up. And there was that taste again. A metallic, rusty flavour that tainted my taste buds.

Oh no, not again!

I knew what was coming next. Sure enough, my breathing increased and my muscles tensed. Lights started swirling around my head as rage pooled in my chest. I'd been right, my episodes were getting stronger and more frequent. The rain got heavier and I blinked it away, struggling to make out what I was seeing. Then I reared back with embarrassment. It was a couple, making out. They were going pretty hard and heavy, the woman's head was thrown back and I heard her gasp as the man's lips locked onto her neck.

That's some love bite he's giving her.

I looked down and was about to turn away when suddenly the woman screamed. I dropped my helmet in surprise. My head whipped back up and my entire body tensed. In a flash I realised, he wasn't kissing her, he was attacking her. That was no scream of pleasure: that was a scream of pain. I didn't hesitate. Finally, it was time to put my violent tendencies to good use. This was what I'd been training for. There was no way I was going to walk on by while a woman was being attacked.

Clenching my fists, I sprang into action. I darted into the alley and stood before them, my body squared off and ready to fight. "Get off her. Right now."

The man growled and removed his mouth from the woman's neck. He was wearing fangs and fake blood dripped from his mouth. She'd also put fake blood and a fake wound on her neck. It was very convincing. It was a shame they hadn't made more of an effort with the rest of their Halloween costumes but I had to hand it to them for dressing as a couple. A vampire and his victim - nice touch.

The woman looked at me and spluttered in terror. "Help me. Please!"

I cocked my head and looked at the man. "You heard the lady. I think she wants you to leave her alone."

He looked at me and snarled. This guy was really going full-on method acting with this vampire thing. I was impressed at his commitment.

"Back away, bitch. This is none of your business." His turned back to the woman, as if I was no more significant than an ant. The woman screamed again and tried to push him off her.

I inhaled and centred my stance. If this guy wanted to go a few rounds, he'd picked the wrong delivery lady, on the wrong night. There was no way, I was letting this rapist simply go back to his rapey business. "Right, that does it. I'm giving you one more warning. Take your hands off the lady. Step away from her, or I'll make you." All at once, my rage started to lift and a feeling of clarity descended upon me. I assessed his physique and started figuring out the best way to take him down. I'd sparred with guys bigger than him before. Sure, he had the advantage of size, but I'd bet he hadn't seen the inside of a gym in a long, long time. I'd bet even more that he'd never done any fight training.

He looked at me dismissively. Then his expression changed. He stared deeply into my face. His eyes took on a haunting, glassy quality which I found strangely mesmerising. When he spoke again, his voice was soft and lilting - almost comforting. "Walk away. You were never here. You never saw me here. You will have no memory of any of this."

I creased my eyes at him. "Listen, dude. Whatever 'David Blaine' hypnosis shit you're into, it's not working on me. So I say again: leave the lady alone or I *will* hurt you. I may not look like much but believe me, I can bring the pain."

The man shook his head slightly and blinked at me, as if offended. "Oh, will you just fuck off!"

He may as well have pressed the big red button, painted with the words, 'nuclear detonator - do not press'.

I launched myself at him, flying through the air like a cannon ball. As I leapt, patterns of light swirled around me and once again, I tasted something metallic. Time seemed to slow down and as it did, I saw lights that I hadn't seen before. The lights I normally saw were orange but these were silvery and they seemed to be coming from the man. I felt my face crease with confusion but I was simultaneously seized by an instinct I couldn't understand. I had a powerful urge to open my mouth. It was a feeling I couldn't suppress or ignore. I opened my mouth and the silvery light poured into me. It felt gloopy and warm, as if it was a physical substance. A feeling of raw energy flooded my body and I felt more confident than I ever had done before. I landed in front of him, crouching in a lunge. My fists touched the ground, supporting my weight on straight arms. I flexed my muscles and twisted my neck. It clicked and cracked as my shoulders rippled with force. Power surged through me. I sensed that I was stronger, faster, more agile. It was a feeling I'd yearned for my entire life and now here it was. I felt invincible. I raised my head and looked at the man from beneath my brow. I cocked my head to the side and smiled. Then I pounced on him.

Consumed by blood lust, I sank my fingernails deep into his flesh. He responded by slashing at my forearm, creating a nasty gash. Blood blossomed from my wound but I didn't care. I was dimly aware of the woman screaming beside us as she sank to the ground. But I wasn't focused on her. All my attention was on the man. I had him in my grasp and he was going to pay for attacking a woman. I'd make him suffer. I wasn't a little girl anymore and I would never stand by and watch, mutely, ever again. I opened my mouth, baring my teeth, like a wild animal. I was a predator and he was my prey.

Then I caught sight of the man's eyes. His fake teeth must have fallen off as his canines were normal now. He looked at me with an expression of unbridled terror. Grabbing me around the waist, he slammed me into the wall sideways. He pressed one cold, clammy hand against the side of my head and ground it into the wall. I growled at him. He clenched his fingers into my hair, pulled my head back and smashed it into the wall, once more. I saw stars but it only added to my fury. Then with, what seemed like a colossal effort, he wrenched himself free of me and sprinted off. I whirled around, my muscles primed to follow him. But he was already out of sight. He moved faster than anyone I'd ever seen.

How is he doing that?

Had I imagined how fast he'd moved? I was certainly feeling a little strange. I was clearly having another episode But it was unlike any episode I'd ever had before. As I watched him disappear, into the night, I caught sight of a woman, on top of the building opposite. In spite of the darkness, I could make out her every feature. She was as small as a child, with bobbed, dark hair and an expression of grim determination. She stood, watching me, her coat flapping open in the wind. Our eyes met for a moment and some kind of understanding passed between us. It was as if I knew this woman. She felt like family and yet, I was certain, I had never seen her before. I watched as she leapt, through the skyline, onto the adjacent building and then bounded off, over the rooftops. I rubbed my eyes in disbelief.

This night is getting stranger and stranger.

Now that the man had gone, exhaustion took over me. And something else - disorientation. He'd hit my head pretty hard and my vision was blurring. I had a pounding headache. I touched my head and felt something warm and sticky. Bringing my fingers down, towards my face, I saw they were wet with blood. Shaking my head, I blinked and tried to come back to myself. I looked down at the woman, slumped in the dirty, wet gutter. She cowered away from me. "P...p... please, don't hurt me."

I looked at her, in confusion, and took a step forward. My legs felt shaky. My former strength and power had completely deserted me and I realised I probably had concussion.

"Please. I have children." She held her hands in front of her face to shield herself.

"I'm not going to hurt you, lady. I was helping you. It's that guy you need to worry about. Mr. Rapey McRapeFace."

She began to shake, tears were rolling down her face. "Wh...whatever you say. Just please, let me go. I won't tell anyone wh.. what you are."

"What do you mean, what I am?"

"Exactly. I won't tell anyone."

I had no idea what she was talking about. Perhaps she'd had too much to drink. Highly likely, on a Friday night, in London. Or maybe she was just crazy. I played along with her delusion. "Okay, yeah, sure. Don't tell anyone."

She got up slowly, trembling all the while. Clutching her handbag close to her chest, like a protective shield, she sidestepped her way out of the alley, as if exiting a tiger's cage. She kept her eyes on me the entire time. It was almost as if she expected me to attack her. I couldn't believe how weird she was acting. I'd just saved her from a sexual predator and she was acting as if I was the one she should be scared of. As soon as she was clear of me, she ran off, in the opposite direction, to my bike. She was running as if her life depended on it. I stared at her back, feeling detached and numb. I was probably in shock.

At that moment, I remembered the takeaway, still in my bike and my chest deflated. It would be ice cold by now and my pay would be docked. Could this night get any worse? *That's what I get for helping someone.*

As I put my hand up and pulled it down my face, I felt something wet touch my nose. It was then that I remembered my forearm. I looked at it. There was a nasty gash that was dripping blood all over the pavement. As I looked at the blood, my vision started to blur. I panicked as I realised I wouldn't even be able to make it to the hospital. I was already feeling weak. I swooned and put my hands on my knees to steady myself. Gritting my teeth, I fumbled in my pocket for my phone. My heart was thumping as I dialled 999.

The operator answered and I heard her curt voice ask, "what service please?"

"Ambulance, corner of City Road and Oakley..." I didn't make it to the end of my sentence. Darkness clouded my eyes and my vision shrank to the size of a pinprick as I sank to the floor, unconscious.

4

Opening my eyes, I squinted as a bright, fluorescent, light shone directly into my face. For a few moments, I had no idea where I was or how I'd got here. Then it all came back to me: the attempted rape I'd stopped, the fight, the strange woman on the rooftop, the entire surreal episode. The air was heavy with the scent of disinfectant and overcooked vegetables. All hospitals smelt like that. Looking down, I lifted my forearms. They felt like they were made of lead. There was an IV tube sticking out of one arm and my mouth tasted like arse. But most of all, my head felt like I was the wrong side of a three-day drinking bender. I groaned and tried to shift higher on my bed. Opening and closing my mouth, my tongue had the texture of sandpaper. I was so thirsty, I could barely even lick my lips.

"Nurse" I whispered. My vocal chords were not playing along. I tried harder. "Nurse." Nope, still too feeble. I briefly considered hoisting myself higher to see if I could reach the red chord but immediately discounted it. I was too weak. And I was groggy. Was that from my injuries or had they given me meds? My eyelids were still heavy but I didn't want to sleep. I wanted to know how long I'd been here. And just how badly I'd been injured by that bastard. As I went over the events again, I couldn't believe that I'd saved that woman from a rapist and then she'd abandoned me. Practically sprinting away from me. The least I would've expected from her was a little human kindness. Perhaps, I dunno, calling the ambulance. Honestly, what was wrong with people in this city?

As I ruminated on my terrible evening, my eyes began to drift closed. In a semi dream state, I saw the door opening and the blurry outline of a man, in a white coat, entering the room. Light poured in, around him, from the corridor outside, creating a kind of halo that spread out around his head. He paused at the door and took a step backwards, as if considering something, then he entered. As he came closer, he blocked out the light and I opened my eyes wider. He stood over my bed, reading my chart and I forced my eyes to focus on him. In spite of my mental fog, my breath caught in my throat.

Holy cow!

He was the hottest guy I'd ever seen in my life.

As he read, I studied his features. He was tall and athletic, with thick dark hair cut short but with a slightly curled quiff that looked entirely natural. It was the kind of quiff most men gelled their hair to emulate. His clear, pale-brown skin was coated with dark stubble, covering his chin. He had a strongly defined jaw and I watched it clench slightly as he read. His lips were a perfect cupids bow and his chin had a subtle cleft.

He half smiled as his dark brown eyes flicked over to meet mine. I caught the scent of his aftershave - complex yet subtle, giving him an air of elegance and sophistication. I gulped, wishing I could've met him in better circumstances than in a hospital bed, wearing a gown which would expose my arse if I stood up.

"Bree - right?" His voice was deep and husky, with ever such a slight indian accent.

I nodded.

"You had a lucky escape. That was some beating you took."

When I attempted speech, all that came out was a squeak. *Damn my dry throat.* "Am I?" I coughed, clearing my voice from sounding like that of a lifelong smoker. "I mean... What's the damage, doc?"

He put down the chart and raised his eyebrows. "Well, aside from the wound to your arm, you have concussion. We've done a cat scan and it's nothing serious. We've bandaged you up and given you medication for the pain but you'll have to stay overnight for observation."

I frowned. "I see." I lifted my arm slightly. "What's the IV for?"

"Oh, just fluids."

I had another thought. "But what happens if I need to go to the toilet?"

He raked a hand through his perfect hair. "Don't worry about that, we put a catheter in."

My eyes flew open. "What?! Erm... did you put it...?"

He interrupted me, laughing slightly. "No, no, the nurses did that." He twinkled his delicious eyes at me. "Your dignity is still intact. Besides, I'm a doctor. I've seen it all before."

I felt my cheeks grow warm and I cleared my throat again, eager to change the subject. "Could you get me some water please? I'm really thirsty."

"Sure, I'll ask the nurse to bring some in when I leave."

He looked down at me, his eyes a mixture of curiosity and compassion and something else that I couldn't quite work out. My eyes flitted to his left hand.

No wedding ring. I wonder how old he is? Late twenties? Early thirties? I bet he has a girlfriend.

He was still looking at me. "May I ask how it happened? The ambulance found you alone, in the middle of the street. Were you mugged?"

Hmm. How had it happened? What was the simplest way of answering that question? "I was attacked."

He folded his arms and I noticed how his white coat strained against his ample biceps. "Attacked?"

I gulped. "Well, not exactly attacked. I saw a woman being attacked - a man was trying to rape her. I went to help her and me and the man kind of... fought."

He frowned. "Hold on a minute. You're telling me that you, a woman, who looks about half my weight, waded in and attacked a man?... At night?... On your own?"

I laughed nervously. "I guess it does sound a little reckless."

He looked up at the ceiling then back at me. "Why didn't you just call the police?"

I started fiddling with my blanket. "I dunno. It just, didn't occur to me." I couldn't meet his gaze but I knew he was still looking at me. Something about him made me want to confide in him but the truth was way stranger than a lie. I couldn't tell him the whole truth, as much as I wanted to. I lifted my head slightly, looking at him from underneath my lashes. In his presence, I felt a strange mixture of desire, comfort and vulnerability.

He walked over to grab the chair that was at the side of the room. Then came over and sat down beside me. He just looked at me, waiting.

I creased my brows. "What are you doing? Aren't you really busy?"

He nodded. "I am."

"Shouldn't you be attending to other patients?"

He nodded again and smiled slightly. "I should."

I knew what he was doing. He knew I was lying and he was going to wait here until he'd got the truth out of me. "Why do you care what happened to me anyway?"

"It's my job to care. I'm a doctor."

Now he was the one lying but I couldn't work out why. Most men were easy to read. The way their gaze settled, lecherously over the curves of my body. The way their eyes lit up and swept over me, as I entered a room. The way their heads turned and their lips parted as I walked past. Even when they were trying not to be obvious, they still were. But this guy was an enigma. He didn't look at me with obvious desire and yet he cared about what had happened to me. Why?

There was only one way to find out - tell him a bit more of the truth and see what happened.

"If I tell you what really happened, do you promise not to admit me to a mental ward?"

His eyes softened. "I'm sorry Bree. I can't promise that. I have a duty of care to my patients. If what you tell me gives me cause to believe you're a danger to yourself, or to others, I have to get you admitted."

I breathed deeply and nodded as a rush of emotions come to my throat. I couldn't risk being admitted. Couldn't have my life become what my mother's life had become. An image of her towards the end flashed into my mind. She'd been a wreck, physically destroyed by years of violence at the hands of my shitbag of a father. And mentally broken by the depression and delusions that had tortured her before she'd eventually taken her own life. Waves of pain and guilt radiated across my heart, as they always did, when I thought of my mother. I should've done more for her, I should've been there for her. Frank told me all the time that I shouldn't blame myself, that I was just a child. But his words were like used chewing gum, easily spat out but not easily digested. I couldn't accept that I couldn't have stopped my mother's suicide. And I'd never forgive my father for what he'd done to her - to all of us. My mother wasn't the only one who'd borne the brunt of his fists.

Tears pricked at my eyes as I sniffed and bit my lip, tasting blood. When I looked up again, the doctor's eyes had taken on a serenely beautiful, glassy quality and he clenched his jaw. He seemed to be fighting with himself as he reached forward, handing me a tissue from a box on the side table. The expression on his face was a mixture of curiosity and something darker - almost feral and I clenched my thighs together and swallowed.

He leaned forward slightly, just close enough that his breath caressed my neck. "I'll tell you what. Why don't you trust me to do what's right for you? You may think I'll never believe the truth but I've been around for a while. I might surprise you." His voice had a quality that was sonorous yet engaging. Something about him made me want to please him. I could have listened to that voice all night. Was this what people meant when they talked about a doctor's bedside manner? This guy had a bedside manner all right.

His gaze crawled, lazily up my face to meet my eyes. There was something in his expression that drew me in, begging me to trust him. I sensed that he was invested in me, in my story, and it was more than just professional interest.

He lowered his voice to just above a whisper. It was like a silky invitation, charming me into doing his bidding. "Aren't you fed up of hiding who you really are?"

I widened my eyes and sucked in a breath of surprise. It was as if he'd read my mind. Surely he couldn't possibly know that I spent every day fighting urges to maim and kill people. He couldn't know that I hid a core part of myself and had been since I was a little girl. Yet he'd articulated exactly what I was thinking and feeling. I *was* tired of it. Tired of the constant battle between my instincts and what society expected of me. Tired of the fear of being found out. Tired of having nobody to talk to. I'd carried the burden my entire life. I couldn't imagine what it would be like to live normally, without fear, like everyone else. The fact that he'd encapsulated my thoughts into a simple sentence was a sign. It was time to talk and he was the person to talk to. As I submerged myself in his warm, dark, inviting gaze, I got a strong sense that he understood. It was as much confirmation as my gut needed. I decided to tell him everything. I just hoped I was making the right decision.

THE DOCTOR LOOKED at me with a mixture of concern and incredulity. "And you say this rapist ran off after you fought him. Why do you think he ran off? Surely he was stronger than you?"

I looked down at the blankets. "It's difficult to explain. In that moment, it felt like I was much stronger than I am normally. I felt really powerful - almost godlike. Maybe my confidence scared him away?"

He scratched his chin and my eyes went to the delicious cleft in it - he really did have movie star hotness. "Your confidence, right..." His eyes roamed to the middle-distance. "Was there anything else unusual about this man? Anything at all that you can remember?"

Jeez, this guy is thorough with his investigation. "What are you, a doctor or a policeman?"

He looked a little flustered and backtracked "A good doctor isn't just concerned with the physical well-being of a patient. You've had a traumatic experience tonight and I'm sure you need to talk to someone about it."

Why did that question seem to bother him? Maybe I was imagining it...

He touched my hand lightly, his dark eyes drenched with concern. "You know, you can talk to me. That's why I'm here."

Perhaps it was residual emotion from the trauma or maybe just exhaustion but his caring manner made my already watery eyes tear up again. I sniffed and wiped them with the tissue he'd given me. It had been a long time since anyone had been that kind to me. In London, people were always in such a rush and nobody was interested in making friends, or even having a chat. In this city, unless you had something that people wanted, they didn't give a shit about you. Why was he being so nice to me? His kindness made me want to confide in him. But could I trust him not to think I was a nutter and get me admitted? I hesitated before continuing, fiddling with my blanket, as I looked down. "This is going to sound kind of crazy but he moved quicker than anyone I've ever seen in my life. Like, it took him a couple of seconds to be hundreds of metres away."

He blinked at me, weighing up my words but oddly, he didn't seem surprised.

"I dunno, he'd already hit my head at that point so maybe I hallucinated it."

"Possibly." He kept looking at me, as if expecting more.

"There was one thing that really bothered me though. The woman. She was terrified of me. She acted as if I was even more dangerous than him. I mean, I went out on a limb to save her, almost got myself killed. A 'thank you' would've been nice. But she sprinted away from me like I was a house on fire."

He leant forward. "That's strange. Did she say anything at all to indicate why she'd been so scared?"

I shook my head, trying to remember exactly what she'd said. "She wasn't making any sense. I thought she may have had too much to drink but she didn't seem drunk. She was going on about 'not telling anyone what I was if I'd just let her go'. The whole thing was super weird."

His mouth slackened as he stared at me, seemingly in shock.

"What?" I asked.

He quickly closed his mouth, shifting in his chair, as he cleared his throat. "Well, people in London can be pretty strange. Maybe you're right, she could've been drinking."

I cocked my head to the side. He was covering up something. What I'd just said had affected him in some way, but why?

He'd apparently heard enough because he abruptly changed the topic. "Your accent, you're Irish, right? It's a beautiful country, I'm sure you miss it a lot." His gaze drifted up and down my face then rested on my lips.

Realising how dry they were, I licked them and he blinked, slowly.

I smiled shyly. *He's checking me out.* "Sometimes. But coming to London was a long-held dream for me. I'm happy to be here. Sure, it's expensive and hard work and people are way less friendly but there are so many more opportunities here." My eyes met his, seeking the camaraderie of a shared immigrant experience.

He held my gaze, smiling back at me in a way that made my pulse quicken. "I can't argue with that. What about your family, do they still live in Ireland?"

Oh God!

My family was the last thing I wanted to discuss and a flash of pain fluttered through my stomach as I bit my lip.

He noticed. "Sorry, I didn't mean to pry..."

"No, it's okay. I have an older brother, Frank, who lives here. I see him all the time. Then I have an aunt and uncle in Ireland who I'm close to. But my Mam and Dad... aren't around anymore." I fiddled with my blanket again, avoiding his penetrating gaze.

"I'm so sorry. Did it happen recently?"

"Actually my Dad isn't dead but he may as well be, as far as I'm concerned. He's in prison and we're estranged. My Mam died when I was eleven years old."

I pursed my lips, trying to staunch the foul emotions from overwhelming me. But it was no use. The pain would always mount me, like a wild animal, the grief clawing into my stomach and tearing chunks off my fragile heart. No matter how much time passed, it still hurt so much. My eyes filled with tears.

He reached forward, arresting the memories with the light touch of his hand, on mine. I stopped fiddling with the blanket and looked at him, wiping my eye as I sniffed. "I'm sorry, I..."

He stared deeply into my eyes. "Losing a parent is one of the loneliest experiences in the world, especially for a child." His sympathetic expression sent waves of longing through my chest.

I cleared my throat but my voice still came out as a broken whisper. "It was a long time ago."

He held his gaze. "And I bet it hurts the same as if it had been yesterday."

Yes! That's exactly how it felt. He understood me so well. His words washed over me like a soothing balm. Who was this guy and why was he being so nice to me? Surely this went way beyond what was required of him, as a doctor. Was it wishful thinking to hope that he actually liked me?

I looked at him from underneath my lashes, taking in his dreamy eyes and chiselled features. "What's your name?"

"I'm Doctor Nikhil Chetty. You can call me Nik." He flashed me a model-worthy smile and I felt my cheeks grow warm.

"What about you? Where are you from?"

He smiled at me. "I'm from India originally but I've lived here for many years."

"Do you have a... family here?" Really I was fishing to find out if he had a wife and kids.

His eyes sparkled with mischievous curiosity. "No. No family. My Mum and Dad died a long time ago. No wife, no kids, no brothers, sisters or girlfriend. Just me and my career."

"Doesn't sound like much fun."

"Oh I wouldn't say that. It has its moments." He twinkled his eyes at me, as if to indicate that *I* was his moment. His eyes briefly darkened with desire and a shiver passed over my spine. I tilted my head to one side, allowing a moment of yearning to pass between us as I locked my gaze on his. There was something about him that made me feel like I was coming home. I breathed deeply and closed my eyes, wishing I could stay with him all night. I felt connected to him in a way I didn't normally, with men who I'd just met.

But all at once, the spell was broken. Raking his fingers through his thick hair, he stood up, with a sigh.

A stab of disappointment pierced my centre. "Are you going?"

"I'm afraid so. I have other patients to treat."

"Will I see you again before I leave?"

"Maybe. But I can't promise anything."

My heart dropped into my belly. He was fobbing me off, I wouldn't see him again.

But then he hesitated by the door. "I tell you what. If I don't manage to see you again before you leave. I'll look you up and we could go for coffee or something."

I inhaled sharply, unable to stop my excitement from showing in my voice. "I'd really like that. You have my address on file, right?"

He nodded and dipped his head. "It was nice meeting you, Bree Ryan."

Then he left. I sank down into the bed, my insides bubbling over. Doctor Nik Chetty was the best looking and most exciting man I'd ever met and it seemed like he was actually interested in me. But would he still feel the same way when he found out what a basket case I was?

5

I sat, in the laundrette, watching my clothes go round the dryer, the same as I did every Saturday. The warmth and whirring of the machines was comforting after the night I'd had and my thoughts soon turned to Nik. He hadn't come to see me again before I'd been released from the hospital and I wondered if I'd ever see him again. Had he been serious when he'd suggested meeting up for coffee? It wasn't just that he was smoking hot. He'd been so kind to me. Listening to my story and believing me - even the parts that sounded really crazy. He hadn't once laughed or dismissed what I was saying. But more than that he'd treated me as an equal, as if he understood my struggles and wanted to help. A ripple of desire coursed through me as I thought of the way the light had hit his eyes, through the hospital room blinds, as he smiled. I remembered the way his hands had moved through his hair. He'd looked at me with curiosity and a hint of flirtatiousness which I found irresistible. It was as if he was unaware of the devastating effect he had on women. Why did he want to know so much about me? Was he really just doing his job, like he said? Or was he interested in me? Towards the end of our chat, I thought I'd picked up a vibe of attraction but then he'd abruptly got up and left. Now, I wondered if was just wishful thinking.

I was brought out of my reverie by the beeping of the dryer, ending its cycle. I looked up, and at the same time, two women entered. One of them was as short as a child, with bobbed brown hair. The other was an older, black lady, with grey-flecked hair, cut in a short back and sides. Perhaps they were a couple. They sat down near the door and watched me. I felt the hairs on the back of my neck stand up. Something about this felt wrong. Why didn't they have any dirty clothes with them? There was only one dryer that had been going - mine. So they weren't here to collect clothes. I shook the suspicion from my head. I was being paranoid. It was probably mild PTSD from my skirmish, the night before - perhaps even the effects of the pain medication. There were plenty of reasons why they could be in here. Maybe they worked here, or knew someone who did. Or maybe they were just sheltering from the wind for a bit. Anyway, why should I care? Saturday was my get-shit-done day and I wasn't going to let a bit of residual trauma, from a delivery night gone wrong, get in the way of doing my chores.

I stood up and walked towards the machine. With a tug, the machine door opened and I started bundling my clothes into my laundry bag. Mixed in with my stuff, was a long-past-white pair of men's underpants, containing multiple holes that had been left in there by the last person. Wrinkling my nose in disgust, I picked them up between my thumb and forefinger and tossed them aside.

Great! Some stranger's grundies went round an entire cycle with my stuff.

I reminded myself to check the machine more carefully before using it next time. As I lifted my bag, I noticed that the women were still watching me. Their gaze followed me as I walked past them and left. After walking a few metres, down the windswept main road, I looked back. I wasn't surprised to see they were following me. Was it just a coincidence? I quickened my pace. They quickened their pace. Then it occurred to me that we were on a main road. There was no reason why I should be cowed by them. I stopped dead in my tracks and whirled around.

"Are you following me?"

The women looked at each other in surprise. They hadn't been expecting me to confront them. The shorter woman closed the distance between us, in the blink of an eye. I heard a whoosh and felt hard metal snap onto my hands. When I looked down I saw that I had dropped my laundry bag and was wearing handcuffs.

"What the?.."

"Don't worry, Bree, we're not here to hurt you," she said.

"How did you do that?"

The women exchanged a glance I couldn't interpret. The older woman smiled at me and hitched up her trousers. "We need you to come with us and this is the quickest way." She had a Jamaican accent.

"Come with you? Who are you?"

"We'll explain when we get there" She bent down and picked up my laundry bag.

"When we get where?"

The shorter woman moved her hands and I saw orange lights coming out of them. They were the same lights I regularly saw around me. Was I having another episode? But then I looked at her face and my mouth dropped open. Her eyes were focussing on the lights.

She can see them too!

She muttered softly, her lips barely moving. A feeling of oppressive heaviness took over my limbs, as if I was being dragged into quick sand. It spread from my feet, through my legs and belly, into my torso and finally reached my face and eyes. I couldn't move, I couldn't speak and all I wanted to do was go to sleep. The drowsiness was deeper than any I'd ever experienced and it was impossible to resist. I wanted to run away, to scream for help, but I was both mute and paralysed. My leg and back muscles suddenly felt as if they'd turned to liquid. I slid down to the floor, my eyes drifting closed as the darkness of a deep and dreamless sleep overcame me.

I awoke to find myself handcuffed and tied to a chair, in an abandoned warehouse. The two women were sitting in front of me. I bucked at my restraints, knowing it would probably be pointless: I was proved right. The older woman sat back, with her right ankle rested on her left knee. She had the easy, confident body language of someone without a shred of guilt. I scowled at her. The younger woman leaned forward, with her arms crossed. Her expression was intense and determined. She radiated a passionate fervour and I frowned, wondering what her cause was.

"Who are you and what do you want?"

The younger woman stood up. "I am Morgana and this is Evelyn." She had a strong German accent.

Evelyn did a fake theatrical bow in her chair.

"We apologise for taking you captive. If there was any other way, we would've done it. But we've found this to be the easiest method in cases like this."

"In cases like what?"

She took a deep breath. "We call you the ignoranti - you haven't been taught of your birth right and have no idea what you are or how to harness your powers."

Okay, now I knew they were crazy. Perhaps members of an enlightenment cult. I looked around for signs of religious ritual. I couldn't see any but that didn't mean they weren't there. My gaze searched the large space, before resting upon a fire door, at the back. They probably had a load of candles and crystals in a room back there. New agers, that was what my money was on. Whackjob new agers, intent on evangelising me to their cause. My mind whirled as I assessed my options for escape. Which one of these nutters was carrying the keys to my handcuffs? Neither of them looked like they trained regularly. I could probably take them both down, at the same time, if they got close enough.

Evelyn's eyes sparkled. She chuckled softly before speaking. "You're sitting there planning your escape right now, aren't you?"

My cheeks heated, as my eyes darted from side to side.

"Don't waste your mental energy. Even if you could get away, we would quickly put you to sleep again, like we did back there."

I blinked at her and frowned. "Yeah, about that. How did you do that, anyway?"

Morgana answered. "That's part of what we have to tell you." She leant forward and clasped her hands in front of her. "You see, you've lived your whole life believing that you are a normal girl. From a normal family."

Inside I bristled. If my family was 'normal' I was a parrot's uncle.

She continued. "But that's not true. You're something far more precious and valuable. You are one of us. You are an arcane witch." Her eyes flashed with excitement as she said the last words.

My face slackened. "Am I supposed to know what that means?"

"We're an elite race of witches. We use runes, incantations and spells to draw powers from the world around us and from the beings around us. We can take on the powers of other creatures."

Ah so they're wicca nutjobs. I was close with the new agers.

The wannabe witch walked closer to me and looked me dead in the eyes. "Do I look familiar to you?"

I narrowed my eyes as I studied her face, searching my memories. She did kind of look like I'd seen her somewhere before, but where?...

Of course!

How could I have forgotten. She had been standing on the rooftop, watching, the previous night, when I'd stopped the rapist. "You were there, on the rooftop last night."

She nodded. "Did you not wonder, at the time, how it was that you were able to make out my face, at night, from such a distance?"

I thought back to the incident. In the back of my mind, I had thought it was strange but it had all happened so fast. Then I got injured and went to hospital, where I got distracted by the dishy doctor... But as she spelled it out to me, the impossibility of my super-advanced vision slapped me in the face.

She continued. "Yes, you're beginning to awaken to the truth. I see it in your eyes. I'll pose another question for you. Did you not think it was strange that a grown man, twice your size, ran away from you and soon after, the woman you'd saved did the same?"

Now, the strangeness of it was all too obvious. I nodded slowly, my voice coming out as a whisper, almost as if I was in a trance. "I assumed he was scared by my confidence... I thought she'd been drinking. I..."

She shook her head. "You were rationalising, you still are. It's what the human world teaches us to do, to explain that which we cannot. Anyone else would've done the same in your position. But we're here to tell you that there is another explanation - one that makes far more sense." She paused, gauging my reaction before continuing. "That man was a vampire."

My mouth opened and closed a few times, like a fish. "Wasn't he just wearing a Halloween costume?"

Her expression was deadly serious. "No."

Evelyn took over. "He was a vampire. He'd probably glamoured the woman he was with into going with him."

I raised one eyebrow. "Glamoured?"

"Vampire mind control - it doesn't work on witches but regular humans are very susceptible to it."

Morgana clenched her fists. "Bree, vampires are real and deadly. As arcane witches, it is our sacred duty to seek out and kill the foul creatures, wherever we find them. They are a scourge upon the earth. They can't and won't ever live peacefully with humans. If we don't kill all of them now, they'll takeover the planet and soon we'll just be livestock - bred to feed them."

I looked from Morgana to Evelyn and back to Morgana. "How do you know my name?"

She began pacing up and down with her hands behind her back. She wore the same long coat that she'd worn the night before and as she turned, it whipped around her, making her look like a character from a graphic novel. "We've spent the time since yesterday using our resources to find out as much as we can about you. In addition to our arcane powers, we have an extensive network of useful connections. Last night, I was performing my regular, vampire-hunting duties when I spotted the creature attacking the woman. I was about to intervene when you appeared. I watched as you manifested your powers spontaneously. You took on his strength and speed. Perhaps you didn't realise but you moved at least fifty metres in less than the blink of an eye. Then you fought him with inhuman strength- strength that you'd magically borrowed from him. The woman witnessed all this and assumed you were also a vampire."

She turned back and looked at me, assessing my reaction. I looked up at the ceiling. I didn't know what to think. This was all too much. It wasn't just that it sounded bat-shit crazy, it was everything the last couple of days had taken out of me. The loss of my job, being attacked and almost dying, ending up in hospital. I needed time to process it all. I wished they would just go away and leave me alone. But I had to admit that some of what they were saying seemed to make sense. If this was some kind of con, it was one of the weirdest and most imaginative I'd ever come across. The fact that Morgana had played with lights that looked just like the lights I'd always seen, added weight to the whole thing. There was no way she could know about that. I'd never told anyone. But I still had doubts and these must've been written all over my face because Morgana leaned in closer and delivered the killing blow.

"We understand your struggles. We know that every time you walk past a vampire, you have a powerful urge to kill it. We know this because we experience that urge too." She clenched her fist and her eyes flashed. "But instead of fighting against it, we embrace it."

That floored me and she knew it.

She continued, in a tone of quiet confidence. "You've spent your life wondering why you have these impulses to harm others. Well rest assured, these impulses are not wrong. You don't want to kill and hurt humans. Every time you've experienced these feelings, you've been in the presence of a vampire."

Her words were compelling and I so wanted to believe her. I'd spent my whole life wishing there was some other explanation for my episodes. Any explanation other than the simplest and most rational one: that I was crazy, just like my Mam. Maybe that was the problem. I wanted this too much. Perhaps this entire encounter was a delusion - part of my escalating mental illness. But it all seemed so real.

I looked at her, allowing myself to indulge the fantasy a bit longer. "Even if I believe you - and I'm not saying I do, what do you want from me? Why bring me here? Why tie me up?"

Evelyn's eyes went to half mast as she lifted her chin. "We'll gladly untie you, if you promise not to use your powers against us. We're on the same side, Bree."

I guffawed. "Use my powers? I don't even know how to use my powers"

Morgana lifted her index finger. "You do. You're able to manifest them spontaneously, most likely in response to a perceived threat. But your abilities are unstable, untrained and unfocussed. We cannot allow you to continue walking around in the human world, using magic in such a way. You risk exposing not only yourself but all of us."

Evelyn added, "many humans are as scared of witches as they are of vampires. 'Witch hunt' isn't an idle expression, you know. If we get discovered, it could mean death."

"But couldn't you just magic your way out of trouble?" I made a rainbow shape in the air with fluttering fingers and then immediately felt embarrassed.

She chuckled at my reaction then her expression turned serious as she shook her head. "We are forbidden from using magic to harm humans."

"What - even if they're harming you?"

"Even then."

If these women were completely nuts, they didn't seem like they wanted to hurt me. Then there was also the distinct possibility that they weren't even real - just figments of my diseased mind. "Okay, I promise."

Evelyn walked over, unlocked my handcuffs and untied the rope. I rubbed my wrists and stayed seated. I had no idea where we were but that wouldn't be too much of a problem. I'd just ask someone on the street where the nearest tube station was.

But it appeared Morgana wasn't finished. "Now. Next steps. You are to come with us to the Arcane Realm where you will be trained in the subtle art of arcane magic."

I shook my hands in front of my face. "Whoa, whoa, whoa! Whatever and wherever this 'Arcane Realm' is, I'm not going."

She blinked at me. "Why not?"

This woman was completely mad. "I have a life here. I have a job...."

"You lost your job two days ago."

Shit! They really do know everything about me. But then, they would do if they were hallucinations.

I played along. "Okay but still. I have rent to pay and a new job to find and a side hustle delivering takeaways."

She waved her hand in front of her face dismissively. "What you describe are trifles that must be abandoned immediately." She strode over and crouched down in front of me, resting her elbows on her knees as she stared at me intensely. "I don't know how else we can impress upon you, the seriousness of our task. If we don't kill all vampires, the world, as we know it, will cease to exist. We need every arcane witch to join our ranks. You are squandering your gifts in the human world and you must stop, right now. Moreover, it's not safe for you. You've already attacked one vampire, who you, regrettably, didn't kill. He was close enough to get a good whiff of your signature scent. We've since learnt that he is a member of the 'Draculs' - a dangerous vampire gang. Make no mistake, this creature will track you down, together with his vampire kin, and exsanguinate you, at the earliest opportunity."

I shuddered but held firm. "I can look after myself."

She scoffed. "You think you can but really, you have no idea. You got lucky last night. You manifested your powers spontaneously but next time you may not. And I won't be there to rescue you. Every day arcane witches go missing or get killed by vampires. Within the last few weeks, in your own district, a young witch, by the name of Rosa Knight, went missing - presumed dead."

A chill went up my spine. "I thought you said you were keeping an eye on me?"

Evelyn stared at me. "If you decide to turn your back on us, on your own kind, and try to live your life as a regular human, we won't try and stop you. We'll leave you alone - we can even make you forget any of this ever happened. We can't force you to join us. It has to be your decision. But remember - the vampires will still know you exist and they'll still be after you."

I looked down at my feet. There was something about the way that she looked at me. Something almost maternal and fierce, that made me think I might be making a mistake. But at the same time, I wasn't about to give up on my life in London and skip off to mythical witch-land with these two crackpots.

I tried something else. "How do I know any of this is real? I had a head injury last night and I struggle with..."

Morgana finished my sentence for me. "...with what you think is mental illness but is actually your natural arcane witch instincts."

I blushed. "Yes, whatever. With *that*."

Evelyn sighed and exchanged a look with Morgana before looking back at me. Her dark brown eyes softened with kindness. "You're a staunch materialist, huh? I can see we're going to have our work cut out for us. "Without warning, she walked forward and rapidly swished her hands over my left hip.

I cried out in pain. "Aargh! What the..?" I undid the fly of my jeans and pulled them down slightly, at one side, to see she'd burnt a shape into my hip. It was a pentagram with the top triangle missing. "How did you do that?"

Her eyes glittered. "Magic. It's the arcane symbol. It doesn't mean anything to humans."

Morgana tapped her foot, impatiently. "Now that you know this is real - will you come with us?"

"No!"

She furrowed her brow and huffed at Evelyn.

Evelyn's reaction was more measured. "We can see you need time to think about this. It's a lot to process. We'll leave you with this." She handed me a business card. I turned it over between my thumb and forefinger. It was so ordinary. I don't know what I'd expected, perhaps more magic.

"Call us when you've made a decision. But in the meantime, *be careful*. Don't let any strangers into your flat. We know you have a balcony. Keep an eye out for who is watching your home. We suspect that dracul vampires may already be making moves towards you. If that happens, consider it a confirmation that what we've said is true and that you're better off with us."

I took the card from her and nodded. Standing up, I slipped it in the back pocket of my jeans.

"I'll also leave you with these." She waved her hands and a set of three, identical, silver knives appeared in her hands. It was a cool trick but it could easily have been sleight of hand - no different to any other magician, plying their trade for tips, in Covent Garden market.

She handed the knives to me.

"Are they magic?"

"Not by themselves but they are useful. Vampires can only be killed with silver or wooden stakes or knives." She paused, then looked at the ceiling, adding as an after thought. "Or silver bullets. Or decapitated." She looked at me. "Keep these knives on you at all times. Then, if you do get attacked, while you're out and about, you'll be able to defend yourself."

It seemed pretty crazy but I took the knives - at the very least, they'd come in handy as pretty steak knives... not that any of us could afford to buy steak, in our flat - but a girl can dream.

I tucked the knives into the inside pocket of my jacket. Was I foolish to even consider their proposal? They could be even more dangerous than the so-called vampires they claimed to fight against. I suddenly felt very alone and very far from Dunmoney. Two days ago, I'd thought my biggest problem was finding a job. But now I realised the world was a lot bigger and more mysterious than I'd ever realised. As I closed my eyes, I thought of the terror in the eyes of the woman I'd saved. She had seemed more scared of me than of the man I'd saved her from. I couldn't help but wonder: who were the real monsters here, the vampires or the arcane witches?

6

My breath came out in rhythmic beats, in time to my pounding feet as I ran along the pathway of Hackney Downs park. Unlike almost every other runner, I never wore headphones when I ran. They made me feel vulnerable - I wouldn't be able to hear someone coming up behind me with headphones on. I never wanted to put myself in a position where I was unable to defend myself. Increasing my pace, I ran under a row of trees, relishing the crunch of leaves beneath my feet. The cold wind was a welcome pick-me-up against my bare arms. Soon it would be too cold to run without a jumper or coat and it was just on the edge of biting now but I preferred being slightly cold. I found it refreshing.

Today's run was particularly welcome. I'd always found running an excellent way to problem-solve and clear my mind. And right now, my mind was full of turmoil. As much as I'd tried to forget about the witches and their insistence that I join them, I'd found my thoughts turning to them again and again. When I'd got home, after meeting them, I'd dumped the knives in the kitchen drawer, with all the other cutlery - I didn't seriously believe that any vampires were coming after me. Hell, I still didn't really believe they existed, although I knew that my encounter with the witches had been real.

The arcane symbol had formed a blister, on my hip and I'd covered it with a plaster to stop it bursting over my tracksuit bottoms. There was no way I could dismiss the encounter as a hallucination with a permanent reminder branded into my flesh. If their visit had been real, did that mean everything they said had been real? Or could they just be crazy witches who, although they had some real power, were delusional in their belief of vampires? And even if what they'd told me was the truth, Evelyn had made it clear that I didn't have to go with them. They'd prefer it if I did but I still had a choice and right now, I just wanted to get on with my life. If there really was some secret war being waged between witches and vampires, as far as I was concerned, it wasn't my fight. I'd been raised as a normal girl and right now, there were more things keeping me in London. Especially one dreamy doctor, who I hadn't been able to get off my mind since I'd met him in hospital.

As I thought of Nik, the exertion of my run seemed to melt away and I broke into a cheesy grin that made a passing couple look at me strangely. I forced my expression back to neutral. Really, I had to get a grip. This was a serious crush and it was embarrassing. I'd even tried a bit of facebook stalking but he was annoyingly absent from social media. I shook my head - I mean honestly, who on earth wasn't on social media in this day and age? Even my grandmother had a facebook account and she was in her seventies. At least he was listed on the hospital website but there were no photos. I'd dug a little deeper, eventually finding a photo from a medical conference a few years back. He looked exactly the same and I'd returned to that site, to gaze longingly at him, several times over the weekend. I was acting like a gushing teenage girl, at a boy band concert. He'd probably forgotten all about me. His coffee suggestion was likely just something he'd said to make me feel better. Guys like him had women falling at their feet every day of the week. To me he was my knight in shining armour. He'd healed me and listened to me, when I'd needed it the most. But to him I was just another patient.

Those old familiar feelings of inadequacy and rejection surged through me, making me break into a sprint, in an attempt to block out the pain. Why would a doctor be interested in an unemployed gig economy worker anyway? He was way out of my league. Disappointment scored my insides and I sniffed. Maybe I didn't need this kind of distraction anyway. I was supposed to be looking for another job.

I ran past a man, walking his dog and I got an immediate rush of anger as the intense urge to attack him overcame me. I ran faster, and the urge diminished. Was that man a vampire? I turned back to look at him. He looked normal enough. Plus it was broad daylight - vampires couldn't walk in the sunlight, could they? The sky was grey and thickly veiled by clouds. Was that enough cover that vampires could walk around? I slowed to a jog and then stopped, before turning to run back in the direction I'd come. The man was walking up ahead, his dog padding along at his side. An image of me plunging a stake into his chest flooded my mind and a red mist of rage descended over my vision. This time, as I ran slower past him, I turned and made eye contact. His eyes widened slightly and he jerked backwards - he was scared! Or was it just my imagination? Perhaps I should challenge him directly? No - if I was wrong, I'd look like a complete lunatic. I picked up my pace again, leaving the man alone. As I turned back to look at him, one last time, I saw his shoulders slump slightly. Was he relieved?

I shook my head, in an effort to clear it. That man was probably just a normal bloke, out walking his dog and the reason why he was scared was because I was menacingly glaring at him. Evelyn and Morgana's visit, coupled with their warnings about vampires, had made me paranoid. Now, wherever I went I imagined eyes on me. I couldn't walk along the street without thinking people were following me. My rage episodes were getting more frequent and harder to manage. If I didn't get this stuff out of my mind, I was in danger of becoming obsessed or even hospitalised.

I rounded a corner, deciding to take the longer route. It passed underneath a railway bridge and deeper into a wooded area of the park. The wind whistled behind my back, pushing me forward as dirt blew into my eyes. I squinted and rubbed the dirt away, my vision blurring slightly. As I came out from beneath the railway bridge, I suddenly heard other footsteps running behind me. A funny, ominous feeling entered my stomach and I turned to see two men, running side-by-side. One of them was skinny, balding, with thin lips and a greyish palor to his skin. The other was younger and heavy set, wearing a woollen hat. They were running at a moderate pace but my uneasiness increased. They hadn't been behind me before I passed under the bridge. It was almost as if they'd materialised out of thin air. I increased my pace and then turned around once more. A third man had appeared next to them and when I looked at his face, my blood went cold: it was the man who I'd stopped from raping the woman, on Friday night.

There was no mistaking him. Tall, with dirty blonde hair, swept over on top, nondescript eyes that were set too close together and a chin that disappeared into his neck. Put together, his features made him look like a turkey. My heart thumped in my chest. It was exactly as Morgana and Evelyn had warned me. They'd said that he'd come back to find me, along with his buddies and now here he was. But they wouldn't attack me in broad daylight, in a busy London park, would they?

I turned once more and saw the turkey curl his thin lips up at one corner. I gasped as adrenaline coursed through me. It was a smirk that left no doubt in my mind that he wished me harm - they all did. Then, without any communication between them, they took to a flat out sprint.

I may as well have been jolted with electricity. I yelped and bolted through the park, as fast as my legs could carry me. Colours and shapes flashed past. The gusty wind pelted leaves and twigs at me from every direction. I didn't even know where I was running to, such was my panic. All I knew was that I was being pursued by three creeps who were possibly vampires.

I didn't look back as my feet thundered along the gravel. My breaths came out in heavy rasping gasps. I was so terrified. My eyes streamed and my fists clenched as I pumped my arms back and forth. Rounding a corner, I bumped into a large doberman and went skidding to the ground, landing in a patch of wet soil. I scrambled to standing and looked around. There was nobody behind me. Had I imagined the whole thing? The dog's owner tutted and gave me a dirty look as he tugged the doberman's lead, to get it away from me.

"Sorry," I whispered, between wheezing breaths. Panting, I rested my hands on my knees as I bent over to get my breath back. The flat-out sprint had really knocked me. I saw stars and felt sick. My mouth was dry and my legs were shaking.

I stayed hunched over, waiting for my heart rate to recover. It started steadily slowing down and I became aware of more sounds than just the pounding of my blood through my ears. Nearby traffic competed with birdsong and the sounds of children playing on the swings, behind me. I wiped tears from my eyes and tried to calm down. I was still shaking. The men had disappeared. Was it possible I'd imagined them? Perhaps I shouldn't be running this soon after a head injury... Or were they really vampires, coming to get their revenge, just as Evelyn and Morgana had warned? I just didn't know who to trust or what to believe anymore. No, that wasn't true. There was one person I'd met recently who I trusted, even though he was little more than a stranger.

Doctor Nik Chetty.

Then, as if my thoughts had summoned him, I caught a whiff of a familiar scent. It was a subtle, metallic smell, mixed with a rich, intoxicating aftershave.

It couldn't be, could it?

I looked up to see him, walking towards me. He was smiling and holding a water bottle. The wind passed through his thick hair, making it whirl in different directions. He was even hotter than I'd remembered and I caught my lip between my teeth. My heart pounded in my chest, but now, more from the sight of him than from the run. I was glad that my face would still be red. He wouldn't be able to tell if I started blushing.

"Well, well, well. Fancy bumping into you here." He flashed a smile that could charm the pants off a nun. Then his smile dropped as he saw my expression. "Are you okay? You look... upset."

I pursed my lips. "I'm fine, I just... ran a bit too hard today, that's all."

He looked me up and down, his face etched with concern. "You should take it easy. It was only two days ago that you were concussed and injured."

I sniffed and smiled shyly "Yes doctor. But you know, I feel fine now." Fluttering my eyelashes, in what I hoped was an alluring way, I added, "what are you doing around here anyway?"

"I was visiting a friend nearby." He seemed eager to change the subject. "How about the pain? Are you still taking pain killers?"

"No, I don't need them anymore, I'm totally fine, honest."

"Good." He looked me up and down, his eyes hovering over my muddy tracksuit pants. "Did you fall over?"

"Yeah, sort of..." I hesitated. "I bumped into a dog and slipped over on some loose soil back there."

His eyes considered me for a moment. "You really do seem to be in the wars lately, don't you. You should be more careful." His gaze lingered over me and he clenched his jaw before his mouth curved up on one side. "Now that I'm here, why don't we go for that coffee? Unless you have other plans?" His eyes held mine and I felt a tingle of warmth spread over my body.

I nodded. "No... I mean yes." *Oh Lord!* "I mean, I don't have any other plans, let's go. But I need to have a quick shower first."

"Sure. Is half an hour long enough? I'll meet you outside Hackney Downs overground station and we can walk to one of the cafes in Dalston."

"Sounds good." I exhaled, suddenly realising that I'd been holding my breath.

I couldn't believe this was really happening. When he'd mentioned coffee at the hospital, I thought it was just something he was saying to be nice. He probably invited all his patients for coffee with him - and then promptly forgot all about them. But here he was, as good as his word.

He narrowed his eyes at me. "You're not going to stand me up are you?"

I grinned. "Why would I do that?"

He lifted his chin. "Just checking. I'll see you in a bit then."

"You can count on it." I ran off, looking at him behind me as I went, unable to stop a goofy grin from invading my face. He stood, watching me run, a smile playing at his lips as his hair blew wildly in the wind.

I showered, changed, put on light make up and the jumper which Agota said brought out my eyes the best. Agota watched me with a sly smile on her face, as I was giving my hair one final adjustment in our bedroom mirror.

"Must be someone nice for you to be making this kind of an effort on a Sunday morning," she probed.

"Uh huh," I answered, giving nothing away. I hadn't told her about Nik yet. For some reason, I wanted to keep him to myself for a bit longer. He wasn't just some tinder hookup. He felt like a man of quality and substance. It was irrational but I felt like I'd jinx it by talking about it. And after all, I didn't know what 'it' was. This might just be a friendly coffee between acquaintances.

Please let it not be just a friendly coffee between acquaintances.

I grabbed my bag and my coat and rushed out the door. "See you later. Bye."

Outside Hackney Downs station, Nik stood, with his back to me. He turned around as I got nearer, his eyes travelling up and down my body. He opened his mouth and I thought he was about to give me a compliment but then he closed it again.

He looked up the road. "You know this area better than I do. Do you have any suggestions?"

"Yeah. There's a nice cafe at the top of Ridley Road. Let's go there."

He raised one arm forward. "Lead on."

Nik put his hands in his coat pockets and walked beside me. He was more formal than the gym rats I was used to hanging out with. Was it because he was older or was this just his personality?

He wasted no time in making small talk. "How long have you lived around here?"

"About six months. I lived with my brother for a few weeks, when I first arrived in London and then I found my flatshare."

"Do you like it?"

"It's not exactly Buckingham Palace but it'll do. I get on well with my flatmates and I can afford it. Plus it's a new build so it's in good condition."

"What about the security?"

I looked at him sideways. "Security? Do you mean like, is it safe from crime?"

His eyes moved from left to right. "From crime, erm, yes. Do you feel safe there?"

I hesitated. I always had done before but since the incident on Friday night and then the visit from the so-called witches, I'd started noticing strange people hanging around outside. Then there was the thing with the weird men, chasing me at the park, just now. I couldn't tell Nik any of that though. "Safe enough I suppose." My voice trailed off at the end.

He looked at me. "You don't sound very sure."

I looked down at the ground as I walked. What was he getting at? Did he know something? Was he in league with the witches? Or was he just weirdly interested in security? Perhaps he was one of those people who imagined dangers around every street corner. But he didn't come across as a nervous type. I decided to be completely blunt. "Nik. It's not all that normal to ask about security you know. It almost seems like you know something."

His voice came out stilted. "Like I know something about what?"

"I don't know - you tell me."

He raised his shoulders and took a deep breath. "Okay, I'll level with you. The truth is... I didn't bump into you randomly in the park today. I came looking for you."

I stopped and folded my arms as I looked at him with my eyebrows raised. "You came looking for me?"

He stopped in front of me. "Yes. I told you I would find your address so we could go out for coffee."

I unfolded my arms as I felt a blush radiate across my cheeks. "Oh, right. Yes you did."

"When you weren't at home, I went to the park, to kill the time until you got back… I saw you."

I blinked at him. "You saw me?"

"I saw you sprinting away from some men." His dark brown eyes were etched with concern. He looked at me from underneath his lashes. "Did you know them?"

Well, at least now I know they were real. "No."

"Then why did you run from them?"

I raised my voice, in protest. "Because they were chasing me."

He paused. "Bree - I can't help you if you won't tell me the truth."

"Who says I need helping?"

He sighed. "Alright, you're tough, I can agree with that. But you're not invincible…."

I felt a shiver go up my spine at his use of the word 'invincible'. It was as if he could read my mind. He always knew exactly the right thing to say.

He continued. "Why don't you tell me what's going on."

I looked up at the sky. "If I told you, you would never believe me."

He chuckled softly. "That's what you said in the hospital."

"Yeah well, whatever I told you there, this is even crazier."

WE REACHED my favourite coffee shop and I pushed the door open. The smell of roasting coffee beans immediately hit me as I was enveloped in the warmth of the cafe. Soft music played and the bearded guy behind the counter smiled and nodded towards us, as we entered.

Nik turned to look at me. "What are you having?"

"Flat white please."

He turned back to the barrista. "One flat white and one black americano please - large cups."

I looked around for somewhere to sit and made my way over to a small corner table, with wooden chairs. Nik joined me a few moments later and placed my coffee in front of me.

"Alright Bree. You were about to tell me why you think those guys were after you."

I put my forehead into my hands then looked at him. "I did recognise one of those guys - it was the guy who I stopped the other night."

"The rapist?"

"Yes."

He frowned. "Are you sure? It seems strange that he would chase after you in a park." He looked at me kindly but his features were suffused with doubt. He thought I was delusional. I had to set him straight. But how? I couldn't very well tell him that some so-called witches had told me the guy was a vampire and that I believed he was chasing me to exsanguinate me, together with his vampire friends. So I went for the next best thing. "I think that guy and the other two, he was with, are part of a dodgy gang or something. And now they've got it in for me. That's not all. I think people are watching my flat."

He raised his eyebrows but not in a way that suggested he didn't believe me, rather in a way that suggested he was concerned about me. Was he concerned about me because he thought I was crazy or did he actually believe me?

He leaned back and folded his arms. His eyes lingered on my lips and a shiver of excitement went up my spine. "Have you shared these concerns with anyone else?"

"No," I said quietly. "I don't think anyone else would believe me. Perhaps I'm just being paranoid."

His smile dropped. "You're not being paranoid. You should always take your gut feelings seriously, Bree. Your instincts are there to protect you. If you think you're being watched or followed and that you're in danger, then I believe you."

His gaze moved up and down my face, taking in each of my

features. He had the languid body language of someone who was in total control of the situation. I felt way out of my depth. There was something about Nik... he was smooth and experienced. He was sophisticated and worldly in a way that most guys I'd met, who were around his age, were not. He exuded charisma, confidence and wisdom. I couldn't imagine him ever rushing or being flustered. In his presence, I felt special. I felt his urbane tranquility rub off on me. It was a feeling I liked and I wished I could stay under the comforting warmth of his gaze forever.

I smiled shyly at him. "You're quite a charmer, aren't you."

He laughed and looked a little embarrassed. "I wouldn't say that."

Emboldened by his modesty, I looked directly into his dark brown eyes. "I would."

His eyes softened with a slight look of sadness, followed by desire and then guilt, before he looked away.

What was that all about?

This guy was complicated. Maybe he was married? I looked down at his left hand again, searching for a tan line, on his ring finger. I couldn't see one.

He sipped his coffee, looking at me searchingly. "What do you do for a living?"

I sighed and wrinkled my nose.

"That bad, huh?"

I smiled, bitterly. "It's not that it's just... I lost my job on Thursday. I got fired for getting into a fight with a co-worker." I wasn't exactly covering myself in glory here. I wouldn't be surprised if this made him run a mile. Put together with my possible mental illness and recklessness with getting into fights, on deserted streets with strangers, I may as well have been wearing a sign that said, 'Beware: Bunny boiler.'

But he didn't seem phased. "Wow! You've really been having a shit time of it lately, haven't you."

I nodded, once again grateful for his kindness. The depth of his attention on me, made me feel cherished and important. I'd never felt like that before.

"What do you do - what did you do?"

"I'm a Social Media Marketing Executive."

His eyes misted over. "Social Media Marketing Executive. That's one of those jobs that didn't even exist when I went to university."

I frowned at him. "Really? You don't look that old."

His eyes widened, as if he'd said something wrong. Then he shifted in his seat and corrected his expression. "I'm not. I'm twenty seven. But technological advancement came to India late."

"Why did you leave India?"

"I came here on a medical visa. At that time, the UK government was giving out a lot of visas to foreign doctors, to plug a skills gap in the National Health Service."

He picked up his spoon and stirred his coffee - an action that seemed redundant since I hadn't seen him add sugar. It made me wonder if he had restless hands and was more nervous than he seemed. "Your family still live in Ireland though, mostly, right?"

He seemed to be very interested in my family and I felt my heckles rise at what was starting to feel like an interrogation. What was it that he wanted to know exactly? Unable to keep the irritation from my voice, I replied curtly. "I told you that back at the hospital."

He sighed, evidently aware that he'd taken it too far - whatever 'it' was. "Sorry if my questions seem a little personal. I just find you… fascinating."

I felt myself blush and smile, at the compliment.

He continued. "You seem to have advanced fighting skills. It might be worth your while investigating where you got your abilities from." His beautiful face seemed to implore me. I recognised worry in that face and I wanted to take his cares away. Even though we were scarcely more than strangers, I wanted to know him and I wanted him to know me. What's more, I already felt like he knew me.

But I had to set him straight. "I know where I got my abilities from. I do mixed martial arts training several times a week and I've been doing it for years. My brother is a personal trainer, we often spar together."

He stared at me, seeming almost to dismiss what I'd just said.

"Right but I'm talking more about the fight abilities you used the other night, when you were stopping the attempted rape."

I cocked my head to one side. He seemed to be implying that there was something special about my abilities that night. First those two crazy wannabe-witches, and now him. He was looking at me strangely - reading me. I got the feeling that he was trying to assess just how far he could push me. Who was this guy?

"You should research your ancestry, Bree. Try to find out if there's anything unusual in your family line, anything that your older family members may have kept from you."

I interrupted him. "If you know something about me then I'd appreciate you telling me."

His eyes met mine. "I don't know anything for sure."

"But you suspect, right? What do you suspect?"

He hesitated and took a deep breath. "I suspect you may be something really special." He paused and opened his mouth. I thought he was going to say something else but then he closed it again.

I felt as though my whole centre of gravity was shifting as my thoughts raced, trying to work out what the hell was going on. Was he in league with the witches? He must be. What else could he mean? But then, if he was, why not just spit it out? Could men even be witches? Hot men, with smouldering gazes that left me losing my train of thought?....I tilted my head, letting my eyes rest on his.

He cocked his head to the side, mirroring my actions. The heat in his eyes made me shiver, as he gazed at me, drinking in my features. He was hauntingly beautiful. His voice came out in mesmerising tones and his dark eyes grew glassy. "Can I see you again - perhaps tomorrow night, if you're free?"

A date? He was asking me on a date.

"That would be nice," I squeaked, cursing my inarticulate response. Why couldn't I have sounded more enthusiastic or better yet, nonchalant - as if hot guys asked me out every day? Spoiler alert: they didn't.

Thankfully he seemed not to notice as he gave me his phone. "Here, punch your number in and I'll give you a call to meet up."

I took his phone and added my number, glancing up at him as I finished. He was draining his coffee cup. "I have to go but remember what I said. Research your family lineage. It's the best advice I can give you."

He put on his coat and walked out, giving me a nod and wave, as he left. He was such an enigma. I felt as if he was somehow involved in all the weird stuff that was happening to me but couldn't yet work out his role. Even though I wanted to learn more about him, I was scared of what I might discover if I did.

7

"How was it?" Agota asked as I slung my bag on my bed and collapsed beside it.

I scrunched my face up. "It was nice but also weird."

She sat up. "In what way?"

"I dunno. I can't work this guy out. He's really nice and handsome, smart and kind..." My voice trailed off as I remembered how nice he'd been to me in the hospital.

"I know that face. You really like him."

"Yes but there are things about him that I don't fully trust. I get the feeling that he's hiding something from me and that's never a good thing, where men are concerned."

"What makes you think that?"

"Well, for starters, he pretty much insisted that I research my family ancestry but he wouldn't give me a straight answer as to why. That's pretty strange, right?"

Agota's eyes moved from left to right. "Could he be a history buff?"

"No. It's something else. It's like he's trying to protect me by giving me what he sees as helpful advice - but why is it helpful?"

I scratched my head and looked down at the floor. I knew it was no use talking to Agota when I'd only given her half the picture. I hadn't told her the full extent of how I'd got my injuries the other day. She thought it was a straight forward fight. I hadn't told her about any of the weird powers I'd apparently used. Nor had I told her about my visit by the witches or their claim that I was one of them. It wasn't that I didn't trust her - far from it. I just didn't think she'd believe me.

Agota looked at me. "Maybe you should just follow his advice. It can't hurt. And if you do find out anything unusual, it might give you an insight into his motives."

"Yeah, that's what I was thinking."

"You could start by discussing it with Frank." Agota's eyes softened and sparkled, in the way that they always did when she said my brother's name. "How is Frank anyway?" she asked.

I grinned. "Still single, if that's what you're really asking. Honestly, I don't know why you don't just ask him out."

"I can't do that. Then I'll never know if he just went out with me because I was a sure thing. I want *him* to do the chasing, not the other way around."

I rolled my eyes. "That'll never happen. Women throw themselves at him, at the gym, all the time. Plus, he's too busy working to think about dating."

Her smile dropped. "I've got no chance, have I."

"I wouldn't say, 'no chance'. Actually, I think he fancies you. He's just lazy. What you need to do is amplify your assets when you're next in his presence."

Agota's eyes dropped to half-mast. "Bree, you know English is my second language, please translate what you just said to regular speak."

"I mean, dress in a way that no man can resist and flirt it up a storm, the next time he's here."

She looked skeptical. "And you think that'll work?"

"Oh it'll work. He just needs a little nudge."

"A little nudge, right..." She smiled and did a little sigh. "That is one fine-looking brother you have there, Bree."

I blinked at her. "He's the same brother who used to sit on my face while farting."

"He can sit on my face anytime."

"Eurgh, enough already. Seriously, I think I just threw up in my mouth a little bit."

My phone started ringing and I grabbed my bag and looked at it. It was Frank. "Talk of the devil." I gestured to Agota that I was going outside and answered as I walked to the balcony.

"Hey Frank, what's up?"

"I was just calling to see how you're feeling. How is your forearm?"

"Oh it's healing nicely thanks. I might even be able to come back to training by Tuesday."

"Don't come back too soon. You know the increase in blood pressure, when you exercise, could open the wound back up again."

"Yes, I know. I'll take it easy when I do come back." I paused for a second, thinking how best to phrase my next question. "Hey, Frank, do you know much about our family history? I mean, beyond Mam and Dad?"

"Um, a bit. There's not much to tell really, nothing that you don't already know. Why do you ask?"

"Was there anything unusual that you can remember, from our childhood, or anything strange, or different, about any of our family members?"

"Other than that we were as dysfunctional as all hell? Actually even that seems pretty normal, as far as I've learnt. Maybe not quite as dysfunctional as our family was but most people's childhoods were fucked up in some way or other."

"So you never saw anything that you couldn't explain? Anything that seemed… I dunno, magical or supernatural?"

He paused. "Okay, now you're creeping me out. What is this all about?"

I sighed. "Well, on Friday night, when I was helping that woman… I felt like I had more strength and power than I normally do. It's hard to explain."

"You were traumatised and suffered a head injury. You were probably just confused."

"Yeah, maybe." I murmured.

"Besides, if you want to know more about our family history, you're asking the wrong person. You should speak to Aunt Siobhan. She knows tons of stuff about our past."

Of course! Aunt Siobhan. Why hadn't I thought of that. She was Mam's sister. She and Uncle Paddy had stepped in and raised us after Mam died. She had a fascination with the old Irish ways and was known as a bit of a new age crackpot around where we'd grown up. Aunt Siobhan never met a piece of gossip she wasn't all over. If anyone knew what was different about our family, it would be her.

"Thanks. That's a good idea. I don't know why I didn't think of her."

"I don't know how you can forget about her. The thought of her stew and dumplings gives me an actual physical feeling of loss, every time I think of it. I can almost taste it now. Mmm."

"Aw Frank. You know you can come around here for stew and dumplings anytime. In fact, Agota makes a mean Hungarian ghoulash."

He sucked his breath in sharply. "Beautiful and a good cook. When can I come over?"

"Anytime. You're the one with the busy work schedule, you tell us."

"Okay, I'll check my diary and let you know. I better go, a client has just turned up. I'll speak to you later, sis."

"K. Bye." I hung up the phone and walked through to our bedroom. Agota was still lying on her bed.

"You owe me big time."

She sat up with a look of excitement. "He's coming over?"

"He's expecting Hungarian ghoulash so, if you don't know how to make it, I suggest you learn, very quickly."

She smirked. "I know how to make it. What kind of Hungarian woman can't make ghoulash?"

"He's going to look at his diary and let me know when."

Her eyes lit up. "You're the best Bree"

I held up one forefinger. "In return, I want to borrow your black top for my date with Nik tomorrow night."

"The lacy one?"

I nodded, "yup."

"It's a deal." She scrambled off the bed and walked over to where I stood, shaking my hand, as she looked me in the eyes.

Needing time to think, I walked out of the bedroom and went to put the kettle on. Now I just had to call Aunt Siobhan. But for some reason, I felt nervous about that. Deep down, I knew that Aunt Siobhan held the keys to all my family secrets. Some of them were painful and some of them were things I didn't want to know and may not recover from. Was I really ready for whatever it was she would tell me?

I TEXTED Aunt Siobhan and arranged a video call meeting. That evening, sitting on the sofa, sipping my tea, I listened to the call tone and watched the screen of my laptop, waiting for Aunt Siobhan to answer.

Her ruddy face came onto the screen, strawberry blonde hair flecked with grey and tied in a loose bun. "Bree! It's so good to see you How are you?" She sounded so Irish. I hadn't remembered her accent being so strong when I'd lived with her and Uncle Paddy. Did I sound like that to Londoners? Or was I already losing my accent?

"I'm well thanks Aunty, how are you and Uncle Paddy?" We had a loose arrangement that I would call on Sundays. By 'loose' I meant that I called about once every three weeks. But they were so nice, they never complained or made me feel guilty about living my life. Aunt Siobhan had told me that she understood I needed to explore the world on my own, flex my freedom, without them constantly butting it.

She smiled warmly. "Oh you know us. We're keeping well enough. How is work?"

I bit my lip. "Well actually... I got fired. I'm looking for a new job."

Her mouth fell open. "Fired? How did that happen?"

"It was that dickwad, Rafferty. I finally had enough and punched him on the nose."

She cocked an eyebrow, she didn't seem surprised. "He had it coming, he did. You'll find another job soon, intelligent, hard working girl like yourself."

"And that's not all. I sort of had an incident on Friday night. I got into a fight with a man - I caught him trying to attack a woman. Anyway, to cut a long story short, I ended up in hospital."

Her hands flung to her face as she made a sharp intake of breath. "Why didn't you tell us sooner? If I'd known..."

I interrupted, eager not to get off the topic. "It's okay, I wasn't seriously hurt, a bit of concussion and a cut on my arm. The thing is - I fought pretty hard and I was just wondering if there's any family history of... of special skills, advanced fighting and that kind of thing?"

She paused. "Well you know about your Dad."

I felt the familiar knot of pain I always did when my Father's violent tendencies were brought up. He was in prison for assault. It would've been bad enough if he'd restricted his abuse to strangers. But he hadn't. My childhood memories were littered with occasions in which I was hiding in cupboards, too terrified to come out, as he beat my mother black and blue. Then there were the darker memories, ones in which I was on the receiving end and Frank was desperately trying to stand up for me. I'd never been scared of monsters growing up - because I had a real one living at home with me. I shook my head, forcing my thoughts back to the present. "Yeah, anything else?"

She stared at me, her eyes flitting left to right in a way that made my stomach feel uneasy.

"Aunt Siobhan - what is it?"

She couldn't look me in the eyes. "Listen, if you want to learn more about your family, why don't you come back and visit us sometime soon. I don't think these kinds of conversations are best done over a video call."

What did she mean 'these kinds of conversations'? I challenged her. "I can't afford to come right now. What is it you're not telling me?"

"Maybe I shouldn't say anything. It's just a hunch, nothing more."

"What?"

"I still think this should wait until..."

"Tell me!"

She took a deep breath. "Alright. After your brother was born, your Mam and Dad went through a rough patch."

I humphed. "Some people would say their entire relationship was a 'rough patch'."

"I wouldn't disagree but they weren't always like that. When they first got together they were so in love. Anyway, I think your Dad was jealous of your brother's place in your Mam's heart. After Frank's birth, your Dad started staying out later at the pub. Your Mam started spending time with other friends. She got close to one male friend in particular and I've always wondered if..."

The uneasy feeling in my stomach increased. Was this conversation going where I thought it was? I waited for her to finish the sentence.

"If she had an affair. In some ways you and Frank are very similar but I think that's because you grew up together. In a lot of other ways, you're very different. Frank has many talents but he doesn't have your gifts of sight."

Aunt Siobhan had always believed I had the gift of sight. I didn't know why she thought this - I'd never told her about the lights that I saw. But she had a way of reading people. I sometimes wondered if she had the gift of sight herself. Although I'd never admitted what I saw, she'd always talked about my clairvoyance as if it was fact - as obvious as the sun rising at dawn and setting at dusk.

I wasn't as surprised or hurt by her words as I would've expected.

But then, I hated my father. To hear that he may not be my biological father was welcome news, so much the better if it turned out to be true. "Who was he?"

"Not someone you know. He left Dunmoney when you were very young. Maybe he left because he didn't want to cause any further problems for your family."

"Do you know how I can contact him?"

"I could probably find out if you want. But Sweetheart, what has brought on this sudden interest?"

I looked up at the ceiling. Should I just tell her? Since Mam died, she was the closest thing to a mother that I had and if I confided in anyone, it should be her. She'd also be the least likely to think I was crazy. She already believed in magic and witches and the whole shebang. She'd always believed in them. But something still made me hold back. So I told her as much of the truth as I felt comfortable with.

"You've always said I have gifts. Maybe I do. And if I do, I want to find out where they come from. I'm just trying to figure out who I really am." What I didn't tell her was the thing I really wanted to figure out.

Is Nik somehow involved in all of this?

I ended the video call and walked onto the balcony, still sipping my tea. Across the road, one of my neighbours stood on his balcony, smoking a cigarette. I'd seen him often, on that same balcony - he must be a chain smoker... or was he watching me? On the street below, a black cab was parked opposite. Was it my imagination or was that cab always parked there? With the driver always in it? I shook the thought from my head. Since the witches had visited, I was starting to imagine vampires everywhere. But as I thought this, I looked down and saw a figure, definitely watching me, from the shadows of a building. He was wearing a flatcap and as his face turned, the moonlight caught his features.

Is that Nik?!

I squinted and leant forward but the man scurried away. Had it been him? I dismissed the thought. It must be someone who looked similar. He'd already asked me out and I'd said yes. Why would he be watching my flat? As I went back inside, an uneasy feeling entered my stomach. Who was the real Dr Nik Chetty?

8

It was Monday night and I was waiting outside Hampstead station. My conversation with Aunt Siobhan had given me a lot to think about. She'd admitted it was just a hunch but at some point, I'd have to dig deeper to see if it was true. Our chat had caused me to rehash old family memories, looking for any signs that what she believed was true. She was right, I was different from Frank in many ways but physically, we were quite similar. We'd both inherited our mother's fair hair and facial features. If I tracked down the man who Aunt Siobhan believed may be my father, would he know the truth? Would my mother have told him about me? I looked towards the sky, as if seeking guidance, from a God I'd never trusted or fully believed in.

As I looked back down, a group of teenagers wandered past, dressed in Halloween costumes. I put my hands in my jacket pockets to warm them up, then withdrew my phone and frowned. No message from Nik to say he was running late. I furrowed my brow. Was he going to stand me up? But as I looked back up, there he was, exiting the tube station. A broad grin spread across his face as he spotted me and an explosion of butterflies assaulted my insides.

He walked over and leaned forward to kiss my cheek. "Hi."

His lips felt warm and soft on my face and his stubble grazed my skin as he pulled away. I suppressed an impulse to touch the spot he had kissed. A warm glow spread through my belly as I smiled, shyly at him, suddenly feeling awkward.

His gaze moved up and down my body, taking in my carefully selected outfit of fitted jeans and red top. "You look beautiful."

Beautiful! "Thanks." A gust of wind blew my hair into my face and I tucked it behind my ear.

"Shall we?" he gestured for me to start walking, in the direction of the park but hung back slightly to allow me to go first. He was such a gentleman!

As we walked, I felt his warm presence beside me. My eyes flitted towards him. I should say something. "How was your day?" I blurted out.

He shrugged. "Not bad. Busy, same as most days. How about yours?"

I raised my hand and twisted it from side to side. "Same really. I hung out with my flatmates, applied for some jobs, read through some rejection emails." I gave a rue smile.

"Don't worry, you'll find something soon."

"Yeah, that's what everyone says but anyway..." I didn't want to spend the evening talking about my problems. " I phoned my Aunt Siobhan yesterday and asked her about my family history."

He straightened up. "Really? What did she say?"

"She actually has a hunch that the man who I spent my entire life calling 'Dad' may not be my father."

He stared into space. "Hmm, that is interesting..."

I looked at him sideways, narrowing my eyes. He was being pretty callous considering I'd found out something that would be really upsetting to most people.

He cleared his throat. "... And also shocking. How do you feel about it?"

I shrugged. "Well, there's no love lost between me and my Dad so I'm not heart broken."

He softened his voice. "But still though, it must've given you a lot to think about. Even if your relationship with your father isn't good, that piece of news would upset anyone."

"Yeah, I suppose so..." My voice trailed off. He was going out of his way to show the best version of himself. Isn't that what all men did when they went on dates? But I sensed that he was doing it for another reason than simply getting his leg over. What was beneath his mask?

Nik studied me, as if sensing how far he could pursue this subject. "Did your Aunt tell you who she thinks your real father is?"

"Not yet. She's going to try and track him down and then give me his contact details."

"But is she sure?"

"No but if it's true, Mam probably told him. Now that she's dead there's no reason for my real Dad to lie."

I didn't want to dwell on my family. "Enough about me, I want to know more about you. Do you like living in the UK? What did you think of life here when you first arrived?"

He raised his eyebrows. "It was really different and pretty tough at first but I think I adapted pretty quickly and now I couldn't imagine going back to India. This is home for me. At the end of the day, the world is a small place and people are people, wherever you go."

I hunched my shoulders and sighed. "I'd love to go to India. It's pretty much at the top of my bucket list in terms of places to visit before I die."

He chuckled. "Yeah, it's an interesting place. But London is amazing too. There's so much to do here, you have all the theatres and restaurants and nightclubs...."

"Talking of which. Where are we going? You were very mysterious on the phone earlier."

"I'm not telling you yet. I want it to be a surprise." He twinkled his eyes at me in a way that made me swoon.

Walking to the side of the road, he stuck his arm out, at the approaching black cab.

The taxi swerved to a halt, beside us and the driver wound down his window. "Where to, Guvnor?" His cockney accent was thick.

"West Heath Road please?" Nik replied, opening the door for me to get in. I stepped inside then shuffled over to make space for him to sit beside me. He shut the door and the cab drove off.

As we drove, I looked at the large houses that loomed on either side of the wide road. This area was known as millionaires' row. Fancy sports cars and SUVs were parked in every driveway. The people who walked by wore either business suits or expensive looking evening clothes - like they were on their way to the theatre. It was a world that was so far removed from the one I lived in. In my world, I struggled to afford new shoes and pay the rent. Most of these people probably worked in the City, making huge amounts of money and employing the likes of me to do their clerical work for tiny wages. "I don't come around here often," I commented, as I looked back from the window, at Nik.

"No, me neither. I often forget how posh it is around here."

This lit my curiosity. "Where do you live?"

"I have an apartment in Balham."

I laughed. "Yeah, that's a bit different from Hampstead. It's still pretty expensive there though, isn't it? But then I suppose you are a doctor." I punched him playfully on the bicep, noting, in the process, that it was rock hard. Was the rest of his body just as solid? An image of myself stripping off his jacket and shirt and straddling him, right here in the taxi, flashed into my mind. Shaking it away, I swallowed, as heat rose up my cheeks.

Interrupting my thoughts, the driver called through to the back. "Whereabouts do you want me to stop?"

Nik leant forward. "Anywhere around here is fine, thanks."

He pulled over and Nik handed him a bank note before we got out.

We made our way towards our surprise destination. I had no clue where we could be going. There wasn't much in Hampstead apart from community restaurants and pubs. It was a residential area with very little going on at night. Nik walked close enough to me that our hands brushed. My breath caught in my throat and I shivered as I pulled my coat up closer, around my ears.

"Cold?" he asked.

"A bit." I nodded.

"Here." He took off his coat and placed it, tenderly around my shoulders.

I touched his hand lightly as he put it on me and looked at him. "But aren't you going to be cold?"

"Nah, I'm made of tough stuff." He squared his shoulders off and pounded one fist on his chest, making me giggle.

His gaze hovered over my lips. "You have a lovely laugh."

I kept my eyes on his. I couldn't have looked away even if I'd wanted to.

His large, dark eyes were filled with concern and longing and such depth and beauty. Breaking the spell, he coughed and looked away quickly.

"Thanks." I looked down, biting my lip. I wished he would give in to his obvious feelings for me. Why was he holding back? What was he scared of?

WE CAME OVER A SLIGHT INCLINE, on the street and emerged on the other side to a large dome-shaped building in front of us. I looked at Nik, quizzically. A smile twitched at his lips.

"What is that place?" I pointed at the building.

"It's Hampstead Observatory."

I raised one eyebrow. "Observatory? Do you mean, like, for star-gazing?"

His smile broadened. "That's exactly what it's for."

I broke into a grin. "Is that where we're going?"

He nodded. "Uh huh."

A frisson of excitement bubbled up in my centre. This was *so* cool! But as we neared, I frowned as I saw that the door was closed. A guard stood to one side. "Can anyone go inside or do you need a membership?" I asked. "It doesn't even look open."

He smirked at me. "It's not.

My mouth dropped open. "Then how are we going to get in?"

Nik's smirk turned to a smile of quiet confidence. "Let's just say that the guard owes me a favour."

I chuckled. "Did you save his life, or something?"

He cocked an eyebrow. "Something like that." As he touched me lightly on the arm, tingles went up my spine. "It's best that you wait here. These negotiations might be a little delicate."

It sounded a bit strange but I shrugged and did as he asked. Waiting under a street lamp, I watched him walk over to the guard. The man held a torch up towards his face and scowled as Nik approached. It almost looked like there was beef between them as the guard's body language did not look at all friendly. But then, as Nik got closer, I saw the man soften as his face took on a placid expression. He obviously knew Nik as he was nodding and smiling to everything he said. Then Nik turned back to me and beckoned me over. "Come on."

I walked towards him, my breath coming out in white plumes, in front of my face. When I reached the front door, the guard was unlocking it, without a word.

"Hi." I smiled at him, feeling self-conscious. The guard looked at me with a slightly vacant expression on his face. He must be tired but it was strange that he didn't reply to my greeting or even acknowledge me.

Another rude, Londoner.

I shrugged off his behaviour and stepped inside, with Nik following behind me.

Once inside, he flipped on the lights and I looked up into a high, concave ceiling. Steps on either side, led up to a large platform, on which was placed a huge, white, metal telescope. A smile crept to my lips. Ever since I was a little girl, I'd loved to look at the stars at night. Almost every night I'd stared out of my bedroom window, at the sky, wishing a visitor from the stars would rescue me from my shitty life. No one ever came but my love of star gazing had persisted.

I had to admit, I was impressed. Nik was one classy guy. No other man had ever thought to take me somewhere like this and I'd never seen stars through a telescope before. However this night played out, this date would be one to remember.

I looked to the side and noticed Nik studying my reaction. "Let's go." He said, as he took my hand in his and led me up the stairs. His hand was large, warm and slightly rougher than expected. I wondered if his callouses came from lifting weights. But I didn't want to ask him the world's most cheesiest 'do-you-work-out?' pick up line. I thought of another way to phrase it. "You have rough hands, for a doctor."

He looked at me. "I wasn't always a doctor. I had my fair share of manual labour jobs, when I was younger."

I frowned. He wouldn't still have callouses from those by now, surely?

He noticed my expression and added. "And I do lift weights."

I felt my body relax slightly, glad to have found something that we had in common. "Me too. I'm really into my training. I lift weights as well as the running and fight training."

His eyes did a quick sweep of my body before he simply replied. "It shows."

As he turned away I couldn't stop myself from grinning. I didn't often think about how my training made my body look. For me it was about self-defence but it was certainly nice to get complimented, especially by someone as sexy as Nik.

We reached the top floor and Nik walked around, pressing various buttons. The telescope made a whirring noise, as it turned on and a panel in the roof started to move, creating a viewing hole.

"Now." He touched both of my shoulders lightly and shifted me into position. "You stand underneath this and look through there." He moved it down slightly so that I didn't have to stand on my tiptoes to look.

As I put the telescope to my eye and looked through it, I gasped. It was breath-taking. Living in London, surrounded by light pollution, I had no idea just how many stars were out there. I'd seen more stars in Dunmoney, for sure but even there, it was nothing like this. There was an infinite smattering of stars, moons and planets, myriad galaxies and a rapid succession of shooting stars. Normally I was lucky if I saw one a year. I laughed with delight.

"What do you think?" Nik was close enough to me that his warm breath tickled my neck hairs. I breathed in his subtle smell of aftershave. He sounded nervous which was sweetly uncharacteristic of his behaviour around me so far. It was nice to know that he wasn't always calm and assured. Nicer still to know that he cared about what I thought. I took my eye away from the telescope and beamed at him. "It's the most amazing thing I've ever seen in my life"

His shoulders relaxed, as his eyes twinkled at me. "It's pretty cool, right."

"What made you think of coming here?"

He shrugged. "I dunno, I've always found it relaxing to look at the night sky, when I have stuff on my mind." His eyes met mine and he gave me a knowing look. A frisson of understanding passed between us. I spent almost every night, standing on my balcony, looking at the stars. But he wouldn't know that... Unless he'd been watching my flat. A cold feeling worked its way up my spine and I tensed and pursed my lips. My suspicion from the previous night re-entered my mind. I'd thought I'd seen him, skulking in the shadows, outside my flat. But then I'd dismissed it as just someone who looked similar. What if it had actually been him? Was he a stalker? I suddenly realised I was in a very quiet place, with a guy I hardly knew. I took a step backwards and cleared my throat, feeling the blood drain from my face.

His smile dropped. "What's wrong?"

"Um, it's just... " there was no easy way to say it so I just bluntly accused him. "Have you been watching my flat?"

His eyes shifted from left to right, guiltily and I felt my eyes widen. "You have, haven't you." I felt sick and started for the stairs. I didn't know this guy at all and he was clearly a complete weirdo. He rushed after me and stopped me at the top of the stairs, blocking my way, with his large frame. This only made me feel more intimidated and I clenched my fists.

"Wait, Bree, it's not what you think."

"What is it then." I raised my eyebrows and folded my arms, tapping my foot as I waited for his explanation.

He ran his fingers through his hair. His eyes met mine. "I agree with you. About the rapist. About him being part of a gang, and about him watching you. I've been worried about you so I came to check out your flat. I only did it the one time." The pitch of his voice raised slightly as his shoulders came closer to his ears. "I'm a busy doctor, I don't have time to stalk anyone."

I furrowed my brow. "But... how did you know about the guy being part of a gang. What made you think of it?" *Especially since I made that part up.*

He realised his error and back-peddled, fast. "I phrased that badly. What I mean is, he's involved with some shady people. I'm part of a sort of...vigilante group. We have information on the types of groups he's part of. I knew he'd come for you sooner or later, and I just wanted to make sure you didn't get hurt again."

I felt myself relax slightly. What he said, at least sounded believable and if his motive was protecting me, I couldn't exactly object to that.

He took a step closer, his eyes glistening. Reaching one hand up, he cautiously tucked a strand of hair, that had come loose, behind my ear. His movements had such tenderness. "I like you, Bree.... I care about you. I'd never do anything to hurt you." His expression was suffused with longing. "I know we haven't known each other long but... I want to know you better. I want to protect you."

My breath hitched as I gazed into his beautiful brown eyes. "I don't need protecting." I whispered.

He moved his hand to cup the back of my neck. "We all need protecting from something. Maybe you just haven't figured out what it is yet." He moved closer to me and dipped his head down. His breath felt warm, against my face, and smelt deeply masculine in a way that made me swoon. His thumb, softly rubbed the hair at the nape of my neck. He cocked his head to one side and his gaze moved up and down my face. There was a look of intense desire, in his eyes. The only sound was the whirring of the telescope and the beating of my heart. Hesitantly, he dipped his head lower and brought his lips to mine. His chest relaxed, against me, with a slight shiver as he moved closer. His warm, large body, enclosed mine and my body melted into his. I sighed as he deepened his kiss, his tongue exploring mine. He tasted sweet and clean - like he'd just brushed his teeth. All thoughts left my head as I became aware of only him. His taste, his touch, his rough hands, exploring the back of my neck and moving down my body to squeeze me closer.

It had been so long since I'd been kissed by someone I really wanted and heat surged through me. I let out a slight moan and clenched my thighs as his hands travelled lower, squeezing my bum cheeks. I wanted him so badly, it was almost painful. We were all alone. Except for the guard, there wasn't a soul anywhere near. We could've done anything we wanted. But I knew it was too soon. Every fibre of my being ached for him but I had to stop myself. I wanted our first time to be special and I sensed that he felt the same. He pulled back, reluctantly, sucking on my bottom lip as his eyes hungrily drank in my features. He reached up and touched my cheek as he took a deep, steadying breath. "God you're beautiful."

I smiled and tilted my head to one side, as I raised one eyebrow. "So was this your plan? Take me star gazing and then seduce me with an earth-shattering kiss?"

He smirked. "Earth shattering?"

"Don't get too cocky. The jury's still out on whether or not you're a creepy stalker."

He sighed and brought his arm around me. "I'll win you over, you'll see..." And then he hastily added. "...and I am absolutely not a creepy stalker." He took my hand and pulled me back over to the telescope. "Anyway, I haven't had my turn yet."

As he adjusted the telescope, to take a look, I studied him. He was certainly the best looking guy I'd ever been out with. And also the most successful. I mean, he was a doctor, for christ's sake. It didn't get much more successful than that. A smile crept to my lips as I thought of how much fun, Aunt Siobhan would have, spreading the news, far and wide, that I was dating a doctor. And he was a phenomenal kisser. If that was any indication of what he was like between the sheets, I hoped this relationship would go the distance. But he still had secrets. He hadn't told me everything about why he'd been watching my flat. What was the 'vigilante group' he was part of and how was it linked to the man Evelyn and Morgana believed was a vampire? As I looked at his dreamy body and perfect, chiselled face, I couldn't help but wonder. When he said that we all needed protecting from something.

Was the thing I needed protecting from, actually him?

9

Waking up on Tuesday morning, I was relieved that Agota hadn't returned from her night shift yet. Nor had she been home when I'd got back from my date with Nik, the night before. She would want to know every detail and the truth was, I was still trying to work out my feelings. I liked him, that was for sure. Drawing my knees up, towards my chest, I hugged them, as I thought of *that* kiss. The way he'd tasted and felt, had permeated my thoughts so thoroughly that, even though I couldn't clearly remember my dreams, I knew they'd been about him.

Stretching with a yawn, I got out of bed and walked towards the shower, my thoughts still in turmoil. As the hot water splashed onto my face and hair, I couldn't stop thinking about Nik. What was he doing right now? Was he thinking about me? Did he know how much I liked him? The depth of my attraction, must be obvious, even though I tried to hold part of myself back. In spite of how much I wanted him, physically, I couldn't trust him. He was hiding something and I had to find out what that was before I could ever fully give myself to him. I'd already caught him in a few little lies and they could only be a marker to bigger lies that were as yet unearthed.

Getting out of the shower, I flung some clothes on, without forethought. There was nothing to dress up for. I'd spend today, at home, trawling the internet job sites, before my Eatsapp shift started later. As I walked to the kitchen, to put the kettle on and make some toast, keys jangled at the front door. A moment later Agota came in.

"Hey, Bree." A knowing look crept onto her face.

My voice came out higher than normal. "Hey, how was your night?"

"Never mind about my night, how was *your* night?"

I smiled shyly, as I flicked the kettle on, put a couple of pieces of toast into the toaster and got out a plate. "It was really nice."

She frowned. "Just 'nice'?"

My smile broadened as I gushed. "Okay, it was amazing! He took me star gazing - to Hampstead observatory. We looked at the stars under a telescope. It was the most thoughtful place anyone has ever taken me, on a date." I hugged my arms around my chest and stared, dreamily into the middle distance.

"Wow, that sounds really romantic."

I walked to the fridge to get the butter. "It was and then we kissed."

"And?..."

"And it was like the world stopped turning. I can feel myself falling for him in a big way." I frowned and Agota's brow creased.

"But, that's a good thing, right? He likes you, you like him. Why are you frowning?"

The kettle switch flipped off and I took out a couple of mugs, adding the teabags and then the water. Pouring milk into the tea, I handed one mug to Agota, while I picked up mine and blew on it. "It's complicated." I paused and looked up at the ceiling, thinking of how to explain. "I can feel him holding back, almost as if he's trying not to fall for me, like he feels guilty or something. At first I thought he might be married but I don't think it's that - which makes me even more worried. What could be worse than being married?"

She wrinkled her face in confusion. "Perhaps you're imagining it. He could be scared of getting hurt. You could be creating a complication where there is none."

I raised my eyebrows and put my hands on my hips. "Well he also admitted to watching our flat."

Agota almost spat our her tea. "He did what?!"

"Yeah, that was my reaction. He said he was worried about me. That he believed the guy who attacked me on Friday night was linked to some shady people and that these people might come after me."

The toast popped up and I got a knife out of the drawer and started spreading butter on it.

Agota scratched her head. "Why would he think that? It sounds pretty far-fetched."

"He says he's part of some kind of vigilante group and they have access to information that normal people don't have." The story sounded even more bizarre without the knowledge of the details I was keeping hidden from her. I'd told her and everyone else I knew, that Friday night had been a simple mugging. It was just simpler. I couldn't tell Agota the whole truth. She already thought I was a bit fragile. I didn't want her thinking I was certifiable. I looked at her as I bit into my toast, waiting for her to share her thoughts.

"I don't know what to think, Bree. This all sounds like something out of a movie. I guess my question would be - what is your gut telling you. Do you trust this guy?"

I held my cup of tea in my hands, like a security blanket. "I just don't know. My gut tells me that he's a good person, who would never hurt me, intentionally."

"Maybe that's as much as you need to know, right now. You can figure the other stuff out as you get to know him better." She blew on her tea and sipped it, as she looked at me from under her lashes. "Are you going to see him again?"

I nodded. "I want to... it might be a mistake but..."

She held up her hand and blinked. "Stop. Don't overthink it. Your first reaction was that you want to see him again. Your eyes light up every time you talk about him. Why not just enjoy it for now and don't worry too much about where it might lead?"

Our conversation was interrupted by the doorbell ringing. I looked at my watch. It was eight thirty a.m.

Who could that be at this hour in the morning?

Leaving my toast on the kitchen counter, I walked to the front door. I picked up the intercom phone and looked at the blurry display screen. Outside, Conor, grinned and waved at me. He was holding a large bouquet of flowers. My face cracked into a smile, which I knew he couldn't see. "Conor. Come on up." I put the phone down and walked to the front door, to unlock it. A few moments later he knocked on the door and then opened it.

"Good morning, ladies." He handed me the flowers, then nodded at Agota. She smiled back, politely then picked up her tea and went to sit on the sofa, in the open-plan living space. She picked up a magazine and started flipping through it. But I knew she was listening to every word we said.

I brought my attention back to Conor. "Aw, you brought me flowers. What's the occasion?"

"I was showing an apartment, just around the corner and I wanted to check on how you were doing."

"First lunch and now flowers. You really are spoiling me." I walked over to grab the water jug from the cupboard - we didn't own a vase. As I filled the jug with water, I got the kitchen scissors out of the cutlery drawer, and started snipping the ends off the stalks.

Conor watched me, with concern in his eyes. "I heard about what happened, on Friday night, from Frank. Why didn't you call me?"

I thought for a moment. Actually, I'd been so consumed by the events which followed the incident, that it hadn't even entered my mind to call Conor. But I knew that admitting this would hurt his feeling so I went for the easiest thing I could think of.

"I meant to call you but I've been busy. I met someone nice while I was in hospital."

Conor blinked at me and his face flushed ever so slightly. "You met someone? What, another patient or something?"

I couldn't stop myself from smiling. "No. One of the doctors. He took me out on a date last night."

Conor's mouth dropped open. "When you're still recovering from a brutal attack? That's not exactly what I'd call responsible. A doctor should know better."

His judgmental tone riled me and I felt myself tense. "It was only a mild concussion and wrist wound - which is now healing nicely." I rolled up the sleeve of my jumper and held my arm up for him to inspect.

The wound was covered by a bandage but nevertheless, Conor sucked air through his teeth. "Ooh, that looks nasty."

I waved my hand dismissively. "It's fine. I barely remember it's there now. I just have to keep it dry, when I'm in the shower."

He looked down at my tea. "Have you just put the kettle on? I'd love a brew."

"Oh, sure thing."

He walked over to sit on the chair, facing Agota on the sofa, while I made his tea. "Have you just got back from work? I expect you're ready for bed, aren't you?"

Agota smiled at him. "I always need a little time to wind down after my shift, before I go to sleep."

"Makes sense." He looked up at me as I walked through from the kitchen area and handed him his tea. Then I got my tea and toast and curled up on the sofa, next to Agota.

"So, this doctor." His eyes flashed. "Tell me more."

I hunched my shoulders up towards my ears as I sighed. "His name's Nik. He's kind and intelligent, charming, handsome..." My voice trailed off as I allowed myself to get lost in the memories of his smoking hotness.

Conor smiled curtly. "The full package, in other words."

I laughed. "Yes." I looked at him. "At least something good came out of the shitty experience I had."

"Thank God for small mercies," he replied, his lip curling with sarcasm and an intensity of bitterness which took me by surprise. A cold feeling penetrated my insides and I started to regret having told him.

But as soon as this thought entered my head, he quickly corrected his expression and sipped his tea, evidently eager to change the topic. "How's the job hunt going?"

"Ah you know... it's early days. There's loads out there." *But nothing that I actually want.* "I'm sure I'll find something soon." I took a bite of toast.

Conor's eyes moved from left to right and then widened. "Hey, you could try applying to a few consultancy firms. I heard Trewinsky's is doing a big recruitment drive at the moment."

I raised one skeptical eyebrow. "Isn't it super competitive to get into there?"

He shrugged. "It's worth a try. If you don't ask, you don't get, right?"

"I suppose so..."

He drained his tea. "Anyway, I better be off, I have another viewing to get to. But I'm glad you're okay. I'll call you later." He half smiled but his body sagged and I felt a bit guilty, for some reason. He waved at Agota before turning to leave. "See you soon, Agota."

"Yep, have a good day, Conor."

I saw him out then came back to the living room. Agota followed me with her eyes as I came back to sit next to her, on the sofa.

"Why on earth did you tell him about Nik?"

I creased my brow. "Why wouldn't I?"

She brought her hands up in front of her, "Because it's obvious he has the hots for you, that's why."

My mouth dropped open. "Who, Conor? No. He's just an old friend."

"An old friend who is in love with you."

I rolled my eyes and took a sip of tea. "You sound just like Frank"

"Well he's right. I can't believe you don't see it."

"I don't see it, because it's not true. We've known each other for years. Surely if he liked me, he would've said something by now."

"He's playing the long game. He knows he's been friendzoned, and now he's trying to get you to think of him as more. Think about it, he took you out to lunch on Friday..."

"To cheer me up because I'd just lost my job."

"... And now he brings you flowers, at eight thirty on a weekday morning."

"Because he heard I was attacked and spent the night in hospital on Friday."

She shook her head. "Those are all excuses. I'm telling you, his motive can be found inside your knickers."

I scrunched up my face. "Eurgh. I could never think of him in that way. He's more like a brother to me."

"Well, you can believe what you want but I see the way he looks at you."

I finished my toast. "You're wrong."

She sighed. "If you say so. Anyway, I'm exhausted. I'm going to bed."

"Okay, sleep well."

As I watched her walk towards the bedroom, I picked up my tea and considered what she'd said. Frank had always thought Conor fancied me. It was the main reason why he didn't trust him. Frank was a 'what-you-see-is-what-you-get' type of man and he couldn't stand people who he thought had hidden agendas. It was so different from the way he himself operated. I thought of how Conor had looked as I'd walked him out. He'd seemed weary and defeated. Then, when I'd told him about Nik, there'd been an angry edge to his reaction. As I thought about it more and more, I began to accept that Frank and Agota may be right. And if they were, it might be better that I distance myself from Conor. I would never feel the same way about him, as he did about me and knowing this, yet continuing to spend so much time with him, was cruel. Even though I wasn't attracted to him, I did care about him deeply - he was one of my best friends. But I was willing to let that friendship slide if it spared his feelings and allowed him to move on and find someone who could make him happy.

My thoughts drifted to interactions I'd had with him over the years. Little hints he'd given here and there. If I was honest with myself, I'd always known he had feelings for me but I'd been in denial. I knew that accepting the truth would mean having to give him up as a friend and I didn't want to. I'd been selfish. I thought of how hard it would be to start icing him out. How much it would hurt him. But wouldn't it hurt him more to have me finally and fully reject him, when the time came? The look of pain and anger, that had swept over his features, as I'd told him about Nik had sent a feeling of dread creeping through me. I might be willing to cut Conor out of my life, to spare his feelings but I suspected it might be too late for that.

Whether I kept him in my life or not, I had a terrible feeling that Conor would not accept losing me.

10

The days until my next agreed date with Nik passed achingly slowly. But Thursday night finally arrived and I was buzzing with excitement as I looked through the intercom to see Nik, waiting for me. "I'll be down in a minute."

"Okay." His voice crackled through.

I inspected myself one last time, in the mirror, by the front door. I'd chosen my ripped jeans, a fluffy jumper and a tassled, black leather jacket. I'd picked it up in a charity shop but it scrubbed up pretty well. I finished it off by tousling my pink hair so that it fell around my shoulders and applying a bit of smudgy eye make up. Satisfied with my look I called out to my flatmates and left, skipping down the stairs, two at a time.

When I spotted him, my breath caught in my chest. His honey-kissed complexion stood out against a crisp white shirt, jeans and black bomber jacket.

I opened the door and leaned in to kiss him, lightly, on the lips. He tasted sweet, like peppermint - he'd brushed his teeth before meeting me. The smell of his familiar aftershave wafted over me.

"Hey." His heart-breaking smile completely disarmed me.

Looking down, I tucked my hair behind one ear, as I asked. "Where are we off to?"

He put his hands in his pockets, a look of slight discomfort crossing his face - maybe he was cold? "I thought we'd go to Altitude, in the city. Do you know it?"

I shook my head.

"It's a top floor bar, it has a beautiful view."

"Sounds good."

"Come on, let's go." He walked briskly, taking strides that were too big for me to keep up. I tottered by his side. He seemed anxious - was he nervous? I couldn't imagine why, this wasn't even our first date. But then, as we rounded the corner, towards Dalston, he slowed his pace.

I glanced at him, sideways. "Are you okay?"

He turned to face me, smiling brightly. "Never better, why?"

"You just seemed a little... agitated back there, that's all. I was wondering if you'd had a bad day or something."

He gulped. "Sorry, I sometimes forget how much longer my legs are. Please tell me if I'm walking too fast for you, I'm often not aware." He slowed right down. "Is this better?"

I opened my mouth wide and put my hands on my hips. "I'm not a geriatric you know. I can walk at a normal pace - just not the speed walk you were doing back there."

He chuckled. "Okay, got it. Anyway, we won't be walking for long. The first taxi we see, we're grabbing it."

As I looked up and down the road, a taxi approached, its lights blinding us as it ramped a slight hill. I stuck my arm out and it swerved to stop beside us. The driver wound down his window, and smiled. But as I turned to Nik, he'd gone pale. Something was definitely up with him.

"Actually, it's a lovely evening, maybe we should walk?"

I gawped at him. It was *not* a lovely evening. "Are you serious? The City is miles away. It would take us at least an hour to get there on foot. Anyway, I'm not wearing the right footwear for that kind of a hike."

He looked down at my cuban-heeled ankle boots. They were made for dancing, not walking.

With a tight smile, he dropped the subject. "You're right. I don't know what I was thinking."

The taxi driver's lips curled up slowly, in a way that was insincere and oily. His smile was one of challenge rather than genuine positive feelings. Confused, I looked from the driver to Nik and back again. Something unspoken passed between them but I couldn't work out what. His crow like eyes flashed at Nik. "Where to?"

Nik cleared his throat, a look of palpable contempt on his face. "Altitude bar, on King William's Street, please."

Dismissing the weird atmosphere between them, I hopped in, flattening my back against the leather clad seats. The driver immediately locked the doors, glancing at me, in his rearview mirror, as he did so. As soon as we were inside, it hit me. A feeling of rage that swept through my core, igniting every nerve cell and consuming my thoughts with a murderous urge, all directed at the taxi driver. My mind flitted back to my encounter with the Arcane witches and what Morgana had told me about my episodes. She'd said that my powerful urges meant that I was in the presence of a vampire. Could this man be a vampire? I glared at him, studying his odious features. He was balding, with a beaky nose and small, deep set eyes.

Clenching my fists, I looked out of the window, focussing on my breaths, in an effort to stay calm. The instinct to hurt him was so strong, I ground my jaw, willing the episode to go away. Why did this have to happen now, when I was on a hot date? I flicked my eyes towards Nik. He still seemed on edge - perhaps he'd noticed my weird behaviour. I was relieved when the taxi driver spoke, distracting me, from my dark fantasies.

"Nice night for it, isn't it?"

Nik's eyes settled on the man. "Indeed." He smiled but his eyes remained cold and I had the distinct impression that Nik hated him too - but why? Did they know each other from somewhere?

I looked at Nik, trying to work out what was going on with him. "You're very quiet tonight. What's on your mind?"

He rubbed his face with both hands. "Am I? Sorry, it was just a busy day at the hospital, that's all."

I swallowed, suddenly feeling guilty. Of course, sometimes he'd be out of sorts - I could only imagine how hard his job was. "You must have to deal with some terrible things. I don't know how you doctors do it. All that blood... and losing patients. Don't you get traumatised?"

He shrugged. "You get used to the blood." He gritted his teeth and flicked his gaze towards the driver who was, inexplicably smirking at him, as if they were sharing an 'in' joke. Nik looked back at me and carried on. "Over the years, you learn to think of a human being, more as... just a body. That sounds cold-hearted but it's the best way to treat them, especially when their injuries are severe. If I got emotionally involved with every patient who passed through my doors, I wouldn't be able to do my job." His eyes filled with sincerity. I could tell he really loved his job and this made him even more attractive to me. What could be more heroic than a man who saved lives every day, for a living?

I fluttered my eyelashes at him, in a way that I hoped was alluring. "But you got involved with me."

He lowered his voice to just above a whisper. "You're different."

His gaze travelled down my frame, for just a second, making a shiver go up my spine, before he looked away. It was as if he didn't trust himself with me. Why couldn't I work him out?

Suddenly, he became agitated again as he shuffled forward in his seat to address the cab driver. "This isn't the way to Altitude - you should've turned back there."

The driver looked at us in the mirror. "They're doing roadworks over by Aldgate. Traffic is a nightmare around there. This way is quicker, trust me."

Nik narrowed his eyes at the man, as though he didn't believe him. Clenching his jaw, he seemed to be wrestling with himself. He definitely had some sort of beef with the driver.

Nik tore his attention away from the man, to face me. "Anyway, enough about my day. How was your day? What did you get up to?"

I scrunched up my nose. "Nothing much. Just more job hunting."

He nodded and his shoulders visibly sagged with relief, as we turned towards King William's Street. We pulled up outside Altitude and got out. Nik paid the driver, practically throwing money at his face as if he couldn't wait to be out of his presence.

The driver apparently didn't notice. "Thank you very much, Sir." He tilted his head towards him. But Nik returned a murderous gaze, as if he wanted to punch the man in the face. I couldn't understand his bizarre behaviour but nor was it obvious enough for me to call out. Perhaps he'd just had a stressful day, as he'd said.

As the cab drove off, he put his arm around me and I brushed the incident aside, looking forward to spending an evening with him, as we went inside.

∼

∼

ONCE WE GOT INSIDE, Nik relaxed and I forgot about his weird behaviour in the cab. Then, after a magical evening of laughter and soul-sharing, we left the warmth of the bar and stepped out onto the windy street. Standing near the edge of the road, we tried to hail a cab. A taxi approached and I raised my arm to hail it. But Nik grabbed it down so forcefully that he almost pulled my arm out of its socket.

I whirled around, my eyes blazing at him. "What's wrong?"

A range of emotions struggled for dominance on his face. "Nothing. It's just… such a pleasant evening. I thought we could walk for a bit." He was a terrible liar. His eyes flitted towards the approaching taxi, his expression that of a hunted animal.

I wasn't buying this bullshit. "Pleasant? It is not pleasant - it's windy and cold and horrible. What's really going on?"

I could see the cogs of his mind turning as he raced to settle on an acceptable explanation. Why couldn't he just tell me the truth?

"Don't get in that taxi. I don't like the look of the driver." He blurted it out in one breath.

I squinted, in the semi-darkness, unable to make out the driver. "How can you see him from this distance?"

He faltered. "I... I can't, I just have a bad feeling, that's all." His agitation seemed to increase, the closer the cab got.

This was ridiculous. "Come on, you're being paranoid. He's a professional black cab driver. Aren't they all registered?"

Nik's face dissolved into something akin to panic as the cab stopped beside us.

He gulped, closing his eyes briefly as the front, passenger window wound down, with a whirring noise. I did a double take as I saw that it was the same taxi driver from before. The man must have still been in the area...

Or had he waited for us?

An uneasy feeling spread through me. But I pushed the irrational thought to one side. Now *I* was being paranoid. The driver smiled at Nik with the same, weird, knowing look he'd given him before. Less a smile and more a smirk. "Good evening again Sir, where to?"

Fed up with the sludge-like atmosphere, I strode forward and opened the door, smiling back at Nik. "Come on, what are you waiting for?"

Nik had gone pale. He stood, routed to the spot, looking from me, to the driver and back at me again. Was he about to have some kind of fit? I started to wonder if he was suffering the onset of some type of mental breakdown. Then, without warning, he lurched forward and slammed the door closed. He grabbed me and almost threw me away from the cab, without bothering to give an explanation, to either myself, or the driver. He half walked, half ran, dragging me along as he held my arm in a vice-like grip.

He's lost his mind - or maybe this is the real him? A violent psychopath!

For the first time I started to feel genuinely scared. I looked from left to right, there was barely anyone about. "Ow! You're hurting me." I winced and tried to release my arm.

He relaxed his grip slightly and I tore my arm out of his grasp, rounding on him. "Have you gone mad? What is wrong with you. Tell me now or I'm going home and you can forget about seeing me again."

We were now far back from the road, standing next to a skyscraper, the security guard visible through the glass doors. I felt a rush of gratitude that I wasn't completely alone with Nik who was becoming more and more unhinged by the minute..

His hands were shaking as he ran his fingers through his hair and took a deep breath. "That taxi driver. He means us both harm."

My eyes narrowed. "What makes you think that?"

"Because... there's no easy way to explain." He looked up at the sky and then back at me. "This is not a joke. I'm not trying to toy with you. I just want to protect you and keep you safe. That taxi driver is..."

A feeling of doom spread through me. I knew what he was going to say, I'd known it the minute I'd got into his cab earlier and felt the onset of my rage episode. "Is what?"

"He's a vampire."

It was as if time stood still and the only thing that my mind registered were Nik's lips, forming the words that I'd dreaded yet expected.

He gulped then continued. "Vampires are real, they live all around us." he paused, assessing my reaction. I know I should've feigned surprise but I'd never been a good actor.

"Go on," I replied softly, a cold feeling spreading over my limbs as I crossed my arms.

"It's not like in the movies where they explode if they go in sunlight and recoil at garlic and can't stand the sight of crucifixes. They are just like regular people, living normal lives. But they can only survive on human blood and they live for centuries. They're stronger, faster, heal quicker and are altogether more powerful than humans." He stopped and looked down at me, his brow furrowed, pain etched across his perfect features.

"How do you know all this?" I replied, desperate to know yet afraid of what the answer might be.

He opened and closed his mouth a few times then met my gaze, a mixture of longing and sadness, in his eyes. Taking a deep breath, he said, "the reason why I know all this is because I..."

He didn't get to finish his sentence. With a loud revving of its engine, the black cab reappeared. It mounted the pavement, bumping into the edge of a bus stop, just beside us. Nik grabbed me and dived out of the way, crushing my body under his as we hit the hard, cold pavement. The cab doors opened and two, burly men got out of the back seat. The cab driver got out of the front and joined them. One of them licked his lips and the other cracked his knuckles, as they advanced on us. Icy claws of fear clutched at my insides as I looked at Nik.

Scrambling to his feet, he pulled me up, beside me. A glassy look of hate that I'd never seen before, entered his eyes, as he growled at the advancing men. I didn't know who to fear more - the cab driver and his built-like-tanks buddies, or this strange, animalistic man, Nik had suddenly become.

Then he looked at me. "Run!" he yelled, yanking my arm as we took off. As we ran, our pursuers seemed to move with lightning speed. They surrounded us in the seconds it took for us to get a few metres.

Nik whipped his head from side to side, as if trying to work out which one was the weakest. We'd fled far away from the security guard and were now completely alone, on a deserted side street. The taxi driver painted an oily smile on his face as he addressed Nik. "Just give us the girl and we'll leave you alone. We won't hurt her."

"Bullshit." he snarled.

He shrugged. "Have it your way."

They were at his side instantly, powering punches and kicks into him as he crumpled to the ground. I screamed, instinct telling me to run but my heart telling me to stay and help him.

"Bree, run!" He managed to lift his head and another fist flew into his face, blood spraying from his lip. Nik punched one of the goliaths, hard, in the nose but it was like the man was made of stone. There was barely any reaction. One of them kicked Nik in the face, hard enough that his head ricocheted backwards but he righted himself and carried on fighting. That kind of a blow would normally cause a man to pass out. My hands flew to my face and I staggered backwards, appalled at the level of violence I was witnessing. This was a far cry from the sparring that I regularly engaged in. These guys fought like they really wanted to kill each other and I struggled to match what I was seeing with the tender, compassionate man, who I'd come to know since he'd treated me, in the hospital. It was three against one and there was no way Nik could hold them off forever. As the blows reigned down on him, he crouched down, into a protective ball, his hands covering his head.

My heart thumped in my chest as I fumbled in my bag, for my phone. I had to call the police. These men were going to kill him, if I didn't do something. There was no way I could take them on alone - even I wasn't that reckless. But then, as my fingers found my phone, it was as if something in the air shifted, causing me to look back up. I couldn't explain what had changed but I felt it, like sound waves but ones I could feel rather than hear. My skin tingled as if static electricity was passing over me.

Nik suddenly roared, bursting through the men. It seemed as if he'd grown in size, his muscles flexing as he threw each one off. He snarled and twirled around. Then he closed his eyes and breathed deeply.

The men were staggering to their feet and moving towards him again but he opened his eyes and looked at them, in the same way a wolf looks at a deer.

He lifted his head and growled deeply. The sound punctuated the cold, still, night air and in that moment, my heart froze.

There, inside his mouth were two, perfectly pointed white fangs, where his canine teeth should've been. They hadn't been there before - they'd just appeared. I started to shake as the terrible realisation seeped into my mind.

Nik is a vampire!

11

I felt numb. I couldn't move but merely watched, in mute terror. The other men now also all had fangs. Is that how it worked? Did fighting cause them to appear? Or had it been the smell of blood, from the fight? But a vampire's fangs wouldn't appear from the sight of vampire blood, would it? I had no idea. Everything I knew about vampires, I'd learnt from films.

Nik bared his fangs at the other vampires. His manner was that of a wild predator, I barely recognised him.

The taxi driver looked at his friends, a look of irritation on his face. "Just our bloody luck. He's risen to the source. We can't fight him like this, it's not worth it."

Risen to the source? I had no idea what that meant.

The knuckle-cracking vampire looked at Nik in dismay. "But what about the girl?"

"We'll take her some other time. Come on, let's go." He beckoned for them to follow him into the cab and they sped off, into the night.

Nik took a deep breath and visibly deflated, seeming to decrease in size, once more. He turned around, looking for me.

I didn't want him anywhere near me and backed away as he reached out his hand.

A look of confusion flitted across his face and then his hands flew up to his mouth as if he could cover up what he was.

"Get away from me!" I shouted, walking backwards, with one arm outstretched, like a weapon.

"Bree, wait, I can explain."

I shook my head, shock and disbelief, flooding my synapses. Lights danced around my head and silvery lights came out of Nik. Reality was muted, my shock and fear, blocking out my logical reasoning. I was barely aware of what I was doing, acting in pure survival mode. He was about to cover up his actions in more lies and I didn't want to hear them. I just wanted to get away from him - far, far away.

I turned and bolted, running faster than I'd ever run before. The city rushed past me, a blur of lights and movements. Spurred on by the pain of his lies, I poured all my poisonous emotions into my legs, barely feeling my muscles or the ground as I thundered towards home.

How could I keep seeing Nik now? Slowing to a jog, I realised I was already near Dalston. Looking at my watch, I'd made the distance in a few minutes. I frowned and shook my watch - that couldn't be right? Maybe it wasn't working properly? But I didn't have the energy to think about it any further. Anger and disappointment consumed me. He must've thought I was such an idiot. He'd played me for a fool. I gritted my teeth as I thought of what a sick bastard he was. Was this what he did for kicks? Get human girls to fall for him and then bite them, when their guard was down? Salty tears stung at my eyes as I slowed to a brisk walk.

Adrenaline still coursed through me and my entire body was tense. Now, with my senses on high alert, everywhere I looked, I saw vampires. I saw them coming out of pubs, laughing as they looked at me, dark intent in their eyes. I saw them driving buses and I saw them simply walking along the street. I was trapped in a nightmare, I couldn't wake up from. The world was sodden with them. Was it possible that all this was a mental delusion? Perhaps brought on by my head injury or the stress of the past week? Could I just discount what I'd seen and bury my head back in the sand? I wished I could but I knew that was impossible. I knew what I saw was real and more than that, I'd always known that Nik was hiding something *big*. Something even worse than being married. Now that I knew what it was, the crushing disappointment enveloped me like hot tar.

Nik is a vampire

He'd lied to me. Was he in cahoots with the vampire I'd fought with? Had it all been part of some elaborate, grand plan to get revenge on me? But if that were true, why did he fight, so viciously, in my defence, back there? He'd returned to the topic of my security and safety again and again, during the few times we'd been together. Now I knew why. He knew that vampires were after me. Everything the witches had said had been true. I could no longer dismiss them as two loons. They'd been telling the truth about vampires. And if they'd told the truth about that, then I had to accept that they'd told the truth about me too.

I was an Arcane witch, with the power to do magic and the destiny to hunt vampires. Me and Nik were natural enemies. But why didn't I feel an impulse to hurt him? It didn't make any sense.

As I reached my neighbourhood, I saw a marked increase in the number of vampires. I couldn't believe I had been blind to it for so long. It was like I was waking from a coma and seeing clearly for the first time. The scales had fallen from my eyes. Everything I'd ever been told about the world, was a lie. My sense of self and my perception of reality, began to unravel. I gripped my elbows, my breath coming out in fast, shallow gasps. The city lights seemed too bright, the sounds, too loud. I felt dizzy. I stopped to grab hold of a railing, at the side of the road, bending over to catch my breath.

"Are you okay?" A young woman stopped and bent down, her eyes full of concern. I reared back as she touched my shoulder, lightly. She was a vampire. The same cloying smell of rust, that I'd smelt, when Nik's fangs had protruded, covered her.

"Get off me." I snapped, jerking my shoulder away from her.

She looked hurt and stumbled backwards. I didn't care. I had to get away from her. I had to get home, where it was safe. But was it safe? Was anywhere safe? This was exactly what Nik had been talking about. I wasn't safe in my flat. I wasn't safe anywhere. As long as vampires walked the earth, I wasn't safe.

I sped up my pace until I was almost jogging and reached my apartment block in a few minutes. Before I opened the front door, I turned to look at my street. I saw vampires everywhere. Two in the shop, opposite my building. One, simply standing, watching me, from across the street. Another pretending to wash his car. They were all watching me, furtively but deliberately. I opened the door, making sure it closed behind me, then raced up the stairs , too impatient to wait for the lift. I fumbled with the key, in the lock, cursing out loud, before I finally got inside. Taking in a large, healing breath of relief, I stood, with my back against the flat front door for a few moments. I was a mess and I had to gain my composure before seeing my flatmates.

As my breathing returned to normal, I walked through to the lounge. Agota was moving around in our room. She wasn't working tonight, which I normally would've been happy about but tonight was different. I wasn't ready to face her yet. She would ask me how my date with Nik had gone. What could I say? She'd always been very good at reading people, she'd know I was lying, if I just said, 'fine'.

"Hi." Her cheery voice called through, from the bedroom. Her mood was fathoms above how I felt. Then all at once, I knew what I should say.

I walked through to the bedroom, not bothering to hide my emotions.

Agota's smile dropped when she saw me. "What's wrong?"

"Me and Nik had a fight."

Her face creased with confusion. "Already? You've been seeing each other for less than a week. What was it about?"

I sighed and hugged myself. "He's not the man I thought he was. It's just as I thought, he has secrets. Things so deep, I can't even talk about them."

Her face softened, with sympathy. "Oh no! I'm so sorry. I know how much you liked him. Do you think it's over for good, with no possibility of patching things up?"

I bit my lip and shook my head slightly. "I think so... I dunno, it's really complicated."

She half smiled. "Do you want a glass of wine? I bought a bottle of cheap plonk earlier. It tastes like lighter fuel but it still gets you pissed."

For a brief moment, I considered it. But my head still spun from the alcohol I'd had at the bar with Nik. Plus, I didn't really want to get drunk. I wanted a clear head and space to think. "No thanks, Agota. I'm just going to go on the balcony for a bit."

She nodded. Both my flatmates understood that when I went on the balcony, it was my thinking time, and that I should be left alone.

As I walked through the hallway, I rubbed my eyes, then remembered I was wearing make up. All of a sudden, my eyelashes felt weighed down by the mascara. I felt way older than my twenty two years. I was already bone tired and my makeup was making me feel even worse. It had to come off, immediately. I pivoted in the direction of the bathroom and looked at myself in the mirror. My large, blue eyes were bloodshot and puffy. My pale skin was blotchy, even with foundation on. And my shoulder-length, pink hair, normally straight, was bedraggled and windswept - but not in a good way. All in all, I looked terrible. I grabbed the cotton wool pads and make up remover, from the medicine cabinet and got to work, cleaning my face. When I'd finished, I washed my face again with soap and water, then patted it dry and put on my cheap, no-name brand moisturiser. The face that stared back at me was still blotchy and emotionally ravaged but at least it was fresh and clean.

I walked to the kitchen, poured myself a large glass of water, which I downed, before walking out onto the balcony. I was starting to feel human again. But was I actually human? Were arcane witches human? Or superhuman? Or another breed entirely? Morgana and Evelyn had looked human but their abilities had seemed far from normal. And what about their assessment of me? Since I'd met them, I'd thought a lot about the way my abilities had manifested, to protect me, that Friday night, in front of the vampire. But they hadn't manifested tonight? At least not at first. I'd made it back home far quicker than normal so I was fairly certain that I'd manifested my powers to borrow super-speed, from the vampires.

The vampires.

As the thought came to me, I felt a clutch of fear, then sadness, shoot through my centre. Nik had tried to tell me I wasn't safe but he'd left out the fact that I wasn't safe *with him*. He'd told me as much as he could, without revealing what he was. I just hadn't listened. I'd wanted to believe the best of him because - and as the thought hit me, I felt my eyes widen.

I already had feelings for him.

Keeping him in my life was insanity. But letting him go felt even worse.

As I looked out at the street below, I saw vampires everywhere. The air was thick with the smell of rust and decay. Why hadn't I ever smelt that on Nik before? But then I had. I'd smelt a metallic undertone, to his aftershave, that, at the time, I'd found inviting. Anger flashed through me, at the thought he'd deliberately put on an aftershave that he knew would cloak what he really was. He was a liar and a cheat, a manipulative bastard. And yet, I still wanted him. Even now, in my anger, I longed for him. Even knowing what he was. I didn't understand myself. I didn't understand any of this.

Closing my eyes, I wished I could take a break from life. I was overwhelmed, with no one to turn to. I couldn't talk about this with anyone. Not Frank, not Agota and certainly not Conor. What was going on, in my life, right now, was too out there, even for Aunt Siobhan. I felt so alone. I was desperate to share this with someone - anyone, who would understand.

My thoughts were disturbed by the sound of the front door being opened. Giggling and two sets of footsteps, one of them stumbling, hit my ears. Then the sound of a male voice, asking to use the bathroom. Tallulah's voice responded. So she'd brought someone home? And on the worst possible night, from my perspective. Now I'd have to either stay in my room or make small talk. I felt physically sick at the thought of making small talk so I left the balcony, closing the door behind me as I walked towards my room. I'd almost made it when the bathroom door opened and a tall, very good looking, black man came out.

Damnit! Now I have to at least greet him.

That was the shortest pee break in the history of mankind. He must have the bladder of a mouse.

"Hi, I'm Derek." He extended his hand and as he did so, I recoiled.

Derek was a vampire.

I SMILED CURTLY, folding my arms across my chest. "Bree."

Tallulah came out of her room. "Ah, I see you've met Derek."

I narrowed my eyes at him. "So, where did you two meet?"

Tallulah gushed as she swayed. "At the Brick Lane Social. It was amazing there tonight, the DJ was on point."

She was clearly too shit-faced to notice my discomfort. I wanted to get as far away from Derek as was humanly possible but if I fled to my room, I'd be leaving a vampire, in my flat, alone with my friend. He could murder her and then come and find me and Agota. Plus, it was too much of a coincidence. Tallulah, had endured such a dating dry spell, there were probably cobwebs in her vi-jay-jay. Now, after months of no one, she'd suddenly met a handsome vampire. He was a honey trap - he had to be.

She put a steadying hand onto the wall and suddenly went a subtle shade of green. "Eurgh, I don't feel so good. I think I'm going to be..."

She didn't finish her sentence as she dashed off to the toilet. The sound of violent puking rang out through the flat.

Derek's eyes darkened as he looked me up and down. I wanted to punch his smug, bastard lights out. He didn't bother with small talk and it was obvious why. He was here to hurt me. Tallulah had just been the means by which to get inside. I adopted a fighting stance.

Damnit!

Why had I left the silver knives in the kitchen cutlery drawer! If what I'd learnt about vampires, from Hollywood, was true, I'd never get to the kitchen before he got to me. But I was bloody well going to try.

Flexing my shoulders, I clenched my fists. In response he ground his jaw. I could tell that this mother fucker, wasn't going down easily. I flicked my gaze to the side, down the corridor, in the direction of the kitchen knives. In that same moment, Derek lunged at me, his fangs protruding as he went for my jugular. I leapt out of the way, darting down the corridor towards the kitchen. But he was in front of me, in the blink of an eye. Panic seized me as I realised how vulnerable I was, in the presence of this predator. Apparently I had the power to make mince meat out of him but how the hell did I make that power work? With mounting dread, I realised that Evelyn and Morgana had been right - without proper training, in how to use my arcane powers, I was just a puny human woman.

Not yet willing to accept defeat, I charged into him, ramming his chest with the top of my head. It was like I'd head butted a stone wall and I saw stars. Derek chuckled as if I was a toddler, throwing a tantrum about something trivial. His reaction enraged me and I saw the familiar, orangey lights, dancing around my head. I was taken back to last Friday night. I'd seen lights then too but what had I done next? It had all happened so fast, I couldn't remember and certainly not now - with the threat of imminent and grisly death hanging over me.

Then, an idea suddenly pinged, in my head. My fight training kicked in. I dropped and rolled, standing up near the sink. Glancing into the sink, I knew what I would see and thank God, our messy habits hadn't let me down. There, in the washing up bowl, lay a mountain of dirty dishes and cutlery. Glistening, within the pile was one of the silver knives, smeared with butter. Perfect! My fingers touched the knife, about to pick it up.

But he was already upon me. His fangs were at my neck, just piercing the skin, when Tallulah staggered in. Her appearance briefly distracted him and he pulled back.

Her hands flew to her face. "Derek! What the fuck do you think you're doing?" Her face went bright red and her eyes bulged.

I realised how this must look to her. She'd walked in and seen her hook up, with his mouth clamped around my neck. She thought we were getting it on - the same as I had, when I'd seen the vampire attack the woman last Friday night.

Derek had decided to drop the pretence. He snarled at her, not bothering to hide his fangs. Tallulah screamed and bolted towards her bedroom, slamming the door behind her. The sound of subtle whimpering, could be heard.

Wow! I wouldn't want her in my platoon. First sign of the enemy and she runs for cover.

Next, Agota appeared. "What's going on out here? ... what the..." Her eyes widened and she stopped dead in her tracks at the sight of Derek and his offensive fangs.

Derek shrugged. "Two for the price of one." His eyes glittered as he looked at me. "But you first."

I lunged for the knife, grabbing it, at last, then swirling around to slash at him. Blood sprayed across the white kitchen walls as I made contact with his cheek. Some of it got into my mouth and I gagged at the metallic, rust-like taste.

His hand flew up to his face, as blood dripped through his fingers. "You'll pay for that, bitch."

He leapt into the air, almost hitting the ceiling as he came down onto my shoulders. His weight crushed me to the floor, where he pinned both my wrists back. The knife clattered out of my hands. Agota picked it up and held it towards us both. Her hands were shaking. I knew she didn't have it in her to stab him, even though I was, silently, praying she would.

"G...Get off her. Right now" Her voice quivered.

The vampire seemed amused by this and his shoulders shook with mirth, weakening him slightly. It was just the chance I needed. I bucked up my hips, turning him over, in the same way I'd practiced again and again, with Janice, in the gym. Now I was on top.

"Throw me the knife!" I shouted at Agota.

She threw it way too hard and I ducked as it sailed past me, planting itself into a kitchen cupboard door and out of my reach.

Shit! What are the odds?...

Her face crumpled. "Sorry."

A cruel smile of victory lit up Derek's face as he bucked his hips and rolled over. He was on me once more. But then something happened that I never would've seen coming. Tallulah came crashing out of her room, holding the iron, in her hands. She belted him across the head, hard enough that he went flying across the room. He crashed into the coffee table, shattering it. Glass flew everywhere, a piece of it hit me, in the shoulder. Pain lanced through me and I winced as I looked down to see blood, spreading out across my shirt. I looked back up to see that another piece of glass had lodged into the TV and another piece had hit the window. It slowly cracked and then collapsed to the ground, in a shower of glass. Wind blew leaves and rain into the flat. I looked, from the window, back at Tallulah, in shock and awe. I never would've guessed she had *that* in her. She was a bit out of shape but by God she was strong.

For a blessed moment, I thought Derek was unconscious but I was wrong. He groaned then sat up. Agota sprinted towards the kitchen and started rifling through the drawers. She'd wisely assessed that it would be quicker to get a new knife than to dislodge the other one from the kitchen cupboard door.

"Get one of the silver ones, Agota!" I shouted.

But would she be quick enough? Derek was already back on his feet and walking, unsteadily towards me, his face tight with determination.

I staggered backwards, stumbling over the remains of the coffee table. There was no way out. Derek was blocking my path to the front door so my only option was to either attack him or try and jump from the balcony. I didn't fancy my chances, from the second floor, especially with a gash in my shoulder. Tallulah and Agota were behind him, standing next to each other. Agota had found another kitchen knife and started advancing towards him, with Tallulah just behind her. But then he turned and made eye contact with both of them. His voice took on a deep, sonorous quality.

"You do not want to attack me. We are friends. Do you understand?"

In horror, I saw Agota's hand go slack as the knife drooped towards the floor and a vacant look entered her eyes. I recognised that look. It was the same expression I'd seen on the face of the guard when Nik had taken me to the observatory and I realised that he'd used the same mind control to gain access.

Derek continued, his voice soothing and melodic. "Good girl. Now, the lady behind me is your enemy, she wants to hurt you, she wants to hurt me and I'm your friend. You will help me to kill her. Yes?"

Oh fuck!

Agota strode robotically towards me. Tallulah marched towards the cupboard door, dislodging the knife before turning towards me. All traces of inebriation had completely vanished. Even with the puking, she couldn't have got so together so quickly - it was the vampire mind control, it must have the power to override drunkenness. Tallulah reached me first, stabbing out at me, with her knife. But I was too quick for her. I ducked, barrelling into her legs to bring her down. As she fell, she dropped the knife, I grabbed it and slashed at her arm. My intention was to cut her lightly, hoping that it would break the spell. But in my distress, I slashed too deep. Blood spurted out of her arm, causing Derek to hiss in excitement, his eyes flashing in a way that turned my stomach.

With her mind still under Derek's control, Tallulah barely noticed her arm. She slipped in her own blood as she scrambled up to standing. Then she advanced on me again, blood flowing from her arm all over the floor and sofa.

Derek's lips curled up into a triumphant smile as Agota and Tallulah flanked him, like two dishevelled zombie assassins. He moved slowly this time, licking his lips, clearly relishing the fear I was exuding. Tallulah was already starting to look pale. She wouldn't last long without medical attention but that was the least of my concerns. As the three of them got closer and closer, I thought of my brother, Frank. I thought of my Aunt Siobhan and Uncle Paddy and I thought of my dead Mum. I'd be seeing her very soon. Derek was now close enough that I felt the heat of his body and saw the pupils in his eyes, dilate. Just as he reached out to grab me, I thought of my father in prison - the abusive bastard who'd raised me. I'd never find out if he was my real father or not. I'd never get to spit on his grave.

Derek grabbed me and sank his fangs into my neck. White hot pain rushed through my body and I screamed and writhed. Agota and Tallulah were behind him. I was dimly aware of Tallulah passing out, but my consciousness began to dim as Derek drained the life force from me.

12

Floating in a black sea of stars, the cosmos swirled around me. Space and time were irrelevant. I was insubstantial and at peace.

Then, I heard a voice saying, "Bree, it's not your time."

My consciousness snapped back into my body. A thrumming vibration, pulsed through my being. Strong hands held me and my eyelids fluttered open. The vibration was the thudding of feet, thundering along the pavement. A man was holding me in his arms, as he sprinted.

His voice came out again, this time louder. "Stay with me, Bree. Don't die on me."

Nik!

A rush of euphoria and bottomless relief flooded my awareness and I forced my eyes open.

"You came for me." I whispered, my eyelids feeling unbearably heavy. In the back of my mind, I remembered being angry at him, for some reason but I couldn't focus on it, right now.

His head jolted towards me. "You're awake!" He slowed to a jog then turned to a quiet side street and crouched down, still holding me. "I couldn't stay away, I just knew those Dracul bastards would send someone and I was right."

I tried to speak but instead, I coughed and felt whoozy, the world dimmed again.

"There's no time for this. I have to get you to safety." Nik stood up and started running again. I wanted to ask him where he was taking me but I was too weak. I drifted, in and out of consciousness until, at last, I felt myself being placed into a warm, dry bed.

An Italian-accented, female voice spoke with Nik in urgent, hushed tones.

"What were you thinking? Bringing her back here?"

"What choice did I have? I can't take her to a hospital. How would I explain the fang marks and blood loss? I can't risk being outed."

"But she needs a blood transfusion."

"I know that!"

"Well, where are you going to get the blood from?"

"I'll have to steal some from the hospital."

"Can you do that?"

"It's fine - stuff goes missing all the time. I'll steal or borrow whatever else I need from there too. But she won't last long enough for me to get back. I'll have to heal her a little with my blood"

The woman sounded shocked. "Are you sure? There's no telling what effect it could have on her."

"We have no choice. It's either that or she dies."

It was the last thing I heard before I lapsed back into oblivion.

THE PITTER PATTER of rain against the window, competed with the nearby cooing of pigeons and distant traffic noises. I opened my eyes to see an unfamiliar ceiling, decorated with mildewed seventies wallpaper and grime. For a moment I had no memory of where I was or what I was doing here. And then I tried to sit up and winced as it all came back to me. Vampire Derek and his mind-controlled accomplices, otherwise known as my two flatmates. Then Nik had rescued me. But I still didn't know where I was or how long I'd been out for. My movements were restricted by a canula, sticking into my hand, attached to a drip by a tube. The bedroom door opened and a dark-haired woman came in. When she saw me awake, she immediately tensed up, flattening herself against the wall. I frowned at her, in confusion. She stepped towards me slowly, as if approaching an agitated man with a gun.

"How do you feel?" Her voice came out hesitant and unsure and I wondered what her issue was - it seemed to be with me but I didn't know why.

"Like shit," I croaked.

"And how about emotionally?"

It was a strange question to ask and once again, I felt my brows furrow. "Um, a little freaked out I suppose."

Her body visibly deflated. She was relieved. Why was she relieved? It was like she was terrified of me. Surely, I should be the one who was scared. I was the one in a bed, in strange surroundings, recovering from a vampire attack.

I recognised her voice as the same lady who had been in conversation with Nik when I'd been brought here. Now more at ease, she brushed her dark hair away from her face. "Well, you should eat something, it will make you feel better. What would you like?"

I'd always been the type to wake up ravenous and as soon as she mentioned food, my stomach grumbled, in response. "I dunno, pizza, maybe?"

"Excellent choice. I'll send someone to get some for you."

My brain was still groggy but nevertheless one question sprang immediately to mind. "Where's Nik?"

"He had to go to work. He'll be back as soon as his shift finishes."

"When's that?"

"It's eleven in the morning now. He'll be back sometime after five pm."

"Why aren't you at work?"

She sighed, a look of sadness passing over her face. "I don't work a regular day job anymore."

She drew up a battered old wooden chair from the side of my bed and brought it closer to me. As she sat down, she felt my forehead. Her palm was cool and soft.

"Are you a doctor too?"

"No. My name is Carlotta, I'm a molecular biologist. Nik and I are old friends."

As soon as she said this, I wondered if she was his ex. She was certainly beautiful, with long, silky dark hair, large brown eyes and very red lips. How could I ask without seeming like a jealous girlfriend? "How did you meet him?"

She chuckled slightly then blew air out of her mouth. "That is a long story."

"Does it have a short version?" I cocked one eyebrow.

She narrowed her eyes at me, a smile, flirting at her lips. "You're wondering if we were ever together, aren't you?"

There were clearly no flies on Carlotta and I felt myself blush.

"Don't worry. He's all yours."

Her dark eyes studied me for a moment. "Can I ask you a more personal question?"

"Sure. Go ahead."

"Do you feel any anger when you're around Nik? Any feelings of rage or... this might sound weird but - any urges to kill him?"

I stared at her. She was laying her cards on the table. She knew I fantasised about killing vampires and that meant she knew what I was. And if she knew, it was likely that Nik knew too. He'd never hinted at it though... Or had he? As I replayed back conversations we'd had, I realised he probably did know. He'd suggested that my fighting skills were somehow abnormal and he'd advised me to research my family. Did that mean arcane witch powers ran in families? And if they did, how did he know that?

I looked back at Carlotta. Her behaviour on the way into the room - she'd been scared and if she'd been scared it must be because... I felt my eyes widen. "You're a vampire!"

I couldn't stop my mouth from dropping open. She looked so ordinary and I didn't have the kill instinct around her at all. I wondered if it was the effects of the medication or a similar kind of anomaly to that which I experienced around Nik.

She gave a rue smile. "You can close your mouth. We don't all look like blood thirsty criminals, you know. After all, you didn't realise Nik was a vampire when you first met him, did you?"

I raised my eyebrows. "No, I guess not."

"And you didn't answer my question. Do you want to kill us or not?"

I met her gaze. "No."

She cocked her head to the side, resting her cheek between her thumb and forefinger. "Why do you think that is?"

I shrugged. "I have no idea."

Her gaze shifted. "I wonder if it's because we're vegans."

"You're what?"

She looked at me, crossing one leg over the other. "Vegans. I developed a product called Vital8. I also sell it on the dark web - that's how we fund ourselves. It's synthetic human blood made from genetically engineered rice. Vampires can live off it indefinitely. When I met Nik, he was attempting to bite a human. I stopped him and introduced him to Vital8. That was five years ago. He's been vegan ever since."

If what she was saying was true, Nik didn't feed off humans to survive. Could this be a trap? But then, she had no reason to lie. After all, if they wanted to feed off me, why would they save my life? They had ample opportunity to just finish me off, after Nik rescued me from Derek.

Something was still bothering me. "You know what I am, don't you."

She nodded. "An arcane witch."

I narrowed my eyes. "If you knew that about me, why did you let me in?"

She shrugged. "I wasn't exactly thrilled about the idea but I know you haven't been trained in how to use your powers - you stumbled upon them by accident. That means you're not allied with an arcane witch group so we're safe from slaughter, at least for the time being.

When you go we'll find a new location." She flicked her hair. "Plus Nik can be pretty persuasive."

I looked down, suddenly feeling like the world's biggest fool. "Has he always known what I was?"

She nodded.

"How?"

"Arcane witches have a very distinctive smell, which vampires can detect."

I looked away, taking in what she'd said. He knew and yet he'd still saved my life. He must know how dangerous it was for him to be around me and yet he was dating me. None of this made any sense. What did he want from me?

I looked around my dilapidated surroundings. The torn carpet was covered in stains and patches of gravel. There were holes and pigeon shit on the walls - God knows where the pigeons came in from. There must be a window missing somewhere.

"Where are we?"

Carlotta smiled sadly at me. "This is the ahimsa vampire hideout. We have to stay in old abandoned wrecks and move regularly because the dracul vampires have bounties out on most of us - you too now, I guess."

There's that word again. 'Dracul'. The witches had mentioned them.

I furrowed my eyebrows. "Who are the Draculs?"

"They're a fascist vampire gang - the largest in the world. Their power extends across borders and they have vampires in politics, in businesses, in schools - everywhere. The leader of the group is a man called Hugh Beaufort. He is a centuries-old billionaire vampire. But his property empire and antiques and art dealerships are all money laundering fronts for the real way he makes his money - human trafficking, mostly immigrant women and children, to supply other vampires with live human blood. The ultimate aim of the Draculs is world domination. They believe that vampires are a superior species and that humans should be kept and bred as cattle - to feed us."

"Whoa! That's some dark shit."

"Yes it is." She bit her lip. "They see us as a threat to their plans. If we keep turning vampires vegan - which we do, then it weakens their power base. Also, there's some historic animosity between me and Hugh Beaufort. His daughter joined our movement. I didn't know she was his daughter at the time. Then she got killed in a battle against them - she didn't realise he was a Dracul."

"This is like something out of a movie."

She rubbed her temples with one hand. "It gets worse. Hugh was determined to enact revenge on me so he ordered a hit against my fiance, Noah - a human. I thought I could keep him safe." She gritted her teeth and gulped as her eyes got misty. "I was wrong."

I felt the pain radiating out of her, causing a lump of sympathy to form in my throat. "You mean he died?"

She nodded, her face contorting with grief. She dipped her head as a single tear hit the ground, splashing in the dust, at her feet.

I didn't know what to say. I had just met this woman and she'd shared what must be one of the most painful experiences of her life with me. And why? Just because I'd asked her for the truth. She didn't have to tell me all of that. She could've left out the part about her dead fiancé. I sensed that Carlotta was a straight talker, someone who didn't keep secrets. I'd forgotten what it was like to be around people who weren't afraid to wear their heart on their sleeve. Being around someone who trusted me enough to share her pain with me, reminded me of home and I suddenly wished I could see Aunt Siobhan and Uncle Paddy.

"Could I make a phone call?"

Carlotta's face grew tight but her voice was soft and tender. "I'm sorry Bree, I can't allow that. The Draculs could trace your cell phone signal. We've switched your phone off and you can't use it. I have it in safe keeping for now." She stroked hair out of my face in a way that was maternal and I wondered if she'd ever had any children during her human days. Could vampires have children? There was so much that I had to learn.

"You said you're 'ahimsa vampires'. What does that mean?"

"Ahimsa is a sanskrit word which means 'non-harming'. It just means that we live our lives trying our best not to harm the innocent. In addition to being vegans, we only kill or hurt, in self-defence."

"Kind of like Buddhists?"

"Yes, in mindset, although we're not a religious group. We're more a type of.... Social activism group."

Her explanation made me feel way better about dating Nik. It meant that my instincts, about him being safe and kind, had not been totally wrong.

Carlotta continued. "Listen, I know you have so many questions but you still need to rest. I'll send someone to get you some pizza but why don't you get some more sleep. We can talk later - when Nik gets back. I'll bring in a glass of water - I'm sure your throat is dry."

She was right, my throat was almost burning. Did she know that because she'd inflicted these same injuries on humans in the past? She seemed so kind and gentle, it was hard to imagine her baring her fangs at my neck, in the same way that Derek had. She turned to leave the room and I snuggled into the bed, closing my eyes. As I began to drift off, my thoughts turned to my flat and my flatmates. What had happened to Agota and Tallulah? Were they still alive? And what about my flat. It had been completely trashed. I groaned at the thought of this. All the furniture in the flat belonged to the landlord. Not only would we lose our deposit, we'd have to pay more over the top - thousands.

Now I had no job, debts and a fascist vampire hit squad after me.

13

I woke up to the smell of pepperoni pizza. It was being held under my nose by a pale, slim woman, about my age and height, with purple hair, undercut at the side and flicked over her face. Steel piercings glinted in her nose and several in her ears and chunky rings adorned her fingers.

"Good afternoon, witch. I bring you food." She shook the pizza enticingly, a friendly smile on her face. I wasn't used to being called 'witch' in a scenario that wasn't aggressive. But actually, it had a nice ring to it - it made me feel like a badass. Plus, anyone who woke me up with pizza was alright, in my book.

Hoisting myself up, I grabbed the pizza, mumbling thanks.

"Wow! You really are hungry, aren't you."

I took a slice and offered one to her.

She backed away as if I'd wrapped up my own poo in a box and was offering it to her, as a thoughtful gift. "Whoa! I'm a vampire, isn't it obvious to you?"

"Not really. The smell of pizza blocked out your scent."

She looked confused. "But don't you also get these mad rage fits, around vampires?"

"Yeah but I'm starting to think that they don't happen around vegan vampires - you're vegan, right?"

Her shoulders relaxed slightly. "Yes I am - we all are here."

"I know. Carlotta already explained that to me."

The woman perched herself on the corner of my bed. "Well I've gotta say, that certainly makes it easier to be around you. I'm Viv by the way, I'm the security and IT expert here which usually means hacking." She looked towards the door and raised her voice. "Lance, you can come in now. She's harmless."

A man with a goatee and ponytail entered and stood near the door, raising his hand as he whispered, "hi".

Viv looked back at me. "He didn't use to be like this but he recently lost a close friend to an arcane witch vampire hunter - it's made him extra cautious."

My face fell. "Oh God! I'm sorry, that's... awful."

Viv stared into the middle distance. "We never even would've found out it had happened - we turn to dust when we die."

Lance interrupted, his voice coming out in haunting tones that spoke of his pain and loss. "He disappeared one day and I just knew. I knew... I asked Viv to hack into local security cameras. It took days to uncover the truth." He looked down, gulping back tears. "He was a gentle soul, he loved video games and collected manga figures."

A moment of silence passed over us. I didn't know what to say. These vampires weren't a threat to humans - after all, they didn't hunt us. But arcane witches had sworn to kill all vampires, they didn't see any distinction between Ahimsa vampires and non-vegan groups such as the Draculs. I could see this was painful for Lance and I felt really bad that this had been done by one of my kind, so I changed the topic. "What is your speciality then?"

He perked up. "I do the electrics and plumbing for any new hideouts we find. Me and Viv go way back. We use to share a squat in South London."

I took a bite of pizza. "And now?"

"Now we move around as a unit, with Carlotta and some of the other founding Ahimsa members - wherever we're safe from the Draculs."

"Are they really that intent on flushing you out?" I took another bite.

Lance looked philosophical. "You know, I often wonder if they really are or if it's just become a petty competition, at this point. I mean, why else waste resources persecuting a bunch of pacifists? It doesn't make much sense to me."

"Hmm, well life as an arcane witch isn't that much safer, I can tell you."

His eyes dropped to half mast. "But you guys are rumoured to be the toughest fighters on the planet."

I shrugged. "And yet I'm still lying here, recovering from a vampire attack which almost killed me. Arcane witches also go missing all the time - killed or kidnapped by vampires."

Viv's head whipped towards me. "What?! Which vampire would be crazy enough to take on a arcane witch? I run a mile at the slightest whiff of almonds."

I frowned. "Almonds?"

She explained. "Yeah, that's what you smell like. Like cyanide but even more dangerous to us." She gave a rue smile. "I always hated almonds anyway."

Lance added. "Whoever told you that witches are being snatched is a liar as far as I'm concerned."

"A couple of arcane witches told me. Didn't seem like they were lying to me. They said that the witch who hunts vampires in my neighbourhood went missing recently. Rosa something or other... Rosa Knight."

Viv's eye's widened. "You live near Dalston, right?"

I nodded.

"That must be why Dracul presence has increased around there, recently. She's not there to hunt anymore so it's an oasis of live human blood."

"How do you know that Dracul presence has increased?" I bit into another slice of pizza.

"We monitor security cameras around the area constantly. We also have ahimsa vampires on the streets who report to us."

Lance clarified. "We have to keep tabs on them. It's our best protection against attack. As soon as we get word they may be moving against us, we abandon our location and move to a new one. We've done this countless times over the years."

"But why don't you just kill them all? You're not sworn against harming vampires too, are you?"

Lance chuckled. "Remind me not to get on your bad side. Actually, we are sworn not to harm other vampires - unless in self-defence which includes defence against other innocents."

I looked up at the ceiling. "Wouldn't this qualify because if you don't kill them, they will harm humans?"

Viv shook her head. "It's more complicated than that. Many vampires, Draculs included, only drink what they need to survive, never killing humans and glamouring away the memories of those who they drink from. It's still wrong but I would argue that taking another life is worse. We don't kill vampires unless we have to - we prefer a soft approach of sedating them then convincing them that synthetic blood is a better choice. It's healthier for them, it tastes better and it's certainly better for humans."

I chewed on my pizza, mulling over what she'd said. I hadn't expected vampires to be so... self-reflective. But why wouldn't they be? My opinion of them had been shaped by what I'd watched on TV and read in books and it was clear that I had a lot to learn.

Lance looked at me. "Do you like reggae?"

I broke into a grin. "Who doesn't?"

"Then I have a treat for you. I've been meaning to test out some new speakers that I bought..." his voice trailed off as he left the room.

I looked at Viv. "Can I ask you a question?"

"Sure."

"Why did you bring in my pizza if you thought there was a chance that I'd hurt you?"

Her mouth curved up at one side. "I've always been a bit of a risk-taker. How do you think I ended up as a vampire in the first place?"

"How did you end up as a vampire in the first place?"

She closed her eyes and shuddered. "Psycho girlfriend who turned out to be a vampire. She couldn't live without me so she turned me."

"Okay, you win the prize for worst relationship ever.... You're not still together are you?"

"No. She got staked by a hunter, soon after she turned me."

The irony of this tickled me and apparently Viv too. She looked at me and we both cracked up. I really liked this woman.

"Oh, by the way, your clothes were covered in blood and we're the same size so you're wearing my pyjamas."

I hadn't even considered that and I looked down to see navy pyjamas with pirate ships on them.

"I'll find you something better to change into, when you're ready to get up."

"Thanks." I smiled at her.

"I better go check on the security cameras, see you in a bit."

As I watched her leave, I reflected that I'd already been shown more kindness here than I had been by humans, the entire time I'd been in London. Here, I wasn't a weirdo with strange rages and mental instabilities, here I was understood and accepted. I could see why Nik had been drawn to them. A knot of tension went through my centre, as I thought of Nik. I still hadn't processed how I felt about him. If he'd lied about something so fundamental - what else had he lied about? And could I ever trust him again?

THE REST of my day was spent recuperating and chatting to Viv, Lance and Carlotta. There were other ahimsas in the building and some of them passed through to say hello and introduce themselves. I was touched at the level of trust they all put into me already. Carlotta showed me the Vital8 blood that they drank and told me a bit about the process by which she created it. She was so inspiring. I'd always wished I could've been better at science and maths - maybe then I could've studied mechanical engineering and be making pots of cash now instead of drifting from one crappy, dead-end job to another.

With everything that had been going on, my job hunting had been put on the back burner and if I was honest with myself, my heart wasn't fully in it. I was beginning to have doubts about what I'd studied. Spending time with Nik and Carlotta made me realise how fluffy and shallow my intended career path was. Nik saved lives for a living. Carlotta had created a form of synthetic blood, thereby saving countless human and vampire lives. In contrast, I had studied to spend my days selling products and doing shout outs for events. I sighed. It just felt like I had more to offer the world and I was selling myself short by not pursuing something more meaningful. Okay, I didn't know what that was yet but I wanted to find out.

"Earth to Bree - it's your turn, dum-dum!" Viv prodded me in the ribs, waving her hand of cards across my face.

"Sorry, I was miles away." I looked at my cards and picked up a new one. *Hmm. Jack of spades.* I replaced it with my jack of clubs.

"Ha ha suckers!" Lance placed a full suit of hearts down. "I win."

Viv pouted.

"In your face!" He pointed at her, waving his cards in glee.

"Not fair! It's a fix - you used magic." I scowled at him.

"Nice try! Vampires can't do magic so you lost for realz, sweetheart!"

I looked at Viv. "Is that true?"

She nodded. "Afraid so."

As I sucked my teeth, I heard footsteps, coming up from the basement. My heart thumped with apprehension and my throat felt dry. Nik's handsome, smiling face, appeared, as he walked up the stairs. His eyes displayed a mixture of relief and concern.

"Hi," I whispered.

His gaze travelled up and down my body and I self-consciously, readjusted my pyjama neckline. When he looked back up to my face, his eyes glittered, then smouldered. I swear the temperature of the room went up several degrees. How could I stay angry at a man who looked at me like that?

"I'm glad to see they fed you then?" He began.

I nodded, suddenly feeling shy. "How was your day?"

"Oh you know, busy, boring, the usual. How are you feeling?"

"So much better." I tried to get up and then winced as the canula jerked my hand back.

He rushed towards me. "Hey, take it easy."

"When can I take this thing out?"

He looked at the empty bag of fluids, hanging above the tube extending from my hand. "I'll take it out now for you. Let me just wash up first and I'll be right back."

Nik reappeared a few moments later carrying a bag of medical supplies. As he entered, Viv looked from me back at him and then at me again. Then she got up and made a loud show of needing to check the electrics, giving Lance a pointed look. He took the obvious hint and mumbled something incoherent before leaving too.

Nik sat down on a stool at the side of my chair and placed my hand on his lap as he put his gloves on. Looking at me, he touched the canula slightly then asked, "Have you had enough to eat and drink?"

I looked at him from under my lashes, in a way I hoped was alluring. "Yes thanks. Everyone's been super nice to me."

Then, without warning he tore off the plaster, covering the needle.

Balls! That hurt.

I gasped, suppressing the urge to curse. "You could've warned me"

"Then it would've hurt more." He carried on talking to me as he worked. "They're not what you would've expected from a bunch of vampires, huh?"

I blushed and looked down. "No, I guess not."

He removed the needle then pressed down with a cotton wool pad. "What else have you learnt that was unexpected?"

I looked up towards the ceiling as I pursed my lips. "Hmm, let me see. You're vegan. You can go out during the day but you get burnt really easily so you have to be careful. Crucifixes don't affect you. Neither does garlic."

I looked at him, proudly, gauging his reaction.

He raised his eyebrows. "Not bad for a start. Anything else?"

"You're not immortal, you just live for a really really long time - about five hundred years, was it?"

He nodded. "For turned vampires, for hybrids and born vampires, it's longer."

I smiled and tilted my head to the side. "And you can have children.... With vampires or humans." My eyes lingered on his. Not long enough to scare him but long enough to make him understand that this fact mattered to me. I couldn't ignore the frisson of joy that had raced through me, as Carlotta had told me that. But we were still on shaky ground after the events of the past few days. He may have saved my life but he still had some making up to do to get totally back into my good books.

He studiously cleaned the wound one final time then put another plaster over it. Was he avoiding eye contact or just being thorough? "Carlotta had a human boyfriend, did she tell you that?"

My face fell. "Yes, it was awful, he got killed by the Draculs."

He sighed, a defeated look entering his eyes. "So you know the risks involved with being with me?"

I bit my lip and nodded, looking down at my lap. He was trying to put me down gently by making a link between our relationship and the tragic way in which Carlotta's had ended.

His words came out in one short, rush of breath. "I'm sorry Bree. I'm so sorry."

I whipped my head back up. "Are you breaking up with me?"

His mouth opened then closed, as if I'd caught him off guard. "What? No?! I mean, we're not a couple... are we?"

How could he be so callous as to say that out loud, when we hadn't even discussed it. My eyes started to well with tears. I couldn't believe I was letting him get to me - and showing him how much I cared by crying. He'd been about as careful, with my heart, as a dog is careful with a leftover leg of lamb that's been absent-mindedly left on the kitchen table. I sniffed and wiped away a tear, suddenly wishing I could be alone.

"Wait, do you want us to be... a couple?" His tone was cautious, searching.

My tears seemed to shrink back inside as hope surged through me. I caught my bottom lip in-between my teeth and smiled at him, gazing into his eyes. At that moment Viv and Lance came rushing back in.

Viv's face was tight and flushed. "Sorry to break up the party, but we have a big problem."

∼

I FROWNED, "WHAT?"

She held up her phone and pressed play on a news clip. It was the six o'clock news. A reporter was standing in front of my apartment block.

Residents of Hackney are today reeling after a serious assault was committed on two young women by their own flatmate. The young women, Tallulah Jones and Agota Varga, are both recovering in hospital. One of them is being treated for life-threatening injuries.

An image of Agota and Tallulah came onto the screen. They looked happy and wholesome.

Nobody knows exactly what made Bree Ryan go on the rampage and perform such a brutal and unprovoked attack against people who were supposed to be her friends. But a source told us that she'd recently been fired from her job, for violently attacking a colleague.

Now my image came onto the screen. They'd chosen the most unflattering photo and my large eyes displayed a sheen of frenzy that they didn't normally have.

Police are now looking for anybody who can give any information as to the whereabouts of Ms. Ryan. She should be considered extremely dangerous and possibly mentally unwell. Anybody with any information is urged to phone the hotline below.

A number scrolled along the bottom of the screen. Viv flipped off the phone and made eye contact with me and then Nik.

My mouth dropped open as I felt my blood boil. "Those lying pieces of shit! And they call themselves my friends!"

Nik's eyes softened with kindness, as he looked at me. "Bree, your flatmates probably aren't lying - at least not as far as they believe." His tone was gentle. "They've been glamoured by Draculs. They really believe that you attacked them."

I blinked at him, trying to comprehend what he'd said.

He continued. "Think about it, what is easier to believe, for most humans? That a vampire glamoured you into trying to kill your flatmate and you got hurt in the fight? Or that your flatmate, who has always been a little different, had a psychotic break and attacked you?"

My shoulders sagged - I understood the logic of what he was saying. "Great! So now I'm on the run from the police as well as the Draculs?!"

Viv replied quietly. "Fuck your life, right?"

"Fuck my life big time." I looked down, trying to hide the fact that my eyes were starting to well with tears again.

Nik rushed to my side, touching my shoulder lightly. "Hey, please don't cry. It'll be alright."

Clenching my fists, I couldn't stop myself from raising my voice. "How? How will it be alright? Do I just call Agota and Tallulah and tell them the vampire glamour is a lie?"

Lance chuckled and Viv elbowed him in the ribs causing him to cough a few times before stopping.

Nik gave them a look before turning back at me. "Not quite but there is a way to break a vampire glamour…"

Hope and excitement surged through me.

"…You have to kill the vampire who performed it."

My face dropped. "I have to kill Derek?"

"Not necessarily you, anyone can kill him. The point is, once he dies, his glamours no longer have any power."

I brushed hair out of my face. "Couldn't you just glamour Agota and Tallulah back to the truth again?"

He shook his head. "I'm afraid not. I can't break another vampire's glamour - without killing him."

"But... but, why didn't you kill him? How did you get me away from him?"

He shifted awkwardly, his face flushing. "You were unconscious, almost dead, on the floor. I fought Derek, got him down, had a stake at his heart. Then the evil bastard glamoured Agota to hold a knife to her own neck. She would've killed herself. He correctly guessed that I wouldn't allow that to happen. I was forced to let him go. She dropped the knife then passed out, as soon as he left - a strong vampire glamour can have that effect on humans sometimes."

I sat up straighter. "How badly hurt was she?"

He shrugged and raised his hands. "I wish I knew. I left her in a trashed flat, with significant injuries. I called an ambulance and checked her pulse but I didn't have time to treat her - I couldn't anyway without my medical supplies."

This was unbelievable. My eyes widened. "So you just left her there?"

He implored me with his eyes. "I couldn't take her with us. I considered it but it's too risky, involving normal humans in our world. Plus I had to get you to safety, that was my main concern. The police sirens were already sounding. They would've taken me into custody and then the Draculs would have sent someone else to finish the job Derek started. They would've killed you, I couldn't risk that."

I put my head in my hands. "Derek left me almost dead and then made me the sucker to take the fall for Agota's and Tallulah's injuries. It sounds like one or both of them could actually die - then I'll be wanted for murder!"

He knelt closer and touched my hand softly. "I admit, it's not the best position to be in. But you'll get through this." Then he corrected himself. "*We'll* get through this."

I looked up, tentatively, sniffing away my watery eyes. "We?"

"Yes of course. I'll help you however I can, we all will. We're already at war with the Draculs anyway."

This man was amazing. It was a knight-in-shining-armour

moment and I wanted him so much right now. I softened my eyes at him and smiled. I was grateful for his help but it still didn't take away the fact that I was now wanted by the police. It felt as if I was a tiny fish, in the middle of a shoal, with a ring of sharks, circling around me. Sooner or later, the sharks were going to get me but which would it be? The police? Or the Draculs?

14

Once Carlotta heard that I was wanted by the police, she became even less enthusiastic about me staying there. I couldn't blame her - she had a whole community to protect. All the Ahimsas had been so kind to me, I couldn't put them at risk by continuing to stay with them. But I also didn't really have many other options.

That night, Nik insisted on staying by my bedside, to watch as I slept. He said vampires didn't need as much sleep as humans. By the next day, I was already starting to feel strong enough to start considering my next move. I couldn't stay with the Ahimsas but where else could I go? Staying with my brother was out of the question. That's the first place the police would look. Ditto, going back to Ireland. And I didn't have enough money for a hotel.

Nik sat on the edge of my bed. "You could always stay... with me." The effort in his face as he tried to keep his expression casual and his tone neutral was something I didn't miss. After just a few days I'd already learnt how to read him so well. Part of me jumped for joy and wanted to accept straight away. But I couldn't be so selfish. So far Nik had managed to fly under the radar of the Draculs, maintaining his double life as a respectable doctor by day and ahimsa activist by night. If I stayed with him and the Draculs found me there, that would put him squarely in their sights.

Still wrestling between what my heart desired and what my head knew was the right decision, I started to answer him. "Oh Nik, I…"

Holding one hand up, he interrupted me. "Just hear me out. We can leave here via the storm drains - it's how we usually escape when the Draculs are after us. If they don't see us leave, they won't know where we've gone." He looked deeply into my eyes. "I can keep you safe, I know I can."

I wanted to believe him, I really did but his suggestion sounded too much like wishful thinking. "It's not just the Draculs though, is it. The police are also after me. If I get recognised, I'll get reported and…"

"And I can glamour any policeman, who takes the statement, or human, who sees you, into forgetting that they ever did." His gaze roamed up and down my face. "What's your answer?"

"I don't know, I need time to think about it."

"I understand." He looked down, an aching sadness flickering across his features. When he looked back at me, his beautiful dark brown eyes burned with a heat that made my breath hitch. In his gaze I saw hunger but also something else - guilt. He looked down at his lap, "I'm sorry Bree… I'm sorry that I'm a vampire." His voice was filled with regret.

His sadness tore my heart from my chest. "It's not your fault."

"Isn't it?" He snarled, his tone bitter and resentful. He sighed, looking up at the ceiling, a pained expression on his face. "Sorry, I didn't mean to snap at you, it's just… I don't think you fully realise what that means - I need human blood to survive. I'm vegan now but in the past I've…"

I held up my hand and shushed him. "We've all done things we're not proud of. What you did back then, you did to survive, and as soon as you had an alternative, you changed. You didn't have to, that was your choice."

His features softened, his dreamy eyes, becoming suffused with gratitude.

I reached out and cupped his stubble, lifting his chin to look deep into his eyes. "You're a good person Nik and I forgive you for lying to me. Life dealt you a shitty hand, I'm sure you didn't choose to become a vampire."

He shook his head. "No, I certainly didn't but... I still blame myself."

I bit my lip. "Do you mind telling me how it happened?"

His eyes widened. "Are you sure you want to know?"

I nodded and waited.

He picked up one of the water bottles, Viv had left on the table and opened it before handing it to me. "Here."

"Thanks." I took a sip.

Then he opened another bottle and took a sip, as he stared into space. He softened his voice and deepened his breathing. "Most of what I told you, about my childhood in India, was true. I left out any parts that would identify the fact that I've been on this earth for eighty four years."

My eyes widened. "You're eighty four years old?!"

"Yes. But vampires age very slowly." He gulped and took a deep breath. "In India, in those days, we were married off, by our parents, as soon as possible. My family found a wife, for me, when I was twenty two. She was nice enough but we didn't love each other and, as a result, we didn't have any children. Over the years, my family put more and more pressure on us, to provide grandchildren. But it never happened. Then, when I was twenty five, I got a job as a laboratory technician. It was an excellent opportunity for me. I didn't come from money or a high caste so me and my family were all very happy. This job allowed me to make the excuse of working late, every night. So that's what I did - to avoid coming home to a loveless marriage. I also started having a few drinks, alone, in the lab, before coming home." He leant forward and took a sip of water. "One night, I was walking home late and I was approached by a woman, who I now know, was a vampire. She was beautiful, the most beautiful woman I'd ever seen. I'd had a few drinks, as normal and..." He took a deep breath. "I'm not proud of myself but she lured me to her home. When we got there, she attacked me, draining me, to the point of death. As my life ebbed away, under her fangs, I thought of my family, I thought of my wife. Even though I didn't love her, she didn't deserve a husband like me. I felt that this was my punishment for how badly I'd been treating her and I accepted my death." His expression darkened. "But death was not what came. The vampire, turned me into one of her kind - against my will." He laughed bitterly and looked down at his feet. "She said I was too handsome to die." He looked up at me, his eyes filled with sorrow.

"Nik, that's so awful."

But he wasn't finished. "After I was turned, I went home to my wife and actually told her the truth. Of course, she was terrified and no longer wanted anything to do with me. She insisted I divorce her but I refused. Divorce carries a big stigma for women in India and I didn't want her to suffer anymore, because of me. I suggested that I leave India and go and find work in Europe - that way, I could still provide for her by sending money home to her, each month. Husbands leaving their wives to work overseas was quite common. Nobody would ever find out what I'd become. It was an acceptable solution." He took another sip of water, gulping it down along with his emotions. "Getting over here would be hard though. The vampire who sired me had connections within immigration and she pulled some strings."

"What was it like? When you first arrived?"

"Much harder than I'd expected. I'd saved a bit of money, but that was quickly used up. Britain was very racist in those days and getting a job as a lab technician wasn't possible. I got a job, working as a cleaner, in a hotel. The job paid very little but I was allowed to board there. I started saving, little by little. It took me decades, because I was also sending money home to my wife. Eventually, I'd saved enough to study medicine and - well, you know the rest."

I stared at him. It was quite a story but I knew that it was true. "Where is your wife now?"

"She died ten years ago." He looked at the floor, guilt filling his features.

"Hey, you did your best for her. At least you provided for her and weren't ever, actually unfaithful."

"But I wanted to be - that's why I went with the vampire in the first place. If I hadn't been weak, this never would've happened to me."

He looked so anguished. I could only imagine how many times he'd relived that day, wishing he'd made a different decision. I whispered. "You're just trying to do the best with what you've been given. None of us are perfect."

He nodded, closing his eyes as he breathed deeply. "I'm sorry I lied to you. I just thought... I dunno, I just wanted to be normal for a while. The way you looked at me - it made me believe the fantasy. I wanted to tell you, I was going to..." His voice trailed off and his expression was drenched with shame.

In that moment I realised that I couldn't carry on being angry at him. Not even a little bit. He'd lied to me because the world would never accept him as he was now. He'd lied because he felt like he had no choice. I knew what it was like to be an outcast just because you were different and I sure as hell wasn't going to feel any negative way about Nik for trying to pretend he was just a normal guy. Isn't that what I'd been doing my whole life? Pretending to be a normal girl. As I looked at him, I understood that being with him meant accepting every part of him - especially the vampire part - and I wanted to be with him.

"It's okay Nik. I understand why you lied." I touched his face and smiled.

He moved closer, until our faces were inches apart, close enough that I could lean forward and touch my forehead to his.

His voice came out raspy and cracked. "How did I ever get so lucky?"

I revelled in a moment of bliss before whipping my head back up, as something suddenly occurred to me. "Just don't ever bite me, will you?"

His mouth dropped open in offence. "I wouldn't dream of it.... Could I just have a little nip?"

I slapped him across the chest, hard as he started laughing.

"I was joking! The idea of feeding off you disgusts me."

"Hey!" I pouted, putting my hands on my hips. *He didn't have to take it that far!*

He swiftly backtracked. "Not just you - any live human. I'm a committed vegan." He leant forward, nuzzling his nose into my neck.

His warm, soft lips, contrasted with his rough stubble in a way that made my entire body feel as though a static electric charge was rippling over my skin.

He breathed deeply, as if trying to inhale me. "I'm sure you'd be the most delicious human I'd ever tasted but I will never know because the only way I'm ever going to taste you is like this." He kissed my neck lightly, then trailed kisses up the side of my face, finally sucking on my lips, gently. As he stroked my cheek and gazed into my eyes, I felt the last shreds of resistance dissolve, like sugar, in hot tea.

The heat in his eyes tore through me like an iron rod. He kissed me again, this time more deeply. I moaned softly, fisting his hair with one of my hands as the other hand weaved its way down to stroke his wash board abs. His smell was intoxicating - I knew I shouldn't feel this way about him. I should feel revolted and enraged, in his presence, but maybe that's what made it so exquisite. I closed my eyes, allowing my head to fall back, exposing my neck. If Nik wanted to bite me, now there was nothing stopping him. I wanted him. I wanted to peel off his layers and feel his hands squeezing my thighs, as I wrapped them around his middle.

Suddenly, he pulled away, a look of apology, in his eyes.

He doesn't want me.

The thought lanced my heart like a spear and I bit my lip, tearing my gaze away from his.

He turned my head back towards him, pulling my chin, softly, with his fingers. Then he brought my hands up to his lips as he kissed my fingertips. "I want you, believe me, I want you."

I twinkled my eyes at him. "Then why not take…"

He interrupted. "I want our first time to be special, not in some mouldy, derelict building, surrounded by pigeon faeces. Not with you recovering from a traumatic exsanguination. Does that make sense?"

I sighed and nodded.

He smiled and stroked my hair. "Have you made you decision, then?"

I sat up. "About what?"

"About coming back to mine?"

I smiled, mischievously. I'd been unsure about going to his flat before but now I was starting to change my mind. If this his way of getting me into bed, I was so up for it.

He carried on. "It was wrong of me to bring you here in the first place but I had to make a split second judgement call to save your life. This is closer to yours than my flat is. You'd lost a lot of blood. I had to act fast."

I frowned. "Don't the Draculs know about your flat too?"

He shook his head. "I don't think so. There are hundreds of ahimsa vampires and I'm not well-known, like Carlotta. I mean, sure, there's a risk that they know about me and my flat but it's a lesser risk than staying here."

I looked down, a cold feeling spreading through my belly. This so did not sound like he was just trying to get his leg over…Bummer.

"What's wrong?" He asked.

I lifted my head. "Nothing. It's just… are you only inviting me to your flat because I'm in danger here?"

"No, of course not! I would've invited you anyway." He ran his fingers through his thick hair, blowing out breath.

He had a pained look on his face and I wondered if he thought I was hard work. Were human women harder to handle than vampire women? Had he had a lot of human women? What about vampires? There was still so much that I didn't know about him.

He broke my thoughts. "Listen, this is hard for me. I'm not good at this. I don't know how to behave - I don't date. I have no idea how these things are done these days."

I burst out laughing. "You sound like you're about a hundred years old."

His face became deadly serious. "I'm close to that."

My face dropped. "Erm, right, of course. Sorry, I wasn't thinking." I wished the ground could swallow me up.

He reached out and touched my cheek. I felt my blush deepen as I softened into his touch, revelling in the feeling of his rough hands on my soft skin. His eyes became languid and I ached with desire for him, once more. He leaned in for another kiss, our lips almost reaching...

Boom!

I went flying through the air. Dust, debris and fire, tore through the flat. Pain ripped through my body, before everything went black.

15

Dazed and bruised, I forced myself to my feet. A sharp, ringing noise, crowded out all other sounds and my vision was blurred. I sniffed away a runny nose, then realised it was blood. But I couldn't think about that now. One thought pierced my consciousness, brushing away any other concerns.

Nik

Holding my nose to staunch the bleeding, I wafted away smoke and dust, scrambling over chunks of brick and concrete as I tried to find him. I'd landed awkwardly and my neck hurt, as I turned it from side to side. The blast had come from outside, which meant we were under attack. Could it be the Draculs? Perhaps a grenade, thrown by one of them? My stomach clenched with fear and nausea, as I realised that Derek, or other vampires just like him, would soon be entering. Unfamiliar, angry voices, barked orders as footsteps got closer. My heart pounded in my chest and my throat felt dry and hoarse.

The outline of the first vampire, with the others, either side of him, approached me, like a shadow, through the dust. My eyes darted from left to right, searching the rubble for any sign of Nik. It wasn't just that I feared for his safety, it was something else. An instinct and a drive that I couldn't ignore. Something deep within me told me that I just had to find him - that he was the solution to defending myself against these hostile vampires.

Then I got a feeling - almost like something calling to me from the corner of the room. Something or *someone*. There he was, passed out, his body sprawled over debris, his connection to me, beaconing me, like a lighthouse to a ship. I raced towards him. In the same moment, the dust cleared and the vampires saw me. They charged towards me at the same time as I sprinted to him. Adrenaline surged through me. I had to get to him first. But we were outnumbered and none of them were injured.

The vampires got there first. A woman with a pinched, hard face threw some kind of net over me. It felt like the net weighed a tonne except the texture was like gravel-embedded slime. A coldness spread over my limbs and I sank to the floor. My muscles felt like jelly. I tried to stand and collapsed. Gritting my teeth, I tried again but it was no use. The net defeated my every attempt.

The vampire leader, a tall, skinny, dark-haired man, shook his head at me. "We're not just going to stand and watch as you gain powers from your vampire boyfriend, witch. And don't think you can get any from us either." He touched the net that draped over me. "Obsidian." It meant nothing to me but I guessed it was some sort of a way to block me from drawing their powers.

I glared at him. "What do you want?"

"Isn't it obvious? We want you." In the same breath, all three of them lunged at me. I was still recovering from my last vampire attack and didn't have the strength to fight one of them, let alone three.

Blood pumped, audibly through my ears as time slowed down. Beads of sweat broke out on my forehead and I started to shake. Holding out a defensive arm, I crumpled to the floor, cocooning myself, in a crouching ball as I silently prayed.

Wake up Nik - wake up!

Realising that I was in no condition to fight, the skinny leader scooped me up and flung me over his shoulder. My body flopped, like a rag doll. The smell of vampire and my own fear was overpowering and I gagged.

"Come on, let's go." His tone and manner was nonchalant, as if this was an everyday job for him. Where were they taking me and what would they do to me once we got there? He walked towards the hole, that had once been a wall and all hope dissolved within me.

But then, a voice called out, clear and determined, from the corner of the room. "Let her go, you Dracul scum."

Relief flooded through me. Nik was awake! Finally!

"Why would we do that? She's the reason why we're here."

Nik clenched his fists and gritted his teeth. His eyes held murderous intent, all aimed at the Draculs.

The skinny leader continued. "You didn't think we'd gone to all this trouble for a bunch of crusty, misguided vegan vampires, did you?" He gave a sickening laugh of victory and his cronies joined him.

Something seemed to flip, within Nik. He roared with rage and charged into them, at lightning speed, ramming the leader with his body.

The skinny vampire was knocked to the side and dropped me. I landed awkwardly, on a pile of bricks and I heard a sickening crack which I fervently hoped wasn't my back breaking. But as I wriggled my toes and turned my head, I realised the click had improved my neck. It had also thrown the net off me. Strength, power and vitality flooded my body.

The leader's face turned dark red and he glared at Nik. "Get him."

Then, all three vampires were upon him, raining kicks and punches and bites, from every direction. Anger started building up inside me as violence and blood, filled the air. The Draculs had forgotten all about me so lost were they in the blood lust of attacking Nik. I had to help him but how? Closing my eyes, I thought back to the night I'd first seen his fangs. I'd drawn on his powers that night, sprinting miles home, in seconds. How had I done it exactly?

The Draculs were still pummelling him. I felt the pain of each hit to Nik as if it was being dealt to me. I had to help him. Taking a deep breath, I focused on him and became aware of a feeling of raw power, spreading through me. It rose from deep within my pelvis, travelling, with a tingling sensation, up my spine. My vision cleared and my mind calmed down to the speed of infinity. I became aware of everything and nothing. Orangey lights spiralled around me. Intertwined with those, were the silvery lights that I now recognised and remembered were Nik's. Opening my mouth, the power rushed through me.

I stood up, clicked my neck, one final time and stepped towards them, like an avenging high priestess of death. Unleashing my powers, I barrelled through them with a terrifying scream that would give the scariest horror-story villain nightmares. I flung the Draculs off Nik, tossing them aside, like dirty washing.

Whipping my head towards him, I shouted, "Nik, run!" Then I turned back to my foes, picking up a brick to bash into one of their faces. He went spiralling into the wall behind him. Excitement soared through me as I spied a broken piece of chair leg. It had snapped into a point.

"Rah!" The skinny leader launched himself at my legs. But I dropped and rolled, grabbing the makeshift stake at the same time. I was too quick for him. His eyes widened in terror as he realised, too late, that I was beneath him, with a stake in my hand. I sat up, jabbing into his chest and his terrified eyes disintegrated as he turned to dust and blew away in the wind. The other two Draculs, looked at each other. Then, realising they'd met their match, they darted for the street. They almost made it, through the large hole, where the door had once been. But once again, I was too quick for them. Sprinting towards them, I bounded, into the air, landing inches in front of one and staking him, before I whirled the same arm around to stake the other. My body relaxed slightly, the tension of the fight over and I closed my eyes and exhaled deeply. I revelled in victory and a feeling of deep satisfaction. An urge I'd spent my life denying, had finally been fulfilled. I was both exulted and terrified.

As I opened my eyes, it felt like all the anger and fire that had been in me previously was gone. It was replaced by a serenity such as I had never felt before. I looked at Nik and let out a long satisfied sigh.

My happiness was brief though, for in the next moment, his face dropped. "What's wrong?"

His acute hearing had picked up that which I could not. "There are more footsteps, lots more. They're moving too fast to be human."

I gulped as his anguished gaze met mine. We both guessed what this meant.

Dracul reinforcements!

OH SHIT!

"Don't these bastards ever give up?" I shouted at Nik, as the next group of Dracul vampires advanced on us. I was exhausted. My body was covered in wounds. I had nothing left to give and now I had to take on an army. But just as my shoulders sagged in defeat, the rest of the Ahimsas started emerging from within the building. They were all armed. Some held makeshift stakes, others held silver chains in gloved hands, a few even had guns.

My gaze went straight to Lance and Viv, at the front of the group. Gratitude filled my heart. They could've ran to the next hideout, made their getaway as I knew they usually did in such circumstances. But instead they'd come to help us and not just Lance and Viv but all the Ahimsas. This was what a family should be like. Always there for each other, always protecting each other.

I didn't have time to give it anymore thought as the first Dracul reached me. He formed a fist and brought it towards my face, with full force. Years of fight training reflexes kicked in and I dodged it, swerving to the side as I delivered a swift chop to the side of his torso. The soft spot where his kidneys should've been, instead felt like pure rock and I winced in pain as the shock reverberated through my wrist and up my forearm.

Another vampire jumped on my back from behind. She put something around my neck and I gagged and cried out as I staggered around, trying to shake her off. Was she going to strangle me to death? But instead I felt a click and a feeling of cold, rough, thin metal. I elbowed her sharply in the ribs but she barely reacted. She was way stronger than me and for the first time genuine fear twisted my guts.

"Get off me." I screamed as she bared her fangs at my jugular. She was just about to sink them into my flesh when another vampire shouted.

"What are you doing, you idiot? Hugh wants her alive and untouched."

The vampire swore under her breath and jumped off, catching hold of my hair in one hand as she threw me towards the ground. Pain blossomed across my lips as they made contact with the hard tarmac.

The female vampire spat at me. "Not so tough now, without your arcane powers, are you. *Bitch!*"

What did she mean? I was still an arcane witch - wasn't I? That was the problem. I didn't really know how or why my powers worked. I had sort of twigged that they were linked to the lights that I'd always seen. But I couldn't yet summon the lights on command and they seemed to randomly fuck off just when I needed them the most.... Like now for example.

Not willing to give up, I scrambled to my feet. I may not be able to control my powers yet but I could still fight like a gladiator. Assuming a fighting stance, I twirled around, delivering a powerful, roundhouse kick to the vampire who had just spat at me. Her diminutive frame went flying through the air and she landed, with a satisfying crunch. But in seconds she'd picked herself up. Her shoulder joint was dislocated and I curled my lips in disgust as she clicked it back into place, without so much as a blink. In less than a second she was upon me again. This time, two burly male vampires came to her assistance. They grabbed me, by the arms, holding me with a vice-like grip that was impossible to get loose from.

I whipped my head from side to side. All around me, Ahimsas were fighting Draculs. It was a massive street brawl. Suddenly, a cloud of dust appeared, indicating that a vampire had been dispatched. I squirmed, trying to get free from the vampires ,who were holding me, as I looked around desperately, for Nik. I spotted him on the edges of the fight and felt like weeping with relief. He locked eyes on me. "Bree! Get out of h... *Oof!*" His sentence was knocked out by a brutal jab, administered to his nose. Blood sprayed out, hitting another vampire on the shoulder.

I closed my eyes, unable to bear seeing him get hurt.

The female vampire got a mobile phone out of her pocket and spoke into it. "We've got the girl, let's go."

The other burly vampires nodded and they started dragging me off, in the direction they'd come from. I screamed and thrashed about, kicking, twisting, head butting, whatever I could to get free. But it was no use. They were too strong and my powers were not coming to the party.

The words, she'd uttered, acted like petrol on a fire as they were picked up by Nik's sensitive ears. His eyes grew black and he roared. He seemed to grow in size as he threw the vampire he was fighting off him and punched his way through several others. All at once, the fight grew in intensity. I watched as, one by one, each vampire entered the same, feral state of primal anger and violence.

The vampires who had captured me remained calm, however. Dust, gravel and blood flew in all directions, blurring my vision. Then, through the noise and violence, a black van came screeching around the corner. It stopped beside me and the back doors flew open. I was bundled into the back. The last thing I saw as the doors shut was Nik's face, stricken with grief as he watched me being taken. Then the van drove off.

The Draculs had finally got me.

16

The dark interior of the van stank of old blood mixed with sweat and the rust-like stench of the vampires surrounding me. I knew there was one sitting either side of me. I'd seen them getting in before me but I couldn't see them now. The windows into the front had been blacked up to prevent me from seeing where we were going.

"Where are you taking me?" I tried.

They ignored me.

"Why me? What do you want from me? At least tell me that?"

Silence. They didn't even make conversation with each other. I could make out muffled conversation from the front of the van but couldn't work out what was being said.

I gave up trying to get any information out of them and instead, sat in terror, flinching each time one of them moved. There was also some kind of crazy cold, weakness, seeping into my body. My muscles ached but it wasn't just from the fight, it was more like the kind of ache from an approaching bout of flu. Perhaps I was getting sick? My throat did feel kind of scratchy and I sniffed away a runny nose. Damnit! If I had flu, it would seriously hinder my chances of escaping these bastards.

I reached up to touch the dog collar like metal band around my neck. It was encrusted with something course, like tiny gems or sand and felt cold and heavy around my neck. I fingered it, trying to remove it. But it wouldn't budge. It was attached at the back with some type of metal lock. What was it made of anyway? I started to panic and coughed, breathing deeply as I yanked at it, in desperation. After several minutes of useless flailing around, I gave up and slumped down lower, blowing my hair out of my face. Not only was the dog collar locked in place, it was also getting heavier and heavier. I imagined poison, leaching out of it and through my pores. I shook the paranoid thoughts from my head. If they wanted to kill me, there were easier ways of doing it. Plus that other vampire had said that Hugh wanted me alive and untouched.

I thought back to the conversation I'd had with Carlotta. Hugh Beaufort was a human trafficker who supplied other vampires with live humans to feed on. Is that why they'd taken me? Was I going to be added to Beaufort's stable of humans? But why had they gone to so much trouble to take me? Surely there were other humans out there who would've been way easier to capture. *Hugh wants her alive and untouched.* He wanted me specifically. Why?

The sounds of London gave me some comfort from my dark ruminations and I listened carefully, trying to work out where we were. Buses driving past, a distant police siren, a man shouting in a guttural language - perhaps Arabic? It didn't matter, I was still no closer to guessing where we were or where we were going. Each time the van turned a corner, I tried to see if I could catch any glimmer of light or location but it was no use, I couldn't see a thing.

After a while the sounds of the city gave way to less traffic and the purring sound of an engine on a motorway. We were either heading to the suburbs or out of London altogether. The thought made my spirits sink. The further away from central London we were, the harder it would be for me to escape.

Cold dread covered my body like wet clay. I was feeling sicker and sicker and the cold dog collar wasn't helping. Now my nose was blocked and running and my throat felt like I'd swallowed hot gravel.

My thoughts turned as dark as the interior of the van. I would die, exsanguinated by blood thirsty monsters. My family would never find out what had happened to me and I'd never be able to clear my name. People back home would probably think I'd gone off the deep end, in London and gone crazy, like my Mam, just as they'd always thought I would. My eyes welled with tears and I sniffed. As I swallowed, I winced with pain - it was as if shards of glass were shredding my throat. Assaulted by my own dark thoughts, I curled up into a ball and wept.

AFTER A WHILE, the van started to slow down and the traffic noise subsided. We must be on quieter, residential streets. As we turned, the sound of pebbles, crunched underneath the tyres. The driver parked the van and I was rough housed out by one of the burly vampires who had put me inside. He was well built, with a bent nose and cauliflower ears. He must have been a fighter or maybe, a rugby player, when he was a human. Cauliflower ears noticed me studying him and licked his lips before winking at me, lasciviously. I curled my lips in disgust. He pushed me forward and I stepped onto a vast driveway, surrounded by trees and well kept grounds. Up ahead stood a mansion that was big enough to be a hotel. Were we still in London? I couldn't tell but with a house this big, it was unlikely. I looked up at the sky and saw the familiar, lack of stars I saw from my balcony. If it wasn't London, it was close.

Illuminated by lights, all the way along the driveway, two men stood waiting on a grand set of sandstone steps, which led up to the front door. They wore black business suits with ear pieces, making them look like celebrity bodyguards. Their hard, angular faces looked incapable of smiling.

The man on the right had dark brown hair, slicked back with gel. His dark eyes flashed with malevolence as they looked me up and down. His gaze contained an unholy mixture of lust and contempt and he looked away, briefly when I met his expression with defiance.

The man on the left had white blonde, heavily-gelled hair, translucent, pale skin and a pointy nose. He reached up to touch his ear piece and I noticed an expensive-looking, platinum, chronometer watch glinting at his wrist. His piercing blue eyes fixed on me, in a manner of a carnivore marking his prey. "Good Evening Ms Ryan. My name is Peterson. This is my associate, Mitchell." A white plume of breath emanated from his thin lips. "We are your bodyguards. We've come to escort you to your guest suite." I hadn't expected the Swedish accent that came out of his mouth but it explained his blonde features.

I raised a skeptical eyebrow. "Guest?"

His smile didn't reach his eyes. "Mr Beaufort will explain everything over dinner. Come along."

They walked forward and grabbed each of my arms, leading me onwards. I tried to struggle but by now I was weak, sweating and felt like I had a temperature. My feet dragged, marking a trail of bare soil, through the pebbled driveway, as my head lolled. I could barely keep my eyes open.

Mitchell barked a curt order at the Draculs who had transported me here. "Leave." His tone and general manner reminded me of an attack dog.

They got back into the van. My spirits sank lower as I watched my means of escape speeding down the driveway, off into the night.

Mitchell propped me up as Peterson pressed the doorbell and waited, with his hands behind his back. The door opened and a mid-thirties, fair-complexioned black woman with jet black, straightened hair, tied up into a messy bun stood there. She wiped her hands on a white apron, tied at her waist. "Ah Ms Ryan, you've arrived." She had a thick, west country accent. Was she a vampire? A quick whiff in her direction told me she was human! My curiosity was peaked and my eyes immediately went to her neck but I saw no bite marks there.

She leaned forward and grabbed my upper arm, causing me to flinch. "Don't worry, I don't bite. I'm one of Mr Beaufort's cooks - you can call me Sally. Normally Jethro, the butler would answer the door but he's attending to some other guests of Mr Beaufort. Come on then." She pulled me into the hallway. Mitchell and Peterson followed, silently behind. Inside, I was greeted by the sight of polished oak floorboards, covered by a large, persian rug and a huge chandelier, which dangled above a central staircase. Oil paintings hung on each wall and soft classical music played around me. The warmth of the house made my muscles instantly relax but I still felt the discomfort of the choker, weighing heavily on my neck. The Draculs had implied that it was a means of blocking my powers and I felt the truth of this with every step I took. It was as if my very life force was draining from me, along with my powers.

Maybe Sally could get it off? She seemed friendly. It was worth a try. "Could you get this thing off me?"

She pursed her lips and fiddled with her hands, inside her apron. "Oh no. I couldn't do that. I wouldn't even know how to. You'll have to wait for Mr Beaufort. He'll be joining you for dinner."

I felt my eyes widen. *Dinner?* Was I the dinner? The icy hand of fear seeped through my core as my gaze darted, from left to right. My belly did somersaults and my palms felt clammy. The imposing figures of the two bodyguards were still behind me - there was no way I could escape.

"Do you like shepherd's pie?" Sally turned around and smiled, knowingly, at me.

Did I?!

I'd never been one to lose my appetite due to emotional distress and today was no different. In spite of my fear, my stomach rumbled as my nostrils picked out the enticing smell of buttery mashed potato mixed with rich beef and gravy.

But wait - if Beaufort was a vampire, why did he need a cook? Once again I wondered if I was the dinner. Was this what he did? Capture and then 'invite' humans over to his house as his 'guests', before enriching their blood, with good food and draining them? My legs got even weaker and I wiped sweat from my face. I was reminded of the children's fable of Hansel and Gretel, only in my story, I didn't have a clever sibling, with me, to free me from the cannibal's clutches.

If Beaufort planned to devour me, I was alone and powerless to stop him.

17

Sally led me up the stairs and along a corridor, past door, after door. What immediately struck me was just how many of these doors had huge vampire bodyguards, dressed exactly the same as Mitchell and Peterson, standing outside them. Who were they guarding?

Plush carpets cushioned my weary feet and from the hallway, a grandfather clock chimed eleven. A man came out of one room, carrying bedding. He dipped his head slightly at me, as he walked past. I didn't detect any scent of metal. He was probably another human servant. Just how many servants did Beaufort have?

"Do you live here, Sally?" I asked.

"Yes. We're fifty five full time, house and garden servants here, in total. Then there are also live-in vampire guards, like Mitchell and Peterson."

Live-in vampire guards. How was Beaufort feeding them? I gulped back a knot of fear. Was I being prepared for their consumption?

Sally continued. "I've run you a bath and laid out some clothes for you. Get washed and changed and then Mitchell and Peterson will bring you down for dinner."

"But what about my choker? I can't get it off."

"Don't worry, you can bathe with that on," she cheerily replied.

I rolled my eyes and pouted. This woman was playing along with the lie that I was a guest but I was their prisoner, no doubt about it.

She opened a door and my jaw dropped at the sight of the bathroom inside. I'd never seen a posher room. For starters, it was as large as my entire flat. White, marble floors and walls reflected the soft spot lighting. Steps led down to a huge, plunge pool, lined with mosaics and filled with bubbles. This formed the centrepiece of the room. To the side was a chaise lounge, upholstered in gold brocade. Several toiletries and a hair dryer were artfully arranged on a large, gold mirrored basin. In front of the plunge pool, lay a large, shaggy bath mat. An antique chair was draped with an expensive-looking outfit. Sally gestured towards the clothes. "These should fit you. I'll leave you to get on with it now."

She ignored my scowl and left, locking the door behind her. I walked around the room, inspecting it for weapons. Perhaps I could smash up one of the chairs and use the broken wooden legs as stakes? I thought of Mitchell and Peterson outside the front door. It wasn't likely that I'd be able to take them both out, at the same time. Not without my powers. Besides which, I wasn't at the top of my game. I was exhausted and covered in blood, ash and grime.

The deep warm water of the bath called to me, inviting me to soothe my sore muscles in its shadowy depths. The smell of lavender mixed with hot steam, calmed my senses and smoothed the jagged edges of my mind. As much as I felt weak and pathetic for accepting the trojan horse this vampire was offering me, I wanted that bath. Goddamnit, I wanted it so badly, it hurt. Without allowing myself anymore time to change my mind, I stripped off my filthy clothes and stepped into the water. It was deep enough that I could submerge all the way to my chest, whilst standing. The temperature was perfect and, in spite of my suspicions, I couldn't help but close my eyes in bliss as I luxuriated in the warmth, lapping at my breasts. Wading over to the side of the pool, I sat on a mosaic bench. A mini golden shelf, set into the side of the bath, contained a new bar of soap. I grabbed it and started lathering myself up. It was the most exquisitely scented soap I had ever used. Next, I did the same with the shampoo and conditioner. Each bottle was of a brand I'd never heard of before. Probably something really exclusive that wasn't for sale at the regular shops where I bought my no-brand haircare products.

After washing, I lay, floating in the water, staring at the Renaissance art, painted on the ceiling, as I planned my next move. My fever symptoms were starting to subside, with the hot water but I still felt weak. The obsidian choker was wrapped around my throat like metal shackles around the feet of a prisoner. Even if I did manage to escape, how would I get the bloody thing off? It was made of solid metal. Could the witches help me? I gritted my teeth as regret flooded through me. Why hadn't I gone with them when I'd still had the chance? I'd dithered over it and now my indecision would be my undoing. I was stuck in a house surrounded by vampires in God-knows-where and they planned to do God-knows-what to me but whatever it was, it was against my will and was probably going to end with my death. I thought of Frank and Aunt Siobhan and Uncle Paddy. Would they ever find out what had happened to me? Or would the Draculs glamour everyone into thinking that I'd run away or... committed suicide? Intense anguish rushed through me and I dragged my hands down my face. It would break my brother's heart if he thought I'd killed myself. I had to get out of here.

Knock, knock, knock.

My hands instinctively flew up to cover my naked breasts as I whipped my head up to look at the door.

"Are you almost finished? The food is ready and we don't want it getting cold, do we." Sally's voice called through the door.

I cleared my throat, before answering. "I'll be out soon." Her voice had broken my dark thoughts. I had to pull myself together. If I was going to get out of here, I had to think fast and keep my wits about me. I scrambled out of the bath and patted myself dry, using the fluffy, white towel, left on the chair. Then I slipped the clothes on and sat down in front of the mirror, to dry my hair. It was the first time since Derek had bitten me that I'd seen my reflection and now I reached my hand up to my neck, to trace the puncture wounds his fangs had left behind. My fingers trailed down to touch the dog collar, lower down on my neck and a wave of anger passed through me. I'd find an opportunity to get out of here - I had to. There must be silver knives or wooden objects around the dining area and now that I had bathed and rested, I was ready to take on these bastards. Powers or no powers, I wasn't going to just lay down and let them kill me.

A few minutes later, with my hair still damp, I decided it was good enough and opened the door.

"I'm ready." I said to Peterson and Mitchell. Mitchell's eyes flashed at me lasciviously and I wrapped my arms around myself. I hated the way that creep looked at me. They led me a different way, down a narrower, darker staircase and we went along a passageway and through a set of double doors, emerging into a large dining room. Soft lighting and candles cast long shadows of the greek statues and ferns that decorated the sides of the room. Artwork adorned each wall. Classical music drifted through speakers at each corner. A long table was set out with one place setting, and a steaming plate of food, at the far end. My mouth began to water as the smell of shepherd's pie instantly transported me back to Aunt Siobhan's cooking. This time, I didn't wait to be told, I sat down and got stuck in.

Sweet Jesus!

She'd used chunks of real steak and lamb - no cheap, frozen mince meat in this dish. I closed my eyes as the rich, meaty flavour, combined with buttery potatoes to create a mouth-gasm. My entire body relaxed as my ravenous belly finally found satisfaction. Mitchell and Peterson stood a few metres away but I was too absorbed in the meal to think about getting away. Food would have to come first - then I could make my escape.

I was just about to shovel another delicious forkful, into my mouth, when the double doors opened and a man walked in. As soon as I saw him, every hair on my arms stood on end and I gulped as I put my fork down. My heart thumped in my chest and it felt like all the air had gone out of my lungs. He had a face that I would never forget. Not because there was anything unusual about it. Quite the opposite, his slightly sagging flesh, topped with salt and pepper hair made him look like any other rich, middle-aged guy. But I'd seen him before and my reaction to him then had been even more severe than my reaction now. This was the man who had walked into the steak restaurant I'd gone to last week, with Conor. Bile rose up my throat as he smiled at me, his perfect teeth glinting brightly out of his tanned face. Everything about him sickened me. His chinos and relaxed dress shirt, unbuttoned at the top to reveal a few grey curling hairs, screamed oily, misplaced vanity.

Reaching me in a few heartbeats, he extended a chubby, dry hand. "Hugh Beaufort. It's nice to finally meet you." His clipped, upper-class accent grated on me.

My top lip curled in disgust as I ignored his hand and sucked air through my teeth. "I can't say the feeling is mutual."

He started laughing. "They said you'd be feisty. That's good. I like a challenge."

I recoiled at his sleazy use of the word 'challenge'. Was he seriously hitting on me?

He took a seat, next to me, at the head of the table, stretching out his legs as he turned to face me. "Have you been treated well so far?"

"Not really. I was kidnapped, had a power-leeching dog collar locked to my neck, before being brought here, against my will."

"I apologise about the manner in which you were invited to be my guest, everything will become clear to you in time, trust me."

I glared at him. I'd sooner trust a convicted felon.

He softened his eyes and tone, as if speaking to a child. "Your bath, clothes and food? I trust it has all been to your liking?"

I was done pandering to this shitbag's sense of entitlement. If he wanted a conversation with me, he better start telling me the truth, and fast. I folded my arms. "What exactly do you want from me? Why am I here? Why do I have this thing on?" I gestured to my neck.

He raised his hands. "It's a precaution, my angel. The flu-like symptoms are a side effect that will pass soon, once your body adjusts -they've probably already started to wane."

As I considered his words, I realised that he was right. I was starting to feel a bit better.

He continued. "We wouldn't want you using your powers to slaughter the entire household now, would we? We've discovered that obsidian, does for you arcane witches, what kryptonite did for superman. It blocks your arcane powers and makes you physically weaker. Transforming you from a lion, to a kitten." He reached out and stroked a lock of my hair.

I flinched. "Don't touch me."

His eyes took on an insincere sadness. "You're angry, I don't blame you. But you know, I can actually help you. I can make sure you get everything your heart desires."

I dropped my eyes to half mast. "How would you know what I want? And why would I trust you?"

He raised his eyebrows. "Oh we know a lot more than you realise - probably a lot more than anyone else, in this world. And as to why you would trust me. Well it's quite simple, my angel. I will start by giving you a small taste of what you want. Call it a show of faith, if you will."

He shouted out. "You can bring him in now."

A smaller door, at the other end of the room opened and two burly men pushed another, man out. The man was in chains, dirty, ragged and bloody. They threw him across the floor and his clanking chains, echoed through the space. He raised his head and locked eyes with me and I gasped.

Derek the vampire!

I instinctively recoiled.

"Don't listen to a word he says, he's a lying piece of shi..." Derek's words were lost in a spray of blood as one of the larger vampires kicked him in the face. He howled, like a wounded dog and scrambled back up, onto his knees.

"Thank you, Williams." Beaufort replied, not looking at Derek as he poured himself a glass of water. "As for you, you miserable half-wit, if I hear one more word out of you, I'll have you executed. Is that understood?"

Derek's eyes flashed with hatred but he kept quiet.

"Take him away. She's seen enough." He wafted his hand in the air, dismissively and Derek was dragged back out again.

Beaufort turned to me, a smile of smug, self-satisfaction painted on his face. "As I was saying. I will give you Derek, as a gift, to do with as you will."

I crossed my arms. "Why would you do that?"

"Because I want us to be friends and friends give each other gifts, don't they."

I suppressed the urge to sigh out loud. It was clear Beaufort was the type to deal in half-truths. Okay, if I had to play it his way, I would, for the time being. I gave him a tight smile. "And what 'gifts' do you expect in return?"

He shook his head and tutted at me, in an infuriatingly patronising manner. "Such a transactional girl. Why should I want anything in return? Why can't I just be a nice person who wants to help out a damsel in distress?"

My blood boiled over. Slamming my hands on the table I glared at him. "Why don't you remove my collar and then we'll see just how much of a *damsel* I am!"

Beaufort gave a slow clap as he chuckled. "That's the spirit! Actually, I am going to remove your collar. In a closely confined, secure room, alone, with Derek." He leaned forward and put his hands on the table, his cold, blue eyes bored into mine. "And I want nothing in return...." He stood up to leave, ".... Yet."

I slumped back in my chair. So that was his game. He wanted me indebted to him. But if this slimeball thought I'd ever pay him back, he had another thing coming. He stood up and walked towards the double doors then turned to look back at me. "Goodnight Bree. We'll talk more in the morning."

I started to panic and held out my hand. "Wait"

He turned back, an infuriating smirk on his face.

"Am I...are you going to feed on me?"

He stared at me, blinking, letting the seconds tick by in silence, relishing my discomfort. Finally he answered. "I've forbidden all of the vampires in this house from biting you. No harm will come to you, as long as you play by the rules."

"What rules?"

But Beaufort ignored me, he was already walking out.

"What RULES?" I shouted, spittle flying out of my mouth as I banged my fists on the table.

"Goodnight Bree" He called back, his voice echoing as he entered the corridor and the doors swung shut, behind him.

Steadying my breath, I picked up my knife and fork and started to slowly finish my meal. But the food tasted like ash in my mouth. Nevertheless I chewed in silence, with the imposing figures of Mitchell and Peterson standing sentinel at the side of the room. I thought back to the day I'd first seen Beaufort. He'd made eye contact with me and I'd seen fear in his eyes. That meant he knew what I was, even before I did. Is that when he'd first set his sights on me? He wanted an arcane witch - why? It was maddening that I knew so little and this made me even more vulnerable. I was his prisoner but it was clear that wasn't enough for him. He wanted to make me squirm, he wanted power, he was getting off on this. I was trapped, in a mansion full of vampires. Nobody had harmed me yet but that almost made it worse. The impending sense of doom was unbearable. It was like being dangled by a rope over crocodile infested waters and hearing the rope snapping, one thread at a time. When was the rope going to break completely? When was I going to be cast to these crocodiles and torn apart, piece by piece?

18

After dinner, Mitchell and Peterson led me upstairs, to a large bedroom. It was done up like Elton John's wet dream, with a large four-poster bed, antique dressing table and chair, large gilt-framed mirror and expensive persian rug, covering dark floorboards. Elaborately-patterned, designer wallpaper adorned the walls. There was also an en suite bathroom, decorated a bit like the one I'd been in earlier except this one had a shower, toilet and basin. I walked around the bedroom, checking the floorboards to see if any of them were loose - they'd make good weapons. But sadly, no such luck. Then I tossed open the velvet curtains, I checked the windows. They were nailed shut. I looked out, across the clear, moonlit night, to see the vast english countryside. Rolling hills and the odd cluster of woodland and, crucially, not a single house or light, as far as the eye could see.

Bollocks! I stamped my foot and slumped down in the chair. I'd never felt more impotent.

My tired face stared back at me, from the mirror. I was clean and smelt beautiful but no amount of washing and expensive toiletries could erase the trauma of the past few days. Reaching towards my collar, I craned forward, inspecting it closely. Tiny black crystals were embedded into dark metal. I had to find a way of getting this thing off. If I didn't, I risked being forced to spend the rest of my life here, as a prisoner of that scuzz bucket, Beaufort. I clenched my fist.

No way! I will escape. Or Nik will come for me.

Or would he? Was I that valuable to him? It felt like it, when I was with him but I was beginning to have my doubts. Our relationship had been complicated from the start and maybe now, I was too much of a liability for Nik to have in his life. The Ahimsas already spent their lives constantly looking over their shoulders for Draculs. Perhaps Carlotta was, at this very moment, advising him to cut me loose. A wave of pain coursed through my chest at the thought of him tossing me aside. And it probably would be that easy for him. I was just another girl, of the many that he must've had and would have, during his very long life. What was he doing right now? Was he thinking of me? He'd warned me that I had to be careful and he'd been right.

Tears welled at my eyes and I sniffed and wiped them away. I had to be strong. If I fell apart, I had no chance of escape. I couldn't rely on the slim chance that Nik would rescue me. I had to find out as much as I could about Beaufort. What his strengths were, what his weaknesses were and most of all - what he really wanted from me. I was bone tired and wished I could get a good night's sleep. But could I trust what Beaufort had said? Would I really be safe from vampire attacks here or should I sleep with one eye open?

I got up and walked over to the bed. Spreading my hands across the soft sheets, I couldn't help but be a little impressed. It was perfectly made, with hospital-tucked corners, fluffy feather pillows and a plump eiderdown. Everything about this place seemed designed to delight but why? Why did Beaufort care what I thought? Where did he keep the humans he fed off? And did they also get this kind of deluxe treatment?

I crept towards the door and opened it a crack. Mitchell and Peterson were still outside. Nik had told me vampires didn't need much sleep. They'd probably stand there all night. Peterson turned towards me, he'd taken off his glasses and his dark eyes flashed a warning. "Goodnight Ms Ryan."

Giving him a murderous glare, I slammed the door shut. "Goodnight, arseholes." I screamed at the closed door, as I stormed over to the bed.

Blowing a strand of pink hair from my face, with a loud huff, I collapsed onto the eiderdown. A puff of air released from the bedding, which for some reason made me feel even angrier. Then, as I looked at the antique dressing table, I decided I'd had enough. I got up and strode towards it. Squatting down, I lifted it up and was about to hurl it over when I heard....

"I hope you're not about to damage my Louis the Sixteenth dressing table." It was Beaufort's voice.

I dropped the dressing table and whipped my head from side to side, searching for the source. Then I spotted tiny speakers, disguised as lights, at two ends of the bedroom ceiling. But where was the camera?

"What do you expect?" I snapped. "I'm not gonna go to sleep in a dracul vampire's house, without arming myself."

"Ah. So your plan is to smash up my dressing table and use the broken wood as stakes. Am I right?"

I pursed my lips and folded my arms, glaring at the speakers, in florid silence.

"Mitchell and Peterson would disarm you before you even realise they've entered the room. All you will accomplish is destroying a very rare and priceless antique. I'm sure you'll agree with me, that would be a shame."

His treacle-lined voice had the same effect on me, as someone insulting my mother. I thumped both fists onto the dressing table. "The biggest shame here, is that you hide behind security staff and speaker systems, instead of taking me on, one-on-one, in a fair fight. Because when that day comes, I promise you, that the rare and priceless antique I'll be destroying is YOU!"

There was a brief pause and then he replied. "You're tired Bree.

Get some sleep. No harm will come to you tonight. We'll talk more in the morning." The intercom clicked off.

I hated him. The veneer of politeness masked a man who, instinct told me, was capable of unspeakable acts of depravity. Even worse than that - he was a coward. He'd been terrified of me, when he'd seen me at the restaurant. But now, surrounded by his henchmen, he talked big. I'd get my own back on him. Whatever *this* was, I'd find a way out and then I'd enjoy watching him suffer.

Resigned to my fate, for now, I checked under the pillows and was not surprised to find a set of luxe pyjamas, in my size. Unbuttoning my shirt, I stopped at the second button - was he watching me get changed? He probably was, the pervert! Add that to the list of things I hated about him. I stomped towards the bathroom. He probably had cameras in there too but it felt more private. I changed into the pyjamas and then brushed my teeth with the new toothbrush and toothpaste on the basin. Then I got into bed, still seething. But against my expectations, I soon felt my eyelids get heavier. And as they did, one thought drifted through my sleepy head.

You may have the upper hand for now, Beaufort. But not for long. Not for long...

I SLEPT the dreamless sleep of the truly exhausted and awoke feeling like I'd just closed my eyes for a moment. However, the sound of birdsong and the sunlight filtering through the crack in the curtains, told me it was morning. Suddenly remembering where I was, I sat bolt upright. Now I'd had a good night's sleep, my thoughts were clearer, my body was stronger, I felt more positive about my situation.

Yes. Today is a good day for breaking out of a vampire's lair!

I jumped out of bed and was just about to get into the shower when there was a knock on my bedroom door. I stiffened. "Who is it?"

"My name is Darla. Mr Beaufort has assigned me as your personal maid. May I come in?"

Personal maid? What in the hell was going on here? "Sure." I answered weakly, hoping it wasn't another vampire.

A pretty, young woman with dark curly hair, slicked back into a tidy ponytail, entered. She had a smattering of freckles across the light brown skin of her nose and cheeks and her eyes twinkled as she smiled at me. In one hand, she pulled a small wheelie suitcase. Draped over the other arm, was a pile of clothes, on hangers, with the tags still on. As she came closer I gawped at the price of one of the shirts. It cost more than my monthly rent. Darla held up the shirt against my cheek. "It suits your colouring. Mr Beaufort will like that." As her hand brushed against my face, I sniffed but detected no vampire scent. Darla was human. My eyes flicked immediately to her neck - no bite marks.

I wasn't going to let the opportunity to pump her for information slip past but I was aware that Beaufort could be listening and watching us and I didn't want to get her into trouble. I kept my questions as neutral as possible. "Why have I been assigned a maid?"

She smiled as she pulled the suitcase over to the dressing table. "Mr Beaufort likes all of his favoured humans in the house to have a personal maid."

I creased my brow. "Favoured humans?" How many humans were here? And on what basis did Beaufort select the humans he favoured? "Do you have a maid?"

She laughed slightly, as if I'd said something ridiculous. "Oh no. I'm one of the house servants."

I studied her. She looked normal enough but what human, in their right mind, would choose to come and work for a vampire? "Did you know he was a vampire when you started working here?" I asked.

She swallowed and her chest rose and fell a little faster. "No." Her haunted expression left little doubt in my mind - she was scared. Her eyes darted to the speakers and then back at me, as if she was sending me a silent warning.

But I wasn't about to give up that easily. "Why don't you find another job?"

A look of pain flashed across her features but she ignored the question. "Right. Time for you to get into the shower. Put these on." She dumped the pile of clothes into my arms. "Then when you get out I'll do your hair and make up."

She turned away from me, as if trying to avoid my accusing eyes. Reluctantly, I went to the en suite bathroom and did as she'd instructed. It was clear that Darla either wouldn't or couldn't tell me more than she had. But I was determined to keep trying.

After my shower, I walked back into the bedroom.

Darla stood behind the chair, at the dressing table and patted the backrest. "Come take a seat over here." She opened the suitcase and took out a blow dryer, hairbrush and curling tongs. My eyes immediately went to the curling tongs. The metal lever would make an excellent weapon. It was unlikely to be made of silver so it wouldn't kill any vampires but it could maim them and buy me a few seconds. I glanced into the suitcase that lay open, on the floor. Inside I spotted hair pins. Perhaps I could swipe one and use it to pick the lock on my collar? I wouldn't do it right away, I'd talk to her for a while first, get her to relax, before choosing my moment carefully.

Darla plugged in the hair dryer and switched it on. Holding the dryer in one hand, she waved it over my head as she brushed my hair with the other hand. I decided to start casually, asking simple questions before working up to what I really wanted to know. "How long have you worked here?"

"It'll be five years in January." Her voice sounded weary and defeated.

Eyeing her in the mirror, her face seemed to take on a sad, wistful expression. "Did you answer a job advert or?..."

She gave a brief, bitter laugh. "I used to work for myself, getting clients through a beauty app." As she talked her eyes grew misty. "I was hired to come here and do a job for one of Mr. Beaufort's parties. It was a lot of money, I felt really lucky to have won the work. And he," her voice cracked. "Let's just say when he finds someone whose skills he likes, he doesn't let that person go." Her eyes widened meaningfully on the last few words.

What was she trying to tell me? Was she a prisoner here too, just like me? "Do you live here, like Sally?"

She nodded, looking down at the floor as she bit her lip. It looked like she was trying to stop herself from crying. But then she corrected her expression and took a deep breath as she fluttered her lips. "I think if we curl the ends, like this." She held up a lock of my hair, and wound it round the curling tongs. When she let go, it had formed a beautiful loose corkscrew which she teased out, with her fingers. "That will really suit you. What do you think?" There was genuine concern in her voice and I sensed that, whether or not she wanted to be here, she was good at her job and took real pride in her work.

"Yeah, that looks really nice."

She nodded proudly and started work on the rest of my locks. "What about you, how did you end up here?"

Her question surprised me but I wasn't going to lie about it. Flattening my eyes, I replied, "I was kidnapped and brought here against my will."

She hesitated, for just a moment, the slightest crease disturbing her forehead before she carried on. "That's unusual. Most of the people who come here do so voluntarily..." She switched off the blow dryer and lowered her voice to a whisper. "... At first." I almost missed what she said, it was so quiet - certainly quieter than what the speaker system could pick up. Her gaze flicked to mine and then quickly away again, as she bent down to put the hair dryer and hair brush away.

She was being careful - telling me just enough that I understood the humans here were prisoners. Even though our conversation had been surface level, I already liked Darla. She was trusting me when she barely even knew me. That took balls.

I thought carefully of what else I could ask. "The grounds of the estate look huge. How big is it?"

"Oh it runs for miles in all directions. If you want to explore the estate, just ask Mr Beaufort and he'll let you. Do you ever go running?"

I nodded, enthusiastically.

"Then why not ask if you can go for a run? You'll have to take your bodyguards of course."

Of course. But Darla understood what I was thinking. Exploring the grounds was the first step. Maybe during the run I could do something to shake off Mitchell and Peterson. Or, even better, find a well-shaped stick to stake one or both of them with.

Darla finished curling my hair and put the curling tongs back into her suitcase. I couldn't help glancing to the side and she noticed my line of sight.

"The tongs are made from heat-resistant plastic. They snap pretty easily." Her voice had a tone of resignation that suggested she'd previously had this exact same idea. If the tongs were plastic, they'd be no good for staking vampires. Inwardly cursing, I reasoned that it should've been obvious. No vampire would arm his human captives with potential weapons.

Bending down, she took the makeup box out of the suitcase and started applying cream over my face. "Your skin is a little dry. What moisturiser do you use?"

I raised one eyebrow. "Er, whatever I can afford, which is normally the shop's own no-name brand."

She chuckled. "Well, one thing you will get here is access to top of the line products. Mr Beaufort likes his pets to look well-groomed." She emphasised the word 'pets' and 'well-groomed' in a way that sent a shiver down my spine. Is that what I was here? A pet? Darla clearly thought so. But if I was a pet. What was she? Just a servant? As she bent forward to dab concealer onto my lower eyes, I whispered. "Do the vampires feed on you?"

She whispered back, quickly, her eyes wild with fear. "No. I'm not a blood slave."

Blood slave? What the hell!

I broke out in goosebumps as my mind went into overdrive. So far I'd learnt that there were some humans who were pets - Darla thought I was one of these. Then there were human servants, like Sally and Darla. And a third class of humans - blood slaves.

I didn't want to get Darla into trouble. She'd probably already risked a lot by telling me what she had done so I decided to stop the questions for now. If she was going to be my personal maid, I'd have time to find out more later.

Grabbing a huge brush, Darla dusted powder all over my face before crouching down in front of me, to shape my eyebrows. As I looked in the mirror, my face already looked way better than it normally did, when I did my own makeup. She had a real talent. "Where did you learn to do makeup like this?"

Her tone lifted, telling me that this was a topic she enjoyed. "I went to beauty college. As a child I was always doing my dolls' hair. That's all I ever wanted to do - make them look pretty. When I left school it was an obvious choice for me." She withdrew the mascara brush from its tube. "Look up."

I did as instructed and she started applying mascara to my top and bottom lashes. "I didn't know what I wanted to do when I was growing up. That's probably why I've ended up drifting from one, dead-end, office junior role to another. You're really lucky."

Her face crumpled and she looked like she was about to cry. "Lucky, right."

I gulped, aware that I'd put my foot in my mouth. She would be lucky if she wasn't a vampire's prisoner. Was she even paid? I suspected not. And coupled with her use of the term 'blood slave' I guessed that she too was a slave - kept here against her will, performing work for no pay. Even though I'd told myself I'd asked enough for today, I couldn't resist asking one final question. "What's the pay like?"

She shook her head, her eyes welling with tears, confirming what I'd suspected without uttering a word. The desolation was written all over her face. But Sally, Beaufort's cook, had seemed so cheerful. Had that been an act, a survival mechanism? And if I was a 'pet' what special privileges did that give me, other than maid service?

Darla put the final touches on my face and stepped aside to show me in the mirror.

"I look amazing!"

She smiled. "Thanks. Now you're ready for your first day in Beaufort Heights." Seeing my frown, she explained. "That's the name of this mansion - your home for the foreseeable future." Her tone dripped with sarcasm but she looked at me with pity and compassion.

I tried to infuse my returning smile with as much gratitude as I could. Holding her hand, I squeezed it lightly and looked into her eyes. "Thank you." I wanted her to know that I wasn't only thanking her for doing my hair and make up.

She nodded and zipped up the suitcase, as she began walking out. Her shoulders slumped and her footsteps seemed heavy on the wooden floors. It was only then that I remembered I hadn't swiped any of the hair pins, as I'd been planning. *Damnit!* I'd have to wait until tomorrow - if I lasted that long. But the way Darla had described it, I wasn't here to be fed on. The question still remained.

What was I here for?

19

After Darla left, Beaufort's voice came through the speaker system. "Peterson and Mitchell will accompany you down to breakfast. Then they'll take you to meet me, in my study."

Study. This guy really liked to play Lord of the Manor.

The smell of eggs and bacon wafted towards my nostrils and my stomach growled. Without my mobile phone, I had no idea what the time was or how long I'd slept. But I did need to eat.

As I'd suspected, Mitchell and Peterson were still standing in the same place I'd left them, the night before.

Looking at each of them, I said, "Let's go then". The sleep had improved my mood heaps and I had to admit, as far as being kept prisoner went, this could be a lot worse. At least I wasn't a 'blood slave'. An image of Derek, as he'd advanced towards me, fangs bared, flashed into my mind and I shuddered as I remembered the pain of his canines piercing my flesh. But the luxury of my 'prison cell' worried me. It felt like Beaufort was lulling me into a false sense of security. I was more determined than ever to get some proper answers out of him.

After breakfast, Mitchell and Peterson led me to Beaufort's study.

As we approached, a dark-skinned black lady was led out of the room, sandwiched between two vampire guards, a look of anguish on her face as she clutched her neck. I tried to see if there was a bite mark, underneath her hand but I couldn't see between the guards. However, I sniffed, as she passed, and when I got no hint of metal, I knew she was human.

My two vampire bodyguards waited outside and I went in. Row upon row of dusty, old books, lined the walls of the dark, oak-panelled room. Beaufort stood behind a large desk with more antique chairs in front. He was facing the floor to ceiling windows which looked out, over his estate.

As I entered, he turned and smiled, gesturing towards one of the chairs. "Please, take a seat." He held a dark grey handkerchief, in one of his hands, and he tucked it back into his pocket. I curled my lips in disgust. He'd just fed on that lady, I was sure of it. He'd probably just used that handkerchief to wipe blood from his mouth.

But I wasn't here to accuse him of drinking from humans - I already knew he did that. Nor did I want to waste any more time with the polite chit-chat bollocks, he'd started with, the day before. So I launched straight into the interrogation. "Why am I here? I'm obviously your prisoner so why are you treating me so well? What's your agenda?"

Beaufort's lips turned upwards but the smile didn't reach his eyes. He sat down, on the other side of the desk, facing me and steepled his fingers as he pursed his lips. He was thinking how to start. Was he nervous? He was! This was unbelievable!

"You know, it can be a very lonely life, being a vampire."

I rolled my eyes and folded my arms. "My heart bleeds for you."

His head jerked slightly. "I'm not after your pity. I merely mean to explain your role in all of this." He waved his hands around as if to indicate his house, his possessions, his world.

I creased my eyes, in confusion. What exactly was he getting at?

"I had a daughter you know and a wife." He tilted his head, studying me, looking for any signs that I knew his story. I kept my face neutral.

His expression darkened. "My daughter was taken from me, by a vicious, cruel wench who still hasn't paid for what she did to me." Rubbing his forehead, he sighed. "I wanted to try again for another child. But my wife didn't agree. She said that Lucy - that was our daughter's name, was irreplaceable. The strain of grief finally tore us apart and she left me."

I hissed at him. "Maybe she left you because you're a human-trafficking piece of pond scum."

He pursed his lips. "Look, I know you've spent time with the Ahimsas and they've filled your head with lies about me and my organisation. I want to set the record straight which is why I've invited you to..."

I interrupted. "Abducted me."

He continued. "Why I wanted you to spend time here."

I'd had about as much as I could take of his double speak. Slamming my hands on the desk, I glared at him. "Okay Boomer. I've sat here listening to your sob story. Let me play you a serenade on the world's tiniest violin." I stuck my chin out, raised my eyebrows and mimed a violin at my shoulder. "But what I'm still waiting for is exactly what you want, from *me*!" I spat out the last word, no longer caring that I was alone, in the study of a vicious apex predator.

"I want you to give me an heir."

The words tumbled out of his mouth so quickly and quietly that I wasn't sure I'd heard him correctly.

"Sorry, what did you say? It sounded like you said you want me to give you..." I hesitated and he finished my sentence.

"... An heir." An aching sadness filled his eyes as they met mine. But I felt no compassion for him.

This time there was no mistaking what he'd said. So he *was* a filthy pervert. I knew it! He simply wanted to jump my bones, same as most other guys did. But he was old enough to be my grandfather, probably great, great, great grandfather if I counted his years on earth.

He held his hands up, in a placatory manner and I realised that my jaw had dropped open.

"It's not what you think."

I blew air out of my mouth. "Not what I think? Really? Because it sounds to me like you just propositioned a woman young enough to be your granddaughter."

"That's not why I want you to produce my heir."

I folded my arms again and tapped my fingers against the sides of my torso. "Go on then. I'm waiting."

His eyes glazed over. "Lucy was a special child. She was an arch vampire - a pureblood, produced by two vampire parents. Such progeny are difficult to create - vampires are not as fertile as humans. I want a child as special as she was." He looked at me. "A witch-vampire hybrid would be the most powerful being on the planet. My resources are vast and I know for certain, this has never been done before."

I guffawed. "Yes. And there's a reason for that." I leaned forward. "Witches hate you. I'd sooner mate with a squid than with you."

He gave the same tight smile he'd given me earlier. "You only say that because you don't know me. Give me a chance and I'll show you that I can be quite charming."

"It's never gonna happen, Beaufort."

"Call me Hugh"

"Like I said. It's never gonna happen, *Beaufort*."

He sighed and stood up. "You may think I'm your biggest enemy but the Ahimsas are using you more than I ever have or ever would."

I stood up and turned away. "I'm not listening to your lies."

"Lies? Why do you think Carlotta gave you refuge? Why do you think Nik asked you out, in the first place?"

I spun round and looked at him, eyes wide. He knew even more than I thought he did.

"Do you think it was because he likes you? No. It was because Carlotta ordered him to. They wanted to find a way to make an alliance with the arcane witches. They've wanted that for the longest time. Nik doesn't care about you. He's even more self-interested than I am. At least I'm being honest with you about what I want. He's lied to you since the beginning and he still is."

His words hit deep, like a punch to the gut. I'd always wondered if Nik really liked me and Beaufort was needling right at my insecurities.

He could see his words had struck a chord and he came around to my side of the desk. "Think about it, my angel. What can Nik give you? What has he already given you? Have you ever been treated as well as you have, since you came here? With me, you would live in the lap of luxury. We wouldn't have to be a couple, you could live your own life but all your desires would be pandered to. You'd simply have to raise our child but there'd be staff to help you, nannies and cleaners, an assistant, whatever you wanted. Other than that, you could fulfil all your dreams. Do you want to travel and see the world? I can pay for that - and it'll be first class, all the way. Perhaps you want to study further? I can make that happen - at the most prestigious universities in the world. Why live a life of toil and struggle when I'm offering you the chance to live as one of the world's elites? Isn't that what every girl ever dreamed of? To be a princess, in a beautiful castle, with a handsome prince at her side?"

As his words, wormed their way into my consciousness, I turned my head slowly towards him. I had to admit, he wasn't horrendous looking. To many older women, he was probably quite a catch. He must've clocked my moment of positive appraisal as he quickly leant forward and touched his lips to my forehead. It was a fatherly kiss and I touched the spot where his lips had been, my head a sea of confusion, tears welling at my eyes.

"I have to go." I whispered, rushing out of the door. There was no way this manipulative fucker was going to see me cry. Half running to my bedroom, the ever-present Mitchell and Peterson strode briskly, behind me.

He'd hit more than a nerve, he'd hit a home run of truths. I'd always wanted someone to protect me and provide for me. Someone who would make all the bad stuff in the world go away. Hugh Beaufort was offering me utopia on a stick and all I had to do was provide a womb, in return. Sure, it meant I had to sleep with him but would that be so bad, in return for a life without cares? It would be so easy to accept his offer and never have to work again. Shit, I'd probably even get one of those high society weddings, with my picture in Hello magazine.

I reached my room and slammed the door shut, sinking against the wooden frame as I stared at the ceiling, breathing deeply. This was the last thing I'd ever expected but it did explain the VIP treatment. I was being buttered up. This was basically one, long seduction technique and, pitifully, I was already falling for it. It felt like there was an angel at one ear, slapping me around the face and telling me to snap out of it and escape already. And a devil at my other ear, whispering sweet nothings about how lovely and carefree a life with this vampire would be.

And I had no idea which of them to listen to.

KNOCK, knock, knock.

"Come in." My voice sounded hesitant. Why was I still scared? Beaufort had laid his cards on the table, I wasn't here to be fed on… but there was a distinct possibility that I could be raped. Two young women entered. One was blonde, the other had jet black hair. They looked about my age, were both slim, gorgeous and wearing bikinis. I sat up on the bed, brushing strands of pink hair away from my face.

"I'm Mel" said the dark-haired one, "and this is Gemma." She gestured towards the blonde who stood, with one hand on her hip, looking me up and down as if I was something nasty the cat had dragged in.

Mel continued. "We're two of the resident humans here at Beaufort Heights." She paused, letting what she'd said sink in. I found my eyes immediately going to their necks. I couldn't see any bite marks. They must be two of the 'pets', as Darla had described it.

She flicked her hair out of her face. "Would you like to come with us to the leisure suite? There's a pool and a jacuzzi, a masseuse and beautician."

"Beautician?" Beaufort really did pamper his pets.

She took my question to be a lack of understanding and helpfully explained. "Yeah. You can get a facial if you want or get your nails done - or both."

Gemma stood, silently glaring at me, beside Mel. She didn't bother to hide her disdain for me. "If you're tired, you can stay here." Her tone of voice suggested that would make her happier but Mel turned to her and gave her a pointed look. "Come on, Gemma, let's make Bree feel welcome, as Hughie asked us to."

Hughie?! I felt like vomiting. "Erm, I don't have a bikini." I mumbled.

"Oh don't worry about that. Hughie will have bought one for you. He always takes care of his girls like that, he's so generous."

His girls...

Mel's eyes softened. "Look, I know this is overwhelming. It was the same for me when I first arrived. But just relax and go with it." Her eyes grew a little sad and distant. "Pretty soon you'll wonder why you ever resisted." She took a deep breath and shook her hair out of her face, as she brightened up her expression. "Besides, what else are you going to do with your day?"

I bit my lip. She was right. I could either stew here, wallowing in self-pity as I tried to plan a hopeless escape. Or I could go and enjoy the spa. Who knows? Perhaps I'd find a way to escape there that had so far evaded me within the four walls of this bedroom. "Will Beaufo... I mean Hugh be there?"

Mel nodded. "Oh yes. And you'll get to meet all the other girls too."

My body straightened. "All what other girls?"

"All his other humans of course."

His pets. His favoured humans.

I was hardly surprised. Of course he had a harem of girls - what billionaire wouldn't? But I couldn't deny that I was curious. These two seemed okay with the arrangement and they didn't seem all that different from me. Had they come here by choice? Were they still here by choice? They'd left the door open and I saw no bodyguards outside. That meant they were free to come and go as they pleased and this fascinated me. What was the draw of 'Hughie' as Mel called him? Was it as simple as money or was there something else?

I scrambled off the bed. "Alright, let's go. It sounds like fun."

Mitchell and Peterson followed the three of us, downstairs two flights, to the ground floor. As I turned around, Mitchell's eyes lingered on me and the other girls in a way that was unsettling and I shuddered. He had shark like eyes, two tiny pricks of dark within his hard face.

I turned back to Mel. "Why don't you have bodyguards?" I asked, gesturing towards the two silent men behind us.

"I did at the start but not anymore. I want to stay here now."

My ears pricked up. "You were brought here by force?"

She smiled. "Not exactly by force. I used to be a model. We got invited to a lot of parties. I was at this one party and got invited to an afterparty in the house of a billionaire. That billionaire was Hugh. He took a liking to me and insisted I stayed." She gulped and looked down.

Darla's words echoed through my mind and fear lanced through me. *When Beaufort finds someone he likes, he doesn't let that person go.*

I began to get an impression of a man who collected humans like some people collected dolls. We walked down a long corridor, the smell of chlorine wafting towards us, from ahead. "Don't you miss your family?"

Her eyelids flickered and she hesitated for just long enough to tell me that she missed them loads. But then she corrected her expression. "Sometimes. I can call them whenever I like but I'm not allowed to talk about what goes on here."

"What would happen if you did."

"I'd get kicked out and nobody wants that. This is paradise."

Paradise?! I couldn't believe what I was hearing. There had to be a catch. Did they even know that Beaufort was a vampire? I asked the question, as bluntly as possible. "Does Hugh feed on you?"

"Nooo!" She extended the word as if it was a ludicrous suggestion. "He has blood slaves for that." She flicked her hair out of her face, nonchalantly.

I was horrified. These women seemed fine with the fact that Beaufort kept humans here as blood slaves, as long as it wasn't them. Had they always been without morals or had they sold them, in exchange for a life of no work and all play? Any notion I'd had that these girls were like me evaporated. I could never stand by and turn a blind eye, as other people were being mistreated. It wasn't how I was built and certainly wasn't how I'd been brought up. To look the other way like that made them complicit in what was going on here. Almost as if they thought they were better than the blood slaves and that was nothing short of delusional.

I asked the other question. "But you sleep with him, right?"

She giggled. "Oh yeah, of course."

I was floored that she was so open about it. I would feel ashamed if I was her. There was something about her that seemed out of place. She walked the walk and talked the talk but I got the impression she was lying about how happy she was here. She'd been unable to stop herself from reacting when I'd asked about her family. But if she missed them that much, all she had to do was purposefully get 'kicked out'. This inconsistency made me question everything she'd said. Would she really get 'kicked out' for breaking the rules? Beaufort had spoken about rules but maybe this was a pre-agreed, reinforcement of the same lies. Had Beaufort coerced her to put on an act for me?

As we walked closer to what I assumed was the leisure suite, soft bossa nova music drifted to my ears along with laughter and voices. Tropical warmth enveloped me as I entered the suite. A man, was doing sprint lengths in the huge pool. Was that Hugh? It was hard to tell with his goggles and swimming cap on. To the side of the pool was a jacuzzi and another man came out of a sauna, wrapping himself up in his dressing gown, just a minute too late to avoid me seeing his ding dong. I looked away and giggled. Looking back up, I noticed waiters milling around, carrying trays of drink and hors d'ouevres. One wall was comprised of floor to ceiling netting and it looked like there was a greenhouse on the other side. Tropical plants grew against the net. Humming birds and large butterflies flitted amongst orchids and ferns. Everywhere I looked I saw beautiful young women and a few men, being pampered. I counted four masseuse's and there were more treatment rooms around the sides of the main suite.

"Wow!" I breathed out. It was an instantaneous reaction.

"Pretty cool, huh?" Mel grabbed my arm. "Come on, let's get your bikini and join in the fun." Gemma trailed, grumpily behind us. She had a face like a slapped arse and it was aimed squarely in my direction.

Mel let go of my arm and walked over to ask another lady who I guessed was a servant - mainly because she was older and not wearing a bikini. The lady nodded, disappeared through one of the doors then came back carrying a bag. She walked over and handed me the bag. "There you go. You can get changed in any of the side rooms that are free. They all have locks on the doors."

I made a mental note. If ever I was desperate to get away from Hugh, I could lock myself in one of these and buy myself at least a few hours. Like everything else I'd been given since arriving here, the bikini was exquisite. Delicate patterns competed with neon colours and gold stitching. The designer label told me that this bikini cost way more than what I would normally spend on a fancy evening dress. With my bikini on, I exited the changing room and spotted Gemma and Mel, milling nearby. They'd probably been instructed to stick close by me.

Mel gave a wide grin and pulled me into the pool. From within a crowd of young women, Hugh Beaufort turned around. His hair was wet and he gave me a dazzling smile, his teeth bright white against his tanned face. Light reflected off the water making his light blue eyes glint.

"Ah Bree, I'm so glad you came, my angel." He waded forward and kissed me on each cheek, making me inwardly gag. "Can I get you something to drink? George..." he clicked his fingers at a nearby waiter and pointed at me. "Get the lady whatever she wants."

"I'll just have a lemonade thanks." I had no intention of losing my wits on alcohol and waking up to find I'd signed my soul over to this incubus.

I expected Hugh to try and pressure me but instead, he merely raised his eyebrows. "As you wish. A lemonade please George. Ice cold." He wiped his face and settled back against some seating that had been fashioned to look like ornamental rocks. "What do you think of my impromptu pool party? I'd love to say that we're holding it in your honour but actually, this is what life is like everyday here. I live life to the fullest." He winked at me, sickeningly and leaned back to take a sip of water, that he'd left on the side.

"Yeah, it seems…. Nice." I smiled weakly.

He laughed. "Nice?! Nice?! My angel - all this could be yours and not only for today, for the rest of your life."

I raised an eyebrow. "Don't you get bored of non-stop parties?"

Mel sidled up to him and leant her chin on his shoulder, looking at me with big eyes. "There's more than just parties, there's horse riding, shopping, casinos, private theatre nights, concerts, restaurants - although the private chefs we get in here are way better."

Hugh interrupted. "And then there's the occasional entertainment that is of a more… exotic variety."

I gulped. Was he talking about sex parties? Please, dear God, don't let him be talking about sex parties. But that would explain why there were also dudes here. He didn't strike me as the type to swing both ways though….

He laughed at me. "Don't look so nervous. I'm talking about when punishment has to be meted out. We still have the rather unpleasant, but necessary, business of finishing off Derek, after all." He took another sip of his water, studying my reaction, from over the rim of his glass. "Like I said. Friends give each other gifts and I really do want us to be friends."

I looked from him to Mel and back again, my head in a sea of turmoil. Here he was, dangling in front of me, the thing that I most wanted. With Derek dead, I'd be able to reclaim my life, move back into my flat, get a job and forget about all this. But even that was a fantasy. I could never walk away and forget about all this. Once he'd given me Derek, I'd be indebted to him and he'd expect payment. He'd expect me to give him a baby. Could I just lie to him and bide my time until he trusted me enough that I was no longer followed around by the two silent henchmen? If I double-crossed him, he'd follow me to the ends of the earth to enact his revenge - his relentless quest to kill Carlotta was proof of that. But with Derek still alive, was I any better off? I was his prisoner, whether Derek lived or died and the worst part about all of this, the part that I could barely even admit to myself was...

I was already beginning to like it here.

20

"Well? Which is it to be?" Hugh blinked at me, expectantly, as if he was asking me which type of biscuits I preferred with my tea. "Do you want to kill Derek yourself or shall I get one of my staff to do it for you?"

I needed more time to think. I knew there were still things that Hugh was hiding from me. "Let's save that for later. I want to enjoy the party for a while first." I smiled at him.

He frowned and then laughed. "You do surprise me. I would've thought you'd be itching to stick a stake into his chest." He clapped his hands together. "Party it is - DJ, turn the music up and play something a little more lively."

Pumping deep house came on and the women, clustered around Hugh, started gyrating. It was surreal. I felt like I'd stumbled onto the set of a music video. I waded out of the pool and sat by the side, watching as I sipped my lemonade. I was way out of my depth. Even if someone else killed Derek, Hugh would see it as a favour that he'd done for me. Everything that I'd heard about this man, before meeting him, was negative but since I'd arrived, I'd only been shown the positive. This entire experience seemed like a carefully controlled piece of theatre - designed to make me think he was a generous, benevolent playboy who just liked to enjoy life. Looking around, I saw only happy, smiling faces. Maybe life as a vampire's plaything wasn't all that bad? I certainly couldn't see any evidence that this man was as evil as the Ahimsas made him out to be.

But then I thought about Darla. The fear in her eyes had been unmistakeable. When I'd asked her if she had a maid, she'd laughed, almost as if the idea was ridiculous. Why? What was it that made Hugh choose certain humans as his playmates while other humans were servants or blood slaves? I looked around the leisure suite at groups of splashing, laughing men and women. Around the side, servants stood milling around.

And that's when it hit me.

It was so obvious, I couldn't believe I'd missed it. The people in the pool were all white. The servants standing around the sides were all lighter shades of brown. I thought back to the woman I'd seen being led from Beaufort's study earlier. She'd been dark skinned. As the unavoidable realisation hit me, I turned my face, left to right, looking for evidence that my suspicion was wrong. I found none. The house was clearly built on a hierarchy of race. White people - typically attractive white girls, were Beaufort's pets or favoured humans. Brown people were his servants and black people were his food.

My heart raced and my throat went dry, in spite of the lemonade. Growing up, there hadn't been many non-white people in my town. But I'd been raised to view everyone as equal. There were a thousand and one ways in which my family was fucked up. But racism wasn't one of them.

Mel swum over and leaned on the edge of the pool. "What are you doing out here all by yourself? Why don't you come and join us?"

"No thanks, I'm feeling a bit... tired."

"Ooh, you should go and get a massage? That'll make you feel better."

My insides were in turmoil. I hated that I was here, enjoying the high life while others around me were slaves. Nevertheless, perhaps I should get the massage. It would give me peace and quiet to work this all out. "You know what, I think I'll do that."

"Go to Sandra - she's the best. She's over in that treatment room. See you later" She did a cutesy wave and twinkled her eyes at me before swimming off.

Grabbing a towel from one of the passing servants, I dried myself off as I walked to the treatment room, Mel had pointed to. A man was just coming out of the room and as he walked past, a whiff of vampire floated past my nostrils. There sure were a lot of vampires in this place - did they all take turns feeding off the blood slaves?

Entering the room, I was greeted by a buxom, fair-skinned black lady, in her mid thirties, with braided hair tied up with a scarf. "Good afternoon. My name's Sandra, may I ask what your name is?"

"I'm Bree."

"Welcome Bree. Don't be shy, come on over. I'll just close the door while you get ready. I need your bikini top off, you can change behind the screen if you wish. Then drape this towel over your body and lie on the massage table, face down. Do you have any injuries I should know about?"

"No but I have quite a few cuts and bruises, as you can see."

"Don't worry. I'll avoid those completely. Do you have any allergies?"

I frowned, wondering what the point of the question was. "No."

"Good. I had one client once, who was allergic to lavender and didn't tell me. She came out in hives. You see, I add a few drops of lavender to my massage oil - helps you to relax."

I smiled, feeling my shoulders already relaxing. Sandra was a chatty one and that was exactly what I needed. I would spend my time milking her for as much information as I could.

I got myself ready and lay face down, on the massage table. Sandra leaned over me, slathering warm oil onto my back and I allowed myself to enjoy the sensations for a moment before asking, "how long have you worked here?"

"It's going on ten years now."

"Wow! You must have seen a lot of changes to the household, in that time?"

"I sure have. I was here when Mr Beaufort was still married and then he lost his Lucy..." Her voice cracked a little. "That poor man has suffered so much."

"It sounds like you had a good relationship with the family."

"Yes. It broke my heart when Lucy died. Such a shock to all of us. She was a sweet girl." She sniffed and reached for a tissue, to wipe her nose. "I'm sorry, I get a little... you know."

I tilted my head to the side and saw her fanning her eyes, with her hands.

"Please don't apologise." I changed the subject. "What's Hugh like to work for?"

She paused for a moment, then went back to rubbing her hands over my back. "He's very kind, very kind indeed." There was something tight and manufactured about her response. She'd been here long enough to learn that dissent wasn't worth it and she was not going to breathe a word of complaint. Her hands moved down to the tops of my thighs and I flinched as she got to a tight spot. "Sorry, I'll go a bit softer."

"That's ok. My hamstrings are really tight - I work out regularly but I've never had a massage before."

"In that case, you're probably going to be sore afterwards then. Drink plenty of water and get a good night's rest. You should have a bath tonight, it helps with the detox process." She slapped the side of my body. "Okay, you can get on your back."

I turned over, pondering the question I was dying to ask. There was no way to ask it delicately so I just went for it. "There are a lot of vampires living here. Does Hugh share his blood slaves with all of them?"

Her face dropped, for just a second and then she corrected her features into the same serene smile, she'd had on her face before. "He is very generous. We all get so well treated - vampires *and* humans." Her eyes filled with fear and then flicked to the ceiling, where I saw tiny cameras. Beaufort was watching us here too. Did he have people permanently monitoring our every move? Or did he just replay the recordings later and mete out punishment to anyone who'd stepped out of line?

I couldn't blame her for towing the party line, to protect herself. If she'd been here ten years, she must've seen a lot and suffered a lot.

Suddenly there was a blast of colder air and I noticed an air vent, in the corner of the room. An eerie sound, like a child crying, blew in with the air. Sandra walked over and shut the vent then dusted off her hands and wiped them on her apron.

"Did you hear that?" I asked.

"What?"

"That. It sounded like crying."

She let out a high-pitched laugh and then cleared her throat, her eyes begging me not to pursue this line of questioning. "It's a very old building, there are lots of weird creaks and groans. Most likely the wooden floorboards, combined with the wind. Or it could be bats, we get those coming in from time to time." Her hands trembled as she placed them back on my body.

Bats?! As if! I dropped the issue. Her behaviour had already given me what I needed. If that sound was bats, I was a ferret's priest. Somewhere, within the bowels of this mansion, there was a child crying. With the size of this place, and the amount of vampires here, he could have hundreds of kids locked away, some of them could be blood slaves. It was no longer just about my survival. I might be the only person who could set these people free. I hadn't worked out how yet but I would - I was determined to. As I lay on that bed, with Sandra pummelling my thighs, I took a deep breath, to steady my emotions.

"All done! How do you feel?"

I did my best to keep my voice light and cheery. "Great! You have magic hands." I started to get up and Sandra laid a gentle hand on my shoulder.

"Don't get up too quickly, you'll get light headed. I'll go and wash up and leave you to get changed. Take as long as you need."

"Thanks Sandra." I waited until she'd left the room and closed the door and then I sat bolt upright. Not caring about the cameras, I scrambled off the bed. I marched over to the air vent and tried to reopen it but it was jammed shut.

Damnit!

I struggled for several minutes, then swore as I tore a nail. My head whipped towards the door at the sound of footsteps approaching. I raced back to the massage bed, acting natural as I put my bikini top back on.

Sandra came back in and smiled at me. "All ready?"

I returned a wan smile. "Yep. See you soon."

She nodded kindly at me. I felt so bad for her. She was being held here against her will, like all the others. I had to help her, I had to help all of them. And I couldn't forget the sound of crying I'd distinctly heard, coming from that vent. Perhaps I could sneak back here later and see if I could hear it again? But would I even be allowed to do that? Would Hugh allow the pretence that I was a guest here extend to me roaming the mansion as I wished? Okay, Mitchell and Peterson would tag along behind me but so far they hadn't stopped me from doing anything.

If only I could just get this damned dog collar off. I closed my eyes and concentrated on the obsidian-coated metal band, as if willing it to break. It lay fixed around my neck, as stubbornly as ever before. I sighed at my own silliness. What did I think would happen? That it would magically pop off? I walked over to rejoin the fake party, my legs feeling as heavy as my heart.

Walking out of the massage room, I felt a heavy sense of inertia settle over my body. The exhaustion and drama of the past few days had really taken their toll on me. But it felt like more than that. Maybe it was the months of working two jobs, for a pittance, in London? Being here felt like a luxury holiday and I found myself starting to feel at home. I was already slotting in, just like all the other girls here. Guilt and shame fought for dominance, within me. Was I eventually destined to shrug off the injustice that existed in this house and simply enjoy life, like Mel and Gemma did?

My gaze found Gemma at the other end of the pool and as I looked at her, she walked over to me.

Her eyes narrowed. "You might be Hugh's favourite for now but he'll soon tire of you, just like he does with all his new pets." She gave a triumphant smile. "Then he'll be mine again." She strode off and I watched her in pity. She really thought I was competition. Was it a severe case of Stockholm syndrome or did she really want to be here? Actually, it seemed like many of the other girls suffered from the same syndrome. I watched as they playfully splashed, fluttered their eyelashes and giggled at Beaufort's lame, Dad jokes. I refused to become like them. It was a pitiful waste of a life. I might not have a clear idea of what I wanted out of life yet but I was damn sure of one thing. My dreams extended way bigger than being a vampire billionaire's mate. I gritted my teeth. If Hugh Beaufort thought he could charm his way into my knickers, with trinkets and parties, he had another think coming.

21

The morning had been such an unpleasant mix of nasty surprises and guilt-lined pampering that by the afternoon, I was desperate to have time to myself, just to think and sort out my complicated emotions. Taking Darla's advice, I asked Hugh if I could go for a run around the grounds. Alone in my room, I slipped on the expensive workout outfit he'd taken great delight in gifting me. The pink lycra catsuit, covered with strategically-placed mesh patches, left little to the imagination. Tying my hair into a high pony, the memory of him clapping his hands together as he blew out the hot air of his inflated opinions made me seethe with anger.

An excellent idea! You should explore the grounds of your new home. After all, we wouldn't want that lovely figure getting flabby.

I squirmed as he almost licked his lips, his gaze crawling over my body, like a poisonous spider. The fact that I had to ask for his permission lit my belly with fury. He thought he was getting to me, that the run was a sign I was starting to adapt to life here. But he was wrong. He was my jailer, nothing more. The day when I'd watch him turn to dust as I stuck a silver knife into his decrepit heart couldn't come soon enough.

Outside my room, Mitchell and Peterson were dressed in

matching black running shorts and a white top. "Ready?" Mitchell asked, his gaze casually checking out my physique, as normal.

I avoided his hungry eyes. "Yes, let's go."

We took off at a rapid pace down the pebbled driveway. The weather was cold enough that I would've had to run fast just to keep warm. But that wasn't the only reason for my quick pace. My emotions twisted inside my belly like curdled milk. As my feet pounded the pebbles, I thought of Darla. She didn't look much older than me and yet she'd spent five years of her life here as a prisoner - no a slave. She wasn't paid and who knows how badly she was treated. The look of fear in her eyes had told me enough. It was the same look I'd seen in Sandra's eyes. Eyes that spoke of horrors witnessed and bodies that trembled with memories of trauma.

The driveway extended for longer than I'd expected. This place was huge, but now, as we neared the gate, Mitchell said, "this way." A wild instinct to sprint towards the gate took hold of me. But it was a ridiculous idea. It looked to be around eight feet high and the top was covered by spikes. Even if I could climb it, Mitchell and Peterson would easily overpower me before I got close. I'd be no match for either their speed or their strength.

Flanked by the huge vampires, I begrudgingly accepted that this run wouldn't offer anything more than information. We turned onto the grassy hills of the estate grounds, pebbles giving way to spongy, well-cut grass, beneath my feet. In the distance I spied a thicket of trees and felt a rush of excitement. There could be fallen logs or pieces of branches that I could use as a stake. The obsidian collar suppressed my powers but I wasn't about to let that stop me. I could take out at least one of these guys, if not both. Then it was just a matter of scaling the gates or finding a weak point in the perimeter walls. Fuelled by the excitement of possible escape, I quickened my pace and made for the thicket.

Mitchell and Peterson looked no more fatigued than they would if they'd been going for a light stroll, but I was panting loudly. As we reached the thicket, my eyes scanned the ground, looking for anything I could use. But there were no fallen pieces larger than useless, flimsy twigs anywhere. Now, Mitchell turned to me, his eyes twinkling with patronising amusement. "If you're planning to find a chunk of wood to stake us with, you'll be disappointed. Mr Beaufort sends vampire staff members to scour the estate, every day, and collect any pieces of wood they find."

I scowled at him, annoyed that he'd read my transparent thoughts. We carried on running, uphill. I had to admit, the estate was breathtaking. Rolling green hills with the odd cluster of trees. In the distance, a small herd of deer grazed on a hillside. Overhead a large bird of prey circled, its golden brown feathers shining in the bright, early winter sunlight. At the top of the hill, I stopped, resting my hands on my knees as I bent over to get my breath back. As I straightened up again, still panting, I noticed a series of simple, small, brick cottages, in the valley. They must've been the original grounds keeper's quarters for this manor house. But it looked like older cottages had been added to, over the years, with newer brick evident on the more recently built dwellings.

"What are those?" I pointed to the houses, looking at Peterson.

"That's where the blood sla... " he corrected himself "... servants live."

My heart seemed to thump in my chest a little quicker. "Can I go and visit them?"

He shook his head. "Mr Beaufort strictly forbids fraternisation between the house humans and the blood servants."

Yeah, I bet. He didn't want to risk an uprising. The hierarchy of the house was partially maintained by Beaufort's pets wilfully ignoring the plight of the blood slaves. If they were allowed to come and see how the other half lived, it might sow seeds of guilt that would turn into dissent.

"Can you tell me anything about them? How do they live? Are they well fed?"

Peterson cleared his throat. "You must ask these questions of Mr Beaufort, we are merely here to accompany you." What a cop out. Beaufort probably had the blood slaves sleeping on filth and eating gruel. He didn't want to damage the image that he was so carefully constructing for me, a fantasy that I'd never believe. If they weren't allowed to take me there, it was because I'd be appalled by what I saw.

I challenged his non-response directly. Looking him squarely in the eyes as I put my hands on my hips. "You're not allowed to talk to me?"

Ignoring my question, Peterson looked towards the lengthening shadows of the setting sun. "It'll be dark soon. We better start heading back." He and Mitchell turned and started a slow jog, back in the direction we'd come, and I reluctantly followed. But as we ran, I took one more look at the row of small brick houses. It was then that a figure came out of one of the cottages. He was tall, with a good posture and very dark skin. From this distance, I couldn't make out his face but I could tell he was staring at us. I sensed his dark eyes contained a mixture of hatred and pain. What would he and others in those houses think of me? Beaufort Heights was full of young, white women who filled their cups with luxury, tainted with the blood of the black humans living down the hill. The man who watched me likely thought I was no different. But he was wrong. I *was* different. I wasn't going to stand by and enjoy an idle pampered life here while other humans suffered. The more I learned of Hugh Beaufort and his house of horrors, the more determined I became to take him down, by any means necessary.

22

That night, I lay in bed, turning over everything I'd learnt, looking for chinks in Beaufort's armour that I could use to escape. The run could be one means. Even if there were no pieces of wood on the floor, that didn't matter. I was strong, I could jump up and grab a branch, tearing it off on the way down to deliver a death strike to one of the vampire bodyguards. But, even if I was successful at pulling off such a complex move, I'd only have time to take out one of them. The other one would quickly disable me before I could kill him. As a human, I was simply too slow and weak to take on even one vampire effectively, let alone two. The answer lay in the obsidian collar. I had to find a way of getting it off. With my arcane powers, I stood a chance of escape, without them I was trapped.

Perhaps I should take up Beaufort's offer of killing Derek? If he removed my collar to allow me to do that, maybe I could find a way of killing more vampires than just Derek. But Beaufort was smart. There's no way he'd remove my collar without covering all his bases first. Hell, I'd probably be put in some kind of nuclear bunker and locked away to duke it out with Derek, alone.

I sighed, frustration stopping my eyes from getting heavy.

Think, Bree, think!

There had to be a way. I'd spotted hair clips in Darla's suitcase. I was already planning to swipe one and see if I could pick the lock of my collar with it. But really, getting myself away wasn't enough for me. I also wanted to rescue the other humans. If I made it out of here and left the other humans to their fate, it would eat me up inside, I'd never forgive myself. That meant I had to plan my escape carefully. I had to find a way of getting messages to the captives down the hill and I had to have a plan coordinated and agreed with them before I made my move. But how would I talk to them? Even the house servants weren't allowed to interact with the blood slaves. No - not house servants, house *slaves*. I wasn't going to fall into the trap of buying into Beaufort's fucked up euphemisms. That's how the grooming began, first by accepting the lifestyle, then by adopting the ideology and finally by agreeing with it and no longer resisting. That was how Mel and Gemma had been manipulated, but I was made of stronger stuff.

My thoughts were disturbed by the sound of tyres on gravel. Scrambling out of bed, I rushed to the window. A dark mercedes was rolling up the driveway. The car stopped and a group of gorgeous, young white women got out. All swishing, straight hair, gleaming skin and graceful limbs. They looked like models - just Hugh's type. I watched as they walked into the house, chatting and laughing. They had no idea what they were getting themselves into. I'd probably be introduced to them tomorrow - the newest edition to Hugh's menagerie of humans. My saliva tasted like bile in my throat. The whole thing sickened me.

Dragging my feet back to bed, my thoughts turned to Nik. What was he doing now? Was he thinking about me? Did he miss me at all? I'd tried not to let what Beaufort has said about him affect me - the man had every reason to lie. But there'd been a ring of truth to his words that I found difficult to ignore. And now, in the darkness of my lonely room, I replayed every interaction I'd had with Nik, looking for evidence that he really cared about me. I wanted to believe that he did and that was the problem. It made it impossible to decipher real emotions on his part from wishful thinking on mine.

A tiny voice cried out in my head. Maybe, I should just accept that Nik wasn't that into me? I shook the dark thought from my mind. The situation I was in was bound to make me feel depressed. But I couldn't give in to that. I had to stay positive, not just for my sake but also the sake of all the other humans in the house - even the other pets. I had a low opinion of the other girls but they were victims too. None of us were free to leave, not really. Even the ones who thought they were had been brainwashed into thinking that life was good here. I pitied them. At least I still had my own mind. They didn't even have that.

Still seeking a solution, something dug at the recesses of my mind and as I turned my attention back to the memory of seeing the blood slaves' houses, I realised what it was. That man had walked out of the house. Nobody had stopped him. That meant they weren't guarded. Nor had I seen any chains binding him. If they weren't guarded and there were no chains, what was keeping them here? Why didn't they escape? During my run, I'd seen that the perimeter of the estate was surrounded by very high, spiked walls, but that couldn't be the only thing stopping them. If I was going to get out of here, I had to find out. I may only have one chance at escape and if I blew it, I could be trapped here forever. I wanted to believe that Nik would miss me, that he'd come and rescue me but actually, I couldn't rely on that. He might just as easily forget about me and move on with his life.

There was only one person I could truly depend upon to get me out of Beaufort Heights: myself.

THE NEXT DAY, Darla came back to help me dress and do my hair and make up. I was surprised by just how happy I was to see her. Spending time with her felt like a small yet precious relief from the fake, vacuous personalities of the favoured humans I was forced to hang around with.

"How was your evening?" She asked, smiling at me.

It amazed me that she managed to keep a positive, sunny disposition, in spite of the shitty hand that life had dealt her. She was incredibly strong and it only made me admire her more. Darla was the type of person I wanted to be when I grew up.

Taking my cue from her, I tried to sound upbeat. "Yeah, it was okay thanks. I did go for that run you suggested."

She raised her eyebrows, laying her suitcase next to the chair where I sat, in front of the dressing table. "Oh you did? What do you think of the estate?"

"Hmm, it's really beautiful... and interesting." I lowered my voice. "Especially the row of brick houses in the valley." I met her eyes and, in them, saw a complex mix of grief, anger and shame.

She bit her lip. "House servants live in the servants quarters downstairs."

My ears pricked up - that could be where the air vent led to. "Do any of the house servants have children?"

A look of aching sadness filled her eyes. "Many of us have been here for years. There are male servants too - butlers, valets, gardeners, and the like. Inevitably this leads to the odd pregnancy. All the children who've been born here have never left the house."

I blinked at her. "What do you mean, they're kept on the estate or?..."

"No, servants aren't allowed to leave the house - not even for exercise. Unless they're assigned an outside job such as gardening."

My jaw dropped open as I let what she'd said sink in. That meant any children who lived here had never felt the sun on their face or the wind in their hair. I thought back to how I'd been, as a child. I loved climbing trees and running through the fields. That this was being denied to the children here was unspeakably cruel. The fact that the house had so many windows made it even worse. They could only gaze upon an expanse of countryside they were forbidden from enjoying.

I whispered. "How can you stand it?"

She shrugged, shaking her head as if to say, *I have no choice.*

Brightening up her features she put on a cheery voice. "Right, what are we doing with your hair today then?"

In the back of my mind, I still planned to swipe some hair pins but maybe I wouldn't have to resort to that. "How about an up do?" I asked, keeping my expression as innocent as possible.

She gave me a look that said. *Do you think I was born yesterday?* "A twisted, high ponytail would look great on you." She started playing with my hair. "Back-combed slightly at the front to give you a fierce quiff, like this see?" She stood aside to show me in the mirror.

"Yep." I nodded enthusiastically, hoping that the style would require pins.

"It'll just need a little hair spray and that's all."

Damnit, she'd read my mind! If she knew I wanted hair pins, she'd watch them like a hawk. But maybe I could still distract her.

Darla started brushing my hair, teasing out the ends with a wide brush.

"What about you? Have you ever had a fling with any of the other servants?"

Her eyes went dreamy and she smiled, her cheeks flushing. I knew that look. "What's his name?" I asked

Her face grew redder and she giggled. "I don't know what you're talking about."

"Come on, fess up Darla. I'm already bored out of my mind here, tell me something juicy."

She stopped brushing and looked at me, in the mirror. "Oh, that's all I am to you, a source of entertainment?"

I squirmed, feeling my own face redden. "No... I didn't mean... I"

She cracked up laughing. "I'm kidding. It's not that I don't want to talk to you, it's just..." her smile faded, replaced by something darker. "It's very new and... Happiness is so hard to come by here." Her eyes grew watery.

I felt shitty. I'd jibed her into talking about something that was hard for her. "It's okay Darla, I understand. You don't want to jinx it by talking about it."

"Yes! That's exactly how it is."

I smiled sadly. "It was the same for me when I first started dating Nik."

Her eyes sparkled. "Ooh. Who's Nik? Even the name sounds enticing. Like a bad boy. Is he someone you'd never want to bring home to meet your parents?"

I nodded. "You could say that." *But not for the reasons you think.* "Actually, he's a doctor."

She frowned as she finished brushing my hair. "That doesn't sound too bad. My Mum would be thrilled if I brought a doctor home. Just how high are your parents' standards?"

I laughed. "It's not his profession that's the problem. He's... unconventional."

"What do you mean like a biker or a goth or something?"

I had to nip this line of questioning in the bud. If she knew I was dating a vampire, her opinion of me would hit rock bottom. I liked Darla and I wanted her to like me too. "Yeah, sort of. It's complicated." I steered the conversation away from the danger zone. "I miss him a lot here. I spend my nights wondering if he feels the same. It was a very new relationship, you know..."

She started backcombing the front of my head. "You're just gonna have to trust him babe. If it's meant to be and he's right for you. He'll wait."

I lowered my voice. "But my stay here doesn't have an end date - what if I never get out?"

She sighed, nodding, in sympathy. "You just have to stay positive, keep hope alive. That's what I do."

She bent down to pick up the pack of hairbands and I briefly considered trying to grab the hair pins. But she'd spot me and if I tried and failed, even once, she'd never be so unguarded around the hair pins again. When I did make my move, I had to make it count.

Standing up again, she twirled my hair into a high pony with a pronounced quiffed fringe which she created my simply pulling some of my backcombed hair out of the band. She then set the do with enough hairspray to make wet noodles stand upright.

Coughing away the cloud of spray, I wafted my hand around and looked in the mirror. She was a true artist. I already looked amazing and she hadn't even started on my make up yet. I kept quiet as she applied my make up, my mind going over options of how to steal the hairpins. By the time she'd finished, I'd come up with a pretty good plan.

She stood the suitcase up as she started doing it up. I half stood up, half leapt forward, as if about to help her. But in the process, I purposefully kicked the suitcase, causing all the contents to spill out over the floor.

"I'm so sorry, let me help you."

"No really, it's okay." She snapped, warning me back, with her eyes.

I spotted the hairpins, mere inches away from me and as her attention was diverted by winding the cord back around the curling tongs, I put my foot on the pins. Withdrawing my foot towards me, the feel of the metal pins gripped beneath my slightly curling toes, I straightened up. "I'm so clumsy."

She eyed me suspiciously, her gaze darting to my hands. I touched my hair, lightly, as if smoothing it one final time, with flat hands. Her body relaxed slightly, I'd quashed her suspicions.

"Same time tomorrow then. Have a good day." She smiled at me as she walked out and I tried my best not to look guilty, smiling back as I kept the hair pins gripped under my foot.

Conscious that the cameras were on me, I waited a good amount of time before retrieving them. Trailing my feet over to the bed, I sat down and casually bent down to scratch my ankle. Hoping that my bent over body would block the view of the camera, I put the pins into my closed fist. Then I walked to the bathroom, where I embedded the pins, deep within the quiff of my hair. Checking myself in the mirror, I was satisfied that they couldn't be seen. I still had no idea if there were cameras in the bathroom but I hoped to God there weren't.

Step one of operation 'Escape from Beaufort Heights' had been successfully completed. But I'd have to wait until tonight to try and pick the lock of my dog collar, under the bed sheets. And I had no experience of picking locks. All I had was determination and persistence. I hoped that would be enough.

23

Another long and tedious lunch... It was hard to imagine anyone who loved the sound of his own voice more than Hugh Beaufort. Whenever anyone else spoke, he merely pretended to listen, while waiting for his turn to speak.

"There I was, alone, on my horse, when two bandits jumped out of the bushes." He paused for effect.

Gemma widened her blue eyes. I'd noticed that she affected a little girl lost routine around Hugh, which he lapped up like ambrosia. "What happened next Hughie?"

'Hughie' surrounded himself with a bunch of giggling airheads. He'd clearly chosen his human companions for their looks, not their intellect or sense of humour... or personality. Their constant fawning of him was already tiresome and I'd only been here a couple of days.

I'd had just about enough of this charade. Butting in, before he could answer Gemma's question, I asked. "Why don't you tell us what year you were born in, Hugh?" I narrowed my eyes at him, curling my lips into an evil smile. His other pets might be in denial about just what an ancient relic he was but I wanted the facts out in the open.

"1756." His voice was deadpan, his expression unflinching.

I stared at him, in part awe, part horror. I don't know why I was surprised. It made total sense. My knowledge of history was sketchy but wasn't the transatlantic slave trade a big thing around then? I sort of remembered it from school.

Getting bolder by the second, I pursued the line of questioning. "Slavery was legal in those days, wasn't it?" I looked him square in the eyes. "Did you ever own slaves?" My gaze flicked briefly to the light brown servants, standing silently around the dining room.

"Yes, many people of my social class did."

Interesting. Now it almost sounded like he was making excuses. But surely he couldn't feel bad about having owned them back then - he still owned them now!

I tilted my head to the side, smiling sweetly as I raised my eyebrows, ensuring that my tone dripped with acid. "Why don't you have any white servants, Hugh?"

The room fell silent. Everyone, around the table, turned and stared at me. Some of them looked at me as if I'd just told a small child santa clause wasn't real.

He narrowed his eyes. "If you have something to say, Bree, just come out and say it. There's no need to dance around the issue with questions."

Crossing my arms, I turned my chair so that I was facing him head on. "Alright, I'll say it. You're a racist, slave-owning piece of shit. You've literally built this house off of the blood of black people. And you groom and rape white girls."

His face turned red. "*I am not* a rapist!"

That was what he objected to the most - out of everything I'd just said? This was too much for me. It was almost farcical. My body started shaking as I burst out laughing. Great, giggling fits that had tears streaming down my face.

"Why's she laughing?" I just about heard Gemma say, from above my hysteria.

Hugh's jaw was so tightly clenched that I thought his ancient teeth might crumble. He was trying so hard to control himself. Why? Hadn't he got the message by now that there was no way, in this multiverse, or the next that I would ever mate with him? It was probably foolish of me to goad him like this but I felt like I had nothing to lose. Part of me thought that if I made him hate me enough, he'd let me go. I knew it was unrealistic but I couldn't have stopped myself from taunting him even if I'd wanted to. It was in my nature to speak the truth and also in my nature to be reckless. This situation was like a pile of tinder made to ignite the best and the worst in me.

Finally, I calmed down enough to wipe my eyes and continue the conversation, which was steadily becoming the most interesting one I'd had in Beaufort's presence. "Leaving the racism aside for one minute - not because I'm letting it go but because I want to talk about the ridiculous statement you've just made. In what way are you *not* a rapist?"

He lowered his voice but the tone was drenched with anger. "I have never taken a woman against her will and I never will. Why would I need to?" He gave a smarmy, teeth-too-bright smile. "Women love me."

Gemma gazed at him, adoringly and he winked at her. She drew her chair closer and started nuzzling into his neck. He tickled under her chin, like an owner, stroking his cat. I could've thrown up. I couldn't believe he hadn't raped any of these women. But it was unlikely any of them would admit it even if he had. He seemed to have all of them so utterly brainwashed.

As I studied him, it occurred to me that I had a once in a lifetime opportunity to get inside the head of an eighteenth-century slave owner and I wasn't going to waste it. "You didn't answer my question. Why don't you have any white servants?"

"White people are less suited to manual labour."

I frowned. "Oh? How so?"

"Black people are less intelligent, everyone knows that."

Wow! There it was, flopped out onto the table, like a stinking dead fish.

"You know there's no scientific evidence for that, right?"

"Science doesn't know everything. If black people were as intelligent as us, they would've never allowed us to enslave them, steal their lands and their minerals."

"They didn't *allow* us, they were brutally enslaved and conquered using gunpowder."

Gemma chose this moment to stop being a vapid spectator and instead score points by trying to hammer home Hugh's argument. It's a pity her intellect wasn't up to the job. "Yeah and who invented gunpowder, huh?" She smirked, proud of herself.

"The *Chinese!*" I spat, gaining a small amount of satisfaction from the way the smile withered on her face.

Hugh patted his hands up and down as if trying to calm a bunch of squabbling children. "Ladies, ladies, there's no need for all this unpleasantness. Let's all just go back to having a nice jolly lunch together." His eyes dropped to half mast, as he looked at me. "Bree, if you're so concerned about the plight of the servants and blood slaves, why don't you go and live amongst them? Go and live in their hovels, down the hill." He leaned forward. "You people today. You think you're so... what's the word you use? *Woke*, that's it, isn't it? But you're very happy to take my gifts, wear the clothes that I've bought for you and eat the lovely food that my chefs prepare. I didn't hear you turning down the personal maid I provided for you."

I felt blood rise to my cheeks as the truth of what he was saying splashed over me like dirty rain water, from a passing car. He was right. I was complicit. Here I was, thinking I was better than him but I'd enjoyed every luxury this house had to offer. I thought I was some kind of crusader, saving the black humans of this house from a racist eighteenth century slave owner. But I was barely any better than him. I was also benefitting from their labour, their blood.

I felt so ashamed, I wanted to run from the room to go and slam my fists into the bed as I burst out in frustrated tears. I was so close to doing that. But then I caught the eye of one of the servants. I didn't know the woman but she was desperately trying to communicate to me with her eyes. They were widening as she subtly nodded her head. I flicked my eyes away quickly. I didn't want her to get into trouble. What was it she was trying to tell me? For the entire meal, all the servants had remained expressionless. Even when Beaufort was saying the vilest of racist things. Yet when he'd given his last little speech, she'd become animated.

Then it hit me.

In a fit of pique, Hugh Beaufort had just offered me a possible escape path. He'd just asked me why I didn't go and live down the hill with the blood slaves. My heart rate sped up as my thoughts raced. I'd be closer to the perimeter fence. Would Mitchell and Peterson come with me? Probably. Even if they did, there were other humans down there - angry humans not Beaufort sycophants like the people around this table. We could stage a rebellion! I gripped my napkin with excitement. But I was getting ahead of myself. I didn't even know if he'd been serious. He could've just been trying to show me up. But if I took him up on the offer, right now, would it show *him* up to have to rescind it?

"Actually, I'd love to go and live down the hill with the blood slaves." As soon as the words were out of my mouth I panicked that I'd made the wrong decision. Did living with them mean becoming a blood slave? The memory of the pain as Derek sank his fangs into my jugular was still very raw and I clutched my napkin even tighter. Flicking my gaze towards the servant who'd spoken to me, with her eyes, I saw that she was now subtly smiling. But was she smiling because this was a good thing that would help me to get free? Or had she set me up? Perhaps she saw this as punishment for a pampered white girl who was partially responsible for her suffering. The ticking of each second, of the clock on the mantelpiece, seemed to last for minutes. Hugh's eyes looked up at the ceiling as he considered his options. Then finally, he looked back at me. "Fine. Have it your way." He sipped his goblet of blood. "Ask Darla to pack some things for you. You'll soon come crawling back when you see what it's like down there."

I didn't know whether to jump for joy or sink to the floor and weep. When would I learn to just keep my big mouth shut? I'd had a plan - okay half a sketchy, ill thought out plan but still, a plan. With my hair-pin lock pick, I could've bided my time, waiting until the opportune moment to strike. Now, I didn't know what I'd find down there. Would I even get anymore opportunities to strike?

But the thing that I held onto was that Darla had told me not even house servants were allowed to interact with the blood slaves. If Beaufort had forbidden it, it must mean there was opportunity in it. I bet none of the other favoured humans had ever been down the hill. I had to think like Darla and be positive about this. Surely it must be easier to escape down there, it had to be.

But then, if it was easier to escape, why had none of the people living down there done so already?

24

After lunch I strode off from the table. I didn't want to spend a single minute more in the company of these despicable people.

But on the way to my room, Mel caught my hand, pulling me aside as she lowered her voice. "What was that back there?"

I curled my lip at her. "I'm not going to apologise for speaking my mind. You are quite happy to live a life of luxury, enjoying pedicures and massages while around you other humans are enslaved. It sickens me that the rest of you are fine with how things are here."

Her eyes narrowed. "That's what you think? That we're all fine with it?"

"What other explanation is there?"

"We're doing our best to *survive!*" She spat out the last word then lowered her voice, and her head, as one of the many vampire guards walked past and glowered at us. She giggled and twirled her hair around one finger, as if gossiping about something inane with me and at that moment, it dawned on me that her entire persona so far had been an act.

Waiting until he'd passed, she dropped the act and continued. "You think you stand a chance against Hugh Beaufort? You think you can defeat him? You have no idea who you're up against. He's had centuries to master this game and he is very, very good at it."

A shiver went down my spine. "What game?" I breathed.

"Manipulating people. Using their weaknesses against them. Getting them to do whatever he wants. All you did back there is show him your weaknesses. You'll lose, Bree. And when you do, you'll be forced to give up all your high and mighty ideals. He'll turn you into one of us, just wait and see."

I balled up my fists. "I don't care what he does to me. I'll never become like you."

Her shoulders sagged at the obvious insult. The look of defeat and hurt in her eyes softened my heart. Perhaps I shouldn't be so quick to judge Mel. She'd probably suffered a lot here. Part of me felt sorry for her. The other part of me wanted to grab her by the shoulders and shake her, tell her to 'wake up' and fight - never stop fighting.

She lifted her sad hazel eyes to meet mine. "I hope you don't become like me. I hope I'm wrong and you're right. But I can tell you that nobody has ever left this house. People don't simply walk out of Beaufort Heights. Once you're here, you're here for life."

Her words settled over me like an ominous dark mist on a summer's night yet even more chilling. She'd been here long enough to have seen what Beaufort was capable of. That's why she acted the dumb party girl. Not because she liked it but because she had to. Which begged the question: what happened to the girls who didn't play along? And by standing up to Beaufort, was I about to find out?

I pulled my arm away from Mel and rushed away from her. Her words had shaken me to my core. Spending time with her meant seeing a visual reminder, in human form of what Hugh Beaufort did to girls.

Alone in my room, I breathed a sigh of relief but my insides were churning. Had I taken on an opponent I was ill-equipped to beat? Mel's words had been unexpected. She'd played her part so well that up until now I'd thought she was completely on his side. What had it taken to break her? What had she already endured here?

My thoughts were disturbed by a gentle knock on the door. "Come in" I called out. I'd already come to recognise the taps as Darla's signature knock and it gave me a feeling of comfort that there was at least one person, in the house, who I felt could be a friend.

Her smile, as she entered, seemed to glow with an extra bit of sparkle this afternoon. "I've come to help you pack."

I took a deep breath. "Yes, thank you. I'm going to go and live down the hill." I tried to keep my voice upbeat but inside I was terrified. The gung ho attitude I'd had over lunch had evaporated and, alone in my room, I couldn't help ruminating over all the poor choices I'd made that had led me to this point. Now I'd not only spend the rest of my life as Beaufort's prisoner, I'd be fed on at the same time - possibly daily, who knows.

Darla carried a small duffel bag, which she placed on the bed. Out of the bag, she withdrew a simple linen shirt and trousers and a rough polyester jumper. "These are the clothes that the blood slaves wear. Mr Beaufort has said that you're welcome to pack any of the other clothes he's bought you, as well as the toiletries."

I thought about this for a minute. "Do the blood slaves have toiletries?"

"They have basic stuff, soap, flannels, toothpaste and toothbrushes."

The martyr in me wanted to forgo all of the trinkets Hugh had given me. That way I could staunch the sickening guilt that had engulfed me when he'd said I'd enjoyed the trappings of his slavery-enriched lifestyle. But I had to be smart. Extra clothing was a good thing - even if just to provide warmth. I wouldn't be surprised if they didn't have heating down there. The toiletries would also come in handy.

"I'll pack them."

She half smiled. "Good idea. In fact, I brought some other items for you to take as gifts." She reached deeper into the bag and withdrew a wide toothed comb, detangling brush, and some other bottles and tubs.

I frowned, picking up one of the bottles. "Hair oil?"

She gave a knowing look "Just trust me on this one."

"Where did you get these from?"

"Mr Beaufort buys them for us."

Registering my look of surprise, she explained further. "He insists that all us house servants keep our hair neatly brushed and tied back - blow-dried straight if we're serving at special events. He says if it's all 'big, wild and woolly' it'll offend his fancy dinner guests." Her eyes flashed with a deep-seated anger.

I realised I'd never even thought about what it took to maintain afro hair. Looking at the tubs and bottles, I didn't recognise any of them. Sometimes, when I was in town, I walked past an afro hair care shop but I'd never been inside one and the pharmacy where I bought my hair products didn't sell any of the bottles that lay on the bed.

Darla has really thought ahead and I was touched by her help. "Thank you."

She smiled as she walked to the wardrobe and started taking down and folding the fancy clothes inside. "I don't often get a chance to help the people down the hill."

I dipped my head. She was reminding me that she wasn't only doing this for me.

"I heard about what you did at lunch." She didn't look at me.

"Oh yeah?" I felt slightly uneasy. Did she approve of what I'd done or was this the part where I got a lecture on how ignorant I was?

She paused and looked at me. "Thank you."

I held her gaze, not speaking. My heart felt warm and fuzzy.

She looked away. "Do you know what you're getting into?"

"Not really."

She stuffed some of the folded clothes into the bag. "And you're doing it anyway? Brave."

"Or foolish."

She shrugged. "He expects you to come 'crawling back', that's what he said, isn't it? If it's too much for you, don't be too proud to do that."

I nodded. She was right but I really hoped I wouldn't have to. I wanted to go down the hill, then over the fence, then never come back.

I lowered my voice. "Why haven't you ever tried to escape?"

Her eyes flicked towards the cameras, which, by now, I'd worked out were in the corners of the room.

The terror in her eyes spoke volumes as she breathed the words. "Who says I haven't?"

"What happened?" I whispered.

Speaking quickly and so quietly that I could barely hear her, she told her story. "Once a week a vampire drives a food delivery truck through the gate. I managed to sneak inside my first week here. As the truck drove towards the gate, my skin started to itch. Then my whole body felt like it was on fire. I didn't know what was happening. The pain was indescribable, worse than anything I've ever felt before and I passed out. When I came around again, I was back here." Her eyes flickered, recalling the memory. "I was beaten to within an inch of my life, as punishment. All the other servants were made to stand and watch."

I covered my mouth with my hand as bile rose to my throat. How could they treat a woman like that? "Did you ever find out what made your body react like that?"

She nodded. "There's some type of spell or curse on the gate and on the perimeter walls. Only vampires can pass through unharmed."

So that's why the blood slaves hadn't escaped. I tilted my head to the side. "That's weird, I didn't think vampires could do magic?"

"Apparently, the spell was put in place by a witch."

My thoughts whirled. I was a witch but should I admit that to her? I hadn't been trained and still was unsure of how to use my magic. But the alternative was not trying at all.

"I'm a witch." I said quietly. As soon as the words were out of my mouth I regretted them. I had no idea if I'd be able to lift the spell. Had I given her false hope? She'd already been through so much here. I shouldn't have offered something I wasn't sure I could deliver.

Her face lit up with excitement. "Then you can lift the spell?"

I gulped, feeling less confident than ever before. "Maybe, I'm not sure."

Mitchell's voice thundered through the door. "Time to go Ms Ryan."

Darla squeezed my hands and nodded at me, her eyes burning with determination. "Good luck. Do what you can, however small that may be."

I nodded, picked up my bag and walked out. Whether or not I could lift the spell, I had to at least try.

MITCHELL AND PETERSON accompanied me as I carried my duffel bag down the hill. I'd changed into the clothes that Darla told me the blood slaves wore, keeping a stash of the designer clothes in my bag. The jumper was scatchy and thin but at least it offered some warmth. Winter was drawing in and the weather grew colder by the day. Turning back, I noticed the pinched, white faces of the favoured humans staring at me from various windows of the mansion. They looked like ghosts - ghosts of the girls they'd once been and maybe, I questioned, spectres of the woman I'd become. I steeled my resolve. That wouldn't happen to me. In spite of what Mel had said, I was stronger than them. I wouldn't let Hugh Beaufort get to me. Adjusting my bag, on my shoulder, I resisted the urge to feel inside my hair, for my precious two hair pins. I couldn't risk the vampire guards guessing that I had something hidden there.

"Are you going to stay with me down there?" I asked Peterson.

"Mr Beaufort requires that you have guards with you at all times."

Mitchell chipped in. "You will need our protection. The Blood slaves are savages. If we aren't there, they will kill you the first chance they get."

Savages.

Mitchell evidently held the same outdated views as his boss. Peterson probably did too. A picture was forming in my mind of Beaufort's Draculs. Carlotta hadn't been exaggerating when she'd described them as a 'fascist vampire gang'. The Draculs I'd encountered so far were all raving white supremacists. It wasn't a stretch to imagine that their hierarchical view of the world extended to thinking that humans were a lesser species who should exist merely as food.

As we walked, I tested this theory on Mitchell. "How did you start working for Mr Beaufort?"

"The Dracul organisation has foot soldiers all over the planet but not many ever get to even meet Mr Beaufort." He lifted his head proudly. "It's a great honour to be selected as one of his personal guards."

His hero-worshipping tone was laughable. "Were you a raving racist loon before you became a vampire or did something happen to your brain during the transition?"

The slap came so hard and fast that I flew through the air. Landing on the muddy grass, I rubbed my cheek, which still smarted from the unexpected blow. My senses were fully alert as Mitchell crouched down, sneering over me. "Listen to me you spoilt little girl. You think you're protected because Mr Beaufort has taken it into his head that you're the best choice to sire his heir." He spat on the ground beside me. "A mistake if you ask me but who am I to question his judgement." He leaned in closer, his rancid breath hot on my face. "You're nothing. You were nothing before you came here and you're even less now that you're sullying yourself by siding with the blood slaves. Mr Beaufort will soon forget about you, and when he does, you're ours. There are no cameras, watching what we do away from the house and believe me, we will do *whatever* we want with you."

His eyes widened with emphasis on the word 'whatever,' then looked me up and down, slowly, in a way that made me feel like boneless.

Peterson stood, staring at the horizon. "Get up," he ordered, without looking at me, his tone as hard and unyielding as his angular face.

I struggled to my feet, slipping in the wet grass.

Peterson took a step closer and lowered his voice to a menacing whisper. "Consider that a warning Ms Ryan." His use of my formal title belied the lack of respect in his tone. His lips curled up into a sneer. "Next time we won't be nearly so gentle."

I swallowed, trying to stop my bottom lip from wobbling. Is this what I'd set myself up for? As fair game to be used and abused by these hateful bodyguards, in whatever way they wanted? I knew that to retaliate would just antagonise them further so for once I held back. Picking up my bag from where it had fallen when Mitchell had slapped me, I hoisted it onto my shoulder. "Let's just get to the slaves' quarters." Inside I was a seething mass of anger mixed with fear. I was starting to feel like I'd made my biggest mistake since coming here.

AS WE APPROACHED THE FIVE, small brick houses that stood in a row, at the bottom of the hill, another vampire guard exited the first house, wiping crimson blood from his lips.

Peterson noticed my look of disgust. "What's the matter Ms Ryan? You know that's what these people are here for, so you better get used to it."

I bit my tongue to stop myself from asking what I really wanted to know. *Are you going to feed on me like that?*

I was too ashamed to ask. I couldn't bare to admit, even to these two evil henchmen that I was scared of being bitten. I didn't want them thinking that I thought myself above the blood slaves. Some of these people had probably endured years of being used as food for the vampires of the household. And here I was unable to face the idea of a single bite.

Peterson opened the door of the first house, without knocking. The front door opened directly into a small room, dirty and cramped, with five people, some standing, some sitting on the floor. They wore the same clothes as me but had no socks or shoes on. They stared at me, as if I was a creature from another planet, watching my every move with a mixture of curiosity and contempt. As I'd predicted, it was very cold.

Mitchell gave me an evil smile. "We'll leave you to get acquainted. Don't get too close." He leaned forward to stick his face into mine. "You never know when one might get drunk to death by accident."

I felt the blood drain from my face and he started laughing. His laughter echoed as he started walking outside.

Before leaving, Peterson turned to me. "Don't get any ideas about escaping. One or both of us will be stationed outside at all times."

"I thought you said I was Mr Beaufort's guest?!" I spat at him, as he walked off. If only my murderous glare could burn a hole in his back. At least they were gone though and, as I looked around the room, it didn't look like this one had cameras. But I'd been caught out before, I'd tread carefully until I knew how things worked down here.

I looked at my new housemates. A man who looked to be in his forties, tall with short, dreadlocked hair, leant against the wall, looking me up and down as if I was pond scum.

"Hi, I'm Bree." I stuck out my hand.

He rolled his eyes slowly down to look at my hand, then back up to my face. "What's the point of introducing yourself. You won't be here long."

I crumpled my hand up and retracted it slightly. "You don't know that."

He sucked his teeth and looked away.

Next to him a young woman, with feline eyes and closely-cropped hair, sighed audibly as she gave me a look of disdain. "Whatever, darling. We know your type. We can spot you a mile away."

I didn't understand what she meant. "Type?"

She explained. "You think you're going to ride in here, on your big white horse and save all the poor black people. Tell me I'm wrong."

I bristled. "Don't you want saving?"

Sitting on the floor, a middle-aged woman with a short, afro, clutched tissues to her neck. She must've been the one the vampire guard had just fed from. Her eyes were angry and accusatory. "You've got a white saviour complex. You think that if you show compassion to us, it absolves you of the privilege you've benefitted from - not just in the house, but in society."

I swallowed, unsure how to respond to this. Nobody made any attempt to fill the awkward silence that followed. I felt my cheeks heat. I'd expected hardship when I came to this house but I'd thought it would come from vampires, not my housemates. In truth, I'd believed they'd be grateful that I'd arrived and it was a sock to the gut to learn that not only were they not grateful - they were hostile.

A teenage boy next to her had longer dreadlocks, he looked at me and half smiled, as he stood up. "I'm Charles Junior, everyone calls me CJ."

My heart melted at his small act of kindness. "It's nice to meet you CJ"

He pointed at a girl on the floor, she looked about eight years old. "That's my sister, Rainie."

"Hi, Rainie," I whispered, cracking a wide grin as she twinkled her pretty dark eyes at me.

I chewed the inside of my mouth, waiting for the adults to introduce themselves to me. When it didn't happen I suddenly remembered the items Darla had suggested I bring. "I erm, brought some hair products with me. Would you like to see?"

"What are we going to do with *your* hair products?" The woman on the floor asked, raising her eyebrows at me, as if I was an idiot.

"Actually, they're for your hair type. Look," hastily taking my bag off my shoulder, I lay it on the floor and rummaged inside for the comb, brush, bottles and tubs. When I took them out the woman's eyes lit up. "Ooh! Finally, I can do my baby's hair properly. Rainie, would you like some cornrows sweetheart?"

Rainie bounced up and down. "Yeah cornrows, cornrows!"

The woman's expression softened as she looked at me. "I'm Paulette," she gestured to the man leaning against the wall. "He's Samuel and she's Grace." She took the tissue off her neck and blood trickled from a nasty bite wound. "It'll heal quicker if I leave it to air out."

I couldn't help but take a step back causing Grace to laugh at me. "You're going to have to get used to the site of bite marks if you stay down here."

I dipped my head. "I've got some cotton wool pads if you like?" Reaching into my bag, I pulled out the packet and handed it to her.

"Thanks." She dabbed at the wound and it started to clot. Looking at me with caution, she asked. "What are you doing down here anyway?"

I glanced at the window. Mitchell and Peterson were nowhere in sight so I walked closer. They lay on the grass, about fifty metres away, playing cards and laughing. Now that they were away from the Beaufort Heights cameras, they weren't taking their guard duties nearly so seriously. All the better for us.

Walking back to the others, I still lowered my voice, mindful of the enhanced hearing of vampires. "I'm planning to break out of here. Not just me - all of us."

Samuel and Grace exchanged a look. "We were right - she does think she can save us."

I was confused. "Look, I don't know anything. I've only been here a few days but the way this place is set up like an eighteenth century plantation sickens me. Please explain to me why you haven't escaped?"

Samuel took a deep breath and turned around, lifting up his back.

I gasped at the deep welts and scars that criss-crossed his skin.

"And that's only the half of it," he said. "Sometimes they kill one of us - to set an example to the others."

Paulette added. "It's impossible to leave here. Beaufort has got a spell put on the perimeter and gate. Humans can come in but we can't go out again."

"Yeah, I heard about the spell."

I wasn't yet sure if I should tell them I was a witch. The truth was, I had no idea if I'd be able to remove the spell or not. If only I'd taken Morgana and Evelyn up on their offer to join them and get properly trained. But then if I'd done that, maybe the Draculs would never have been able to capture me in the first place. There were so many things I wished I'd done differently.

One thing struck me though. There were vampire guards all over the house but none here - except for Mitchell and Peterson, who'd come because of me. "Why don't they guard you, like they do us?"

Samuel gave a bitter smile. "They don't think we're clever enough to escape. And they think we've given up hope."

Ignoring the first statement, I focused on the second. "Have you given up hope?"

"Hell no!" Samuel stood up, clenching his fists. "I've been here nine years but I'll never give up hope. I'll never stop trying to get out of here."

Nine years. The weight of what he'd told me hit me. "How did you end up here?"

"I was a delivery driver. I came to deliver a package here and never made it out again."

I shook my head in disbelief. "Didn't your family ask questions - come looking for you?"

He sighed, a look of deep pain on his face. "We never get the full facts but what we think happens is that the Draculs glamour the police and our families into thinking we're dead." His eyes welled with tears and he sniffed and clenched his jaw, trying to keep them from falling. "I had a fiancee, we were going to get married."

Grace said, "I've spent most of my twenties here. What should've been the best years of my life, a prisoner, being fed on by vampires."

"And you know, vampires don't even need to feed off humans - there's a plant-based alternative now."

All five eyes turned to stare at me. "What did you just say?" Paulette asked.

I nodded. "There's synthetic human blood. It's made by a vampire friend of mine and..."

"A friend of yours?" Paulette balked.

I held my hands up to correct my mistake. "She's a vampire but she's vegan, she doesn't feed off humans anymore."

Her mouth dropped open. "You expect us to trust you when you've just admitted to us that you have vampire friends?"

I bit my lip. "They're not like the Draculs. They've taken a vow of non-harming - a bit like Buddhists."

Paulette pursed her lips. "I don't care what *vow* they say they've taken. Vampires are lying, manipulative monsters. Any friend of a vampire, is no friend of mine." She turned away from me and picked up the comb. "Come on baby, let me do your hair."

Rainie shuffled closer to Paulette to get her hair done. Paulette poured hair oil onto her hand and then rubbed it all over Rainie's scalp. Then she started brushing it, in sections, with the detangling brush.

I watched quietly, aware that the mood had shifted from somewhat amiable back to hostile and mistrustful. I'd royally put my foot in my mouth and wasn't sure how to come back from it. But I knew one thing, if I was going to get out of here, I would need their help to do it and I was determined not to give up.

25

The blood slaves' houses had two rooms. My housemates had divided these up into one room for girls and women and another room for men and boys. There was a communal, concrete washing block at the back, shared by all of the blood slaves, from all of the five houses. I leant that they'd devised a system and took shifts to wash with girls and women going first and then boys and men. My housemates hadn't thawed in their attitude to me, since our earlier conversation and, as the afternoon wore on, I accepted that it may take time to gain their trust. But I wasn't going to waste my opportunity, away from the cameras of Beaufort Heights. The hairpins were still nestled within my quiff, like two rods of hope.

As night drew in, Samuel and CJ retired to their room and Grace handed me a rolled up mattress, and thin blanket, from a pile in the corner.

"Time to make your bed." She said, suppressing a smirk. She was clearly enjoying seeing a favoured human reduced to the same living standards as she had to endure.

I took the mattress from her with a thin smile of acceptance.

Peeking out of the window, I saw that Mitchell and Peterson were still sat on the grass outside. I knew that vampires didn't feel the cold so they wouldn't be bothered by the chill in the air, in the same way that I was. At least their attention wasn't on us. I rolled out my mattress and got under the blanket. Then, I withdrew one of the hair-pins from my quiff and got to work, trying to unpick the lock of my obsidian dog collar. Groping, behind my neck, I twisted the collar around so that the lock was at the front. Then I felt for the tiny key hole and poked the hair pin into it.

I'd never picked a lock before and had no idea what I was doing. But I guessed that it should be quite easy - I'd seen enough films in which people used hair pins to pick locks. It must be a doddle, right? Wrong! I wiggled that hair pin around, trying for long enough that my arm started to ache. By now, the others were asleep and the sound of soft snoring drifted from Rainie. Eventually, the hair pin broke, skewering my finger at the same time.

Ouch! I yelped, then froze, realising I'd been a bit loud.

Rainie turned over and made a soft lapping sound with her mouth but she didn't wake up. Glancing around, it looked like Grace and Paulette were also asleep.

I was about to get out my other hair pin, when suddenly I heard a sound that made me freeze. Heavy footsteps, coming from the front of the house and walking right up to the front door. Fear gripped my heart. Each footstep thundered like a hammer hitting concrete. I didn't move or breathe as the door creaked, slowly open. Other blood slaves wouldn't enter our house, at night so that meant it was a vampire. I thought of the way in which Mitchell had looked at me, lecherous intent in his eyes, since the first day I'd arrived at the house. Away from the cameras, there was nothing to stop him doing whatever he wanted to me - he'd said so himself.

Part of me wanted to shut my eyes and wish the monster away, just like I had done as a child. But I had to look, I had to know who was coming for me. Just as I'd feared, the unmistakable, imposing silhouette of Mitchell, appeared in the room. His metallic vampire scent invaded the room like a noxious gas. My thoughts raced. Should I just get up and run? But he'd easily catch me, within seconds. At least here, if I screamed, maybe, just maybe, my housemates would help me.

Mitchell walked over to my bed and crouched down. The light of the moon illuminated his face and the look of lust, combined with hate that I saw in his expression, chilled me to my core. His breathing was heavy and consistent, there was no hint of alarm in his body language. In contrast, I felt like I was about to lose control of my bladder. My heart thudded in my chest and I gripped my blanket, with clammy hands.

He tilted his head to one side and leaned his face down, putting his lips near my ear. "Shhhh." He drew out the lisping whisper in a way that made him sound like a snake. "Don't be so noisy, there are people sleeping." His tone was jovial but laced with a dark threat. He stroked my hair, tucking it behind my ear. "You know, you're a very pretty girl. You don't belong down here."

By now I was shaking. Tears sprang to my eyes which I jammed shut, to avoid looking at him.

His rancid breath poured over me as he stroked me with sweaty palms. He began to fumble with his belt buckle.

I started to whimper, so afraid I couldn't even scream.

Suddenly, there was a rustle from the other side of the room. Paulette's voice rang out, loud and clear, as she sat up. "Hey! What the fuck do you think you're doing?"

"It's none of your business, slave!" he snarled.

"Oh, I'm making it my business. I'm sure Mr Beaufort would be very interested to hear how you're treating his pet. I'm good friends with his regular blood slave, Yvonne. Just a word in her ear and he'll hear all about it."

Mitchell paused momentarily then sniped back. "He wouldn't believe the likes of you, over me."

She folded her arms and arched one eyebrow. "And you're willing to take that chance, are you?"

Huffing loudly, Mitchell got up to his feet. "Cock teasing little bitch," he muttered under his breath as he stormed out.

I let out a cleansing exhale and sat up. "Thank you so much Paulette - that was amazing!"

"Yeah well, I'm not going to pretend to be sleeping while another woman is being raped in the same room as me."

I was in awe of her. She was so much more vulnerable than me, she could be bitten, or even killed, anytime the vampires felt like it. Yet she'd stuck up for me. "I thought you hated me." I said quietly.

I heard her sigh. "I don't hate you. Of course I don't. I just think you're a bit...ignorant... and misguided. But I can tell you're well-meaning and that counts for a lot."

Inside a small kernel of hope stirred in me. Was she extending a small olive branch, in my direction? "Maybe you could teach me how to be less ignorant?" I offered, my voice rising at the end, hopefully.

She huffed. "It's not our job to teach you how to be anti-racist you know. It's your job to find out." And with that, she turned over and went back to sleep.

I put my head in my hands. *So much for the olive branch...*

SLOP. I looked down at the simple bowl of porridge that had been ladled into my bowl by a scowling vampire guard. I'd learnt that they took turns to come and give us our food, wheeling a food trolley down the hill. The guards hated doing a task they saw as servant's work so they usually left as soon as they'd served us. All except for Mitchell and Peterson. But after Mitchell's performance on my first night here, they'd both kept a bit further away. Whenever I so much as glanced in Mitchell's direction, he looked away, with a mixture of shame and anger in his eyes.

The food was generally cold by the time it reached us but we ate it anyway, knowing it was all we'd get until the next day. I couldn't believe I hadn't noticed this food delivery process during my brief stay at the house. My time had been filled with lunches and pampering, in a way that now made me feel ashamed.

I'd been staying in the blood slaves quarters for three days but I hadn't yet told the other housemates what life was like in Beaufort Heights, for the favoured humans. Now, as we sat on the floor to eat our porridge, Grace asked me. "What's it like up there?"

I paused, chewing my porridge slowly before swallowing. "It's.... really weird. We're treated like a cross between children and pets. Beaufort spares no expense on spoiling his favoured humans. He buys us designer clothes. I was assigned a personal maid. We get massages, manicures, pedicures. I've heard there are also things like horse-riding classes, cinema nights and tennis lessons but I never got to do any of that, I left too soon. The food is exquisite..."

"Damn, Bree! Why do you want to leave? If that was the way I was living, I'd never want to go back to the real world. I'd just stay up there, being waited on hand and foot, like Lady Muck."

I chuckled. "Yeah, it sounds amazing and when I first arrived, I was tempted to stay, I'm not gonna lie. I loved the luxury - I mean, who wouldn't, right? But, it comes with strings attached."

She wrinkled her nose. "You have to sleep with him?"

I nodded.

"Euww! You let that wrinkly old codger put his dick inside you?"

I dropped my spoon and waved my hands in front of my face. "No, no, no! He wanted to but I never let him."

"Why didn't he just do it anyway?" She cocked her head to the side.

"I wondered that too, at first. But it seems like Beaufort has a code of honour against rape or something like that."

She burst out laughing and looked at Samuel. "Hey, you hear that Sam? Boss man up the hill has a 'code of honour' against rape... but not slavery."

I joined in the laughter. "It is pretty ridiculous, isn't it."

Samuel wasn't laughing. "No. It makes perfect sense to me."

"How so?" I asked.

"He's a white supremacist, right? He thinks that black people are inferior to white people - thinks we're more like animals. That's how he justifies treating us like this. But raping a white woman would rattle at his conscience." He spooned some porridge into his mouth then swallowed.

"That doesn't explain why he doesn't rape any black women?" I asked before inhaling with wide eyes. "Wait. He hasn't?...."

Grace interrupted firmly. "No. Not that I've heard." She lowered her voice, "it's the guards you have to worry about."

Looking up from my bowl I saw Mitchell, staring at me. I quickly looked back down at my porridge bowl and shovelled some into my mouth, hoping I hadn't inflamed his unceasing interest.

Samuel answered again. "He thinks we're animals - how many men do you know who want to fuck an animal?" He put his hand to his mouth, a pensive expression on his face. "But why did he let you come down here though? Even house servants aren't allowed to mix with us."

I looked up to the ceiling. "It's a long story but the short version is - I pissed him off enough that during an argument, he said, I put on Hugh's deep, clipped, upper-class English accent *why don't you go and live with the blood slaves if you care about them so much*"

Grace and Samuel both started laughing. "Great accent! Is that how he talks?" Grace asked.

I frowned at them. "You've never met him?"

"No. He has certain blood slaves he likes to drink from, doesn't touch anyone else. Yvonne, in the second house down, is one of his favourites - poor woman."

Samuel looked at her. "It's not like getting bitten by the guards is any better."

Grace nodded. "Probably worse actually."

I could see Samuel's mind was still turning over and I was right.

"Why didn't he just kill you when you refused to sleep with him?"

I took another porridge mouthful, chewing and swallowing, as I thought how best to explain. "I'm a special case. He wants me to give him an heir."

Grace's eyes widened. "He wants you as his baby mamma?"

"Yep."

Samuel blinked. "I didn't think vampires could have children."

"Neither did I but they can, apparently."

"But why you?" Grace asked.

I hesitated. I hadn't yet told any of them what I was. But I couldn't avoid telling them forever and now was as good a time as any. "I'm an arcane witch. He thinks a witch-vampire hybrid baby will be really powerful and he wants his son or daughter to be special. See this?" I pointed to my obsidian neck collar. "It blocks my powers. Arcane witches are specialised, vampire-hunters. If I didn't have it on, I'd be able to kill every vampire mother fucker in this mansion."

Samuel placed his bowl on the floor and got up to take a closer look. "It's locked in place. All we have to do is pick the lock and…"

"I've already tried - and failed."

Grace did a double-take. "How did you try?"

I leaned closer and mouthed. *With a hair pin.*

"Do you have any more?" She whispered.

"One more. I'm too nervous to try it again in case I fail and stuff up our last chance."

She was smiling. "You're not going to fail because you're not going to try. I am." She dusted off her shoulders. "You're looking at the best lock pick this side of London town."

A broad grin spread onto my face as I looked at the beaming faces of Grace and Samuel. It had taken a few days but they were sort of okay with me now. Not only that but we had the beginnings of an escape plan. Now, we just had to find a way of breaking the spell on the perimeter fence and we'd be out of here.

Samuel was one step ahead of me. "If you're a witch, I assume you can break the spell on the perimeter, right?"

I held my hand up in the air and twisted it from side to side. "I'm semi-confident."

"Semi's not good enough. You have to be damn sure."

Grace glared at him. "Lower your voice Samuel, do you want to get us all killed?"

He whispered. "Sorry, it's just - this is too good a chance to mess up. We have to be certain before we try anything."

"I know" I nodded. I stared into space for a while, chewing my last mouthful of food as I mulled it over. "The thing is though. I don't think we're ever going to get that level of certainty. I wish I had a chance to practice it first but if I do that and get caught then we've lost our only chance. Either we try and risk failing or we stay here forever."

Samuel gritted his teeth. "I don't want to spend the rest of my life here."

"Me neither," Grace agreed.

Samuel continued. "We should try to leave on that food truck. It comes every Monday. If we sneak in and stow away in the back, we might be able to overpower the vampire driver then bust all the other blood slaves out too."

I thought about it. I wanted to get all the humans out, not just the blood slaves. But I could come back for everyone else once I was out. The first step was getting free.

I smiled at him. "It's a good plan. With my collar off, overpowering the driver will be easy."

Grace replied. "Then we're agreed." She held her hand out and I placed mine on top. Then Samuel placed his on top of ours. We smiled, conspiratorially, at each other.

Finally, we had the beginnings of an escape plan.

26

Grace picked the lock of my obsidian collar that afternoon but I kept it on around vampires. With the clasp on, it looked like it was still locked in place so wouldn't arouse any suspicions. This would give me a few days to practice my magic before the food truck arrived.

Vampire guards came down the hill fairly regularly to feed from the blood slaves. But any moment when we were alone, I'd practice my magic. Not having had any training, I could only go on instinct. Taking off my dog collar, I watched as the orange lights twirled around me and practiced manipulating them with my hands. Recalling the other times I'd borrowed vampire powers, I went over the steps to inhale their magic, over and over again, in my head. The only unknown at this point was how I would remove the spell from the gate - that part I'd just have to wing. I couldn't risk doing it ahead of time and getting caught. That would derail the entire plan and possibly get me killed.

Monday arrived and we waited anxiously for the food truck. CJ and Rainie were outside playing but actually they were on lookout. Samuel paced, swinging his arms back and forth. He exuded a mixture of nerves and excitement. Grace was quiet and pensive, wringing her hands as she stared into space. Only Paulette was vocal. She didn't trust our plan and wasn't shy about sharing her reservations.

As soon as CJ and Rainie went to play in the other room, she hissed at me. "You're going to get us all killed."

I bit my lip, about to defend myself when Grace stepped in and spoke for me. "Please Paulette. Try and be positive. Do you want to live here as a slave for the rest of your life?"

"No but..."

"I'd rather die trying to escape than live a half life here being tortured and fed on."

Paulette looked down at her lap. "I have young ones to think about. They don't deserve to die."

"None of us do!" Grace countered, raising her voice. Her eyes flicked to the vampire guards outside and she lowered her voice. "But we also don't deserve to live half a miserable life. Let's take a chance on us. Let's choose hope. Can you do that for me?"

Paulette's face crumpled as her eyes filled with tears. "It's just that... you know I've been let down before and..."

Grace knelt beside her and held both her hands. "I know Paulette. But this time it'll be different."

Something in their words caught my attention. "What do you mean, you've been let down before?"

Paulette sniffed. "This isn't the first time we've had a witch come here and promise to get us out."

"What?!" I couldn't believe I was only hearing about this now. "Who? When? What happened?" I could barely get my questions out fast enough.

"Her name was Rose or Rosie..."

"Rosa?" I asked

"Yes that's it. Rosa. She was a pet, just like you, up in the main house." She sniffed again. "Anyway, one night she escaped and came down the hill. Told us she'd break the spell on the gate and then come back for us." Her eyes darkened. "She never came back. She escaped from this place and never helped anyone."

Adrenaline surged through me. As terrible as the story was it was also wonderful. Rosa was an arcane witch, like me. If she'd been successful at lifting the spell on the gate, that meant I could too. For the first time since hatching the plan, I had real faith that we could pull it off.

Crouching down, next to Grace, I looked Paulette in the eyes. "Rosa may have betrayed your trust but I would *never* do that. I promise you, when I leave this place, you're coming with me." I looked each of them in the eyes. "All of you."

CJ and Rainie came in through the back door. CJ was breathless. "It's coming."

I inhaled deeply. "Right, this is it.

The food truck rolled, slowly up the long driveway and I took off my obsidian dog collar. I gasped and shuddered as strength and power rushed through my system. I'd learnt that the collar not only blocked my magic but it also reduced my strength and speed. Even my thought processes were foggier when I was wearing it. Now, with sharpened reflexes, I stood up, clicking my neck from side to side as I strode outside.

Mitchell and Peterson had assumed their usual position of lounging in the grass, playing cards. But as I approached, they sat up, their faces registering first annoyance and then a flicker of fear, as their gaze dropped to my neck. Swirling silvery lights mushroomed around their heads and I willed the power towards me, sucking it into my core. My body seemed to grow in size as my muscles hardened and vitality rippled over my skin.

Mitchell locked eyes with me and his lip curled. My vampire enhanced hearing heard a subtle growl purr over his chest. He sprang to his feet and launched himself at me, flying through the air with arms outstretched. To my eyes he seemed to move in slow motion and I turned and sprinted in the direction of the thicket of trees we'd run past during my first few days here. Reaching it in seconds, Mitchell's footsteps thundered behind me. He was gaining on me fast. I may have vampire powers but he was still way bigger and stronger than me. But it didn't matter: I was smarter.

He lunged at me and I sprang into the air, through the branches of the tree. As I descended, I grabbed one of the branches, snapping it easily before turning, to plunge it into Mitchell's chest. His face froze in a surprised gasp of pain before he disintegrated, blowing away in the wind.

I had no time to celebrate his demise. Peterson wasn't far behind him and in seconds, he was upon me. But when he saw the bloody tree branch in my hand, he faltered, stumbling backwards before he started running away. I took off, in pursuit. There was no way I'd let him warn the rest of the house. Reaching him in seconds, I jumped on top of his shoulders, winding my feet around his torso. Lifting the tree branch, I bought it down towards his chest. But he was quicker than Mitchell. Curling himself up into a defensive ball, he dropped and rolled forwards, shaking me off at the same time. I back flipped through the air, to face him, assuming a fighting stance, my makeshift stake in one hand. We circled each other. Peterson swiped at me and I jumped backwards. Peterson's eyes were filled with such violent intent that I started to doubt myself. He registered the moment of fear, in my eyes and seized upon it, lunging forward to grab me by the neck. He lifted me off the ground and I started to choke, dropping the branch as my vision started to blur.

"You're not as strong as you think you are, little girl." He smiled, licking his lips as his eyes went to my neck.

I flailed my legs around, and clawed at his hand, trying desperately to get him off me. But it was like his hand was coated in oil, I couldn't get a grip. The world began to get fuzzy around the edges as my consciousness started to blur. He lowered me just enough that he could reach my neck. His canines grazed at my skin. My heart pounded like drum beats in my ears. My eyes closed and I felt a sharp prick of pain as his fangs pierced the first layer of my skin.

Then a moment of clarity settled over me. A voice inside my head said.

This is just like the gym, in London, Bree. Imagine this is Janice and you're just sparring.

I opened my eyes, snapped my head back and head butted him, hard.

He staggered back in shock, releasing his grip on me at the same time. I squatted to grab the branch from the floor and hurled myself at him, stabbing him, in the chest, with a warrior cry that bellowed from the core of my being. His form disintegrated before me and his metallic scent wafted past me as dust on the breeze.

This was the danger point. If I could smell Mitchell and Peterson's death dust, the other vampires of the house soon would too. And I was right. A loud beeping alarm sounded from up the hill.

They'd be waiting for me.

But I couldn't let that stop me. I was determined to get out of here. Plus, I'd made a promise and I intended to keep it.

Turning around, I saw Samuel and Grace, rounding up the other blood slaves, as we'd planned. We'd designated a spot, near the gate, where they were to wait. Far enough away that the spell wouldn't affect them.

The beeping got louder as I sprinted up the hill, my magic giving me a vampire's speed, armed with only a tree branch. Within seconds, I was at the house. The first vampire guard was waiting for me on the sandstone steps. Wearing a bulletproof, stab vest and holding a semi-automatic weapon, he opened fire. Time seemed to slow down and I watched as the bullets approached me, in slow motion. Jumping into the air, the bullets whistled beneath my legs before I landed on the ground again. His finger braced on the trigger again but I was already moving forward. With split second speed, I plunged my branch into his neck then pulled it out. He gasped, eyes bulging as he clutched at his bloody neck with one hand, releasing the trigger. I tore his stab vest from his chest and stabbed the branch deep into his centre. His features drifted down to the ground in a pile of dust.

Beep, beep, beep.

Behind him, five more vampire guards all wore the same vests and pointed their semi-automatic rifles at me. I'd only ever seen the weapons in movies and American TV shows but if I'd already taken down one guy, I could take down more. They opened fire at the same time and I sailed into the air, somersaulting to land behind them. Zipping through the front door, I spied an antique sword, nailed to the wall, above a family crested shield. Dropping my tree branch, I soared into the air and ripped the sword off the wall, just in time for the first vampire guard to enter behind me. Swinging my sword at his neck, I decapitated him and he turned to dust.

Beep, beep, beep.

By now, the servants of the house had come to see the commotion. Darla appeared, armed with what looked like the broken leg of a piece of antique furniture. I smiled at her.

"Behind you, Bree!" She called out.

Just in time, I whirled around and drove my sword into a vampire guard's neck. Then springing up, I withdrew my sword and swung it at his head, turning him to particles.

"Darla - get everyone into the food truck. Now!" I shouted, as more vampire guards poured into the mansion entrance hall.

On the stairs above, some of the favoured humans watched, with a mixture of fear, awe and excitement on their faces. I smiled to myself. Soon they'd be free to leave too.

A group of vampire guards opened fire all at the same time. Grabbing the dead guards bulletproof vest, I zipped through the gunfire, dodging bullets as I held up the vest, as a shield, with one hand and swung my sword with my other. I dispatched eight vampire guards and stopped to cock my eyebrow and half smile at the next group, behind them. Their eyes were wild with blood lust as they snarled at me with fangs bared.

Beep, beep, beep.

Suddenly Beaufort's voice rang out of the speaker system. "Give up Bree, you can't possibly kill all of the vampire guards in this house. And even if you did, my pets will never go with you."

"Yeah? We'll see about that."

But as his words filtered through my mind, I realised he was right. All it would take was one mistake and I'd be dead - then the rest of the humans would never get out of here. I had to make a split second judgement call and in that moment, I decided that saving the humans was more important to me than getting revenge on Beaufort.

I leapt into the air, just as the next group of guards opened fire. But this time, I sprang backwards, then dropped and slid to shield myself behind a greek statue. The blare of rapid gunfire rang out as the guards annihilated the statue. But I was already sprinting towards the side patio doors. With lightning speed, I crashed through the glass door, barely noticing the shards of glass that lanced my skin. Fuelled by pure adrenaline, I spied the weapon of a dead vampire, on the grass nearby. I raced towards it and scooped it up before reaching the parked food truck, a moment later. Checking the back of the truck, I gave a satisfied smile and nod at Darla, sitting inside the truck beside scores of other humans. We'd pick up more when we got to the gate. I closed the truck doors then froze.

The crunching of pebbles underfoot had me whirling around to see a vampire behind me. Wearing a retail uniform, and overweight, with longish, greasy brown hair, he didn't look like one of Beaufort's guards.

He lifted up two shaky hands, his eyes wide with terror. "Look, I don't want any trouble. This is just a minimum-wage job for me. I'm unarmed. Please, just let me go home. I'll even drive you out of here."

I narrowed my eyes at him, pointing the gun at his chest. "This is filled with silver bullets." I didn't think it was but he wouldn't know that. "If you make one false move, you're dust, understood?"

He nodded vigorously and side-stepped towards the vehicle, still holding his hands up as he kept his gaze trained on me and my big gun. Truth be told, I wasn't sure I even knew how to shoot the thing. But again, he didn't know that. Keeping my gaze as menacing as possible, I got in beside him. I pointed the gun at him and said in a low, even voice. "Drive."

He didn't hesitate, turning the ignition key, he started the truck. He turned it around the ample driveway, just as another group of guards ran out of the house. They opened fire, raining a hailstorm of bullets onto the truck. Me and the driver ducked as he sped down the hill. As we approached the gate, my skin started to itch and I focused on the orangey lights of my magic, that glittered around me. I didn't know what I was doing but had a hunch that if I borrowed the vampire's powers, it might offer me immunity to the spell. The other humans would pass out but at least I'd be able to get everyone to safety and revive them once we were out.

"Stop here, we have more people to pick up." I commanded.

The vampire obediently complied, idling the engine as the blood slaves, crept out of the bushes, lining the sides of the driveway. I heard the sound of the truck, being opened, from the outside and more people getting in. As soon as it closed, I gave the order. "Let's go." And the vampire driver started driving towards the gate.

Now, with freedom in sight, I focused on the lights of his power. Sucking it into my chest, I felt a tingling sensation as more power flooded through me.

But then my body was gripped by agony. Every nerve ending was tipped in pain as a burning sensation spread over my skin. Screaming and crying came through from the back and a few banging noises. But I could barely focus on what was happening in the back of the truck. My own pain obliterated every other thought from my mind. My vision began to blur and I gritted my teeth.

"Keep driving" I shouted, through a clenched jaw. I realised I hadn't removed the spell but it made no difference. I was determined to make it out of here. Sweat poured down my face and my entire body shook as pain tore through my flesh. It felt like my skin was being ripped off my body.

Hold on Bree, hold on. Just a little longer....

But it was no use. The blurring at the edges of my vision closed in further and further until I could see only a pinprick of reality.

Then everything went black.

27

I came to, tied to a chair, back in Beaufort Heights. Heavy chains secured my ankles to metal shackles and my torso was bound by obsidian-embedded chains. The cold metal of the obsidian dog collar was back around my neck. I felt even weaker than I had the first time they'd put the collar on me.

The odious figure of Hugh Beaufort paced in front of me, his arms behind his back as he held a shaving blade in one hand. We were in a room that I'd never been in before. It was dark, devoid of any decorations or antiques and had a single, dangling light, fitted with a dim bulb, at the centre of the room. The smell of old sweat and blood mingled together in a way that turned my stomach. But most chillingly of all, Darla, Samuel, Grace, Paulette, CJ and Rainie, all stood, bound in chains, in a line against one wall. Vampire guards stood at either side of the group, with guns pointed at them.

The look of terror in their eyes made my insides turn to liquid.

"Ah, you're awake. Good. Time to get started." Beaufort said, his buoyant tone in stark contrast to the horror of the situation. "I'm very disappointed in you, Bree."

Tears sprang to my eyes. "Hugh, please. This was all my idea, the others are innocent. Please let them go."

"Innocent?" He said quietly, a menacing undercurrent of barely-contained anger in his tone. "INNOCENT?!" He roared, unleashing his rage. He strode over to Darla. "This one was stupid enough to leave hair pins within your reach. I saw you take them. Her reckless actions resulted in many of my best guards being murdered by you." He pointed his shaving blade at me.

Darla's eyes widened and she started shaking as tears rolled down her face.

Beaufort lifted his shaving blade, it glinted in the dim light as he walked towards Darla. "What am I to do with you, huh?" He trailed the blade along her neck, not hard enough to draw blood.

She whimpered and started to beg. "P..p..please Mr Beaufort. Please don't hurt me. I didn't know she took the hair pins, I swear."

"LIAR!" He barked. "You conspired with her. Are you stupid enough to think I couldn't hear your whispering, couldn't see your collusion?" He turned around to look at me. "You still don't get it, do you? Nobody leaves Beaufort Heights. Nobody. I see and hear *everything* that happens here."

I glared at him, biting my tongue to stop myself from retorting that Rosa had left. I wasn't in any position to be taunting him, no matter how much I wanted to.

"Anyway," he continued. "You've wasted enough of my time with your snivelling excuses and lies. I'm ready to move to the most interesting part of these proceedings." His blue eyes flashed at me. "The punishment part." He tapped the flat edge of the razor against his lips as his gaze went to the ceiling. "Who should I punish first I wonder?"

My gut clenched as I looked at Rainie. Urine was trickling down her leg and she was crying inconsolably.

"Please, Hugh, just let them go. I'm the only one who should be punished. Just let them go. Please don't hurt them."

He cocked his head to the side, considering my words. I could see he was thoroughly enjoying the power he had, in this moment. He was drunk on it, sucking it up as if it was powdered sugar. He nodded, as if coming to a decision. "Maybe you're right. Maybe I should let them go. After all, good help is so hard to find. Wouldn't you agree, Darla?"

He looked at her, dropping the hand holding the razor, to waist height.

She nodded, biting her lip so hard that she drew blood. Tears streamed freely down her red face and she sniffed and shuddered.

"Then again, maybe not." He said.

"No - wait!" I called out.

But it was too late. His hand slid the razor across Darla's neck and blood flowed down her shirt as her head lolled to one side. Her eyes filled first with shock then dimmed to a lifeless glaze as her soul departed her body.

"Noooo!" I screamed, clenching my fists as white hot rage tore through my chest. "You evil bastard!"

He whirled around and crouched down, in front of me, his face, inches from mine. "This is not my fault, Bree. It's *your* fault. *You* are the one who planned this disastrous escapade so poorly. *You* are the one who failed them all. *You* are the loser here and I am the winner."

Tears rolled down my face as the truth of his words poured over my broken heart. Darla had been my first and only friend in the house. She'd put herself at risk for me. She'd given me hope when I'd been at my lowest. And now she was dead, because of me. She didn't deserve to die. Beaufort was right. I'd failed her and I'd never be able to forgive myself. Waves of grief washed over me, in violent bursts, drenching my insides in poison. I could barely even speak and was only dimly aware of Beaufort standing back up and starting to pace again.

Forcing my consciousness away from my inner pain and back onto him, he turned once more to face me. "But Darla isn't the only one who is going to be punished today. Oh no, that would make me look weak, in front of my vampire guards. And they are so very impressionable, you know. "He smiled at them and they chortled, as if this was a fun way to pass the time. I'd never hated those mindless goons more than I did at this moment.

"Let me see. Who's next?" He walked, agonisingly slowly, staring into the terrified eyes of each human. As he got to Rainie's tear-streaming face, he crouched down.

Paulette cried out, an agonising wail, like she'd been shot in the gut.

Hugh stroked Rainie's face and spoke to her gently, as if he was being kind, which I knew was just more mind games. "How about you little girl? Would you like to get out of here? Would you like to be free?" His smile was oily and insincere.

Her trembling lips slowed down slightly, her tears slowing down and a heart breaking look of hope entered her huge brown eyes. "Yes, sir." She nodded.

His eyes flashed with malevolence, "I know of one way you'll be free."

I gasped as he withdrew the razor, from behind his back, placing it next to her throat.

The hope in her eyes was replaced by terror.

Panic surged through me.

The razor just nicked her flesh and she screamed.

Paulette begged. "No, No. Please don't Sir, please, please."

My thoughts zoned in on the sight of the razor, in his meaty hands. Everything in my life was crystallised into this one point in time. I was more desperate to save this girl's life than I'd ever been about anything. I cared about her life more than I cared about my own and in that split second, I knew what I had to do.

"Stop, Hugh. I'll do it!" I called out.

He withdrew the razor and turned to face me.

Paulette's legs gave out and she sank to the floor, sobbing, in relief.

"What was that, Bree?"

"I said I'll do it." The words came out quietly but I knew he could hear. "I'll give you an heir. I'll have your baby. If you promise not to hurt her, or any of the other blood slaves or servants."

A slow smile of victory spread across his face as he folded the razor away. "That's what I thought you said." He put the razor into his pocket and walked towards me, looking down at me as if I was a piece of dirt, on the floor. "Now, this is what is going to happen. In a moment my guards will lead you to your new living quarters - the dungeons beneath the house."

I felt my eyelids flicker slightly, in surprise.

He explained further. "Oh, you thought you'd still get the royal treatment?" He held up his finger and shook it from side to side, together with his head, as he tutted loudly. "That is reserved for my favoured humans, which of course, you no longer are." He paused to let this sink in and I gritted my teeth, to stop myself from spitting in his face. "You will not resist mating with me. If I get even an iota of an idea that you are resisting," he pointed at Rainie. "She dies. And then her Mum and brother too. In fact all of them." He crouched down and lowered his voice to icy levels. "You see, I'm in charge here and I get to decide who lives and who dies. Not some dirty little Irish savage who is only good for opening her legs, nothing more."

He stood up and clicked his fingers at one of the guards. "You, take them back down the hill." He gestured to the other guard. "And you take this one down to the dungeons." He waved his hand dismissively over Darla's body. "I'll get one of the servants to clean this up."

The utter coldness of his tone and manner, around a human being he'd just murdered, filled my throat with bile.

I thought things couldn't get any worse but just as he was about to leave the room, he turned around and looked at me, smirking. "I knew you'd come around eventually. I planned it perfectly." Then he walked out of the door.

And that's when it hit me. An avalanche of dawning realisation that crashed over me like a tidal wave of sludge. He'd planned this entire thing. He hadn't sent me down the hill in a fit of pique - he'd done it on purpose. He'd seen me stealing the hairpin but had let me keep it. He knew I'd try and break out once I was down the hill. He knew I'd try and take the blood slaves with me. He also knew that by spending time with them, I'd get close to them and then, in my desperation, offer myself to him, in exchange for keeping them alive. He knew I loved Darla - he'd seen us bonding when he watched us through the cameras. That's why he'd killed her first - to break me.

Mel's words rang out in my head.

He's had centuries to master this game and he is very, very good at it.

Game set and match. He'd won and I'd lost. I wanted to roar and pound my fists against the wall. But, still chained up, and soaked with defeat, as I watched Beaufort walk out, all I could do was hang my head and sob bitterly.

28

The entrance to the dungeons was a trapdoor, in the back of the kitchen, leading to a subterranean level. A dank, dark, row of dungeons, each contained a prisoner. Dim, dangling electric bulbs lit the rough, granite walls. My chains rattled, as I shuffled past each cell. The prisoners all seemed to be human although it was hard to tell above the stench. The whole place stank worse than a music festival toilet. Old sweat, mingled with faeces, urine, blood, puke and fear. I tried to breathe through my mouth, barely able to believe that this is where I'd be imprisoned, from now on.

But then I reached one cell and immediately recognised the inhabitant. He was even dirtier and more ragged than when I'd last seen him but he was still unmistakeable. It was Derek, the vampire.

So this is where they've been keeping him.

Now his disgraceful appearance, when I'd first arrived at Beaufort Heights, made sense. He got up and rushed to the bars, his eyes wild. I staggered back stumbling slightly on the uneven ground.

"Get back." The guard who was escorting me barked at him and Derek took a step back but clenched his jaw, glowering at the guard.

"See? I told you Beaufort was a double-crossing snake." He shouted, as I was pushed forward by the guard.

I sighed, it hurt me so much to admit that Derek had been right. Now, compared to the monster that I knew Hugh Beaufort to be, Derek seemed like a cute little pussy cat.

Each cell was about two metres wide and three metres long, with a bucket at the back. The human prisoners either crouched or stood, some of them rocking and muttering, driven mad by the lack of daylight and the squalid conditions. I guessed it made no sense to kill them, when they were useful sources of fresh blood.

We reached an empty cell, a few cells down from Derek's and the vampire guard drew a set of keys out of his pocket, opened the door and shoved me inside. I didn't resist. If I did, Beaufort might kill Rainie. A small voice inside me said I shouldn't give up, should still think about ways to escape but that voice was drowned out by a vast cavern of despair. I felt myself sinking into that cavern and there was very little I could do about it.

The vampire removed my obsidian chains but kept my collar on. Then he left the cell, locking it behind him and I listened, as his footsteps echoed into the distance.

Alone, in my cell, I sank down into a ball, in the corner and allowed tears to roll, silently down my cheeks. I hated myself. I didn't even want to live anymore. Mitchell had been right, I was worthless. I'd been nothing before I arrived and I was even less now. How could I have been so arrogant as to believe that I would actually get out of here, with barely any planning, and not just me but all the other humans too? Now Darla was dead because of me. The accusing look, on Paulette's face, as the vampire guard had led her and the others out of that room, had burned me worse than acid. She was right to look at me like that. It was my fault that we'd failed. I never should've given them false hope. I never should've attempted to break the spell, before I was certain I could do it. I should've planned better, I should've...

"Hey, cry baby!" Derek's voice called out, pulling me from my dark thoughts.

"Leave me alone, Derek. In case you hadn't noticed, I'm not in the mood for a fight."

"Who said anything about fighting? I'm on your side. Now, are you going to sit there crying all day or are you going to start thinking up an escape plan with me?"

I put my head in my hands and exhaled, loudly. The last thing I needed was to have to deal with this dickhead on top of everything else. Slowing my voice down so an idiot like him could understand, I explained. "I can't escape - if I do, Beaufort will kill everyone I've come to care about here."

"And you let him know that you care about people? Well that was a schoolgirl error, if ever there was one."

"Yeah, I know that now, bellend. And thank you for twisting the knife into what is a *very* fresh and *very* raw wound."

He paused and for a few precious moments, I thought he'd decided to shut up and let me go back to my self-pitying wallowing. But I was wrong.

"That's a setback, I must confess. But it's not insurmountable, we can still find a way around it."

Oh, no, no, no. This jerk had to be set straight. "We?! There is no 'we'!"

His voice sounded hurt when he retorted. "Don't be like that Bree. Look, I know we didn't get off to the best start."

This was unbelievable. "*Didn't get off to the best start?* You tried to kill me. Then you glamoured my flatmates into thinking that I'd violently assaulted them. You know that I'm wanted by the police now, don't you? My life is in tatters - it was even before I was kidnapped by Beaufort's henchmen."

This time I waited for his response. If he wanted to make friends and form an alliance, he better start explaining himself and fast.

"I'm not a Dracul vampire," he began.

"Hmmph! You could've fooled me."

"No really, I'm not. I'm a vampire assassin - a professional hitman. I'm not part of any gangs, I prefer to work alone. The Draculs hired me to do what I was told would be a simple job. Attack you, make you think I'd come to kill you, drain you to within an inch of your life, then glamour your flatmates into thinking you'd attacked them."

My eyes widened. The entire thing had been a set up, right from the start. Hugh Beaufort was the most masterful strategist that I'd ever come across.

Derek continued. "It was good money and seemed simple enough so I took the job." He paused, his tone of voice turning to deadly hate. "When I came to collect payment, they kidnapped me, bundled me into the back of a van and brought me here. Beaufort never had any intention of paying me for my work. I was just a pawn in his game."

"The game to get me to agree to have his baby." I whispered.

Derek's vampire ears picked it out easily. "Agree to what?!"

I explained, a little louder. "He wanted me to have his baby. All of this has been for that purpose, all of it. Bringing you here was his first plan - he thought I might agree in exchange for killing you and ending the glamour on my flatmates. But when that didn't work, he saw a better opportunity. He used my own compassion against me."

"That sick bastard." Derek breathed. "I kill people but I do it for money. It's a clean and honest transaction."

I raised an eyebrow at his interpretation of the word 'honest' but I let it slide and carried on listening.

"Beaufort is different, he enjoys manipulating people. He gets off on the power, enjoys the game. I despise him."

"That makes two of us," I replied.

"That's why we can't let him win. Between us, we have to think of a way to take him down." His voice was laden with fervour.

"Do you think I would be here if there was any way we could take him down? I'm here because I'm all out of options."

He fell silent for a few moments before speaking. "What made you think you could get out of here in the first place?"

"Someone else did it - another arcane witch by the name of Rosa Knight. The blood slaves told me she escaped. She promised to come back for them but she never did."

"Then how do you know she escaped? Maybe she got killed trying."

That was true and something I hadn't even considered. I was feeling like more of an idiot by the second.

"But if she offered it, she must've thought she could do it?" I tried.

"Not necessarily - she might have been a chancer, like you. She might have thought she could just wing it and then died when she failed."

I put my head back in my hands. "You're not exactly helping here, Derek. I'm already at a low point and you're just making it worse."

Another voice rang out, an older-sounding man with a deep baritone and clear, upper-class accent. He sounded like a classically-trained actor. "The spell on the perimeter cannot be broken by an arcane witch."

"What? Who is that? Repeat what you just said and add an explanation, please, mate." Derek asked.

"My name is Oliver. I have been a prisoner here for twenty years - not always in the dungeon of course. During my time here, I have acquired a great deal of knowledge and one of them pertains to the maintenance of the perimeter spell. Beaufort has an alliance with the spirit witches - the mothers of all vampires, as you may be aware. Once a year a spirit witch comes to re-ward the perimeter with spirit magic. Breaking the spell requires a spirit witch, with the ability to control the spirits who ward it."

"Are you sure about this?" I asked.

"Absolutely certain. There is no way off this estate without a spirit witch to remove that spell."

My heart sank. I'd never had any chance of escaping and Beaufort had known that. It had all fed into his sick plan. It also meant that Rosa was probably dead, as Derek had suggested.

I dropped my head to my chest, letting myself drown, deep in the lake of my own despair.

29

Clang, clang, clang, clang.

The sound of a metallic bowl being hit loudly, with the back end of a spoon, startled me into full wakefulness. In the dungeons, there was no night and day, no wake or sleep, only a groggy inertia that cloaked me, making me constantly drowsy but never enough for a full, refreshing sleep. The only way to keep track of the days was by delivery of the one meal a day that we were served: lukewarm porridge, the same as the blood slaves got. The vampire guard who brought us our food, took great delight in heralding his arrival by means of the harsh, metallic sound, jarring the peace of the dank dungeons.

By my count, I'd been here five days. Beaufort hadn't yet come to collect on his 'prize'. Was he just busy? Or waiting until my fear had time to fester and reach a fever pitch of infection?

The guard's footsteps travelled in my direction, the squeak of the trolley, grating on my nerves, as he stopped at each cell to slide the bowl underneath. Every so often he'd make a snide, spiteful comment to one of the inhabitants of the cell. The vampire was a low-life parasite, feeding off the misery of those in no position to fight back. The first day I'd been here, I'd been tempted to attack him, as soon as he came to collect my empty bowl. But then I'd thought of Rainie, down the hill, and held myself back. I couldn't have that sweet little girl's death on my conscience. My nightmares were already filled with Darla's angry, accusing face, as she heckled me from the grave, blaming me for the loss of an imagined life she'd never been able to complete. I still couldn't believe she was dead. I'd cried so much, I couldn't cry anymore. Instead, my grief had turned into an ugly morbid thing. A child of wrath, locked away in a holding cage, waiting for the only thing that would bring release - driving a stake through Beaufort's sick heart.

The guard got to me and smirked. He never missed an opportunity to have a pop at me. "It's Bree the merciful." He chuckled, bowing gracefully before sliding the bowl under the door. "Look where your mercy got you. You should've just not given a shit, like all the other pets upstairs."

I took the bowl, glowering at him, but I didn't fight back. I was beginning to wonder if I still could. Was it just because I feared for Rainie's life or had Beaufort really broken me? It didn't matter anyway. I was never getting out of here. If my mind fractured and I became a gibbering, mindless lunatic, like many of the other lost souls in these dungeons, perhaps that would be better. Then, maybe, I could block out the pain of Beaufort's abuse. Did crazy people still feel emotional pain? I hoped not.

He continued his taunting. "Yeah, I bet you wish you were back up there now, don't you. Sipping on fine wine as servants waited on you hand and foot. Getting dressed in silk and getting regular massages." His eyes grew a little misty and I wondered if he too would like a taste of the good life - it certainly appeared that way. His voice even cracked a little at the end. Then he shook his head and snapped out of his reverie. "Anyway, one of us will be down to collect you later."

This got my attention. "What?"

He stroked his bristly grey chin. "Yep. Today's the day, Bree the merciful. It's baby-making time."

I felt the blood drain from my face. "Why today?"

"You're fertile." He leant forward. "We can smell it when you ovulate."

So that's what Beaufort had been waiting for. He knew I was hostile and unpredictable. He didn't want to risk mating with me on random days when I couldn't fall pregnant. This gave me a surge of hope. If he was being cautious around me, that meant he still viewed me as a threat.

Why?

∼

SOME TIME LATER, two vampire guards turned up, handcuffed me and dragged me out of my cell. As we passed Derek's cell, he shouted out. "Tear off his dick."

I smiled at his attempt to cheer me up. During my time here, I'd found out that Derek wasn't half bad. We had a lot in common. Not just the fact that he'd been played by Beaufort, just like I had. We both liked tinkering with motorbikes. Derek had even created his own line of leather motorbike gear, which he described as a 'side hobby'. But the passion in his voice when he spoke of it, made it clear that this was his true calling. He also did MMA fighting. He'd started as a boxer, going professional for a while, before transitioning into a mixed fighting discipline. His attitude towards life was refreshingly carefree. He'd always lived by his own rules, giving zero fucks about breaking the law. And he cheerfully boasted about his skill at nicking cars, which he did 'just for fun'.

I recalled the words he'd spoken to me hours before. *If you ever get out of here, take me with you.* Derek had made me promise and in return, he'd promised to remove the glamour on my flatmates. I doubted either of us would ever get to fulfil our pact but it made me feel better. It was a small act of hope in an otherwise hopeless situation.

Shaking my thoughts back to the grim present, I trailed my feet as I walked. I felt like a condemned man, being led to the gallows. How could Beaufort still believe he wasn't a rapist? This was rape - using coercion, the threat of harming someone I cared about, to force me to sleep with him, that was definitely rape. Being an eighteenth century guy, maybe the definition was different in his day. In his mind, if I wasn't scratching at his face, screaming and thrashing about, as he forced himself inside me, it wasn't rape. Somebody should educate Hugh Beaufort on the many ways in which the world had changed. But then, surrounded by yes men and barbie dolls, who would ever have the balls to do that?

We ascended the steps, opened the trapdoor and entered the main house. I squinted as my eyes adjusted to the bright lights of the kitchen. My gaze darted from left to right, as I walked, looking for anything I could use as a weapon. There was a wooden rolling pin - that would do. But I had no hope of reaching it, handcuffed and with my obsidian collar locked firmly around my neck. With mounting dread I began to accept that this was happening. Hugh Beaufort was going to rape me and I was powerless to stop it.

Rounding the corner, we entered the entrance hall and there he was, standing at the top of the stairs, a smug smile plastered on his odious face. A servant stood, holding a towel, cowering next to him.

"Peugh! I could smell you from half a mile away. Veena here will take you for a bath. I like my lovers to be fresh and clean." His eyes flashed with glee and I felt like throwing up. My footsteps sounded like the toll of a funeral church bell, every step leading me closer to my doom.

We reached the top of the stairs and the vampire guard escorted me and Veena to the luxury bathroom I'd been shown to when I'd first arrived. Leaning close to me, the vampire spat in my ear as he spoke in a sinister whisper. "You should be grateful. It's an honour to mate with Mr Beaufort."

A rush of nausea assaulted me, at the thought of my vampire captor's scraggly, old body, on top of mine. My mouth turned down, as my nose wrinkled. I bet he grunted and snorted, like a pig, when he was shagging.

The vampire continued. "And the likes of you doesn't normally get to have a bath in the master suite." He sneered, pleased with himself.

But trapped in my own tunnel of deep regret, grief and fear, his insults barely touched me. His cheap shots were no match for the depth of my pain.

This time, Veena came into the bathroom with me. Was I on suicide watch? It wouldn't surprise me and, come to think of it, that may be the best revenge for Beaufort. Or, better yet, wait until he'd impregnated me and then kill myself with his bastard child in my belly. I shook the dark thought from my head, barely able to believe what Beaufort had turned me into. I was no longer Bree Ryan. I was a creature of hate and vengeance, my life reduced to a single-point of focus and meaning: to destroy Hugh Beaufort.

I got into the bath, as if in a trance, barely aware of the hot water, lapping around me. It was a stark contrast to how I'd first luxuriated in this bath tub. I yearned for the innocence of the girl I'd been. When I'd first arrived here, I'd been wary but still hopeful and full of fire and passion. Now all that was gone. I lay, listlessly, all thoughts of escape abandoned, bobbing in the warm water, like an abandoned old deck shoe, floating in the waves of a polluted sea. Submerging in the water, I looked up at the renaissance frescoed ceiling, watching as bubbles escaped from my lips. It was so tempting to stay down here, in the quiet of the bath's watery depths, just never come up again and let myself drown.

Strong arms hauled me out of the water. "Back up you come," Veena said. She looked at me with kindness, too terrified to tell me what she really thought but conveying as much as she could through her eyes. Her eyes said 'thank you'. Her eyes said 'sorry'. Her eyes said 'I wish things could have turned out differently' and I gulped and nodded, my eyes welling with tears. I almost couldn't cope with kindness anymore. I'd become so accustomed to heartless jibes and cruelty, from the vampire guards. Her kindness almost hurt more than their insults. Because I knew it was so fleeting and I'd have to give it up and be raped, then return to my underground cave, only to be raped again the next day and every day during my fertile period.

"Let's get you out." Her eyes crinkled in the corners and she held up a towel. I stood up, covering my naked breasts as I shivered. I wasn't cold, I was shaking with shuddering sobs. She wrapped the fluffy towel around me, stroking her arms up and down as she dried me. She was doing her best to comfort me, offer what little solace she could without risking punishment.

My tears flowed faster and now I began to sob out loud, no longer caring enough to hide my pain.

She handed me a pile of elegant clothes. Designer underwear and a floaty, rose-coloured chiffon dress. Why was he bothering to dress me up when his objective was just to knock me up? This facade of civility seemed somehow worse than being roughly pushed up against an alleyway wall. At least that method was more honest. This was rape, however he wanted to dress it up. He could paint my face and swathe me in the softest fabrics. But there was no hiding the cold, hard ugliness of this. He was taking me against my will and I would never forget, nor forgive.

I put the clothes on mechanically and Veena zipped up my dress. It hugged my body like a wisp of smoke, barely containing me. My breasts spilled out of the plunging neckline. And a deep slit in the side, revealed one leg as the fabric spooled around me, the hemline skimming the floor.

Veena got to work with a round brush and hair dryer, styling my long hair into soft waves, that fell around my face. Next she put light make up on me. Dewy lipstick, soft, romantic eyes and a light rosy blush on my cheeks. She'd done me up as a bride but I felt like I was betrothed to Satan and about to be damned through the desecration of the marital bed.

She finished off the look with a diamond earring and necklace set. It was the most beautiful jewellery I'd ever worn. But no amount of pretty, glittery diamonds could light the darkness of my mood.

When she'd finished, she led me by the hand, giving me to the vampire guard, standing sentry outside the bathroom.

"This way." He led me down a darkened passageway. I was sure the lights had been brighter when I'd first arrived. The carpeted floor felt like claws, digging into my soft, exposed soles. By now my tears had dried. I had no more left to give. I'd cried for the hopeful girl I'd been who was now gone. I'd cried for the way in which my honour lay in tatters, destroyed by the shards of my broken promises, made to slaves who would now never know freedom. But most of all I'd cried for Darla. A life so full of promise. A woman so full of vibrancy and joy, her positivity had been a lifeline to me and now she was gone - snuffed out in one senseless act of brutality. The waste was so desolating, it twisted in my soul worse than an arrow being pulled out, tearing through my organs and suffocating my will to fight or to live.

We reached Beaufort's bedroom which, as I would've guessed, was fancier than a prostitute's knickers. He lay in wait, like a preying mantis, scoping out the best position from which to devour her mate. His lust-filled gaze followed me into the room.

Licking his lips appreciatively, he nodded. "Now that's more like it. Now you look like one of my lovers." He beckoned me to join him. The guard unlocked my handcuffs and then retreated, shutting the door behind him.

I sat on the edge of the bed, rubbing my red wrists as I gulped down the tears that threatened to spill once more.

"Oh come on Bree, it's not that bad. I could tell you that I'll be quick but that would be a lie."

I gagged, inwardly groaning.

"But remember your promise. Not a single hint of resistance or..." he made a slashing movement across his neck.

My hand flew to my mouth and I scrunched up my face in disgust and hate. Catching sight of my reflection, in the mirror, opposite his four-poster kingsize bed, a blotchy, tear-streaked girl stared back at me.

He shuffled closer to me, stroking my hair away from my neck. His eyes lingered on my neck and his breathing began to increase. He leaned in and planted a wet, smoochy kiss on my cheek. I recoiled but it didn't deter him. I sat motionless, staring into space, as his nose sniffed behind my ear.

"Mmm. I love the smell of a woman during ovulation. There's

nothing like it." He breathed. "You're in the peak of your womanhood, ripe for impregnating."

My contempt turned to disbelief and I stared at him, wishing I could poison him with the well of hate behind my eyes. How could this guy think that women loved him? For starters his pillow talk stunk worse than week old mackerel, left out in the sun.

Beaufort opened his mouth and I heard a clicking sound as his fangs appeared. Saliva dripped from one of them. Any pretence at decorum he'd previously put on for me, had been tossed aside, in service of his lust. He was a feral beast and he no longer cared to hide it from me. The sight of him, in his true, full vampire form, did something to me. My leg bones felt like they'd disintegrated. I couldn't stand, even though every fibre of my being told me to run. My scream caught in my throat, coming out as a mere whimper. Time seemed to slow down and images of my life flashed before me. Was I even still breathing? I was too scared to tell. My only awareness was of the threat, crawling across the sheets, slowly towards me, savouring my fear and distress. This was the man I'd first seen in the restaurant. This was the monster I'd sensed, beneath the veneer of gentility. This was the real Hugh Beaufort: merciless, tyrannical and bestial.

I scrambled backwards, turning my head from side to side, seeking out anything that could be used as a weapon. He'd asked the guard to remove my handcuffs. Because now it was about more than just 'getting the job done' now he wanted to enjoy it and the way that he enjoyed it best was by inflicting fear as well as pain. He wanted the thrill of the chase. As I turned my head to look back at him, I squealed - he was at my throat. It had taken less than the blink of an eye for him to be there. His manicured fingernails grazed the soft skin of my neck, drawing just the tiniest nick of blood. I cried out and his eyes flashed. He threw his head back and laughed.

"Now we're really having fun!" His eyes glinted with triumph.

I tried to latch onto any idea that might help me but I was a mess - a quivering, gibbering mess. I'd been a fool to think I could handle this vampire. I still couldn't even really use my arcane magic properly. My powers were unpredictable and difficult to control. I should've taken the witches help while I'd still had the chance. This is where my bravado had gotten me. I'd thought I could protect myself against vampires. I thought I was strong and brave. I wasn't. I was a weak little girl, alone in the world, with no clue about how to defend myself.

Beaufort brought his fangs to my neck once more and they danced across my flesh. His hot breath assaulted my nostrils and I squirmed and closed my eyes, praying something would happen - anything to stop him from raping me. Blind panic took over my mind. It fragmented into a chaotic maelstrom of flashing images and abstract thoughts. Was this what was meant by a dissociative state? I no longer felt glued to my body and would've done anything to leave it.

Without warning, Beaufort wrenched my dress from my torso, stripping me to the waist, as he tore the delicate fabric. I cradled my bra-clad breasts in my hands, crossing them protectively over my body as I quivered in time to my own shuddering breaths.

"Mmm, Bree. You look good enough to eat. I don't normally bite my lovers but tonight, I'm going to have to make an exception." He snapped his head back and bared his fangs.

30

In that moment, reality slowed to a standstill and something inside me snapped. I felt a twang, like a rubber band being let go, and it was like my soul just popped out of my body. I exited my physical existence, through the top of my head and flew above where I sat motionless, suspended in time, with Beaufort's snarling, slavering mouth, open and ready to feast on me.

Above my body, I turned my hands over. I existed as a glittering, semi-corporeal being, translucent and insubstantial. The events of the world below seemed less important and real than the events of the world I now inhabited. And what a world it was, swirling, metallic lights whirled around me in spiralling patterns, in every colour of the rainbow. The lights were the source of my powers, I now understood but it felt like so much more. I was made of light and would go back to it after I died. Death seemed not so much an ending but more of a transition. All these thoughts and more drifted through my mind wordlessly, in a transmission of wisdom that seemed to come from the lights themselves.

Then I became aware of more beings around me, thousands of them, more than could be fit into the room my body sat in. Even that room no longer existed. It was an illusion, like the rest of physical reality. The spirits around me drew close, flitting in and out of my body with the playfulness of a child. Some of them had transparent, silvery bodies, like mine but others were just orbs of light, zipping in and out of my sphere of reality. I loved them all just the same and they responded in kind, filling me up with love and strength and power like I'd never felt before. Euphoria rushed over me and a clarity of mind and all at once I snapped back into my body. But this time I wasn't alone. This time, I had the power of a thousand spirits at my beck and call.

It was as if someone hit the 'play' button on reality once more and Hugh's teeth reached my neck but at the same moment, he cried out, his eyes widening in fear as I whipped my head backwards, holding a hand in front of his mouth.

"No!" I didn't recognise my voice - it was like a sonic boom, filled with the voices of a thousand angry spirits, of all ages and generations.

Beaufort's face turned white and he shrank back and started shaking. "It... it can't be. No, it can't be."

The room filled with dazzling light and a penumbra of swirling spirits filled the air around us. The spirits carried me into the air and I floated above the bed. Catching sight of myself in the mirror, I no longer looked human but more like a goddess of destruction. Blazing streaks of iridescence cascaded from my head. My hair flapped outwards, as if blown by an ethereal wind which emanated from the spirit world. My eyes were vengeful and full of fury as I turned them on my vampire abuser.

"Now you die, vampire!"

I pointed a finger at him and white ectoplasm flew out of it, hitting Beaufort in the face. He fell to the floor, screaming and writhing in agony as the fluid began to dissolve his facial features.

Beep, beep, beep.

I looked at the door. Somebody had sounded the alarm. That meant the other vampire guards would be here soon. And I was right.

The door flew open. Outside, a group of around twenty armed

guards stood, dressed in bulletproof stab vests and carrying semi-automatic weapons.

They opened fire. I flew up higher, as the bullets whistled beneath me. But I felt no fear. "Spirits of war, lend me your weapons." I shouted.

All the guns started floating in the air and not just those that the vampires had been holding. It looked like every weapon in the house, including knives, swords and stakes. The vampires stared, open mouthed, petrified by fear. I pointed at one of them and ectoplasm shot into his face. He fell to the floor and started clawing at his face. "Aargh, get it off me, get it off me!"

When they saw this, the other guards looked at each other, then turned and sprinted towards the stairs.

Seeing that I was distracted by the guards, Beaufort rolled and scuttled out of the door, disappearing around the corner.

White hot fury surged through me as I flew after him, with the weapons still floating around me like a macabre cloud. But as I entered the corridor, he was nowhere to be seen.

Veena stood on the corridor, trembling and pale as she looked at what I'd become.

I softened my voice. "You don't have to fear me." Holding out my hand, I lowered to the floor. "Join me." I raised and lowed my hand and the weapons dropped to the floor. I handed a gun to her. "Here - do you know how to use it?"

She nodded enthusiastically. "I used to be in the army."

"Do you know where they keep the silver bullets?" I reasoned they had to have some here in case of attacks from rival vampire groups.

"Yes. I'll go and get them." She sped off, holding her rifle aloft.

By now other servants were gathering around and I handed out weapons to each of them.

But I couldn't wait for Veena to return. I had to go down the hill and make sure Beaufort wasn't carrying out his threat to kill Rainie. Grabbing a sword in one hand and a stake in the other, I flew into the air and shot down the hill, with the speed of a torpedo.

I burst through the door of my former house. But there was no one there. They must have heard the noise and fled, to hide somewhere on the estate. As I moved through the other little, brick houses, I saw it was the same in each one.

I circled over the estate, looking for the blood slaves. As I approached the perimeter fence I saw what Oliver, in the dungeons, had been talking about. Two vast spirits, seething with fury and darkness, hovered over the fence, flying from left to right as if on patrol. I could sense their energy and their power. It was the energy of decay and destruction. The energy of cycles completed and lives ended. These were spirits of death and disease. They'd been shackled to this location for decades and they were very, very angry. Then I realised, they weren't flying because they were on patrol. They were trying to escape, just like everyone else on this estate. As I looked, with spirit vision, I saw what was tethering them - two etheric strings, bendy enough that they could fly around the estate but strong enough not to break.

I flew to the etheric strings and focused my attention on them. "Be gone." I ordered and watched as the strings dissolved back into the spirit world from where they'd come. The spirits changed colour, from dark, blackened red, to vibrant pink. Flying once around my head, they transmitted gratitude, telepathically, then disappeared. Had I done it? Was the spell no longer in place? I had to be sure. I couldn't give any of these captives false hope, like last time. Floating down to the ground, in front of a part of the fence, I approached it cautiously. I felt normal, no itchy skin, no nausea. Placing my sword and stake on the ground, I got right to the fence and grabbed hold of it. It was too tall to climb so I flew to the top, still tracing my fingers over the steel of the fence. Then I landed on the other side. The thrill of success coursed through me. But I wasn't going to stay this side of the fence. I'd made a promise to get everyone out of here and I was going to see it through.

THE NEXT TASK was to find where everyone was hiding. I picked up the sword and stake and headed back into the sky, circling overhead to view the entire scene.

By now there was a gun fight, going on, at the front of the mansion, between vampires and house servants. Would the same thing I'd done before work here? I called out, "spirits of war, lend me your weapons." But nothing happened. It seemed this spirit magic was just as unpredictable and hard to control as arcane magic was. But at least now the servants were armed - it was a fair fight.

I spotted Samuel and Grace crouched behind a makeshift barricade, they'd constructed out of a food trolley. Samuel was firing shots at a vampire, positioned behind a wall, in the mansion. The vampire's head popped into view, he fired a few shots, through the window, which had been relieved of its glass, and then disappeared again. Samuel swore and returned shots at him.

I floated down, to crouch next to them. "Where are the others?"

Grace whipped her head round, startled, then relaxed when she saw it was me. "How did you get there?" She asked.

"I've discovered I have spirit witch powers. That means I've removed the spell from the perimeter fence."

She raised a skeptical eyebrow. "Yeah, you've told us that before and, as you know, it ended really badly."

I patted my hands up and down. "It's different this time. I've tested it and everything. I went over the perimeter fence - nothing happened to me."

Pop, pop, pop. Samuel stopped shooting and turned to me. "Are you serious?"

I nodded, looking him in the eyes.

"Then why are we wasting our time in a gunfight. Let's just get out of here."

Grace added. "Some of the blood slaves are up here fighting. Paulette, CJ, Rainie and all the rest are hiding in the thicket of trees to the West. Do you know which one I mean?"

"Yes, I ran past it during my first few days here." It was a smart choice. They could gather branches to create makeshift stakes and arm themselves against approaching vampires.

Samuel held his body flat behind the trolley as another volley of bullets whistled past. "We need a large vehicle to get out of here."

He was right. I'd heard Beaufort boasting about his garage full of luxury cars but that wouldn't be enough to get all the humans off this estate. By my count there were about one hundred and fifty people here. We'd need at least one bus. The fleeting thought of Beaufort created a murderous reaction within me. Where was the bastard hiding? The thought that he might get away with all the sick things he'd done here, burned a hole inside of me. But this mansion was huge and spending time combing over every nook and cranny to find him, would mean putting all the humans at risk of death or recapture. I needed to prioritise. I could come back and finish Beaufort off once the humans had been safely transported off the estate. But how were we going to do that without a big vehicle?

Then it came to me. "Derek!" I cried out.

"Who?" Grace looked at me in confusion.

"Derek the vampire."

Her face soured.

"No, he's a friendly vampire - he's not part of Beaufort's crew. We formed an alliance after being imprisoned in the dungeons together - he's still there. He knows how to hot wire a car. If he drives one of Beaufort's fancy sports cars off the estate, he can find a bus and glamour the driver into coming back to collect us all."

Samuel smiled at me. "It's a great idea. But he's not taking a sports car - Beaufort has a full-artillery hummer in his garage."

My eyes popped open. "How do you know that?"

"It's what I used on my first escape attempt. Didn't work of course, I couldn't get past the perimeter fence." He took another few shots at the vampire then turned back to me. "But we're going with him. You may have formed an alliance but I'm not trusting our freedom to some random vampire who may not come back for us."

He turned back to take another shot at the vampire.

"Eurgh!" The vampire cried out and then turned to dust.

"Got him" Samuel exclaimed, punching the air with his fist as he held the gun in his other hand. "Right, let's do this. Where are these dungeons?"

"Trapdoor at the back of the kitchen."

"Are there other humans locked up there?" Grace asked.

"Yeah, I'm not sure how many but I'd say about a dozen."

"And what kind of locks are on the doors?"

"Old-fashioned style, with a key in the door."

She smiled. "Easy to pick". She thought for a moment. "I'll come with you, I think they have metal kebab skewers in the kitchen. I've seen the favoured humans eating kebabs at their lawn barbecues."

Samuel nodded. "Okay, I'll cover you and you two start sprinting. Deal?"

"Deal." I could've flown but I didn't want Grace to feel like she was on her own. We were a team and we'd get out of here by sticking together. "We'll get Derek, free the other prisoners and then meet you back here. Do you have enough bullets?"

Samuel held up another cartridge. "Oh yeah." He winked, devilishly. "Ready?"

Me and Grace looked at each other, took a deep breath then nodded.

"On the count of three. One, two, three. Go" He began shooting and we raced towards the side door, with heads down, bullets flying past us. We just made it. Glass and pieces of cement and brick crunched under our feet as we entered the utility room. The mansion was starting to look like a war zone. Bits of plaster hung off the walls. And chandeliers and artworks lay, destroyed, on the floor. Why didn't the vamps just give up and let us leave? Now that the humans were all armed, the vampires were wildly outnumbered.

But I didn't have time to ponder their motives. I offered my sword to Grace and she took it. Then we stalked, slowly, crouching down, as we crept towards the trapdoor, at the back of the kitchen. I held my stake tightly, my heart pounding.

We'd almost made it to the trapdoor when a vampire sprang out from behind a cupboard and slashed at us, with a knife. I ducked and his swipe narrowly missed Grace's torso. But his strike had off-centred his balance. He staggered to the right and Grace took her chance. Swinging the sword at his neck, she decapitated him. He turned to dust in front of me.

"Nice work." I said.

"I don't think there are anymore in here." She sped round the kitchen opening drawers with one hand, holding her sword in the other, until she found what she was looking for. "Got 'em" She said, triumphantly holding up a couple of skewers.

"Why do you need two?"

"In case one breaks," she replied, walking back to me.

I reached down to open the trapdoor. It was locked.

"Hang on." Grace said. She handed the skewers to me then braced the sword in both hands. Lifting it high above her head, she brought it down, with a colossal crash, breaking the lock.

I handed the skewers back to her and opened the latch before descending the steps.

Flicking on the light switch, I called out. "Derek." I heard rustling and then he called back.

"I'm here."

"We're coming for you Derek, hold on."

Grace looked at me. "Let's get him first and then free the others."

I nodded. We had to be smart. Derek was the priority here, getting everybody out depended on getting him out.

We reached Derek's cell and he beamed at me. "You came back for me."

"I said I would, didn't I?"

Grace appeared next to me and started picking the lock.

"Who's this?" He looked Grace up and down, appreciatively.

"Derek, meet Grace" I gestured between them. "Grace - Derek."

"I take it this means you're busting me out of here?"

"Uh huh but we need you to hot wire Beaufort's artillery hummer then drive it out of here, find a bus somewhere en route and glamour the driver into giving you the bus so you can drive back here to pick us all up."

Grace added. "There will probably be vampires firing at you as you leave."

Derek chuckled. "I don't care, I'm ready for it. Been planning how to make my escape from this place for weeks."

"Teamwork makes the dreamwork." I replied.

Grace finished picking the lock and opened the door. "This way Sir." She made a comical bow and he strolled past.

"Would you mind getting this thing off while you're at it?" I gestured to my obsidian dog collar.

"Sure." She poked around inside the lock at the back of my neck, for a moment and I heard a click as it popped open. I tore it from my neck and hurled it to the floor. "What a relief." Energy and power surged back through my body.

"Now to free the others." Grace said. She sped round each of the cells, opening them with the ease of a professional thief.

Derek looked at her in awe. "What a woman."

"Don't get any ideas. I don't think she'd date a vampire."

Derek nodded, stroking his chin as he looked at her picking the locks and releasing the prisoners inside. "But I can be very persuasive."

I frowned at him. "You wouldn't glamour her into dating you, would you?"

He looked appalled. "Of course not! I do have some honour you know."

Grace had just freed Oliver, who I now saw was a big, tall, bear of a black man with salt and pepper hair and a double-chin.

He dusted himself down but it would take more than that to remove the grime he was coated with. "Thank you my dear. I overheard that you have a plan to get us off this godforsaken estate?" He cocked at eyebrow.

"We do indeed Oliver."

"Well let's not waste time chatting." He gestured in Derek's direction. "God forbid this vampire starts getting hungry and attacks us."

Derek scowled at him. "Hey, I'm not some mindless, raving beast -

I can control myself. Besides, I've only just been fed, I won't be hungry again for hours."

"Oliver, do you know the quickest route to Beaufort's garage from here?" I asked.

"Of course. I used to be a butler here you know. It's through the conservatory. Follow me." He beckoned and we all followed. Some of the guys we'd released looked really terrible. I saw signs of PTSD and mental illness. One guy had scratched all his hair off. We'd have to drop the sick people off at a hospital along the way. I wasn't sure of the dynamics of this, in terms of explaining what had happened. The hospital admissions team would want to know how they'd got into such a state. I couldn't deal with that kind of questioning right now. I was desperate to get home. But we couldn't leave them here. Derek would have to glamour the hospital staff.

We got to the garage and I switched on the lights, then froze.

There, in front of us, stood Gemma, wearing a silky negligee and pointing a pistol at us.

31

"Put the gun down, Gemma," I said, dropping my stake and holding my hands in the air.

"Drop the sword." She waved the gun in Grace's direction and Grace dropped it, then held her hands up.

"Why are you doing this? We can all get out of here. We'll take you with us. You're free." I lowered my voice, infusing it with as much kindness as I could. "Don't you want to see your family again?" She wouldn't seriously shoot me, would she? She didn't have it in her. But as I looked at her, clenching her jaw, a look of steel in her eyes, I saw an entirely different woman from the one who'd always behaved as a vacuous airhead around her 'Hughie'.

I tried to reason with her. "Just let us go. In fact - come with us. You don't want to stay here, do you?"

She tossed her blonde hair, keeping the gun trained on me, her arm as still as stone. "Why wouldn't I?"

I creased my forehead. "You can do so much better than this."

"Can I?" she shouted. "You don't know me, you don't know the kind of life I've had. Hugh Beaufort was the best thing that ever happened to me. It was bad enough that he chose you to mate with."

She sniffed. "I knew you'd turn on him one day, I warned him but he wouldn't listen."

Grace looked at Gemma. "You don't need that wrinkly, vampire scumbag. Find a nice young man your own age and..."

"Shut up!" Gemma screamed. She took the safety catch off the gun and pointed it at my head. An icy cold shiver ran up my spine and sweat broke out on my top lip. Everyone was silent. I steadied my nerve and took a slow step forward, praying that she wouldn't shoot me. Softening my face, I reached my hand out slowly. "Listen to me, Gemma, Beaufort never cared about you - he used you."

"No! He loved me! He should've chosen me, not you. I would've given him a baby. I love him." Her lip began to wobble as her baby blue eyes took on a quality of vulnerability.

My heart broke for her. Was it Beaufort's abuse that had made her believe she was worth so little? Or had she been this way before she'd even come here, her low self-esteem making her an easy target for his grooming?

Her wrist softened and I seized my chance. Taking one more step forward, I reached her and closed my hand over the gun. I took it from her hands and passed it to Oliver.

She collapsed into my arms in racking great sobs. "He... he told me I was the most beautiful girl he'd ever seen. He said he loved me." She looked up at me, her features twisting from anguish to confusion then desolation. "You know, I was just fourteen when I came here." She wiped her eyes. "I lied about my age to get a modelling contract. I had to get away from home..." Her eyes clouded over. "... I wasn't happy there." She buried her head in my chest and I stroked her hair. An arrow of familiarity pierced my heart. My home hadn't been happy either. Is that why Beaufort had singled me out? Had he sensed the same in me that he'd seen in Gemma? This was clearly what he did. He found broken, abused girls and lured them in with promises of love, security and riches, creating a fake family and fake love - something these girls all craved. He was pure evil and white hot hate coursed though me. I gritted my teeth, waves of nausea fluttering through my belly as I thought of how that twisted pervert had taken advantage of her. He must've known how young she was. He'd exploited her naivety, sucking the youth and innocence from her as surely as if he'd sucked her blood.

I took a deep breath and pulled away from her, holding her at arms length as I looked her in the eyes. "Come with us." I whispered.

She shook her head. "I can't"

"Yes you can. Put all this behind you and start a new life - I'll help you." I knew it wouldn't be easy but I meant what I said.

She shook her head again.

I didn't push her. She'd been through so much. Looking at her now, I guessed she was in her early twenties. That meant she'd been here for years, at the mercy of his manipulative mind games. Maybe she'd leave one day but she wasn't ready for it yet.

"What about the other girls?" I asked. "Do you think any of them will come with us?"

Gemma's brow furrowed. "I'm not sure, maybe Mel? She already ran off. I think she's hiding on the estate somewhere."

Waiting for a chance to make her escape. I thought.

Gemma's eyes grew distant. "Hugh is very possessive. If you take any of his girls, he'll hunt you to the ends of the earth."

I gritted my teeth. "Yeah well, the feeling is mutual." I didn't explain further, aware that Gemma's feelings for this man were complicated. I was still angry with myself for getting distracted and letting him get away. But he'd get his own. I'd make sure of it. I wouldn't rest until I destroyed him.

With Gemma subdued, I picked up her gun and gave it to Derek. "Just in case." I said, as I picked up my stake again and Grace got her sword.

Derek tucked the gun into the waistband of his dirty jeans and then walked through the extensive garage to the hummer, at the far corner. "Hey Grace, give me one of those skewers, would you?"

She handed one to him and within a matter of minutes, he'd used it to gain access. Then he popped the hood and fiddled with some wires, inside the engine. The hummer roared to life.

Grace looked at him. "I'm coming with you - Samuel too. That's the deal we made with Bree."

He looked at me, "What - you don't trust me?"

I held my hands up in a placatory manner. "I'm not the one who doesn't trust."

Grace pointed her sword in his direction, looking at him with steel in her eyes. "Do you want to get out of here, or not, vampire?"

"Alright, alright, whatever you say." He looked at me. "What are you going to do until we get back?"

I thought for a moment. "Can you give us all a lift down the hill? We've got another group of people we need to connect with."

"Of course. Get in then."

We all climbed in. The inside was huge, big enough for all of us to fit comfortably. But we'd still need that bus to get everyone off the estate.

WE PICKED up Samuel along the way and drove down the hill. By now the gunfire was tailing off. Most of the vampires had been killed and those who hadn't, had run away to hide, like Beaufort. As I had this thought it occurred to me that Oliver might have an idea of where to find him.

"Oliver, I lost Hugh right at the start of the fight. He scurried off, out of his bedroom and then disappeared around a corner. Do you have any idea where he might have gone?"

Oliver looked up at the ceiling then back at me. "The mansion has a subterranean level. Lots of tunnels and dungeons, like the one we were imprisoned in. My guess is, he's hiding in one of them until the coast is clear and he can come out and rebuild his mansion."

The idea of this made my blood boil. That he could just saunter out, as if nothing had happened, and then start capturing and enslaving humans again, at the very same mansion, was too sickening for words. I had to stop him. Not now - now my priority was getting away from here. But I'd make sure I came back as soon as possible. I wanted to be the one to put an end to his modern slavery house of hell. I also wanted to be the one to watch him turn to dust as I drove a stake into his black heart. I owed it to Darla. I owed it to all the people he'd enslaved and abused. But I also owed it to myself.

Derek let me out, further down the hill and I flew across the lawn, in the direction of the thicket of trees. When I got there, I found, not just all the former blood slaves, but many of the house servants and some of the favoured humans too. Mel sat among them, huddled up in a blanket. I met her gaze and smiled. She smiled back, shivering slightly, probably as much from the cold as from the shock of the evening's events. I'd never been in a gunfight before and I doubted Mel or many of these other people had either. It was only when I saw them that I realised I was starting to feel cold myself. I'd been going on adrenaline but now things had calmed down, my exposed torso, clad in only a bra, was not nearly enough for this time of year.

Veena was walking around, handing out blankets and checking on everyone.

"Hey Veena, could I get one of those please?"

"Sure" she walked over and handed one to me.

Wrapping it around myself I asked. "Is this everyone?"

"I think so" she nodded. "We lost a few people." She dipped her head, her eyes growing bitter and glassy.

I held her hand. "You did your best, we all did."

She nodded, then looked back up. "It's been a long time since I've been in active combat like that. I'd forgotten how brutal and bloody it is."

"At least we're all getting out of here."

"How can you be so sure?"

I realised she didn't yet know about the perimeter fence spell. None of them did. I clapped my hands, getting everyone's attention. "Hi everyone. For those of you who don't know me, my name is Bree. I know that some of you have heard that I tried to break out of here and failed. Well, this time, I've successfully removed the perimeter spell."

There was a gasp and twittering of voices as everyone started to speak at once. Then a voice I recognised called out from the back. "How do we know it's for real this time?" Paulette stood up and looked at me. I didn't blame her for the heavy mistrust that I saw in her eyes.

"I've already tested it. I got over the fence and back again, totally unharmed." She still looked doubtful so I continued. "The spell was put in place by a spirit witch. That's why I couldn't break it before because I was trying to use my arcane witch powers. But it turns out I have spirit witch powers too."

Paulette hesitated. "You're going first."

I nodded. "Okay. That's fair."

CJ stood up next to her. "What are we waiting for? Let's leave this shithole."

I explained. "A friend of mine is coming back for us with a bus." I didn't want any nasty surprises for them when Derek came back so I added. "He's a vampire but he was in the dungeons with me. He hates Hugh Beaufort just as much as the rest of us." They still didn't seem convinced so I added one more thing that I thought might clinch the deal. "He's a black man."

The crowd visibly relaxed and started high-fiving and celebrating, in raucous whoops.

CJ shouted out once more. "Did you kill Hugh Beaufort then?"

I gritted my teeth, feeling like he'd poured salt on my wound. "Not yet CJ but I will do. I will do...."

TWO WEEKS later I was back at my flat, packing my bags. It was so good to be home, although I'd only returned briefly to get ready before leaving again to go to the Arcane Realm. I'd never take my flat or my flatmates for granted ever again. It might be tiny and expensive but it was home and my flatmates were my best friends. As I packed, I reflected on just how much I'd been through and how much I'd grown. I wanted to believe it was my strength and smarts that had got me away from Beaufort Heights but if I was honest with myself, a lot of luck had come into play too. A shiver went down my spine as I considered that without some of that luck, I might still be there. Frowning I thought of Gemma who *was* still there. I hoped that one day she would see the light and that when that day came, I, or someone like me, would get her out.

As I packed, I reflected on how everything had turned out. After Derek returned, with the bus, dropping everyone off had taken the entire night. Then me and Derek had parted ways, after exchanging phone numbers. I felt like, after the ordeal we'd been through, we'd be friends for life. Plus, he'd been very interested in where to get synthetic blood from and I'd put him in touch with Carlotta and the rest of the Ahimsas.

I'd decided it still wasn't safe for me to be at home. I needed somewhere I could rest and recover without having to sleep with one eye open. Beaufort could send his henchmen to come back for me at any time. I would've taken Nik up on his offer to stay at his flat, but we both agreed that was too risky. So instead, we got out of London, booking a fortnight in a countryside holiday rental home.

The best surprise had been the jewellery I was still wearing, when I got there. The genuine, Harry Winston necklace and earrings were worth over two hundred and fifty thousand pounds. Derek had helped me sell the set, on the black market, to a buyer who didn't ask any questions. I'd been able to get all the damages to the flat repaired and still had enough money to live on for years, without needing to find a job.

As soon as I'd got to Nik's flat, I'd contacted the police. I couldn't tell them I'd been held by a vampire but I'd told them as much as I thought they'd believe - that Beaufort was a human trafficker and was engaged in modern slavery at his mansion. They'd filed a report and opened an investigation but I hadn't heard anything further. I had a sinking feeling that I never would. Beaufort was the kind of guy who had connections in high places. He could buy or glamour himself out of anything and that meant he was above the law.

"Almost ready?" Agota disturbed my thoughts as she came in and slumped down onto her bed.

"Yep." I walked over to her. "I'll miss you." I gave her a playful punch on the shoulder.

"I'll miss you too - you've only just come back and now you're leaving again." She stared at my bags and back at me, with a hint of regret to her expression. "It's just so crazy to think that a couple of weeks ago, I believed you'd assaulted me." She shook her head. "I was an idiot - as if you'd ever do something like that."

"Don't blame yourself. Vampire glamours are very powerful, no human can resist them. Anyway, at least I'm back and we're cool again now."

Agota agreed. "Yes and now I know that not only are vampires real but you're dating one of them!"

I laughed. "I know, you couldn't make it up, right?"

I figured now that they knew vampires were real, it wouldn't be that much more of a stretch to find out I was a witch. So I'd told Agota and Tallulah everything, including my plan to go to the Arcane Realm and learn how to use my powers properly. I never wanted to put myself in a position where I'd be too ignorant to defend myself against vampires, ever again. If I'd had proper training, I would've known about the dangers of obsidian and how to avoid it.

Agota continued. "Do you know anything at all about this Arcane Realm you're going to train at?"

I twinkled my eyes at her. "Not really. That's what makes it so exciting. I do know one thing though."

"What's that?"

"There are definitely *no* vampires there and that is the kind of peace and quiet that I am really looking forward to."

"I'm sure." She tilted her head, coquettishly. "But there is one vampire you'll miss, right?"

Nik. I was going there partly for him. After my time at Beaufort Heights, we'd had a big heart to heart. He'd levelled with me that he had indeed initially got involved with me as a way of forming an alliance with the arcane witches. But he'd assured me that, even though it had started out as that, it had grown into something much deeper. And the Ahimsas wanted an alliance with the arcane witches so they could destroy the Draculs together - an aim I was more than on board with.

I didn't know what the future held for me and Nik. Our relationship was certainly unconventional but it had a strange kind of logic to it. We worked and that's all I needed to know for now. We could figure out the rest later. But what we all agreed on, Nik, my flatmates and the other Ahimsas, was that I needed to get properly trained on how to use my powers. So, I'd called Morgana and Evelyn and they'd asked me to meet them at a nearby hotel. It made my insides burn with an unmatched fury to think that Hugh Beaufort had got away but he'd get what he deserved, I'd make sure of that. As I packed the last of my bags, I made a promise to myself.

I'm going to learn how to harness my powers and then I'm coming for you Hugh Beaufort. This damsel is going to bring the pain.

BOOK 2 OF THE 'ARCANE WITCHES' series, entitled, 'Charmed Fate' is out now. Want a sneak preview? Turn the page to read chapter 1...

Did you enjoy this book? If so, please write a review on the store front of your choice and Goodreads now and tell all your friends about it.

If you want to stay updated about my latest book releases and get your FREE copy of the prequel to 'Cursed Charm' entitled, 'Vampires Can't be Vegan', join my VIP list! Visit www.jalihenry.com, enter your email address and you'll be the first to know when the next book is released. I'll also email you with exclusive offers of giveaways and promotional deals.

Please come and join my facebook reader group https://www.facebook.com/groups/3128187757251090
Or follow me on Instagram https://www.instagram.com/jalihenry/
Or on TikTok @jalihenryreadsfantasy
Or on Twitter @jalihenry

CHAPTER 1 OF CHARMED FATE

We kept low, our feet crunching on the pristine snow as we crept through the forest. Skeletons of winter trees hung over us like interlocking bones - the rib cage of an undead monster waiting to devour us, if the giant hybrid vampire bats didn't get us first. Hunting for vampette saliva was not the most challenging task Morgana had so far given my coven but it was the most dangerous. When we'd protested, Morgana had said that as our Grandmaster trainer, it was her duty to ensure we were tough enough to withstand the rigours of hand-to-hand combat against vampires, on the streets of every major city in the world. It was not uncommon for ignoranti like us to go missing during such expeditions. This was our first hunting trip. It could also be our last.

Vampette saliva held a special type of magic - the magic of vanishing and transformation. We could use it to create shape-shifting potions and vanishing potion. Both of these were an essential part of an arcane witch's arsenal of magic. If we were to pass our arcane exams, and make it as vampire hunters, we had to have it. All we needed was a few drops. The more of the saliva we collected, the greater number of credits we would gain which would count towards our final rank upon graduation. I needed the extra credits. Having joined the academic year late, I was way behind the rest of my coven and if I didn't get these extra credits, I wouldn't get my vampire hunting license. I'd lose my chance to murder Hugh Beaufort, the world's most evil vampire. The man I'd sworn to kill after he'd murdered my friend Darla, in front of me.

A rustle in the bushes ahead sent an arrow of fear straight to my belly. I froze, swallowing as I clenched my spear harder. My palms were sweaty inside my leather gloves. Hector, at the head of the group turned around. The whites of his eyes reflected brightly, in the light of the moon. His breath came out as a glittery grey plume around his ebony face. He raised one hand, pointing two fingers towards his eyes before pointing in the direction of a cluster of ivy bushes. None of us made a sound. A second rustle was this time accompanied by an unearthly mewling cackle. It was like the sound that squirrels make in the summertime except much deeper. A juddering, staccato yapping that affected me like nails being scraped down a blackboard. My body went rigid and my heart thumped in my chest. Each member of the coven radiated fear. I turned to look at Theo. He looked close to tears, his mousy brown curls stuck to his temples. Next to him, Audrey's mouth was set in a mask of grim determination, she'd tucked her bobbed hair neatly behind her ears - tidy and prim as always. But the flicker of her left eye told me she was as scared as the rest of us. Hector's jaw was firmly clenched. And Scarlet chewed on her lips incessantly, her large dark eyes like two watery pools, about to overflow.

Unable to gain courage from my coven, I closed my eyes, taking a deep breath and willing myself to stay calm. We'd never get the saliva if we panicked. When I opened my eyes again, Scarlet yelped as a dark shape rose from the ivy bushes. The size of a large ape, it spread dark bat wings and screeched, soaring towards us with talons outstretched. My breath caught in my throat as I saw its face. A grotesque snout and rows of sharp teeth, with extended canines bared and ready to bite. Short, pointed ears and freakishly human eyes displaying a keen intelligence that sent a chill through my centre. It was the face of a gargoyle, an inhuman monster feared since time immemorial, but this was no demon. Spirit witches had purposefully created this creature, a genetic prototype for their ultimate creation of vampires. Vampette's were a hybrid of bat and human, birthed of magic and dark sacrifice to the goddess Vampiria.

The vampette swooped, clawing at me with long-nailed human hands. It's talons combed through my hair, pulling slightly as I ducked. At the same time I jabbed upward with my rooticon. The weapon, containing both a spear and grappling claw, was specially designed for hunting vampettes. The creature screamed and jerked upwards, avoiding the sharp point by a few centimetres. It circled round and readied itself for another attack. A black tongue flicked out between thin red lips. Its eyes shone with hunger and desperation. It probably hadn't fed for a long time. People came into these woods seldom. Legends of missing hikers and the beasts which lurked within the forest had spread far and wide. Although the vampettes were contained behind the wards of the Arcane Realm and inaccessible to humans, occasionally the spell grew thin and a monster would escape to terrorise the local community. Over the years, stories of large bats had become fodder for urban legends and paranormal podcasts. The vampette dove, this time on Scarlet. She dropped to the floor and rolled but not quickly enough to avoid one of the creature's talons. It tore at her jacket, creating a nasty rip which just reached her shoulder.

"Aargh" she wailed, clamping her other hand over the shoulder. "The bastard got me."

Audrey's head whipped round. "Oh no! The smell of blood is going to bring more of them to us. We have to get the saliva quickly and then get the hell out of here."

The need for silence was gone. Theo looked at Audrey and shouted, "let's form a phalanx."

Scarlet's brow creased, "a what?"

"A phalanx, you know, like what the Romans did when they went into battle."

Scarlet blinked at him, her face blank.

"Didn't you do roman history at school?" Theo asked.

"No."

Theo cast his eyes skywards and puffed out air. "American education."

The creature swooped on Audrey and she batted it off with her rooticon. "Could we debate the merits or otherwise of UK versus US education later please? Preferably when we don't have giant winged blood suckers trying to kill us?" Her accent always got posher when she was angry. The vampette flew higher, circling as it made a haunting cawing sound. "It's calling its friends." Audrey said.

"How do you know that?" I asked. It wouldn't surprise me if Audrey spoke 'Vampette' alongside all her other talents.

"I read 'Deadly Beasts of the Arcane' before coming here." She explained, with a tone that implied I was lazy for not having done similar preparatory research before arriving at the Arcane Academy.

I tried to ignore the heat that rose within me. Even in this life and death moment, Audrey was a pompous little shit - she just couldn't help herself. But I had bigger things to worry about. She may have been a smug know-it-all but she was also right. Just as Audrey had warned, a group of large, dark shapes appeared in the distance. Was it the flapping of their wings which sent a gust of chilly wind to freeze my core or was it my own fear? The flock of vampettes was approaching quickly. I counted eight - there were only five of us and we were smaller. If we were going to make it out of this forest alive, we had to act quickly.

I looked at Theo. "Phalanx, good thinking. You crouch next to me. Scarlet, you go in the middle and Audrey and Hector at the back. Rooticons up then when they get close we all stab at the same time."

There was no time for debate, we sprang into our positions and crouched down, just as the flock was upon us. The same screeching, unearthly calls came, in a deafening cacophony. It was all I could do to stop myself from dropping my weapon to cover my ears. That's probably exactly what the bastards wanted. They weren't quite as intelligent as humans but they were pretty close. And as pack hunters, they were formidable. The flap of their wings caused the top layer of snow to blow an icy dust around us. I stabbed upwards, dipping my head. My stomach flip-flopped as I anticipated the sharp pain of a claw piercing the skin of my shoulder at any moment. But instead I heard a blood-curdling cry of pain. I whirled my head from left to right, my heart in my mouth. Had one of us been hurt? Breathing a sigh of relief, I realised someone had stabbed a vampette. The creature's cry sounded unsettlingly human and it wailed as it flapped backwards, pushing the air in front of it to move deeper into the trees. It would probably go off somewhere quiet to lick its wounds. At least we had one less to worry about. But we couldn't see them all off like that - we had to collect some saliva.

The injury of one of their flock acted a bit like accelerant on the flames of a fire. The other vampettes bared their teeth, snarling in fury as they circled around us. Breaking formation, they each dove erratically, with deadly speed, clawing at us randomly. Two of them attacked Scarlet at the same time. Had they worked out she was the weakest? As the smallest member of the coven, she had a face and petite body that could be mistaken for a child. Chubby, dimpled rosy cheeks and an innocence to her cherubic features which was enhanced by her blunt cut fringe. One of the vampettes clamped its wizened hands on Scarlet's shoulder and pulled, lifting her off the ground. I leapt up, grabbing her ankle and clinging on with all my might.

"Hold on Scarlet."

Her dark, almond-shaped eyes grew to terrified saucers. She screamed and whimpered, slapping at the creatures talons as she cycled her legs, squirming to get free.

Theo and Audrey were desperately swiping their rooticons from left to right, as if swatting flies. They were each warding off two separate vampette attacks.

The creature holding Scarlet howled as Hector embedded his rooticon into its thigh. He clung onto the shaft of the weapon, gritting his teeth. "Quick, Bree, get the container."

I let go of Scarlet's ankle and the vampette flapped higher, lifting her up into the air once more. Lunging forward, I grabbed hold of her ankle again. "I can't let go." I shouted, ducking as another vampette made a play for me.

"Merde!" Hector swore in French as he spat into the snow. Even through his winter coat, I could see his arms shaking with the effort of containing the creature.

Beside me, Audrey wielded her rooticon like a baseball bat and gave the vampette which was besieging her a colossal whack, sending it whirling into the night sky. Then she jumped forward and grabbed hold of Scarlet's ankle. "Now Bree!" She shouted.

I fumbled in my waist pouch, my heart thudding in my chest. My fingers found the cup-sized, plastic container and I flipped the lid off. Dragging my booted feet through the snow, I stumbled and dropped the container. The other vampettes were getting ready to mount another attack.

Audrey gave an exasperated sigh. "Can you hurry up about it please?"

"I'm trying my best," I snapped. Grabbing the container, I positioned myself beneath the vampette's head.

I focused on his snarling mouth. His slavering jaws glistened with our prize.

Steeling my resolve, I slid beneath the vampette, lying on the snow with my container positioned to collect the liquid which dripped from his gaping maw. The drops fell and I counted. "One, two.... Three."

Hector tightened his grip as the creature flailed around, trying to get free. It still had its claws clenched around Scarlet's shoulder. "How much longer?" She wailed.

Ignoring her I continued counting. "Four, five.... Six...hold on, almost there. Let's try and get ten."

Another vampette swooped on Theo, its claws lifting his woollen hat from his head. He batted it away with his rooticon. "Do you have to be such an over-achiever, Bree?"

"Seven... eight... I just want to make sure this is worth our while... nine."

"Bree!" Audrey's voice was tight with alarm. "There's another flock approaching."

Flicking my eyes in the direction the first flock had approached from, I saw a larger flock flying towards us. I swallowed. "Ten... we still have time... eleven."

"Bree!" Scarlet screamed, the terror in her tone cutting through the frigid air like an ice pick.

"Twelve... almost there... thirteen."

The vampette flock was almost upon us.

"For the love of God woman!" Audrey shouted.

"Fourteen... fifteen."

The flock reached us and Scarlet screamed.

"Sixteen." I looked at Hector. "Let it go."

Hector let go of his spear and I heaved on Scarlet's ankle, using all my weight to stop the vampette from carrying her off. The creature lost its grip. It ricocheted into the air, directly into the path of the first vampette in the flock, which had been preparing to dive for us. The two colossal beasts twisted and tumbled, spiralling into the rest of the flock like a fiendish, demon whirligig.

I clicked the cap tightly shut on the container and looked at the others. "Let's get out of here." I nodded at Audrey. She knew what to do.

Raising her arms, she closed her eyes and conjured a magical portal. Creating Ether portals for instant travel between two locations was something I couldn't yet do but I had to admit, Audrey was excellent at it and as much as I found her annoying, I was glad she was part of our coven. Only one person could enter the portal at a time though and as I looked up, I realised we were too late. The vampettes had regrouped and were about to dive at us again. Cold dread poured through me.

We weren't going to make it.

With a piercing warrior cry, the flock leader reached me. Its warm, stinky breath was hot on my cheek as its teeth connected with my neck.

"Aargh!"

~

Click here to read more

ALSO BY JALI HENRY

Check out my Young Adult Dark Urban Fantasy trilogy. 'World Breacher' is a series like none you've read before. The story follows the lives of two teenagers. Orphan Naledi, who struggles to raise her sisters, in rural Africa and Giada, a newly-damned minion in Hell. When Naledi manifests the magical ability to breach portals through time and space, her world collides with Giada's as they team up to stop a demon from resurrecting on earth. Readers have called it 'Dante's Inferno meets Hunger Games meets His Dark Materials.'

World Breacher Book 1: Called by the Blessed

World Breacher Book 2: Called by the Damned

World Breacher Book 3: Called by the Redeemed